HOT-HOUSE HOMICIDE

The Complete

Cases of Mortimer Jones

1946–49

WILLIAM CAMPBELL GAULT

---

illustrations by Peter Kuhlhoff
and Monroe Eisenberg

cover by Peter Stevens

BLACK MASK
2025

Table of Contents

Hot-House Homicide

Poor old Sylvester Morgan. He'd bought a lot of expensive things for his home and then he acquired an expensive wife, but couldn't keep her—his paunch couldn't quite keep pace with her pulchritude. Morgan tried to do everything in this world for his bride, and when that didn't work he sloughed off his mortal coil to try his luck in the next—with a little help of course, from his murderer.

1

Start, Sweet—End, Bloody

IT STARTED INNOCENTLY enough. I remember there were some kids playing in the street outside. My office is out of the high-rent district, to put it tactfully, and in the kids-in-the-street district and either they were unusually noisy that day or my hearing was unusually sensitive.

At any rate, I went over to close the window, despite the heat. It seemed like a routine case, but he was paying for it, I hoped, and therefore it was worthy of my undivided attention. Money will always get that kind of attention from me.

It seemed to be a standard jealous husband angle, at first.

He was sixty, at least, but he dressed and looked like a man who could still be jealous.

"My wife is considerably younger than I am," he was saying, "but I don't want you to think that that has anything to do with the present situation."

Obligingly, I stopped thinking it had anything to do with the present situation. At least I tried.

"She's in danger, some serious danger. I'm— I'm sure of that."

I put my fingertips together and gave him the thoughtful, speculative look—my scholarly private investigator look. "Can you think of any reason why she wouldn't confide in you?"

"None of the obvious reasons." He looked so trusting, I thought, so clearly a lamb. I thought, *then.*

"You mean—"

A small sound came from Carol's throat, and she swayed. I caught her as she fell.

"I mean it's not infidelity. It might be blackmail, it might be some threat that has arisen out of our relationship, but...."

"Your relationship?" I interrupted.

He smiled gently. "I'm old and wealthy. She's young and beautiful and of—of, let us say, doubtful background."

4 / William Campbell Gault

Let *him* say. I hadn't said it, though I had assumed it. The whole thing became so standard, then. I said: "You want her followed?"

Hesitation, and I realized that that had been an unfortunate choice of words. "Followed" connoted the jealousy angle, the aging-husband-protecting-his-investment angle.

"Some investigation seems to be in order," he admitted. He had his wallet out, a pleasant picture. "I want to know why she goes to the florist shop on the corner of Hubbard and Vine. I want to know what business she has there every Monday afternoon. She rarely buys any flowers."

Business of money changing hands. He rose then, looking like the well-tailored aristocrat he was, and I rose, looking like the cheaply-tailored private eye I am. I accompanied him to the door, voicing assurance, and he left.

Then I went back and opened the window. The voices of the kids returned, and a radio blaring, probably in the cigar store beneath. A couple of blocks away, an automobile horn sounded. Down below, Sylvester Morgan, who had just left my office, was climbing into a yellow Cadillac convertible.

One of the kids was standing next to it, just looking, maybe figuring how long it would take to save up for such a car.

I wondered if it hadn't been a dumb move, leaving the force, just because I didn't like Devine's guts. Devine was chief of homicide. Devine was a louse, figuratively speaking.

Well, domestic troubles for the private dick. Whom does she meet at the florist's, and is he handsome? Is it grounds for divorce? Bring your little troubles to Mortimer Jones, bleeding heart and seeing eye.

Morgan had left a picture. Even discounting the photographer's artistry, it was an eyeful. Blonde, faintly hard, but that would be only in the face, not where it counted. Unless this picture was twenty years old, Morgan had a bargain whatever the price.

Monday afternoon at the florist shop on the corner of Hubbard and Vine.... This was Monday morning, and it was hotter than it had any right to be, and the beer at Mac's would be cool.

Mac said: "Hot, ain't it?" Mac is no stickler for original observation.

A beer, and then another. Listening to the juke box, and listening to Mac argue with a customer about the merits of Billy Conn. Listening to the traffic outside, just killing time until I went over to earn my money at Hubbard and Vine.

I own a Duesenberg. I bought it cheap, and I love it, even though it is an orphan. It's a poor car for shadowing, and it costs me money to keep it in the style to which it has every right to be accustomed. It doesn't make sense, but I own it.

I didn't drive it too near to Hubbard and Vine that afternoon—it would be too easy to spot. I parked it a couple of blocks away, and walked over.

There was a hosiery shop on one corner, and a filling station on the other. There was a grassy plot, a sort of park on the third, right across from the florist, which sported a bench just designed for private detectives who want to keep an eye on the florist to check on blondes. I took out my magazine and sat down on the bench. A newspaper looks too much like the prop for a hotel dick and I was way, way beyond that.

Oh, certainly.

The sun burned my neck, and glared off the magazine, and anyone but a Mongolian idiot would have realized that no sensible man would sit in that unshaded spot just to read a magazine. But I did.

I could feel rivulets of sweat running down my sides, and down my legs. I loosened my tie, unbuttoned my collar, and turned the pages of the magazine slowly, as though I were reading one of Faith Baldwin's stories of secretarial love and executive lust.

Then I saw the yellow Caddy stopping for the light, a block away. I rose casually, buttoned my collar and dried my face as well as I could with my soaked handkerchief, then sauntered across the street.

By this time the Caddy had stopped and parked, and she was getting out. I'd been right. She was soft enough, where it mattered. She was in white linen, no hat. She was all right.

She went into the florists, and I must have followed her by about fifteen seconds at the very most.

There were various flowers of various hues, and undoubtedly various prices. There was an old man, even shorter than I am, with thick-lensed glasses and stooped shoulders and a quiet voice.

There was no blonde.

There was a door, open, leading to a workroom, and there was a door, closed. But no blonde—just me and the old man, an icebox, an array of plants and flowers and the closed door.

I COULDN'T ASK if a girl had come in, so I asked: "Have you any roses?"

Has a florist roses…

"Of course. Long-stemmed?"

"Yes, long-stemmed yellow roses."

No, not yellow, those he didn't have.

Fortunately. How would it look on an expense account, long-stemmed yellow roses? I looked at some other flowers before I left, but they weren't what I wanted. What I had my heart set on was yellow roses, long-stemmed. The price, of course, was no object.

Nobody came out of the closed door. It didn't even open.

I went out into the sunlight again. The park bench hadn't been moved, but to hell with it. That door led to the back of the store, where people lived. There was another door back here, however, and it had a doorbell button to the right of the door. Which I pushed.

No immediate results, but I waited.

The door opened, and a woman stood confronting me, short and slightly stooped, and with the same quiet voice as the man in the front of the shop. She looked at me inquiringly, but without suspicion.

"The census," I explained. "If I could have a minute or two of your time—"

"Come in," she said. So quiet and polite.

A kitchen, big and old-fashioned, with a big table in the middle of it covered with bright oilcloth. A religious calendar on the wall. A sink and stove and old-fashioned ice box. Some chairs, and worn linoleum on the floor. A door leading out of the kitchen, closed, and an open door disclosing some steps. That's where they lived, upstairs.

Well, I had no forms, or anything that resembled forms. I said: "If there has been no change since the last census, I won't need to question you."

She hesitated on that one for a second. Then: "Only my son. He's come—he lives with us now."

I pulled out some paper and a pen. "His name?"

"Jimmy—James."

"And he works where?"

"He—he hasn't found a job, yet. But he's looking…"

A voice from the direction of the steps: "Mom, who's there? Who's that you're talking to?" The sound of feet on the stairs, and then he was framed in the doorway.

Jimmy Dexter.

Twelve to twenty years for armed robbery. I'd done it to him myself, when I'd been on the force. But that was five years back. Someone had done him a favor.

"You," he said. "What the hell are you doing here? The law's got nothing on me. This is my home, you're in, flatfoot, and—"

"I'm not with the department any more."

"Then what the hell are you doing here?"

His mother's voice, then. "Jimmy, calm yourself. He just wants to take the census. He didn't mean any harm."

I think he would have believed it. Only at that moment, the door from the store opened and the old man came in. He said crossly: "What's all the commotion about?" Then he saw me. "Aren't you the gentleman who wanted the yellow roses?"

They were all looking at me now, two of them in bewilderment, and Jimmy in hate.

"I came to see Jimmy," I said. "The rest was all untrue. I feel personally responsible for what happened to Jimmy, and—"

"Get out of here," he said hoarsely. "Get out of here, now, right now!"

It was still hot outside. I walked up two blocks to the Dusy. When I started her, she seemed to chuckle at me, deep in her steel throat, laughing at what a poor liar I was. I pointed her toward the office.

Dexter, Jimmy Dexter, out of the clink. A hot head, Jimmy, and not socially adjusted, as they say. But I'd known worse, lots worse. Jimmy Dexter and the very lovely young Mrs. Morgan.

That was probably it. Youth calls to youth, and so forth. Jimmy had curly hair and flashing eyes. And he was probably glib enough.

The Dusy was still chuckling at me. I parked her a block up from the office because of those kids. They like to blow horns and bounce on seats and slide down fenders. She was ten years old, but the rest of the field hadn't caught up to her yet.

I went into the office and sat in my mahogany chair (used—

Sam's Second-hand Furniture) and brooded. Then I phoned Mike Greb. Mike likes to play detective once in a while, despite his age. He said he'd be right over.

I wondered if this case were important enough to cover the expense of an assistant.

I had the picture on the desk when Mike came in. He took one look at it. "Carol Whitney," he said. He was still puffing from his climb up the steps. Mike carries a lot of weight.

"Carol Whitney," I repeated. "It rings no bells, though she does." I let my mind dwell on that for a moment. Lovely.

"Thrush," he said. "Sang at the Slipper, Jack Zarsze's spot."

"Oh."

"Like honey to a bee, and garbage to a fly, that girl," Mike said. "Men after her all the time, all kinds of men."

The honey part was all right, but Mike shouldn't have mentioned the garbage, I thought. In questionable taste.

"Remember Jimmy Dexter?" I asked him.

He nodded, as I knew he would. "Played the piano, played a lot of piano, that boy."

"No," I said. "You're thinking about the wrong lad. This one is the boy I sent up the river. On that Granville bank job."

"That was later," Mike told me. "That was after he went on the weed. Before that he was about the best in town, maybe second, but not much worse. Never got the breaks, that's all. Stuck there at the Slipper, for peanuts—"

"The Slipper?" I interrupted.

He nodded. "Didn't you know that?"

I didn't. There were a lot of things Mike knew that I didn't, but Mike had been on the Force a long, long time.

"Well," I said, "well, well and again, well."

"You in a rut, or something?" Mike asked. "Change the needle."

The phone rang. I answered it, and was sorry I had. Devine's voice: "See how fast you can get down here, hawkshaw."

"What's cooking?"

"You will be," he said in his unpleasant voice. "Unless you get down here in a hurry, census-taker."

Ouch. I winced inside. But I said: "Any complaints about me can come through the chief."

Oh, the smugness in that voice. "The chief is out of town, or don't you read the papers? Temporarily, I'm it. Now, shall I send the wagon, or—"

"I'll be right down," I said, and hung up. To Mike: "Devine wants to see me, now. I'll be back."

"That louse," Mike said. "I'll wait." He settled his bulk in my mahogany chair.

THE DUSY SNORTED in complete contempt.

"I do the best I can," I said. "Sometimes it isn't enough."

She said something like "huh" only there was the gurgle of gasoline in it.

We moved regally through traffic, me and my high-class car. On Broad, a guy wanted to beat me at a light. They never learn.

Jimmy Dexter was not one to call copper. Never. Mama, then? Or papa? Or Carol Whitney Morgan? What a blue-blood combination of names that was. But her blood would be red. Definitely. Of the people, Mrs. Morgan, down to earth. Earthy, even.

Devine was in the chief's office, looking important, shuffling papers and growling. Throwing his weight around. There's one on every force.

"You," he said, when I came in.

I said nothing.

"Can you drive a truck?"

I shook my head.

"What are you going to do on that sad day when we take your license away from you?"

"Who's *we?*" I wanted to know.

"It can be arranged. Don't worry about that." He paused. "Tell me, just who in hell do you think you are?"

"Mortimer Jones," I answered. "Remember me? I used to work here. I even worked for you, when you got something you couldn't handle. I don't have to drive a truck, *or work for the city.* I can make a living."

Color climbed up into his narrow face. "Don't get out of line."

"I won't, if you won't. If you've a beef, make it. If I want abuse, I'll get married."

"O.K.," heavily. "A florist, on Hubbard and Vine. A plain, every-day businessman, a citizen. You bother him. First you want yellow roses, and then you're the census-taker." Pausing, to look at me more closely. "You were sober, all right?"

I nodded.

"Well?"

How much should I tell him? About Jimmy Dexter? No, he'd served his time. Nor about Sylvester Morgan. "Another citizen," I said, "perhaps even more solid than the florist. Some member of his family went there, and he wanted to know why."

"Maybe, to buy flowers, huh?"

"No."

"You got some names?"

"No."

"Uh-huh." Trying on a thoughtful expression, but it didn't fit. Looking down at the desk, and up at me, like an executive, a leader of men. Then: "You plan on bothering these people any more?"

"Not so they'll notice it."

"This is the first kick we've had on you."

I was silent.

"Is there anything going on there, at that florist's, we should know about?"

"I don't think so."

"O.K. Beat it."

I was at the door, when he said: "I guess you know I hate your guts."

"I'd hate yours, too," I told him, "if you had any."

I went quickly down the hall, past the waiting room, past the switchboard, and out the big, double doors.

The sun was still working. Glen Harvey stood out there, picking his teeth on the taxpayers' time, staying within the shade of the doorway.

"How's business?" he wanted to know.

"Fair," I said, "I make a living." I don't know why I should have lied to Glen, excepting that he looked so well fed.

He nodded back toward the door behind him. "Devine giving you a bad time?"

"He tried."

Glen shook his head sorrowfully. "He's getting hard to live with, awful hard to live with."

Driving back, the Dusy made no comment. Maybe she knew I was in no mood for chatter. Well, Papa had put in the beef, and I couldn't blame him for that. He was a citizen. But if he'd had yellow roses, none of it would have happened.

The shades were down in the office, and Mike still sat in the mahogany chair, reading a detective magazine. He looked up when I came in. "Devine hot about something?"

I sat in the leatherette chair (same store). "Yup." I told him about it, all of it, from the beginning.

"Morgan," he said once, "Sylvester Morgan." Then his broad face screwed up, as though he were trying to remember something.

I finished the story.

"You want me to watch the florist?"

"Unless you've got any better ideas."

"I think, maybe, though it might not tie up. I can't see any tie-up."

I waited. Mike doesn't like to be pushed. Outside, one of the kids used some words no kid should know.

Finally, Mike said: "I'd kind of like to look into this other angle. You going to be here, tonight?"

"I can be. Lots of times, I am."

He got up heavily. "Around ten o'clock. If I'm early, I'll wait. If I'm late, you wait. Might take some digging."

He left then, looking like the south end of an elephant, and I could hear him going slowly down the stairs. If I knew what I knew later, I would have stopped him. But I didn't know it, then.

NOTHING MUCH TO do. Read the magazine Mike had left. Turn on the radio and hear how the Yanks were doing. Check on a guy who'd skipped a hotel bill—a little matter of two hundred and seventeen dollars and forty-five cents.

Then I went over to the window, to see if any of the kids were fighting. I raised the shade, and saw the yellow Cadillac convertible slide into a parking space directly below. The door of the car opened, and one slim leg appeared.

I looked at my hair in the mirror behind my chair. I straightened my tie, wished I had shaved in the morning instead of the night before, and wished I didn't always buy cheap suits.

A moment later my door was pushed open, and she stood framed there. I am a sucker for anything female between twenty and forty which isn't downright repulsive. For her, I could move mountains.

The same white linen, the same proud carriage. The voice was a singer's voice. "I guess you know who I am."

I nodded.

"And why I'm here?"

"Not completely." I indicated the leather chair.

She sat there, and crossed her legs, which was unfair. It made me slightly less sharp, and I'm not too sharp anyway.

"It's about Jimmy Dexter," she said.

No words from me.

"It's not what you probably think." She was studying me now, and I hoped I was at my best. "Or, maybe, *you* don't think it," she continued. "Let's say what most people might think."

I remained silent. Looking was good enough for me.

"What *my husband* might think. He hired you, didn't he?"

There was no percentage in denying it. She knew. I nodded.

"He's a jealous man. He thinks I married him for his money."

"Well?"

She smiled. Nothing phony about her. "Well, I did." She

continued to study me. "I seem to have something men want."

Which was no lie, which was an understatement.

She still was doing all the talking. "Jimmy loved me, I guess, and so did some others. But I never encouraged Jimmy, I want you to understand that. He was stuck there, at the Slipper, tied down by a long-term contract Zarze had stuck him with. He loved me, and he thought it was his lack of money that prevented me from loving him. Can you understand that?"

I could, and I said so. I added: "So, the Granville bank."

"That's right. Also he'd taken up this habit, by then. I guess you know what I mean."

I did. Marijuana, reefers.

"You can see my responsibility?" she wanted to know.

"No," I said.

She leaned forward. "He loved me. That Granville bank business was because of me, so he'd have enough, for me." She laughed, faintly bitter. "I come high."

A frank and direct girl. I didn't have to believe any of this, but I did. She was no fool, but no liar either, I was sure. Maybe it was the way she sat in the chair.

"I married Sylvester Morgan. He bought a lot of decorative things for his home, and he thought I'd fit in with them."

"How does this tie in with Jimmy Dexter?"

"Money," she said. "For a lawyer for Jimmy. For some people here and there. To get him out of that place. And I did, after five years."

"But you don't love him?"

"I don't love anybody," she said, "at the present. I'm not exactly an Elsie Dinsmore, you understand, and I can take the kind of luxury Sylvester offers. But I haven't been in love with anybody for a long, long time." She paused. "Not that it's any of your damned business."

Then we both laughed.

"It's quite a story," I said. "But this interest in Jimmy Dexter—"

"I like to think," she said, "that I know something about music. At any rate, his kind of music, our kind of music. In his field he was the best. He can work anywhere in town, that boy."

"He isn't working now," I said.

She nodded her golden head. "Starting tonight, at the Slipper. And Zarze won't hold him this time. He's going up, way up."

"How about the reef—the habit?"

"He's quit. I've seen him every week for a month, and he's straightened out. I brought him money."

"Every Monday afternoon," I said.

Again, she laughed. "Right. You know all about it, now. You can tell Sylvester, or I can, or neither of us can. I suppose you have to make your report."

"I'll see," I said.

"Money?" she said, doubtfully. "I could buy you off."

I shook my head. "We have very few ethics, but we like to maintain those we have."

Her eyes were sparkling. "Well, so long as you're still on the expense account, why not come over and hear Jimmy's debut? Sylvester wouldn't miss the money, I'm sure."

And with that, she left.

I WATCHED HER climb into the Caddy. And the kids watched her. She opened her bag, and threw a handful of coins out on the sidewalk, and they scrambled. I thought I could hear that laugh of hers as the big, yellow car moved off.

And so ends the Morgan case, I thought. Thus, with simple honors, we shall bury the Morgan case in the dusty file cabinet, in the dim past. I will make no report. It is ended.

So I thought.

The Yanks beat St. Louis that day in the last inning. The kids went in to supper, and I went over to Mac's.

Mac was discussing the Bomber, in his knowing way. "The trouble with Joe," Mac was saying, as if he knew, or as if there was anything the matter with Joe.

I had some beef stew, read the sports page, and some of the front page. Outside, it was muggy, and a faint breeze from the east was trying to work itself up into a wind.

My apartment, so called, consists of a room and a bath. It has a kitchen that pulls out of the wall and a bed that pulls out of the wall, and cockroaches, occasionally, that creep out from under the wall.

In this sumptuous place, I took a shower and shaved. I found some clean socks and a clean shirt and underwear. I dressed carefully in a dark blue suit that had cost me seven dollars more than my usual run of suits. I hadn't walked up as many flights as usual for this one.

Outside, it was starting to drizzle, and I pulled the raincoat out of its compartment in my car. The windshield wipers went click, click, click and the motor went chug, chug, chug as we drove over to Happy Jack Zarze's Slipper Café.

Happy Jack is a misnomer. He doesn't ever smile. He wears double-breasted suits, smokes cigars and scowls, and has more rackets than a Davis Cup player. He has no personality of his own, so he borrowed one from the B pictures—the heavy. He's big enough to get away with it.

He was sitting at a table near the door when I entered. There was a cigar in his mouth and a scowl on his face, and seeing me didn't affect the scowl.

"Hello," I said. "Good evening."

His hello was much smaller, and he put a "copper" on the end of it. Jack never stepped out of character.

Over near the bandstand was another table with two people sitting at it. The man was elderly and wore tails, and the girl was young and blond and was wearing green and more diamonds than I thought decent. Even at this distance, she did things to me.

My upper-class friends, the Sylvester Morgans. What, I wondered, was Sylvester's middle name?

She waved. At me? It couldn't be. But it was. Morgan rose, and came over to meet me. He was smiling. Happy ending to the day, I thought. We will all have a laugh at his unfounded suspicions and I will explain about the census-taking, and we'll laugh, and have a drink. The drink, of course, would be on him. The laugh on me.

He said: "She says you'll explain. She says she doesn't want to cut you out of your fee. Won't you join us?"

The light touch, but it didn't quite come off, I thought. His grip on my elbow was a little too shaky, and he didn't have the proper lilt to his voice. I could have been wrong, but it was worth thinking about.

A white piano on the bandstand, but no musicians as yet.

She had her hair up, and she was smiling, and Morgan was watching me. If I'd been married to her, I'd have been watching, too, with an eagle eye.

I told them all about it. Rather, I told him. She knew. But I pretended to be telling them both, so I could look at her.

We had a drink on it, and a laugh, especially about the census.

Then a young fellow came out onto the stand. A dark slim lad in tails. Curly hair, an intense face, and long, fine, strong-fingered hands.

There was a spotlight on the white piano, on the white face and the white hands. The lad looked at Carol.

"*Diane,*" she said.

That was Frankie Carle's number, I thought. Nobody could touch *him* on that one.

The melody, first, and then it wasn't there any more, just a remembrance in the mind, just sort of haunting you while this kid moved around it with melodies of his own. That couldn't be the pressure of fingers on keys, and felt hammers striking steel wire. This was made somewhere else, this music, where humans didn't live.

O.K., that had been Frankie Carle's number at one time.

He had spent five years in the clink for armed robbery, and now I knew why she wanted him out. He didn't belong in any clink. He didn't belong in this world. And who had put him there, in that cold place? Why, you, Mortimer Jones, when you were one of the city's finest. And aren't you proud?

More music, then, and I forgot I was in the Slipper, or in this town, or even alive. I was nowhere, but it was wonderful.

Happy Jack, that unhappy man, came over a little later to ask if Carol wouldn't sing a number.

Carol looked at Sylvester, who nodded, and she went up to the bandstand and sang *I Walk Alone.*

That was enough for one day, because she was up there in the major leagues, too. We had one more drink, and one more laugh, and then I said good night to them all, including Happy Jack.

It was nearing ten, and Mike would be waiting.

Rain was coming down in ten-quart buckets, and the thunder was like the voice of doom. Lightning in the west, in the east, overhead, and the Dusy seemed to shiver. She's all steel, and she doesn't like lightning. The wipers going click, click and the motor chug, chug and the tires humming a little in the wetness of the night.

Well, I'd tell Mike the whole story, and we'd have a laugh, and maybe a drink. There was a dim light on in my office—that would be the desk lamp. I went up the steps.

I didn't tell Mike the story, or buy him the drink.

Mike Greb was dead.

2

Payment Deferred

SITTING BACK IN my leatherette chair, Mike Greb was—eyes open, slackness in the broad face, and a hole in the middle of his forehead.

Blood, a thick trickle of it, drying along Mike's cheek.

No sound in the office, the sound of the rain outside, and the thunder. Just that dim light, and Mike's staring eyes. I picked up the phone.

Old Doc Walters came, and his bag. Then Glen Harvey and the fingerprint boys, and the guys in white, and in blue uniforms.

And Devine.

He looked from Mike to me, and snapped: "When'd you find him?"

"Ten-fifteen minutes ago. When I called."

Doc Walters thought he had been dead a couple of hours. That meant all those I thought were in the clear, back at the Slipper, weren't. None of them, probably, had been there a couple of hours before.

I don't know why that's the first thing I thought of, only when there's a murder, my mind goes to suspects, and they were all I had at the time. They had all been at Happy Jack's at ten o'clock, but they hadn't been there at eight, probably.

Devine's grating voice, again. "Mike working on something for you?"

I nodded. Then I started to do some heavy thinking because this was one case where I didn't want Devine's interference. He could botch up a case better than anyone I knew. I started thinking of an answer to what I knew would be his next question.

It came. "What? That florist deal?"

"No. A hotel skipper—hooked the Ardmore out of a couple of hundred dollars, and we had a lead that Mike was looking into."

"That wouldn't mean murder."

It wouldn't. And neither would a jealous husband. Or would it?

"Let's see what you got on this skipper."

I gave it to him—Joe Helgeson, con man, bigamist, last seen in a rooming-house district on the west side.

Devine said to Doc Walters: "How close can you fix the time of death, Doc?"

"If I can find out what time he ate," Doc said, "I'll be able to judge it pretty close."

"When we find that out," Devine said, "we'll want to know where *you* were at the time." He was looking at me, but it didn't register right away.

When it did, I contemplated pasting him. But it wouldn't do any good. He was the law, and I most certainly wasn't. Not any more.

They all left, finally.

Still raining out, but the lightning was gone. Blustery and wet, and my feet were soaked just from the short block I walked to the car. I didn't go home. Not tonight.

If Doc knew when Greb had eaten last... There are only a few places Mike ate in. I had paired with him often enough, back in the old days, to know that. Mike was very particular about the quality of the food he put in his stomach, if not the quantity.

Two of them were closed, and the third hadn't seen him. The fourth had. It was a little steak and chop house, on Diversey near the Drive. They had some newspaper trade, and that's why they were open now.

The proprietor said: "Sure. Mike was here. About six o'clock. Had this little guy with him, and I remember noticing it at the time, Mike so big and this guy so—"

I asked: "Anything else about this little man? I mean anything unusual, besides his size?"

"N-no. He was pretty shabby. Looked like a bum to me." Then: "Say, there *was* something. I remember the guy reached for a toothpick, and I noticed the end of his right index finger was missing, about a half inch—just the part the nail covers."

"What'd he wear?"

"A cap. Don't know the color, or the color of his suit."

That's all he had, and that's all I had. Mike had eaten around six, and this little guy with the mutilated index finger had been with him then.

I took that down to Headquarters. Devine was still there, and Doc Walters, and Glen Harvey.

Doc said: "Died between eight and eight-fifteen, in that case."

Devine didn't say anything. He just ignored me, which I preferred.

Harvey left with me. "What's cooking at that florist?" he wanted to know.

It had stopped raining, and we were standing next to the Dusy. "Why?" I said.

"I'm checking him tomorrow. Devine smells a rat."

"He should be used to *that* odor," I said. "Nothing's cooking at the florist that I know of. Jimmy Dexter lives there."

"Who's Jimmy Dexter?" he wanted to know.

But I wasn't going to be the one to enlighten him on that. "He's a piano player," I said. "One of the best." With that I left him.

I'm uneasy in the dark. I won't admit I'm frightened, even to myself, but I am uneasy. I don't like it. My garage is halfway up an alley, and the alley is two blocks from where I live.

The rain had stopped, but the clouds still must have been up there because there was no moon, and no stars. The Dusy's lights swept up the alley, and stopped. I got out, and unlocked the garage doors. I swung them open, went back and drove the Dusy in, then turned off the motor and the lights. I was alone, now, in the silence and the darkness.

Not for me, this. I got out of the car, closed the garage doors, and started to move swiftly down the alley.

A cold voice, in the warm night. "Just a minute."

I started to turn toward the voice, but there was something prodding me in the back. It could have been a pipe or the handle of a frying pan, but I assumed it was a gun. And I was scared.

"Don't turn. I just wanna give you this message. Don't worry about Mike Greb. Mike's dead, and the police can worry about it. Stay out of this whole deal—and live."

I said nothing.

"You got that?"

"I heard you."

"Then just keep walking. Go home and go to bed."

I KEPT WALKING. I wasn't armed, and I was scared, and I didn't know when this voice would change his mind about playing nice. If he turned out to be the impulsive type, he could put a bullet in my back. Or maybe, a knife. I took no chances.

I went home, but I didn't go to bed.

Stay out of this whole deal, the voice had said. But I was in this deal, up to my hips. With Mike dead, there was no other path open that I could see. I have to live with myself.

Well, I had some people. Dexter and Carol and Morgan and Zarze and Pa and Ma Dexter. I was to meet lots of others later, but these were all I had at the time. I sifted them through my mind slowly, trying not to miss anything, but it didn't add up. It didn't spell anything. I also had the voice and the little man with the short index finger. But they were intangibles, as yet.

I made some coffee. I knew I wasn't going to get much sleep, anyway, and I like coffee. It keeps my mind clear. It kept me thinking until about dawn, and then I pulled the bed out of the wall.

Morgan was choking me, and his lovely wife was throwing tennis balls at me, and screaming, and Jimmy Dexter just stood in the background, holding that knife…

The sheet was around my neck, I was wringing wet, and the sun was glaring in my face as though it bore a personal grudge. I had slept four hours, I noticed, but I felt as though I hadn't slept at all.

A cold shower helped some, and I warmed over the coffee that was left. But I was hungry.

I own a few guns, and one of them is just made for warm weather, a Colt Banker's Special. I have a permit for it. I took it along.

The alley didn't scare me this morning. I'm all right when the sun is shining. My friend of steel made no comment on the way to Mac's.

Mac was saying: "Loughran was pretty, but he didn't…" Then he saw me. He said: "Sorry to hear about Mike, Jonesy."

I ordered some bacon and eggs. When Mac brought them, he said: "Anything new?"

I shook my head.

He went back to continue his dissertation on Tommy Loughran.

There were no kids in the street. The guy downstairs in the cigar store was putting a cigarette display in his window. There was a black Lincoln Continental at the curb, and right in front of it a battered Ford.

I never lock my door. I lock what papers should be locked up in my file cabinet, along with my liquor, and the rest of the stuff they can have, if they're that hard up.

Sylvester Morgan was sitting in the leatherette chair when I entered. He had some kind of brown tropical suit on, and there was a very fine Panama hat on my desk. His clothes I should have.

He had a check in his hand, and a smile on his face. "For services rendered," he said, and handed me the check.

It was for a thousand dollars.

I would need to be casual now. This was getting out of the minors, and I would have to be smooth. I sat down in the mahogany chair, tilted back, and lighted a cigarette. Impressive.

I said: "And to be rendered?"

His face was well-trained. The raised eyebrows, the well-bred surprise. "I don't understand."

"A thousand dollars is a lot of money."

"Is it?" As though one sum was the same as another, as though denominations didn't matter.

"It is to me. It's a lot more money than that little job yesterday was worth."

He smiled. "And you thought I was trying to bribe you, or something rather similar to that?"

"I'm trying not to think anything I shouldn't."

"Let's put it this way," he said. "I was terribly worried about my wife, and now it's all cleared up. Nobody was hurt, and—"

"Somebody was hurt," I said, "Somebody was killed." Right in that chair you're sitting in, I thought, but didn't say.

"Killed?" Shock on the face now, but the face still under control. The shock might be simulated.

"Didn't you read this morning's paper?"

"No, I didn't. Is it someone I know?"

"It's a fellow who was working for me. On your case. He was killed in that chair last night. I found him here when I came back from the Slipper."

His face was very grave. "So you thought that's why I gave you the thousand dollars?"

"Not yet, I haven't." Which wasn't completely true. "Maybe you could tell me why the check *is* so big."

"Because everything is all settled. Because I'm a wealthy man, and I was pleased with your work, and I didn't want to go to the police."

"You don't like the police?"

Annoyance in the face now. "I have no reason to dislike them. My affairs are my own, and I thought if one wanted privacy, it would be better to hire a private detective. Besides, I could scarcely ask the police department to check on my wife. It wouldn't be considered as a part of their duties, I'm afraid."

If he had any answers they weren't for me, I could tell. I said: "The thousand dollars is for yesterday, then?"

"That's right. Unless you'd prefer to bill me?"

I shook my head.

"If it's too much, consider the rest as a retainer on your services." He stood up. "I may need you again."

He picked his Panama off the desk, stared a second at the leatherette chair, then his eyes shifted to my face. "Killed here? And you say he was working on—"

I nodded.

"I may need you again," he repeated, and then he was moving toward the door.

I didn't try to stop him. I peered out of the window while he got into the Lincoln and continued watching it until it was out of sight.

An angle, Mike had said, though he didn't know how it would tie up. An angle on Sylvester Morgan? Or somebody who was trying to get to Sylvester Morgan? An angle I didn't know, at any rate.

Somebody was coming up the stairs, somebody with big feet.

My former associate and co-worker, the estimable Devine.

BIG SMILE ON his face. A new approach, I thought. Beware, Mortimer, he's trying to win friends and influence people.

"It's dark in here," he said, looking at the shades which I had drawn against the sun's glare. "You always work in the dark, Shady?"

I winced. Even on the borscht circuit, I'd heard better.

"The chief is back," he continued in his bright voice, "and I'm back to work."

"So—"

"So I was a friend of Mike's, too, remember?"

He was a friend of Mike's. He was like hell.

"And I know how you felt about him. I thought we could pool what we have, and see what it adds up to."

"What've *you* got?" I asked.

"Probably not much that you haven't. I know that Jimmy Dexter lives over there, at that florist's, and that he probably remembers you. I know that Mike spent some time in a rooming house over on Windsor."

This was new. I got the address.

The rest I already knew. He asked: "And what've you got?"

"Nothing. Not a damned thing." Then: "Who saw Mike at this rooming house on Windsor?"

"The cop on the beat. Jarvin. You know him."

I did.

Devine asked: "Who was that in the Lincoln?"

He'd been watching me, I thought. And then curiosity got the better of him, so he comes up here with the fraternal act. What a character.

"Fellow named Morgan," I said. "Sylvester Morgan. A customer."

"Money, huh?"

"Money."

"Anything there, anything we could tie up with Mike?"

"If there is," I told him, "you'll be one of the first to know." I got up and went to the file cabinet. I had some cheap whiskey there I had been trying to get rid of for a month. I produced a couple of glasses.

Devine downed his without even blinking. It was probably one of his favorite brands. I said: "Some of my business has to be confidential. But none of it that concerns Mike can be confidential, and you'll get all of it, as I get it—if I get it."

"I'm glad we understand each other," he said.

I'd always understood *him*.

He left a few minutes later still basking in the good neighbor mood. I threw the empty whiskey bottle in the wastepaper basket, and locked the file cabinet again.

A rooming house on Windsor, I thought.

There was a guy I knew who worked at the morgue, and I phoned him, and told him what I wanted him to do. "It might even look like an accident," I said, "and the papers would probably bury it on an inside page. But you'd give me a buzz, right?"

He said he would.

A rooming house on Windsor. Three stories high, and a basement apartment. Narrow, old, unpainted. Lots of wooden gingerbread in the style of its time, when it hadn't been a rooming house. The basement apartment had an outside entrance, and a sign next to the door—*Rooms*.

It had a doorbell button, too, which I pushed.

She must have weighed about two-fifty, and came about to my shoulder, and I'm not tall. She had some kind of a black, shiny dress on, but maybe it hadn't always been shiny.

"I'm looking for a little fellow," I told her, "who has the tip of his index finger missing on the right hand. He live here?"

"Cops again," she said.

"Not me," I said.

"If he was a friend of yours," she pointed out, "you'd know his name. I ain't so dumb as I look, mister."

"Well," I said, "all right. You don't look dumb to me." I had a ten-dollar bill in my hand now.

"Come in and set," she said.

It was cool inside, and damp. The furniture had fringes on it, and doilies. It was mostly mission oak, outside of the stuffed pieces. There was a chromo on the wall of a lad with a handle-bar mustache, and a wedding picture on the radio. Even then, she hadn't been a lightweight.

"As I told the others," she began, "this Mr. Schmaltz wasn't one to be neighborly. But he always paid his rent, and I didn't figure him for one who'd run out on me like he did—"

"He ran out on you?"

"Didn't you know that?"

I shook my head.

"Last night. He didn't come home, and today I looked in his room, and there wasn't a solitary thing, not even a shirt."

"Nothing?" I said, just by way of insurance. I still had the sawbuck in my hand.

She was chewing her lower lip. "Well," she said, and got up. She waddled off through an archway draped with beads.

When she came back, she was carrying three knives. "I didn't say nothing to them other cops, because I know how they are. They just grab, and call it evidence." She laid the knives on the mission oak table, next to the stained glass lamp. "They were in the back of one of the drawers. He must've forgot 'em. But he owed me a week's rent, and—"

"Sure," I said, "of course."

The knives of his trade. Only one trade for these.

She didn't know anything more about him. Just the name, Vincent Schmaltz, that he'd been there five weeks, didn't seem to be working, and still owed her for that one week. I gave her the ten.

The sun seemed hotter after the damp coolness of that cellar apartment. There was a sedan parked down the street some distance from the rooming house, and somebody was waving at me from the front seat.

It was Glen Harvey. I walked over to him.

"Waiting for him to come back?" I asked.

He nodded. "Devine's idea. I'd give you eight to three he'll never show up here, but Devine said somebody else might turn up, and for me to watch." He was lighting a cigarette. "Anything new with you?"

"No," I lied, "nothing you don't know."

"I was wondering," Harvey said, "if somebody else didn't clean out that room for him. A guy who skips doesn't do such a neat job. There's usually some old newspapers around and a collar button or two. This looked like they were trying to prevent identification, or something."

"I didn't see the room," I said.

Glen squinted at me. "O.K., Jonesy, you spent some time in there, but you weren't interested in the room. What's cooking?"

I shook my head. "Nothing. Would I keep it from a friend?"

Harvey nodded. "You would."

NICE FRIENDS. I went back to the Dusy and tentatively

pointed her back toward the office. But halfway there, I got the idea and swung her around in a U turn. She grumbled a little. U turns don't suit her dignity.

If he'd been a union man, they might have something on him. And the butchers' union was over on Eighth.

There was a skinny, tired-looking guy in the front office, dressed in a shiny serge suit.

Did they, I asked, have a record on their members at this office?

"Yah."

"I've been trying to locate a man named Schmaltz," I told him, "a Vincent Schmaltz. Was a butcher at one time, I'm sure…"

"I don't need to look *him* up," shiny-suit told me. "He's been in here heckling us for work for a month."

"He wasn't working at his trade, then?"

"Nah. He hasn't been behind the counter for a long time. He was selling, wholesale, during the war and I don't think he's worked since."

"This last place he worked was—"

"Sperry and Doane. You know, down there on commission row. They're tied up with that grocery wholesaler next door. I forget the name."

"Well, thanks," I said. And added: "He hasn't been in today bothering you for work, has he?"

"Not today—yet." He looked at me suspiciously. "What are you, a cop or something? This Schmaltz in trouble?"

"The answer to both questions is yes," I told him, and left.

Down on commission row. That would be First Street and Water Street, along the river.

There were all kinds of trucks down there, new and old and big and small, and all of them were parked at an angle, their backs to the commission houses that lined the street.

Sperry and Doane. A small place wedged between a whole-sale grocery house and a fruit-and-vegetable wholesaler.

The truck drivers looked at my Dusy admiringly as I got out. They *know*. They know it has four hundred and twenty cubic inches of displacement, and double overhead cams, and develops two hundred and sixty-five horsepower, *without* the supercharger. They know, and you do, too, now.

Sperry and Doane's wasn't too well lighted, inside. There was a girl at the desk near the front, and some other desks toward the dim rear of the room, but nobody was sitting at them.

Nice bright girl for so gloomy a place. Bright eyes, and bright red hair, and a chipper way of asking: "Could I help you?"

"Business must be bad," I said.

She didn't mind the change of subject. "It isn't. I don't mean it isn't bad, I mean the business *isn't*. We're closing it down."

"We?"

"Well, not *we*. I mean I'm a very small cog, but the people who own it, Grenfell and Morgan. We're right next door, you know."

Grenfell and Morgan. But Morgan is a common name. Just a coincidence, no doubt. No doubt.

Red was saying: "But you're probably not interested in all this. What was it you wanted?"

"I want to travel with you," I said, "to some distant tropical isle. I want to strum some stringed thing that strums and look deep into the azure depths of those lovely eyes and hear you whisper all the things you should whisper."

"That's for later," she said. "What do you want now?"

"The boss."

"That would be next door. Either Mr. Grenfell or Mr. Morgan."

"*Sylvester* Morgan?"

"Hmm-hmm." Looking up. "You know him?"

I nodded. "He wears nice clothes."

"You should see Mr. Grenfell," she said.

I did see Mr. Grenfell. Morgan was out, and Grenfell wasn't busy. His office was only ordinary, but she was right about his clothes. And the diamond ring he wore could have served as a foglight.

He was a medium-sized man, and he had an abrupt directness about him. I asked about Vincent Schmaltz.

Nothing registered in his face. "An employee of ours?"

"At one time. During the war. Sold meat for that place you own next door, Sperry and Doane."

Something in the face now, though hard to analyze. Something like caution, apprehension. "I could have it checked for you." He pressed a button on his desk, and a girl came in. Very ordinary girl. She went to look it up.

Grenfell offered me a cigar, which I refused. He studied his nails, and made some remark about the heat. Then he asked casually: "Aren't you a detective?"

I nodded.

"I thought I remembered the name."

He was lying like hell. I'm not that well known. He knew about me, and he was worried about me.

"Read it somewhere?" I suggested.

He looked puzzled.

"My name," I explained. "You said you remembered it. Did you read about me somewhere? I don't advertise."

The apologetic half smile. "That's—ah—probably an understatement. Morgan told me about you, and that unfortunate trouble you had at your office. It was all in this morning's paper."

The girl came back with a card and a paper, which Grenfell studied. "This is it. Vincent J. Schmaltz. Sold meat for us until the summer of '45. But there's nothing else here that would help, not even an address."

If there *was* anything else there, I knew I wasn't going to see it.

Grenfell said: "Is he in some sort of trouble? I don't mean to pry into your business, you understand, but Morgan tells me that detective who was killed was working on something for him. And now this…" He started over. "I mean, it couldn't be just a coincidence, could it?"

"I don't think so," I said.

"Anything that affects Morgan, in a business way," he said, "affects me. And if you have any information on that score, I'd like to hear it."

"I haven't anything now." I said, "but I might have."

His eyes were probing now. "I want to see it, when you have. I'd pay, of course."

If he was the one, he'd pay. But not in money.

3

Slay-Belle

I THINK HE had some more questions, but I didn't give him any chance to ask them. The less he knew, the better.

I had more to go on now, but not enough. Or maybe I just didn't have sense enough to make a story of what I had. Schmaltz had worked for them, had been seen with Mike. Now Mike was dead, and Schmaltz was missing, Grenfell was worried and Morgan had given me a thousand dollars for one day's work.

There was an angle, but it didn't make sense. Not with people as high in the upper brackets as Grenfell and Morgan. However, I still had an hour before lunch.

I went over to the tax commissioner's office. I showed my badge, argued a little, and threw my weight around. Then I signed for it.

The clerk said: "You understand, of course, these men will be notified that you were given the information."

I nodded. If he could read my name, the way I'd scribbled it, he was a better man than he appeared to be.

Morgan had averaged about nine thousand dollars a year for the past five years, and Grenfell about ten.

Him and his fine suits, I thought. Him and his big cars, his expensive wife and high sounding talk. On nine thousand dollars a year. "I'm a wealthy man." How many times had he said that? And who was he trying to impress? Mortimer Jones, for one, and he had.

So it strengthened my hunch, but it didn't prove anything. There was a good chance that I'd never be able to prove it. Even if I could, how would it tie up with Mike's death, if at all?

The Dusy chuckled a little on the way back to my office. She likes it when I'm puzzled, when I look dumb.

I had lunch at Mac's, before going to the office.

At the office, I got out a bottle of my better whiskey, and poured a good, stout drink. I thought it might help. But it didn't. Nothing came to me, nothing bright. I was on my second drink when I heard the feet on the stairs again. These weren't big feet like Devine's. These were small feet, encased in white kid.

My gaze went up from the shoes, taking their time, taking in all the details of the green Chinese silk dress, so simple—so deceptively simple—and stopping at the green eyes. She wore no hat, as usual. With her hair, she didn't have to.

I rose with my customary suavity.

"Hello," she said.

"Hello."

"Is that your car, that Dusenberg, parked a couple of blocks away?"

So proud I was. "That's right."

"How fast will it go?"

I shrugged in my urbane way. "Hundred and thirty, maybe forty. I've never tried it."

"Would you take me for a ride? Would you let me drive it?"

I reverted to type. I put on my semi-scowl and said: "What's the angle? What have I got that you want?" Meeting her eyes and holding them. "You didn't come down here for that."

She sat in the leatherette chair. "Do you always drink alone?"

I poured her a drink. When I started to put in the seltzer, she shook her head. "Straight."

I sat back in my chair.

She said: "As to your unfounded suspicions, there's nothing I want from you. At least nothing I've thought of. Is there any reason you should dislike me? Am I being too forward for your delicate taste."

"Dislike you?" I said. "Me? Did I say that? I may suspect your intentions, Mrs. Morgan, but—"

"Call me Carol," she said.

"All right. But to get back to my thesis. I am not handsome. I am not rich. I am not well-dressed. All of these you are."

"You're modest," she said. "I like that."

I had another drink, and she did, too.

"Besides," she said, "you have a Dusenberg. I've always wanted one, ever since I can remember."

"You want to buy it?"

"Hmm-hmm."

"It's not for sale."

"How about the ride?"

"Later," I said.

"What are we going to do now?"

"Talk," I said. "About you and Sylvester and a man named Vincent J. Schmaltz. About a man named Grenfell and about Mike Greb."

"Grenfell, I know," she said, "and dear, dear Sylvester, that lovely old man. But Schmaltz—is there really a man by that name?"

"There is."

"I don't know him."

"He worked for your husband, for that Sperry and Doane Company. He sold meat."

"Lots of men work for my husband."

"Shall we talk about *him?*"

"If you like. It's a boring subject."

"Well," I said, "for a man who makes about nine thousand a year, he lives very well. He supports an expensive wife."

She tilted her head to one side, studying me. "Where'd you learn that?"

"It's right, isn't it?"

"I've no idea. That isn't much, is it?"

"By my standards it's enough. But not by yours."

"Let's have another drink," she said.

She could get away with anything because of her beauty, and she knew it. She didn't fear me, or the law, and she'd been around enough of the wrong places to understand that all men, or nearly all, can be handled in the traditional way.

"Mike Greb," I said, "was a friend of mine. And he was working for me. There isn't anything as important to me as finding out who killed him."

Her eyes turned a softer green, and her voice was quiet. "What have I to do with that? You don't think *I* had anything to do with it, do you?"

"You know some things you're not telling me," I accused her. "You're certainly not helping me any."

"O.K. My husband has more money than his income tax shows. It might be dishonest money. I don't know. I don't care. If he stole it, that's *his* crime. I don't ask him any questions about it and I don't intend to. The rest of this business means nothing to me. I don't know a thing about it."

"Then why did you come down here today?"

Smiling again. "I couldn't answer that honestly without losing my maidenly reserve. You wouldn't want that, would you?"

What could I do?

WE WALKED UP to where the Dusy was parked, and she got behind the wheel. She started the motor, and the Dusy purred like a milk-drinking kitten. It almost gloated.

She moved through the gears very nicely. She took it through traffic smartly, with no lost time and no unnecessary manipulating.

A very competent girl, this. She loved money, not for itself alone, but money was power, and that was what she wanted. This Dusy was designed for her. She probably loved other things, too, in her high spirited way, but nothing I could mention in a commercial publication.

Traffic was thinner now. We were coming to the end of the drive, and the beginning of the highway, and ahead was the stretch. The stretch is about five miles of straight broad highway, with no intersections.

"Kick it," I said.

The right foot, which was encased in kid, pressed toward the floorboard, probing for power. The Dusy seemed to settle into stride, and the motor hum rose in a sort of exultation.

No tremble, no strain in this sweetheart of mine. Just a seeking of the pace demanded, and the steadily increasing whine of those eight cylinders and thirty-two valves.

Carol's eyes were on the road ahead. They were bright, unnaturally bright, and I thought she might be trembling. But her hands were steady on the wheel, and she was in complete control. As she would always be.

We went up to seventy, cruising, and then into the eighties. Ahead, there was a truck, and coming from the other direction, a car. The car coming was in the wrong lane.

We went around with no effort, with no pause for indecision, with skill and daring and very fine timing.

The nineties now, and still not straining. Her foot was on the floor, and we were still climbing. I didn't watch the speedometer for a while, and when I did it was way up there.

We were up there, now, where we had no right to be. At that speed anything can happen. The centrifugal force can throw a tire, or an unsteady hand on the wheel could send us off the road before the mind could adjust to it. Well, I thought, nobody lives forever.

We were coming to the end of the stretch now. The motor whine was perceptibly lower. She was letting the compression brake in, gradually.

When we were down where we should be, she asked: "How fast did we go?"

"A hundred and sixteen."

"You said it could do more than that."

"Did I?"

"You lied to me."

"And you to me."

No answer to that.

I said: "You came out here without any directions from me. You know this stretch?"

"Yup. It's a nice piece of road. It helps me when I'm bored, when Sylvester gets tiresome. I like speed. It's a—a—"

"Mental cathartic," I finished for her.

She glanced over at me doubtfully. "What's that?"

"Never mind. Has Sylvester been tiresome today?"

There was a drive-in, and she drove in. "I'd like a coke," she said. "Wouldn't you?"

"You haven't answered my question," I said.

"It's a personal question, too personal."

A buxom lass, wearing too much make-up and a too-tight blue uniform, came to take our order.

"Two cokes," I said. "Big ones."

Carol was grinning. "They cost a nickel more, you know."

"I can make it."

She was still grinning. "All right. Sylvester *was* tiresome. And so are you, now."

"Look, being tiresome is what I get paid for. I'm not one of your panting swains, living only to amuse you, to keep your corner bright. I'm just a guy trying to find out something."

The girl came with our cokes. She put the tray on the door, set the cokes on the tray, and walked away. Carol, watching her, said: "She should wear a girdle."

"She should eat less."

"Kill-joy," she said.

No words from me. Talking with her was like playing a game, a game without objective. It was a game I wouldn't have minded playing under different circumstances. This was no time for games.

We finished our cokes, and the girl came to take the tray. I tipped her more than I should have, hoping Carol would notice, but she didn't.

I got out of the car and went around to the driver's side.

"Slide over," I said. "I'm driving back."

"No."

"It's my car. I don't want you to drive it."

She slid over. She was smiling, and the green eyes were bright. "You can't come to my house and play with my tricycle, or my blocks, or my trains."

"I don't want to come to your house," I said. "I don't want to see you, excepting maybe in court, or in the jug."

"Would you come, if I were in jail? Would you bring me magazines and candy and flowers? Would you bring me a cake, with a big file hidden in it?"

I kicked the starter. The Dusy grumbled a little, at the change in drivers.

I swung around, and headed back. I put her up to forty, and kept her there. My eyes were on the road, and my mind was a blank.

"I'm sorry," she said. "I'm a stinker."

"You're just a girl," I said evenly, "who is in a murder case. You may be guilty, or innocent, but you're in it, up to your lovely neck. You've been lucky. You've always had your own way. You think you can get away with murder, too, and maybe you can. But there is also an outside chance that maybe you can't. In which case you will be treated as all adults are treated who do things against the law. Your—your charms won't make a bit of difference then."

"Libel," she said. "Could I sue you for libel, or slander, if none of these things are true?"

"I don't know. Ask your lawyer."

"I love you when you're so grim."

I said nothing.

"When you play hard to get. Sylvester and I squabbled today, and I came down to your office, hoping to charm you, and you were so nice about letting me drive your car."

I remained silent.

"And now you're being so noble and virile, and I still like it. You certainly must be successful with the ladies."

We were coming into the traffic of the drive now. I moved around various cars, stopped for a light, and turned. But I said nothing.

Through the city's traffic, silently, to the place where I park the Dusy. She got out with me, and walked with me to the office. Her car was parked in front of the building and there was a little kid studying its yellow elegance.

She got in and started the motor. Then she leaned out, smiling, and said: "You don't scare me. Not even a *little* bit." And she drove off.

The kid and I watched her go down the street. "Some babe," the kid said. "Some doll."

"Some babe," I admitted. "Some doll."

"And some car," the kid said.

He should have seen mine.

SLOWLY AND THOUGHTFULLY, I went up the stairs to my office. Actually I was looking more thoughtful than I was being thoughtful. Or rather, I was full of thoughts, but they were leading nowhere. Some babe, some doll…

The glasses we'd been using, before the ride, were still there and I took them over to the sink behind the screen, and washed them. I turned on the radio, but it was all opera (soap).

The top of my desk was gritty, and I dusted it. Then I dusted the window sills and the top of the filing cabinet, and some other places the cleaning woman couldn't have noticed. My desk she leaves alone, anyway, at my specific request.

I washed my hands and dried them. I was doing all this on my own time, I reflected, though that thousand Morgan had given me would cover a lot of days at twenty dollars a day.

During the war, I hadn't been in this town. I'd been in lots of other towns, and in places that had once been towns, doing unpleasant things at low wages with a rifle.

But Mike had been here. And Mike, too, had been doing more or less unpleasant things, at medium wages, and carrying a revolver. (Colt Police Positive Special, 5-inch barrel, blued finish, fixed sights—trigger, hammer spur and stock, all checked—caliber .38).

Mike had specialized most of that time on this one thing. I knew what it was and it tied in, all right. It made sense out of the disappearance of Vincent J. and the wealth of Morgan, and the concern of Grenfell, and the interest of Mrs. Carol Morgan, and Mike, himself, going off on the wrong lead.

I could make a story out of it. I could even include Jimmy Dexter as one of the characters, and give him a reason for being in the cast. It wasn't a story that I wanted, though. That was all in the past. What I wanted was something in the present. What I wanted was a pointing finger, as they say. What I wanted was a murder, not a sordid, ugly story from wartime.

Well, maybe I hadn't met him yet. Maybe there were nooks and crannies and backwaters I hadn't explored. That could be. Maybe I'd *never* meet him—or her.

I took one of the glasses I'd washed, and the bottle, and poured another drink. I looked at my watch, and it was time for the ball game so I turned on the radio.

The phone rang, and I turned it off.

The voice with the music in it. "Still angry?"

"Not particularly."

"Could I see you tonight?"

"Why?"

"It's important. I'm calling from a drugstore. It's about Sylvester, and I *must* see you. You've got to arrange it somehow."

"Where and when?"

"At the Slipper, at nine?"

"All right. We aren't going to talk in circles, though, are we? We're going to get right to the point, and make some sense."

"I wouldn't have phoned," she said, "if it wasn't important."

The line went dead.

I had no further interest in the ball game. I had a faint and ego-gratifying sense of triumph, and I wallowed in it, letting it get bigger. She hadn't been so confident over the phone, so sure of herself. For the first time since I'd known her, she needed help.

Of course, I'd known her only two days. And it might not be help she wanted, not at all. But I liked to think it was.

I was tired. I walked over to the car, and started it. She was still grumbling.

"To hell with you," I said. "I thought you were a female. What's so impressive about her?"

No answer, but the grumbling stopped.

I pulled down all the shades in the apartment, opened all the windows, and pulled the bed out of the wall. I took a cold shower, and tried to get some sleep.

It took a while but it came, finally, without the dreams this time. When I awoke, it was cooler, and my head was clearer, though my mouth tasted the way mothballs smell.

Brushing of the teeth and showering of the body, and humming gaily to myself. Putting on a terrycloth robe and making coffee. Sitting around, drinking the coffee, and reading Saroyan, that talented and uninhibited young Armenian. Like Jimmy Dexter plays the piano, that's the way Saroyan writes.

There was a knock at the door. It could have been the voice, or Vincent J. Schmaltz or Carol, but it was just a bakery man, selling bakery, and I bought some doughnuts to go with the coffee.

After the doughnuts, a cigarette, and after that a little nap. Not sleeping, but dozing, half thinking and feeling satisfied with myself and my agile brain. Because the finger would point tonight, I felt sure. She hadn't phoned just to spend the nickel.

The coolness held, for which I was thankful. The breeze was from the east, and that's the way my windows face. I shaved carefully and didn't nick myself once.

The blue suit, because it was the best I had. This week I'd buy some others. I was fed up with cheap suits, and I had a thousand dollars. I wasn't hungry, so I didn't go to Mac's.

Happy Jack was not in evidence at the Slipper. He was probably in the kitchen or the pantry, chewing out the help, and being mean.

The headwaiter was being head-waiterish. Did I have a reservation? With Dexter playing, they could ask that.

"No," I said, "I was to meet Mrs. Morgan here at nine-thirty, though, and she undoubtedly has a reservation."

Mrs. *Sylvester* Morgan?

I nodded casually, the better to impress him.

"This way, sir." What a difference just a few words make.

The same table, near the bandstand, one of the few vacant tables in the place.

The headwaiter left, and an ordinary working waiter came, and I ordered a drink. Then there was a hush over the place, and applause. I didn't look up. I didn't want to look at him.

Star Dust and *Nola* and *Deep Purple* and a number I didn't recognize but would never forget. This boy, I thought, is making a lot of money for Jack Zarze, and he should be making a lot of money for himself. It's cleaner work than robbing banks, and safer, and it should pay him just about as much.

In one corner of the room, I saw a man who could have been Grenfell of Grenfell and Morgan, but the light wasn't bright enough for me to be sure. Nor was there any reason why he shouldn't be here—any bad reason, I mean.

The room was smoky and dim, except for that spotlight, and the music was soft and persuasive, and I was getting sleepy. I had another drink, as Jimmy left the stand, and the orchestra came on.

A very ordinary orchestra, but people got up to dance, and they danced, according to their skills and their inclinations, and talked, and probably lied to each other and about each other. And they drank, and ate. And I had another drink, and wondered if she would show up, or if it had been a gag.

IT WASN'T A gag. The dancers were off the floor, and I had an uninterrupted view of the doorway, and I saw her come in. In white again, that wheat-colored hair piled high.

The white was linen, but not the garment she had worn the first day. This was a suit, which, though man-tailored, did nothing to detract from her complete and ever-present femininity.

"I'm late," she said.

"You're late," I agreed.

Jade earrings and a jade ring—no other jewelry. "And you're angry again."

"No."

I held her chair, and she sat down. The waiter came, she ordered a drink, and so did I. Her eyes were on my face. "You're well-disciplined, aren't you? You take pride in it."

"Are we going to talk about me? Haven't you something more important to talk about than that?"

"About Sylvester then." Her eyes on mine, her gaze grave and steady. "You said some things about him today, about his having more money than the record shows. Is it true he only made nine thousand dollars last year?"

"That's right," I said, "and for a few years before that."

"How about the other years? He's an old man."

"And he's been in that business most of his adult life. I checked that, too, and these last have been his best years." I lighted a cigarette. "Why this sudden interest in his income? You weren't interested in it this afternoon."

"I know that lots of wealthy men cheat on their income tax. I've heard them brag about it. But what happened this afternoon, after I got home, put a different light on it."

She looked frightened now. I asked: "What happened?"

"He threatened me. He threatened to kill me, or kill himself, if he ever found out that I'd been unfaithful to him. He said that, impossible as I might think it, he could kill if there was any reason to, or any need to. He hinted that it wouldn't be the first time."

"Where do I enter this cozy tableau?" I asked.

"You don't believe me," she said.

I shook my head, "You've never given me any reason to. And though I suspect that your husband is guilty of treason, I doubt if he has the constitution necessary for murder."

"Treason!" Surprise in her lovely face, but no skepticism. She could believe it of him. "That's a strange word to use."

"We won't talk about it, now," I said. "I haven't got all the information I need, yet. Who did your husband suspect?"

"You," she said.

She must have seen the disbelief in my face, for she went on: "That's right. He knew I came to see you yesterday morning, and he knows I came to see you this afternoon."

I didn't believe it. I asked: "He threatened suicide, too?"

She nodded. "He said he'd kill himself, rather than give me up. Do you think he would?"

"I don't know. Did you threaten to leave him?"

She nodded, and the dim light reflected in her golden hair. "I told him I would leave him if he ever got abusive or suspicious."

It made a very plausible story. The ancient dandy and the vital young blonde, the frustration and suicide. It would make a credible story for the newspapers. The tabloids would eat it up. But it was as phony as a Mexican diamond.

I said: "I think we ought to go up and see your husband right now."

She studied me for a minute. "Let me call him, first." She rose and went to the phone booths in the lobby, and I saw her disappear into one of them.

A hush was falling over the room again, then the applause came, and a little later the music, a tune called *Margie* which you might remember.

Then Carol was coming back, across the deserted floor, and there was a frown on that face which hadn't been designed for frowning.

"He says we should come up in an hour," she whispered. "What do you think he means by that?"

I shrugged, and whispered back: "We'll go up in an hour and find out."

The people at the next table looked on us with visible disfavor, as though we'd been laughing in church.

We said no more until Jimmy was through, and the band came back. Then Carol asked: "Do you dance? Or is that too frivolous for you?"

"I dance," I said, and we did.

I don't usually get much enjoyment out of dancing on a nightclub floor, because it's generally crowded, and the bands aren't always good, or the floor. This band wasn't too good, nor was the floor, and it was crowded, but I enjoyed it.

"Still hate me?" We were back at the table.

"The belle of the ball," I said. "Haven't we enough trouble without your going coy on me? Why should I hate you? I've been heckled before, and lied to, and I didn't hate those people. I get a lot of it in my business."

"Still want to put me in the—the jug, wasn't it?"

"If you belong there," I said, "you'll wind up there. A person's luck can last just so long, and you've been pressing yours."

WE SAT AND watched the others dance for a while, and I ate a sandwich. I was just finishing it when Happy Jack Zarze dropped by, counting the house. The scowl was gone from his face, though the cigar was still there. He gave me a hello much bigger than the one of the night before, and there was no "copper" on the end of it.

"Have a drink with us," Carol said.

"I don't usually drink with cops," Jack said, "but I guess that wouldn't mean you any more, would it, Jonesy?"

"Not strictly," I said. "How's business?"

"This one's doing very well. And my other—ah—interests are in good hands," he said.

He'd been drinking and was in that mood called expansive by some, and sloppy by others. These "other—ah—interests" would be the ones outside the law, or on the thin edge of legality.

"That Jimmy boy is fine, isn't he?" he asked me. "He's worth all the money I can pay him."

"He's as good as I've ever heard," I admitted. "I hope he sticks to the piano after this."

"He will. Carol and I will see to that." He gave her a smile as broad as his face, and a look you could put on pancakes. Jack Zarze, night-club owner and out-sized Casanova.

"Carol," I said carefully, "certainly has sacrificed enough for the boy's career. Her own, probably. Don't you think so, Jack?" He didn't answer.

He pretended he hadn't heard, and watched the dancers, rolling that dead cigar in his mouth.

Carol asked: "What did you mean by that?"

"I heard you sing," I said. "That was your profession, wasn't it?"

"And I can go back to it, any time I want," she said.

"Would Sylvester approve?"

"So long as I have Sylvester," she pointed out, "I won't need to go back to it." Which brought the conversation around in a circle again. I gave it up, and helped Jack watch the dancers.

Then Jack put the mangled cigar on the ashtray in the center of the table, and asked Carol would she like to dance, and asked me would I mind. It was agreeable to both of us. Or rather, to all three of us, because he must have liked it, the way he held her.

I put him into the mixer, along with the others, and the mixer revolved in my mind. Then I added Jimmy Dexter. And just because I don't like him, I added Devine, but he was too dumb and I threw him out again.

I got up, and walked over to the men's room, taking a roundabout way of getting there, a way that took me past that dim corner.

It *was* Grenfell who was sitting there at the corner table, and who should be with him but the girl with the red hair, the chipper girl who was all that was left of Sperry and Doane.

"Good evening," I said. "Hello." With my famous smile.

He nodded austerely, the redhead grimaced a grimace which could have meant anything but probably meant nothing, and I continued on to the men's room.

On the way back, I ignored them, with hauteur.

Carol was still dancing with Happy Jack. The band was playing an old number, *Dancing in the Dark.* Remember it? The lights were low, even by Jack's standards. The orchestra knew the number and improvised a little on it, and then the clarinet, which wasn't bad, took a ride on it and did all right.

Good music and pleasant company, a beautiful girl and soft lights, the Dusy waiting for me outside, and money in the bank. I had no reason to be unhappy, but tomorrow they would bury

Mike Greb, and I'd be at the funeral.

I sat at the table, toying with an empty glass, and wondering how it would be, working at Devine's job, getting my checks from the city. The chief would give it to me, I knew, and Devine knew, and that was one reason he had no love for me—though I could and would admit it might not be the only reason.

Carol and Jack returned to the table, and we talked about this and that, but my mind wasn't in it, just my tongue. Finally, Carol said: "It's about time, isn't it?"

I consulted my watch, and it was.

Happy Jack signed the check in a spasm of generosity, and we made our adieus, as they say, and went out into the lovely city night. Lights all around, on the streets going by, and in the windows, and high up on top of buildings bright signs advertising this and that at prices all can afford. That is, of course, all who had the money.

"We'll take my car," Carol said. "I'll bring you back." She looked up at me. "Unless you'd let me drive yours?"

"All right," I said, "but when you get to be thirteen years old, I'm going to start to discipline you."

She was still looking up and I was looking down. It was bright out in the street, but this impulse came, and I kissed her. Which she expected, because she reciprocated in her artful way.

"You and your wiles," I said.

That laugh again, the laugh of a kid at a circus, only more musical, and I didn't think she'd ever been a kid. But, of course, she must have been at one time.

The Dusy coughed into life, and I showed her where to turn on the lights, and we moved out into traffic. Neither of us said anything. I wondered how many men had kissed her, but it wasn't a question you'd ask a married woman of her high and strict standards. No, no, many thousand times, no.

Toward Ardmore Court now, which is the street she lived on. It's a winding, climbing street flanked by beautiful homes and well-kept lawns and has the general tone of the upper classes.

On one of the winds, and halfway up the climb, she stopped the car. This home of hers was about as big as the others—what I could see of it in the street light—and about as expensive, and the lawn may have been as well-kept.

"Italian Renaissance," she offered. "At least that's what Sylvester says, and he wouldn't lie."

"Nice," I said. "Lots of room to swing a cat in, I'll bet."

"Would you like to kiss me again?"

"No," I said, which might have been something of a lie.

We walked up some flagstones set in the lawn, and onto the porch. She put a key in the lock, and we went in. "The servants are out," she said, by way of explaining the key, and impressing me.

An entrance hall, or maybe reception hall, with inlaid flooring, an Oriental rug and a couple of dignified dark wood, high-backed chairs. An arch off this, leading to the living room where there was a light.

"Sylvester?" Carol called softly, as we went through the arch. Sylvester didn't answer. Sylvester was dead.

4

Kindly Omit Flowers

HE WAS SITTING in a maroon wingback chair. His mouth was open, his face livid and mottled, and the eyes were staring in the dim light. There was a coffee table in front of the chair, and a decanter, full, and a glass, empty, on the table.

A small sound came from Carol's throat, and she swayed. I caught her as she fell.

I carried her over to a divan, put her down gently, then went to look for a phone. There was one in the hall, and I called Headquarters.

Then I went back to the living room. I rubbed Carol's wrists, and eventually her eyelids fluttered, and those green eyes were looking into mine.

Her voice was a hoarse whisper. "He's committed suicide, hasn't he? As he threatened to do. And they'll think I—"

"Try not to think of it," I said.

The lights of a car coming up the road illumined the room more brightly for a moment, and then passed on.

"But why would he do that, Jonesy? Do you think he loved me that much?"

"What makes you think it's suicide?" I asked her.

Her eyes looked startled. "Isn't it?"

"I don't know. That's for the police to decide. I called them."

"The police? You don't think it's suicide, then?"

"Suicide is a crime, too. And they'll bring a doctor along."

More lights coming up the Court. The cars stopped and feet sounded on the walk. I went to the door.

Glen Harvey came in, and Doc Walters, and another detective. "Devine'll be along later," Glen said. "We called him at home."

If Devine never came it would be all right with me.

Harvey was looking uncomfortable. Doc and the other detective had gone in, but Harvey lingered at the door with me.

"I'll want to talk to the girl alone, and you later, alone. You understand that, don't you, Jonesy?"

"I'll be out on the porch," I said, "smoking a cigarette."

He looked relieved, as he left me.

There were some chairs on the porch, and I took one of the comfortable ones. The people next door were having a party. I could see them, through the full-length windows, and I could hear them, in the back yard. A house full and a yard full—it must take a lot of cabbage. And liquor. I wondered how it felt to be one of the upper classes.

Across the street, a couple was leaving. The woman's voice was high and shrill. "Now, don't forget Thursday night, Alice. We'll be expecting you there. It wouldn't be any fun without you."

The door closed, and they came down the walk to where a Packard Clipper was parked. They got in and drove away.

Lights began to go out, in the house across the street.

A couple next door was doing a rhumba, while the others in the room drank and watched. They weren't very good, I thought, but the watchers seemed to enjoy it.

A car came up the road, and stopped.

I could see it was Devine when he got out. He came up the

flagstones quickly, then paused on the porch. He could see the glow of my cigarette, I realized, but not me, not clearly.

He came over. "Oh," he said, "you."

"Me."

"You seem to be where the trouble is lately, don't you?"

"That's where a good cop belongs, where the trouble is."

"Are you one of those? You consider yourself a good cop?"

I took my time with that. The way he worded it, I didn't want to seem lacking in modesty. "The chief thinks I am," I said.

There was no sound from him for a moment, though I thought I could hear his breathing. Then he called me a name. But there was no anger, no venom in it, only a sort of defeated tiredness.

I was just a little ashamed of myself. It was rubbing salt in an open wound, what I'd said to him.

"I'll be back later," he said, and went into the house.

He's got to live, I thought, and he does the best he can. He's got a family to support, and he works fifteen hours a day. If he's a moron, it's just the way he was born. Try to be tolerant, Mortimer, try to be a gentleman.

Thinking of gentlemen made me think of Morgan, and I wondered what they'd decided in the house. I turned my chair around, and looked through the window.

Carol was sitting up on the divan, and Devine was standing in front of her. Glen Harvey and Doc Walters were near the body of Sylvester Morgan. Then Doc left, and I could see he was coming to the door, so I turned my chair around again.

Doc came out on the porch, but he didn't look at me. He went down to the ambulance, and when he came back a couple of his boys were with him.

Everything was being done very quietly. No sirens had sounded, no red lights had come flashing up this exclusive street. The people next door and the people across the street didn't suspect and they probably wouldn't until they read the papers in the morning.

In my neighborhood, the sirens would have sounded and the red lights would have gone crazy and everybody would have known, and anyone who wanted to sleep wouldn't have been able to.

Then Glen Harvey came out and lighted a cigarette as I threw mine away. He said: "You'll have to come down in the morning for a statement, of course."

"Of course," I said. I was watching my cigarette glowing on the lawn, on that undoubtedly expensive lawn.

"You got anything to say now?"

"Mrs. Morgan and I came up here to see her husband. He set the time. She phoned from the Slipper, and he said we should come up in an hour. When we did we found him like that."

"You came up here to see him? You had business with him?"

"He was jealous of me. I though I ought to straighten him out on that."

"Jealous?"

"He thought I was trying to make a play for his wife." My cigarette was dying on the lawn now, and then it went out.

"That's a hell of a story, Jonesy."

"I know it," I said. "It's true, though."

"It's the same one she told," he said.

"What are they thinking in there?" I asked, "or is that official business?"

"Doc thinks it's conine. There was a little whiskey left in the glass. The servants were out. He sent them out, and—"

"*He* sent them out?" I asked.

"That's right. That's what she claims, anyway. We'll get hold of them soon's we can. The way it builds up, he was planning this suicide, so he sent them away. He knew his wife was going to be gone, and—"

THERE WAS A voice from the doorway. "All right, Harvey. That's department business. Both of you come in here." Devine.

Glen's cigarette went over to join mine on the lawn, and we followed Devine into the sitting room.

Carol still sat on the divan and her eyes went to mine when I entered. She seemed to have herself under control.

The boys were putting Sylvester on the stretcher, and Harvey stood in front of Carol, so as to block her view. Devine said: "Jealousy seems to be the motive here. That was why Mr. Morgan came down to see you in the first place, wasn't it, Jones?"

"I guess so," I said. "It's about as close as any other reason."

Carol seemed to straighten, and Devine looked at me sharply. "You trying to suggest it might be something else?"

"It might be a rich man worried about his investment," I said, "or worried about his wife, or just nervous generally because of something on his conscience. All I know is that he wanted some work done, and I did it. I don't usually ask for motives."

Carol looked shocked.

"You've already made your mind up, anyway. A simple case of suicide, and you've got a cleaned-up case to your credit. Otherwise, it might mean work."

Carol said: "If you don't think it was suicide, Mr. Jones, perhaps you can let us in on your opinion."

Mr. Jones, that was good. She had perked up considerably. I shook my head. "I haven't got an opinion."

"Then I wouldn't pop off," Devine said, "if I were you."

Glen Harvey coughed, and studied the floor. Carol expelled her breath audibly, almost like a sigh. The front door closed behind Doc Walters, and Devine said: "You told me once that Mike Greb wasn't investigating this case. Are you going to stick to that?"

"Well..." I said.

"We found a thirty-eight here. It could be the gun that killed him. I'll know in another hour. If it is, you were lying to me that night in your office."

"Who found the gun, and where?"

"I found it, in that cigar stand right next to the chair."

"The door of which was open," I said.

He looked at me suspiciously. "Yah. Why?"

"Nothing," I said. "Nothing I should have to tell a cop."

All they needed was a box office. They had the plot and the characters and the scenery and the willing audience. They had all the business.

"Does Doc Walters think it was conine?" I asked.

"That's right," Devine said.

"Rather difficult for a man to get. I know he had the money, and could get it, but it would take some time. Unless, of course, he'd been planning this suicide for some time. But he seemed fairly well satisfied with life the last time I saw him."

Devine said dryly: "I haven't called it suicide that I remember. You're taking a lot for granted." Then: "You want to admit you were lying about what case your friend Mike Greb was working on?"

"Maybe," I said. "I think Mike Greb was working on the same thing he worked on during the war. Only from a different angle. He was off the beam, probably, because he was working against our client, instead of for him. And that's why he died."

Carol's eyes were on my face, puzzled. I thought they were a little frightened, too, but I couldn't be sure. She asked: "Does all that tie in with what you were telling me this afternoon? Do you think my husband was responsible for the death of that detective?"

I believe that was what she wanted me to think. "Indirectly, probably," I said.

"You mean—"

"I don't want to say anything I can't prove," I said. "All I have are hunches, just the obvious things according to how it shapes up. I haven't any accusations to make, or names to name."

Relief on her face, and then she put one hand to her forehead. "It's been a rather harrowing evening. Will there be many more questions tonight, please?"

Devine's voice was practically crawling with servility. "Just a few, Mrs. Morgan." He turned to me. "That's all for you. I'll see you in the morning."

"Of course, Mr. Devine," I said. "Certainly. Anything you say."

Harvey coughed, Devine grunted, and Carol stared wonderingly as I went to the door. I went out into the night. Something was missing, had been missing all evening, and I realized it was the reporters. They should have been thicker than flies. But this was too hush-hush, and they had been kept away. The party was still going on next door, and everybody seemed to be having a good time.

This is democracy, I thought. Who are they to be dancing the rhumba, and dancing it badly, while a man is poisoned next door?

The car Devine was driving was right in back of the Dusy. I went over and started the Dusy's motor. Then I went to Devine's car, opened the door, and found the button.

The sound of the siren went screaming into the night.

Harvey was running down from the doorway, and the windows of the house next door were crammed with rubbernecks as I drove off. The Dusy's chuckle was practically human.

THEY BURIED MIKE at Woodlawn, up near Bay Falls. All the lodge brothers were there, it seemed, and most of the cops I knew, but only one relative, because that was all Mike had left in the way of relatives. He was a nephew, a thin, shabby little man who didn't look sad and didn't look happy. He seemed preoccupied and nervous throughout the whole ceremony.

Glen Harvey drove back with me, after it was over. He was quiet, and he didn't mention the siren incident. He said: "Mike was pretty old, at that, wasn't he?"

"He gave about forty years to the city," I said, "so he couldn't have been any spring chicken."

"I've given 'em twenty-five myself," he said.

I couldn't think of anything to add to that.

"There must be some better way to make a living," he said, then lapsed into silence. He didn't say another word all the way into town.

I went to headquarters with him. Devine wasn't there, but the ballistics man was, and he told me the gun they'd found in

Morgan's home was the gun that had killed Mike Greb. Also Doc Walters had definitely established the poison as conine. So much for that.

I dictated and signed a statement in the chief's office. When I was through, he offered me a cigar, which I refused. He looked out the window, at the end of the cigar he was smoking, and up at me. "Why do you have to be so anti-social?" he said. He was smiling.

I looked as innocent as my face will permit. "Who, me?"

"With Devine. Can't you two get along?"

"Any reason we should?"

He frowned a little and carefully tipped the ash off his cigar into the oversized glass ashtray on his desk. "Well, in the interests of justice—" He paused, considering that. "That's too pompous a word. In the interests of efficiency. I like to consider all the detectives in this city, department and private, as *our* men. I want to cooperate with them, and I expect…"

The voice went on, like an after-dinner speaker, and I listened respectfully, because he was a good man, honest and competent, even though a trifle windy.

When he was through, I said quite humbly: "I'll try, chief. I'll make you proud of me yet."

He looked at me suspiciously.

I asked: "And about Mike Greb?"

"It seems to be finished. The rest of that business would be Federal, wouldn't it?"

"You think Morgan killed him?"

"Morgan had the gun. Morgan's prints were on the gun."

"Nice and clean. No other prints?"

"Ah, I believe so."

Well, nobody was paying me to find out any more. If they were satisfied, I had no reason to kick. The Feds could dig up the rest. Maybe they'd find something and maybe they wouldn't. The Morgan case was finished for the second time.

Only Mike Greb had been working for me.

I went over to Mac's. Mac was saying: "A right hook this guy calls it. How can an orthodox boxer have a *right* hook? Here, I'll show you." Business of placing the customer in a boxer's stance, left foot forward, left hand extended. "Now, try to *hook* a right."

The customer obliged, and saw the error of it. I said: "One beer."

Mac went back behind the bar, and drew it "Hot, ain't it?" he asked.

This is where I came in, I thought. It's hot, and I'm drinking a beer, and… I listened. Yup, I could hear the kids' voices in the street outside. Nice clean prints on Morgan's gun. I got the rhythm of it as it ran through my mind. No business of yours, Mortimer Jones. You want the voice to meet you in the alley again?

The voice, sure. That was a pointing finger, all right. But it was the Fed's business. If they asked me, I'd tell them.

I went up to the office. There was some mail on the floor. An ad from one of the third-floor clothiers, an ad from a loan agency, explaining how good my credit was, and a letter from a farmer kid up around Geneva who wanted to know if my Dusy was for sale yet. Some day that kid would design a car of his own, and then it would be Miller, Dusenberg and him.

I was contemplating a drink, when I heard the feet on the stairs. The steps were even heavier than Devine's. I settled in my chair, and thoughtfully brooded over the letter regarding the soundness of my credit.

He filled the doorway. He was as broad as he was tall, and he was wearing a Palm Beach suit that would have made a complete set of seatcovers for the Dusy. He wore a white shirt, oxford, and a hand-painted tie. Big but not impressive.

He was certainly over thirty, but the face was about sixteen and would probably stay that way until the wrinkles came. His voice was nasal. "I'm Rutherford Morgan, Sylvester's nephew."

Hang on to your hats, I thought. Here we go again. "Sit down, Mr. Morgan," I said politely.

The leatherette chair complained creakingly. It was really too much to expect of a secondhand chair.

"I've been to the police," he said, "but the case is closed as far as they're concerned."

And poor little Rutherford, possible heir, is out in the cold. For the Widow Morgan will get all that lovely green stuff, and that big house (Italian Renaissance) and the two cars.

"My uncle wouldn't commit suicide."

"You represent *all* the relatives, Mr. Morgan?"

"I'm the only one. Outside of—of her."

And if she poisoned him, I thought, you would get the money. Because the criminal cannot profit by his crime. You could get you a nice, sharp young lawyer and then you could live in that big house. Only it would be difficult to maintain on what was left of nine thousand a year. Rutherford didn't know about that, though.

"You think—"

"I think my uncle was murdered."

"By—"

He took out a handkerchief and mopped his wet face. "We don't need to mention any names. If she didn't do it, she had a hand in it."

I studied my nails. "You were working for Uncle Sylvester, weren't you?" he asked.

I nodded.

"Well, now you can work for me. What are your rates?"

"Twenty dollars a day. And expenses." I shook my head. "Look, your uncle made nine thousand dollars a year, but he lived like a millionaire. Do you want an investigation made of that? Do you realize what it means?"

"You know quite a lot about him," he said. He tried a smile of cunning, but it was insipid on that immature face.

"I'm asking if you want to do that to your uncle's memory?"

"I'm not as dumb as I look," he said.

That would have been impossible, I thought. Who else had said that? Oh, yes, the landlady, the mammoth in black.

That smile was still on his face. "Unless you've got some reason for staying out of this deal."

I gulped a big gulp, but managed to say calmly: "I'm probably going to work on it for free, for reasons I'm sure you wouldn't understand. I'm just trying to save you some money, for reasons even I can't understand. Are you getting this?"

"It's coming through."

"If we cut Mrs. Carol Whitney Morgan out of her inheritance, you will be next in line. However, the money that has gone to maintain her sinful elegance will not be found. It will be cash money—in no bank, and in no safety-deposit box, in no way available. I'm not boring you?"

"Not when you talk about money."

"You will get the house, perhaps, and the cars, though they might already be in her name. You might wind up with nothing."

"I'm a guy," he said, "who draws to inside straights."

He probably was, too. Which might explain his present need.

He was reaching into the inner breast pocket of the Palm Beach suit. He brought out a fine alligator wallet and opened it. The bills he took from it were hundreds, and there were five of them in that huge paw.

"My rates," I said again, "are twenty dollars a day."

He shook his head. "If you don't find that my uncle was murdered, you can refund the rest. If you do, it's yours."

The five hundreds were crisp and new, but damp, from his hands. I wrote out a receipt for the money, and on the back of the receipt, a resumé of the terms involved. All business, that's Mortimer Jones.

Then I asked: "Drink?"

He shook his head. "I don't drink."

He didn't drink, but he drew to inside straights. And he was probably taking eighteen months to pay back the five hundred to Curley's Credit Company, easy terms. Oh, well…

His heavy feet went down the stairs, and I poured a drink.

THE PHONE RANG, some time later, and my friend at the morgue said: "You got a crystal ball, Jonesy?"

"Sure, naturally."

"That guy with the short index finger. Anyway, some guy with a short index finger. They fished him out of the river this morning."

"Of course."

"Don't be so smug. What do I do now?"

"Follow me carefully," I said, "and don't miss a word. You call the chief of police. You tell him that Vincent J. Schmaltz is dead. You tell him that Morgan is ambidextrous, and that he probably held Schmaltz under the water with one hand and shot Mike Greb with the other. That will clean everything up."

"Just like that, huh?"

"Just like that. Then drop up here, when you get time, and I'll give you twenty dollars."

"Check?"

"No, cash."

"O.K., but it's a silly way to make twenty dollars."

He should be particular about jobs.

I had another drink, then turned on the radio, and listened to the news. I turned it off, and sat by the window, watching the kids. I opened the phone book, found the number, and called it.

Some woman's voice on the phone, and I asked for Mrs. Morgan.

Who was calling, please?

I told her. "And tell Mrs. Morgan it's very important," I added.

Her voice then, and I didn't detect any sadness in it, as befitted a recently bereaved widow.

"I'd like to talk to you," I said, "at my office. I'd like to explain who killed your husband."

A long silence. I could hear all the noises outside, and a fly buzzing in the office, but nothing from her. Finally: "It will have to be tonight. I've some things to do today, important things."

"All right," I said, "at nine o'clock, here."

The important things she had to do were all by way of making contact, I knew. She had to rehearse her part, and get her lines straight, and assemble the cast. While I was setting the stage.

The phone rang again, as I knew it would, and it was the chief's voice, as I expected. "Do you think you're a comedian, by any chance?"

"N-no."

"What about this Schmaltz? Some punk from the morgue called up and gave me a lot of double-talk about Schmaltz and Mike and Morgan."

"You should know all the answers to that."

"And if I don't, I'd expect some cooperation from someone who does. I don't want—"

"I'm glad you mentioned that," I interrupted. "Cooperation is what I'm seeking," and I went on and on, explaining in just what way I sought it, and when.

Then I hung up, and had another drink (small). I went down to the license bureau to check something, and to the bank to deposit the five hundred, and to the morgue to give the lad the twenty, and back to the office to meet some people. Then home to shower, and to take a short and well-deserved nap.

Second act curtain. Smoking in the outer lobby only.

It was ten minutes to nine, and I'd just had a steak at Mac's, and some fried potatoes, and was sitting in my office, in the mahogany chair, smoking a cigarette.

Next week, *East Lynne*.

Only the desk lamp was on, and it was dim in the room with a third-act dimness, and the smoke from my cigarette wreathed upward from my cigarette in the ray of the lamp.

At five minutes to nine I lighted another.

At three minutes to nine I heard the feet on the stairs, and they were her feet, I could tell. She was three minutes early, and with a woman, that meant something, especially tonight, I figured.

She was in some black and filmy stuff which contrasted beautifully with her hair, and made me sorry I was in this business.

I rose, and indicated the leatherette chair. She took it, studying me the while, and I sat down again, and opened my story.

"Interrupt me," I said, "if I'm wrong."

"Is it going to be a story?"

"It's going to be a story, not too long. Do you mind?"

She shrugged, and lighted a cigarette. "How about a drink?" she asked. "You're not much of a host."

I poured her a drink, and one for me. Then we settled back in the chairs we sat in, she with her legs curled under her, me with my feet on the floor.

"We'll go back," I said, "to the war. To a singer and a piano player working for a racketeer named Jack Zarze, or Happy Jack. Maybe the singer and Happy Jack are like that, and maybe not: It doesn't matter. She was working for him, at any rate. The singer, of course, would be you."

She nodded, and sipped her drink.

"Change of locale," I went on. "Two respectable businessmen, Grenfell and Morgan by name, who have always been respectable, more or less, or at least inside the law. Making nine—ten thousand dollars a year, and paying their bills promptly, and their taxes. But the war comes along, and there's this chance to make it in bundles, in bigger bundles than they'd ever seen.

"It's possible Grenfell wasn't in this, maybe it was just Morgan, but it doesn't really matter.

"This Sperry and Doane set-up was ideal for them, and a lot of money was made. It was black market money, but that, too, is unimportant. It could have been imitation Oriental rugs or hot diamonds or the badger game. The thing was that the money was cash, never accounted for to the government, all in negotiable bills, and there was lots of it."

"Would you know how much?"

"No." I studied her, and her poise was still in evidence. "Do you want to tell me?"

She shook her head. "Maybe later."

"This thing," I went on, "was kept very secret, of course, and maybe only one man heard about it, a man named Happy Jack Zarze, who was well-organized, and had a lot of ears working for him. But where was the money? Blackmail would be a penny ante-game with these kind of stakes in view. So, the singer, a girl men want, and it was arranged, and the marriage was a quiet affair. She would find out where the money was kept, and then there would be no need for blackmail."

SHE SAID QUIETLY: "You're clever, Jonesy."

"I try to be. Now we will come up to the present. From Mike Greb's point of view. He's called into the case, and this combination of Morgan and you and Zarze stirs things in his mind, and he goes off on the wrong lead. During the war, Mike was on loan to the OPA and he's got, or had, a one-track mind, more or less. He looks up a pigeon named Schmaltz who he figures is about ready to chirp, and Zarze, or one of Zarze's boys sees him—and Mike dies. Then the pigeon named Schmaltz dies. In the river, looking just exactly like an accident."

She sipped her drink. "It's all pointing to poor Zarze, isn't it?"

"Right. You see, it had to be an organization, not some misguided businessman with one strike against him. The lad who put a gun in my back in the alley indicates an organization, and this drowning of Schmaltz indicates organizational work. That alley business was the big boner Zarze pulled."

Then I went all out. I took a deep breath and a small sip and said: "About getting Jimmy Dexter out of the clink. You didn't marry Morgan for that, because you married Morgan more than three long years after Jimmy was sent up."

"I lied, didn't I?"

"You do that well. And now, yesterday. Morgan's afraid we're on the trail of this old crime. So are you and Zarze. You explain to Sylvester that Zarze has found out something about him. He gets very, very nervous. Zarze wants to see him, you say. So he sends the servants out, and you go out, and everything is all set up, and Zarze comes in."

"You're guessing," but no certainty in the voice.

"No. I have proof. I don't always work alone." How well I lie.

"Go on."

"They have some drinks, and then you phone home, from the Slipper. Morgan, of course, answers the phone, in the hall. While he's gone, Zarze puts the conine in his drink, and after Sylvester dies, he presses his prints on the gun that killed Mike. Then he leaves and comes down to the Slipper and puts on that big welcome act."

"You can prove this?"

I nodded.

"On the way to the house you kissed me, remember?"

I did.

Her legs were still curled under her, she didn't seem at all perturbed, and she was as beautiful as ever, maybe more. "Did you ever see about a quarter of a million dollars in just ordinary bills, Jonesy? Just tens and twenties and fifties?"

"Mmm, no. It must be an extremely impressive sight."

"It is." Crushing her cigarette out, smiling a little. "I suppose you like your work. This grubby office, and cheap suits, and running down frightened people who don't pay their bills."

Well, I thought, this is the third-act curtain. We have the renunciation scene. I wondered what my answer would be if things were different. I wondered if I hadn't set the stage too well. I'd never know, but it would often worry me.

She stood up. "Would you like to see all this money in all those steel boxes, and maybe kiss me again?"

"No," I said, lying, as usual.

Then there was this man in the door. Maybe not a man, but following the pattern, more or less. Small, and in a tight, white linen suit. Thin, and holding a gun too big for him, and coked to the ears. Tiny Veber, who took dope, who killed for a living, and maybe for the hell of it, too.

One of Zarze's boys, undoubtedly, and the boy who had put that gun in my back in the alley.

I wondered what would have happened if I'd said "yes" instead of "no."

We could have standard detective story finish 1-A, where I jump the gun, feel a searing pain across my temple or thigh or shoulder, while I strangle him to death with my big hands. But my hands aren't big, and I didn't want to strangle him. Once he was off the stuff for a few days, he'd be sure to talk, and talk, and talk…

Carol's eyes were on me, and they weren't happy. Only Tiny's eyes were happy, because this business he liked.

"O.K., boys," I said, and ducked behind the desk.

From the screen around the sink, Glen Harvey stepped out, and from the hall behind, some other boys, and it was quick and clean and very efficient. Very nice cooperation, as they say.

Third-act curtain.

I bought a gabardine suit, and a couvert, both expensive. The big nephew drives the Caddy more than the Lincoln, I think. Tiny Veber talked and talked and talked… My Dusy acted up for a week, but it could have been the valves.

It's a hell of a way to make a living.

The Cold, Cold Ground

*Mortimer Jones, the Duesenberg driving
detective, solves the murder of Flame
Harlin, a hot dame who fixed it so her killer
would end up in the cold, cold ground.*

1

Chills and Thrills

IT WAS EARLY fall, and faintly chilly, outside. In my office, the thermometer was well over seventy, but Miss Townsbury had brought some chill with her.

Make no mistake, form no mental picture because of the 'Miss'. She was between forty and fifty years of age, dressed in some brown and eye-repelling type of ribbed silk. An iceberg, in brown silk. Blue eyes, blue as frozen sea water, and features sharp as icicles, with an icicle's thinness to her spare figure. There was nothing about her to indicate that she had ever melted or would ever melt.

She was telling me about the girl named Flame. Flame was the daughter of her brother's second wife—if you follow me. That is, her brother had married twice. For his second wife, he had married a divorcee. This divorcee had a daughter by her first marriage. This daughter's name was Flame. I hope it's all clear. Flame was missing.

Miss Townsbury had begun to suspect something was amiss when she wrote to Flame (Miss Flame Harlin) at her apartment in town, inviting her to come up and spend a weekend at the Townsbury country place. There had been no answer.

Miss Townsbury had phoned, twice, without success. This morning, she had come to town to do some shopping and had dropped in at the girl's apartment. The accumulation of newspapers and mail at the front door, the accumulation of milk bottles at the rear door, had convinced Miss Townsbury that things were not as they should be. I asked her if she had gone to the police. She shook her head emphatically. "I didn't think it wise to bring them into it, Mr. Jones." She paused. "Not until

The Moose wasn't seeing me. He wasn't seeing anything. Somebody had done a big job with a small gun.

we are sure that Miss Harlin is—really missing." If she wasn't sure, why had she come to me?

At twenty dollars a day (and expenses), I thought it best not to ask that question.

I asked some other questions.

Miss Harlin was an entertainer, a comedienne.

Did she sing? Did she juggle? Did she crack jokes?

She sang. "Though her voice wasn't anything extraordinary, you understand. That doesn't seem necessary, today, however. She had—whatever it is the public wants, today. Her songs were very well received."

I knew what the public wanted, today and every day, and so did she. She was being genteel. I asked: "She isn't married, of course?"

A thin, cool smile. "No. She was engaged, at one time, to a Mr. Rodney Carlton. There's a possibility …" She stopped.

I said: "You think there's a possibility they may have eloped?"

"Eloped?" The gaze came up to meet mine, then moved away. "Eloped? No. I suppose that *could* be a polite phrasing." The gaze direct again. "Miss Harlin, I might remind you, is an entertainer. She has always lived an undisciplined life. Her standards of conduct are theatrical standards. Am I being clear?"

I gave her a reproving glance. I said softly: "You're being completely frank, Miss Townsbury. Have you any reason, other than those, to believe that Miss Harlin might have done what you're suggesting?"

The figure stiffened in my leatherette chair. "None. However, under the circumstances, you can see why I came to a *private* detective."

"The police," I told her, "are very discreet in matters of this kind. You wouldn't need to fear any unpleasant publicity." *Not much*, I thought, *not much*.

The cold eyes surveyed me haughtily. "Are you telling me, in your indirect way, that you don't *want* this case, Mr. Jones?"

I hastened to correct her on that. I explained about ethics, and the necessity for private operatives to cooperate with the police, and the rest of the blarney that gives my work its high moral tone.

She relaxed again, with a rustle of heavy silk. She answered all the rest of my questions quickly and competently. When she rose to leave, she said: "I do think, if you don't discover anything in a reasonable length of time, we should go to the police."

I told her I thought that would be best.

She left, and I went to the window, as is my fashion. There was a Mercedes town car parked at the curb. As she approached it, a tall and dark man in a chauffeur's uniform stepped out of the car to open the door on the curb side. I watched, until the Mercedes moved around the corner with a contemptuous snort from its tail pipe.

Such high-class trade I get in my shabby office. Was it my reputation? The penuriousness of my clients? What it was in this case, I didn't find out until later. Anyway, I decided that I would go and see this Rodney Carlton, first.

Downstairs, I stood on the curb a minute, watching a kid punt a football. It kept sliding off his foot wrong—he wasn't getting directly behind the ball. Well, he had a lot of years ahead of him.

I walked up two blocks, to where the Dusy was parked. I started her elegant motor, and headed her east.

The very-near-east, where the rooming houses are, I passed through. The upper-east, where the fine apartments are, I also passed through. In the far-upper-east, the neighborhood can't make up its mind. There are some new apartments, and some fine old homes. There are some cottages, new and inexpensive, but pleasant and in good taste.

This Rodney Carlton's address was one of the cottages. A low white place, with red shutters, with a red door. With a man in the front yard.

THE MAN HAD a golf club in his hands. It looked like a nine iron. He was trying to chip some balls he had into a wash-tub in the middle of the yard. He'd play each shot carefully and easily, with fine form, but they were all short.

"More wrist," I said. "You're not getting enough wrist into them."

He looked up at me and out at the car. He studied me. Then: "You can't be a collector, not with a Duesenberg. Are you selling insur— Who the hell are you, anyway?"

I shook my head. "My name is Jones, Mortimer Jones. I'm looking for a girl named Flame Harlin."

He stood frozen a moment, a thin, good-looking young man with dark hair, with apprehension in his dark blue eyes. "Flame—she's missing? You—expected to find her here?" He was staring now, and his voice roughened. "Who the hell are you, anyway?"

"I'm a private investigator," I told him quietly. "Miss Townsbury has hired me to locate Miss Harlin, whom she has reason to suspect is missing." What a hell of a sentence that was.

He was still staring. "That old battle-axe hired you? Why should she care? She doesn't give a damn for Flame, either way."

"I wouldn't know about that," I said. "I thought, perhaps, you—"

"Come on in," he said, and started for the door. I followed.

Rodney Carlton indicated a chair, and took one himself. He said: "Miss Harlin and I were engaged, at one time, you understand. But I haven't seen her for a month. How long has she been—been missing?"

"A week," I said, "at the least. I'll know more later." I told him about the papers and the milk, about Miss Townsbury's phone calls and her letter.

When I had finished, he was thoughtful. He was considering something, I could tell. Finally, he said: "I've—" He was blushing. "I've a key to—to Miss Harlin's apartment, if—" He paused. "Could I go along, if we took a look in there?"

"I don't see why not," I said. "It's just as illegal for two to enter as for one. I'd be breaking the law, either way."

He rose. "I guess you private detectives don't worry much about breaking the law. I'll get a coat."

The movies, I thought. *It's the movies that give people those kinds of ideas about us.*

While he went to get his coat, I went quietly on my rubber heels to the desk. He was a poet, I saw. There was a half-born child of his mood this moment in the typewriter. I read:

Deep, where the ground is cold.
Deep, where the sun never shines.
Deep and cold and all alone,
Bury them,
Bury them deep.

Then he was standing beside me, blushing again. "Bad?" he asked.

"I'm no judge," I said.

"I have a small income," he explained. "Thank God I don't need to depend on that stuff for a living."

"I've seen worse," I said, "in print," and hoped he wouldn't ask me where.

When we went out again, the sun was shining, and what had started as an early fall day was now a late summer day. *Bury them, bury them deep…* It stuck with me, for some reason.

The upper east side was where Miss Harlin lived. In a small and neat four-apartment building of stone and frame on a quiet, elm-shaded street. Her apartment was on the second floor.

I saw the papers, there. I pawed through them, and discovered that the earliest was eight days old. You'd think the paper boy would— But that was neither here nor there.

Eight days, then … Rodney Carlton handed me his key, and I fitted it, and the door swung open with a slight squeak.

The sunshine was slanting through the tall windows in the high living room. It was an expensively furnished, spacious and definitely feminine apartment—off-white and pastels the basic motif.

There was a faint and lovely fragrance haunting the air.

Everything was in order, everything shipshape. I asked him: "Did she have a maid? Wouldn't the maid bring in the milk and the papers and pick up the mail downstairs?"

"She has no servants," he said. "She can afford them, all right, but she claims she'd be bored silly all day, if she couldn't clean house."

We went from there to a bathroom in peach, to an ivory dining room, to a bedroom in orchid.

Nothing in the place. No exotic girl with a dagger in her throat, no distinguished gent with a neat hole in his aristocratic forehead, no blood, no mess, no clues at all.

The kitchenette was white tile, with a black rubber tile floor. Not even one dirty dish in the sink, nor one spilled grain of sugar. It was like a display home, all the way through.

I opened the back door and brought in the milk and put it in the refrigerator. There was some cheese in there, some wine, some butter, some cold meats.

There was nothing in the apartment to indicate a hurried trip, to indicate violence. It was as though she was gone for the day. But she'd been gone for eight.

I looked through some drawers. I looked through a scrapbook she kept, of newspaper items about herself. There might be something there. I took it along with me when we left.

RODNEY WAS QUIET, in the car. He was looking sick. I asked: "Do you have a picture of her?" He nodded. "Could I borrow it?"

"Of course." His eyes were straight ahead, on the road. His poet's imagination would be working now, thinking the unthinkable. I said: "Everything may be all right. We're not sure of anything so far."

"Sure," he said. "Sure, of course." The Dusy made no comment, purring softly under her hood, moving quietly through the upper east side to the far upper east side, to the cottage of Rodney Carlton.

I waited in the car while he went in to get the picture. When he brought it out, it was wrapped in brown paper. I didn't open it, but put it on the seat beside me.

"Don't think about it," I said. "We don't know anything."

"Don't think about it?" His voice was ragged. "She was my life, that's all. She was all there is in the world for me."

A typical poetic exaggeration, I thought. He hasn't even seen her for a month, I thought. I drove from there down to headquarters. I went in and up to the second floor, to the Missing Persons Bureau. Old Pop Delaney was behind his mission oak desk in there, manufacturing cheap cigar smoke.

"What d'ya know?" he said. "It's been a long time." He had a round head, topped with snow white hair. He had a smooth face, unwrinkled, though he was crowding seventy. But perhaps he'd never worried—he had always worked for the city. So had I, for a while.

I told him about the need for discretion.

"You get all that carriage trade, don't you?" he asked. "How do you do it, Jonesy?"

I ignored that. I showed him the picture, and looked at it myself for the first time.

A tinted picture. A girl with jet hair and Pacific-blue eyes and with that challenge, that bold and alluring something that makes men aware of the person possessing it, that something more than beauty.

"Hey," Pop said. "All right, huh?" Then he frowned. "This the best you got?"

"It's good enough for me." I said.

"Yeh, but for reproduction, a glossy print would be better. You got any others?"

"Just that," I said.

He rolled the cigar in his mouth, studying the picture. "O.K., I'll do what I can. You can pick this up this afternoon." He continued to roll the cigar and study the picture. He shook his head sadly. "I'm an old man, Jonesy," he said, "an old, old man."

I left him with his dreams.

I was just going through the big entrance door downstairs, when I heard a voice. *The* voice. My worst friend and unkindest critic, the boss of Homicide, Devine.

"What's your hurry, Jones?" he wanted to know.

"No hurry," I said. "That was my usual gait. How are things with you?" As though I cared, as though he couldn't be dying, right at my feet, without my caring.

"O.K.," he said. "No murders, no important ones, anyway. Got a vacation coming up, end of the month." He smiled. "In on business?"

"N-o-o," I lied. "Just dropped in to say 'hello' to some of the boys. I'm glad everything is quiet."

"You never drop in at Homicide any more," he said. "Not mad at us, are you? No hard feelings? We work together, don't we, Jones?"

"Always," I said. "Cooperation, as the Chief says."

"That's right," he said. "Be good, boy."

"I will," I promised. "I'm going to cut my cigarettes down to two packs a day, any day now." I left him, and went out into the sun.

He'd be checking now. He'd be prowling the department, trying to find out my business. He didn't like me. He knew I could have his job, any time I wanted it, and he would never like me. But Pop would tell him nothing. Everyone at the department disliked him as much as I did.

The Dusy chuckled, when I kicked her into life.

Back at the office, I went up the stairs slowly, mulling over all I had seen and heard this morning, searching for a thread to untangle, searching for something that didn't fit, some piece out of the proper focus. I found nothing.

I opened my door quietly. It's never locked.

There was a man sitting in the leatherette chair on the customer's side of my desk. A beefy man with a broad placid face, and eyes without expression. Wearing a cheap blue suit and a blue shirt with a brown tie. Wearing a tough expression he'd seen somewhere. A private operative we're not too proud to have in the trade, a gent named Moose Lundgren.

"What's cooking, Jonesy?" he wanted to know.

"Nothing much." I went over to sit in my mahogany swivel chair. "Murder or two, couple of bank robberies—you know how it is."

He smiled genially. "And hotel skippers and jealous husbands or wives and labor trouble—that's how it is, huh?"

"Not labor trouble," I said. "I leave that alone."

He shrugged his bulky shoulders. "Maybe you can afford to be particular."

I lit a cigarette out of the new pack, and offered him one, which he refused. I asked: "Something on your mind, Moose?"

He expelled his breath through his flabby mouth. "Well, that Harlin dame—"

I tensed, waiting. He seemed to be hesitating. I said: "What about her?"

He smiled. "I saw you leave her apartment. I was watching it, at the time, and I wondered—" Again, he stopped, in his hesitant way. "What you got on her, Jonesy? What's the angle?"

"What's yours?" I countered. "You were watching her apartment? Why?"

He smiled expansively. "Why? Why would I be? For pay, of course. A party hired me to do it."

"How long ago?" I asked him. "When did you start watching it?"

He froze up. That stubborn look came to his pig eyes, and he shook his head. "You ask too many questions."

"You started it," I told him. "I've got more questions than answers—I guarantee you that."

He pulled a cheap cigar out of his breast pocket and took some time biting off the end. He lighted it slowly.

I thought, *he's going to get pompous now. He's going to sound important.*

He said: "This guy I'm working for is a pretty big operator, Jonesy. Kind of short-tempered, too. You and I would work better together."

I laughed. I said: "I'll decide that. Don't try to scare me."

He shrugged, a la Greenstreet. He studied his cigar. Then his muddy eyes met mine. "Val Every," he said, and nothing more.

I was supposed to be impressed. Val Every had grown big with prohibition, and grown no smaller in the years since. I didn't believe he'd need to hire a third rate shamus like Lundgren. He had enough guns of his own.

"He a friend of Miss Harlin's?" I inquired pleasantly.

Moose nodded. "He'd like to be more than that. She worked for him, sang at the Pheasant. He wanted to marry her, Jonesy."

"Marry?" I said, doubtfully. "He wasn't a marrying man, the last I heard. Though he always did all right with the ladies, for a man his age."

"He's only forty-five," Moose said. "I'm telling you, Jones, for this Flame Harlin, he'll go all the way. He's been a sick man since she left. He's nothing to fool with, right now."

"Since she left?" I said. "And when was that, Moose?"

He looked at me quietly a moment. "Week ago. Those papers up in front of her door are eight days old."

"Well," I said, "you know more about it than I do, probably. Or at least as much. What do you want from me?"

"Just who you're working for."

"A client," I told him. "A client who prefers to remain anonymous for the moment."

He rose slowly, and stood regarding his hat. "Are you sure that's what you want me to tell Val, Jonesy?"

"You can tell him anything you want," I said. "He's your client."

Again that shrug, and Moose was walking toward the door.

About halfway there, he turned to look at me. He opened his mouth to say something, and then evidently decided against it. I heard his big feet going down the stairs.

THE MAIL WASN'T much, just some bills. I put them carefully with the others, and went over to Mac's.

I had a beer, first, a small one. I drank it slowly, thinking all the while.

Deep and cold and all alone, I thought, *bury them, bury....*

I didn't realize I was thinking aloud until I saw Mac staring at me.

"Bury who?" Mac said.

"The Dodgers," I said. "Why not?"

"Like hell," Mac said. "Bury the rest of them, instead."

"You got a small steak?" I asked.

He nodded. "Stringy and small, and I don't think it'll have much flavor, but you could call it a steak."

"Cut-rate, no doubt, if it's that bad."

"The standard price."

"Fry it," I told him, "in your inimitable way. Garnish it with onions, and serve it deftly. Then chat with me while I eat it."

"Sure," he said, "I got nothing else to do. I can make a living off you, alone. My other customers don't matter, only to me."

I yawned, and sipped my beer.

When he brought it over, he brought another small beer along. There was only one other customer in the place, and he was nursing a Tom Collins.

"You know Val Every, don't you?" I asked Mac.

"I guess everybody knows him."

"Sure," I said. "But you know him pretty well, don't you?

Didn't you buy beer from him, during prohibition?"

"During prohibition," Mac said stiffly, "I sold roofing."

"Days—and hooch in your blind pig at night. Who you trying to kid, Mac?"

He said nothing, looking haughty.

"All right," I said. "The Dodgers are fine. I hope they always win."

"I had some dealings with Every," Mac admitted. "If you got any with him, talk soft, Jonesy. Don't irritate him."

"I'll try not to. But what I want to know is—would you figure him for the kind of guy who'd want to marry some girl who worked for him?"

Mac shook his head. "I wouldn't figure him to marry *anybody*. With his money, why should he get married? He never has, and he's known some lulus. Why should he change now?"

"Love," I said softly. "The great, basic urge, maybe."

"We weren't talking about love," Mac corrected me. "We were talking about marriage, weren't we?"

"A terrific love," I went on, "for the first time in his life, probably. Would he want to marry the girl?"

"Not Valentine J. Every," Mac said flatly. "No. He wouldn't marry a girl. He wouldn't want to, either. He's very set on the subject. With Every, girls are eighteen cents a dozen, ceiling price."

I ate the rest of my steak in silence. As Mac had prophesied, it was stringy, small and unpalatable.

I ate it like a little Spartan, washing it down with beer.

Mac went down to the other end of the bar and explained to the man behind the Tom Collins why Ruby Bob Fitzimmons would have licked any living heavyweight.

I went back to the office, and phoned the dairy that kept delivering milk to the apartment of Flame Harlin. I told them to stop it until further notice. I did the same with the paper.

When I went out again, the kid was back in the street, and still trying to straighten out his punts.

He was doing a little better.

2

Jones on the Job

THE DAY WAS warm, still, a lovely Indian Summer day. The Dusy's tires sang on the hot asphalt, as I drove over to headquarters. Pop had my picture, ready and waiting.

He also had another customer, so I didn't stop to chat. I could have gone back to the office, to comb through that scrapbook, but it was too nice for that.

I decided to run out and tell Miss Townsbury about the Every angle.

The home that housed Miss Townsbury was a weather-dulled gray stone affair, in a stand of virgin timber near the bay. There was a rolling, tree-studded lawn sweeping down from the front of the house. There were tables under these trees, and chairs. There were people, of both sexes, sitting in the chairs around the tables. Miss Townsbury must be having a party.

The Dusy's big tires crunched the gravel as we rolled majestically up to the front door.

The man on the porch hadn't been there when I drove up. But he was when I stepped from the car.

He was the tall and dark and hard-looking chauffeur. He examined me with a scrutiny I thought out of place. It was a police line-up type of examination.

"Your name?" he said, just like that.

I handed him one of my cards.

"Oh," he said. "Oh, yeah, sure. Didn't mean to be rough, Mr.

Jones, but we had a kidnapping scare here, last week, and—"
He tried a smile. "Miss Townsbury will see you, all right." He
started to walk away.

I said: "Did you notify the police about this attempted
kidnapping?"

"I don't know. You'd have to ask Miss Townsbury." He was
looking out at the Dusy. "That's a lot of car you're driving."

I admitted it was, and he went around the side of the house.

The door was opening now, though I hadn't pressed the bell
button. The butler stood there, looking more like the standard
type of servant, or what I think of as standard. I gave him my
card.

From the lawn, I heard the sound of laughter, both sexes.
The butler came back, and said Miss Townsbury would receive
me, and I followed him into the pleasant, dim coolness of the
house.

Right off the entrance hall, there was a small, high-ceilinged
room, furnished and decorated in a sort of pastel green. Miss
Townsbury was in here, knitting. She still wore the heavy
brown silk. She had added a pair of steel-rimmed spectacles.

"Trouble, Mr. Jones?" she asked mildly. She indicated a chair.

"Information," I said. "Maybe trouble. There's somebody else
looking for Miss Harlin."

The knitting needles stopped for a moment, then continued.
She said. "The police?"

"No," I said. "A man named Val Every, a racketeer."

The needles stopped again, and this time she looked up. "Val
Every? He's looking for … Isn't he her employer? Isn't he the
former bootlegger?"

"The same," I said. "He's got a private operator working on

it. This operative came to see me this noon."

The needles went back to work. "You didn't disclose my name?"

"No. I wondered, though, if we might not offer this detective some money for what information he's gathered. He can be bought. I'm sure of that."

She nodded, not looking up. "I'm willing to pay anything within reason, of course, Mr. Jones, but do you think he would have come to you if he had any information we don't have? He may have come to you for the same purpose."

"He did," I said. "But I've uncovered nothing. I went through her apartment. I talked to Rodney Carlton, and—"

"You talked to him?" There was a harsh note in the muffled voice. "And what did that young man have to say?"

"He knew nothing. He hasn't seen her for a month, he claims."

"He's lying." The needles were resting in her lap, and her frozen blue eyes were glaring into mine. "He knows. He's got her, somewhere. You concentrate on him, Mr. Jones."

"I'll learn all I can," I said. Then: "The chauffeur tells me you almost had a kidnapping here, Miss Townsbury. Do you think it might have anything to do with—"

She shook her head vigorously. "Nothing, Mr. Jones. It was the daughter of one of my guests. It wasn't an attempted kidnapping, it was a threat. Some crank, I'm sure. It's being taken care of."

She evidently didn't want any more conversation on that topic. She went back to her knitting, and I promised, before I left, that I'd keep her informed of all developments.

Outside, the hostless guests were doing very well, merrily

enjoying Miss Townsbury's absence. On a bench near the drive, a slim red-haired girl was sitting, regarding me openly and genially.

"Hello, handsome," she said.

I looked around, but there was no one there. *Me,* she meant.

"Don't be coy," she said. "You *are* handsome, you know. It's nothing to be ashamed of. Even though you're not tall, you're handsome."

Drunk, I thought. "Thank you," I said, and climbed into the car.

She came over, to stand near me. Her eyes were a clear, bright shade of green. I saw the dilated pupils. Not drunk, I thought, no, no, no.

"Are we going for a ride?" she asked. "Shall I get a coat?"

From the porch, the butler's voice cut in sharply. "Telephone, Miss Smith. It's long distance."

Without another word, she turned and walked toward the porch. I started the Dusy, and got out of there.

Going out, I noticed for the first time that the fence around the estate was high, and topped with barbed wire. And that there was a heavy gate, now open. The poplars flanking the fence screened it from casual notice.

I STOPPED TO see Rodney Carlton on the way back. He was out in front again, with the nine iron. He had more wrist in them, now. They were landing in the tub. He didn't look as if he were mourning Miss Harlin's absence much.

He looked up when I got out of the car. "This national detective week, or something?"

"You'll get used to me," I assured him.

"You, maybe, but not that lard-beam that just left. Somebody should tell him about soap."

"Lundgren?" I said.

"That's the man."

"What'd he want?"

"Information. He working for the old girl, too? Isn't one of you enough for her?"

"He's not working for her," I said. "Did you mention Miss Townsbury's name?"

"I did. Let her get a whiff of him. It'll show her how the other half lives."

If Lundgren knew that somebody as wealthy as the Townsbury maiden was interested in Flame Harlin, he'd get ideas. I asked Carlton: "Could I use your phone?"

He nodded toward the door, and went back to his chipping.

I phoned Miss Townsbury. I told her what had happened. I said: "Let me know if he bothers you. Let me know as soon as he does."

She promised she would.

I noticed, on the way out, that there was nothing in the typewriter.

"Drop in again," Carlton told me when I left. But I'm not sure he meant it.

I went back to the office, and studied the scrapbook. It was filled with clippings that may have held memories for her, but were meaningless to me. Just the story of her triumphs, large and small—the story of her climb. Up until eight days ago, she had been the featured attraction at Val Every's elegant and expensive Golden Pheasant Club. There was nothing in there about her background.

About four, Miss Townsbury phoned. She said: "That Lundgren person phoned me for an appointment. I told him I'd send someone over to meet him at his office. You go over and find out what he wants."

"Was he threatening in any way?" I asked.

"He wondered why I hadn't gone to the police."

"Hmmm," I said, in my thoughtful tone. "Well, I'll run right over and set him straight."

I ran right over in the Dusy. It was a grubby building near the warehouse section, containing (on the first floor) a harness maker's shop and (on the second) the office of Elmer E. Lundgren, known in trade as 'Moose'. I hadn't, as a matter of fact, known until this minute that his first name was Elmer.

I went up the worn, wooden steps to the second floor and down a short and cheerless hall to his door. The door was open.

Moose Lundgren was sitting in a huge chair behind his desk, facing the door. His eyes were wide open, and he was staring at me. But he wasn't seeing me. He wasn't seeing anything.

He was dead.

His short thick neck was so heavy that his head hadn't drooped backward or forward. It stood squarely on the big neck. The chair in which he sat had a high back, which effectively supported his bulk. There was a small hole, a very small hole, in the center of his forehead—it looked as though it had been made with a .22 caliber shell. Somebody had done a big job with a small gun.

I kept my eyes from Moose while I phoned the police.

"Who is this calling?" the voice at the other end wanted to know.

I hesitated. Devine will be here, I thought. He'll want to

know what I was doing here. He'll want to know the name of my client. He'll be nasty. But I hesitated only a moment. "Mortimer Jones," I said.

"*You* again," the voice said, and some other things, not printable. "I hope they nail you this time."

I told him about a nice hot place he could go to for the winter, and hung up. I went out into the hall to wait.

Finally, there was the sound of sirens. I was almost happy to hear them, even knowing they meant Devine.

Doc Walters, the M.E., was the first to arrive. There was an interne with him. I nodded toward the door and they went through it.

Then Devine's right hand, Glen Harvey, was there. Glen tried a smile of greeting, but it was pretty sad. "You're always in the middle of these things, aren't you, Jonesy?" he said sadly. "No wonder you give Devine the willies."

"I wasn't going to wait, just for that reason," I told him. "I was going to give a phony name and get out of here, but I thought there might be something I could help with."

Glen nodded toward the office. "Got an angle on this?"

"Only that he was on a job for Val Every. There could be any number of angles on a deal like that."

"Hell, yes," Glen said dismally. Then casually: "How'd you happen to find him?"

"He owed me a sawbuck. I came over to collect it. The door was open—"

"Uh-huh. How'd you know he was on a job for Every? You guys talk over your clients like that?"

Tricky, Glen was getting. I said evenly: "No. I knew it, because he happened to tell me, last time I asked him for the sawbuck. He said that as soon as Every paid him for a job he was doing—"

"Don't you guys work on a retainer?"

"Yes," I said wearily. "We do. Anyway, I do. Try not to sound like the D.A., Glen. It's been a bad day."

"Well, well," somebody said. I knew who it was without looking around. "If it isn't Mr. Jones. Always, at the end of a hot day, just before I'm going to knock off, something'll break. And Mr. Jones will be right in the middle of it."

I turned to face Devine. "We were such friends, this morning," I reminded him. "You're not growing tired of me? I hope there isn't someone else, now."

Glen said: "Easy, boss. Jones has been giving me the story."

Devine was white. He likes people to cower in front of him, to speak quietly and respectfully. He said hoarsely: "He's been giving you the story, all right. He's probably been giving you the business." He was talking to Glen, but looking at me. "Wait right here," he told me. "Right in this spot until I come out."

SOME REPORTERS CAME, the print man, another interne, the man on the beat. Harvey was in with Devine and I had the hall to myself, more or less. I smoked two cigarettes. When the reporters came out to get my part of the story, I repeated what I had told Glen. Then, as I was finishing, Devine came out.

He heard the end of it, and drew me to one side. "You tell them about the Every angle?"

I hadn't, and I shook my head.

The reporters were waiting. Devine said:

"That's all, boys. If anything breaks, you'll get it. That's all we have now."

How he kowtowed to anyone who might do him good. I took my arm out from under his hand. I said: "You won't be needing me right away, will you?"

His thin face was hard. "I will. You in a hurry?"

"I can think of a better place to spend my time," I told him.

"Sure, but I want you now. You can come down to headquarters with me and dictate a statement. What happens to you after that would be up to the Chief. You're his boy, aren't you?"

"I'll ask him," I said. "I'll tell him you think so." Which was baby talk. But he brings out the worst in me.

"You can tell him any damned thing you please," Devine said. "Just come along with me, now."

I went along with him. Outside, the sun was setting fire to the west, and some of the afternoon's heat was gone. The wholesale houses were closing up for the day. People were going home.

And Devine's day might just be beginning, for all he knows, I thought. *He's overworked and over-bossed and underpaid. Maybe he's earned his bad disposition.*

But how about this servility in high places? My less tolerant half argued. *How about his whining when things get rough? How about that, Mortimer, you damned sissy?*

"Shall we go down in my car?" I asked. He nodded.

We climbed in, and I started the motor. There were no words, going down, either pleasant or otherwise. Devine was smoking a cigar and scowling. I kept my eyes on the traffic.

At headquarters, I dictated a statement while Devine went in to see the Chief. When I'd finished, when it was typed and signed, he told me: "The Old Man wants to see you." He didn't look at me.

The Chief was looking out the window when I entered his office. I waited respectfully, making no sound. There would be a speech, in a moment, and I'd listen to that respectfully, too. For he was a good, capable, honest man—if a little verbose.

Then the big, white-thatched head turned toward me. "This is a big town, Morty, a very big town."

I agreed that it was.

He indicated a chair, and I took it. He offered me a cigar, which I refused. He put the tips of his fingers together, and studied his desk top. "If you won't work *for* us, you should work *with* us. We need all the help we can get in a town this size."

"I work with you," I said. "I think you'll remember all the times I've worked with you."

He pursed his lips, and nodded. "Well, yes, when there's a pinch to be made, you call us. But you're working around us, now, aren't you? You won't reveal all you know about this."

"I've told you all I know, Chief."

"Who's your client?"

"That I can't tell you. There's no reason to think it has anything to do with Moose Lundgren's death. His death was overdue. Devine's probably told you why I went over to see Lundgren."

The Chief looked annoyed. "Sure, sure, sure … Even if it's true, it's a hell of a story. I think you went over there to make a deal with him. Maybe you even know who killed him. I'm not believing a word of that fairy tale you told Devine. I want the facts."

I looked down at my hands. "You've got all the facts I can give you," I told him. "Talking won't get us anywhere."

There was a silence. His voice, when it came was low. "I've

never threatened to take your license away from you, have I? Never?"

"I hope you're not threatening it now," I said. "You've got Every to work on. I gave you that. Would you rather have someone a little easier to crack? Is that why you want my client?"

"You know me better than that," he said.

"O.K. I shouldn't have said it. But old Pop Delaney was in on my current deal *this morning,* as soon as I got it. I could have called from Lundgren's office, and then taken a powder. I've been working with the department all day. I've kept one thing secret, the name of my client. The Marines couldn't get that, not from me, on this case, or any case, unless I want to tell them. That's my stand, and that's the way it'll always be."

"Delaney?" he said. "Somebody's missing? You might have told me that before, Morty."

"I thought you'd know," I said. "A girl is missing. A girl named Flame Harlin. She was the featured attraction at Val Every's Golden Pheasant. That I know. That's all I know."

I didn't tell him about Rodney Carlton, because Rodney would lead them to Miss Townsbury.

"O.K.," the Chief said. "We'll go ahead on that as far as we can. If it isn't far enough, I'll be calling you in again. Cooperation is what we want here, boy."

"It's no one-way street," I said, "this cooperation. It works both ways. You might mention that to some of the gang."

He smiled. "Like Devine? He getting in your hair again? Devine's a hard worker, Morty. He puts in a lot of hours."

"All right," I said. "As a taxpayer, I'm not kicking. But if you could just keep him out of my cases. His touch is too heavy."

The Chief smiled again. He'd had a change of mood. "We can't all have your touch," he said. "Some of us are more serious. Some of us work for a living."

GLEN HARVEY WAS out in the corridor, talking to Doc Walters, and I stopped. Glen told me: "It was a .22, all right. What would that spell to you, Jonesy?"

"Some guy had a lot of confidence in his shooting," I said. "Or maybe he was too lazy to carry a heavy gun. It could spell anything."

"Like a woman? That could be a woman's gun, huh?"

"Right. But not between the eyes. A woman who could shoot like that could give exhibitions. You ever meet a woman who could place one like that?"

"Not lately," Glen said. "What'd the Old Man want?"

"Just my views on how to improve the department," I said. "Homicide stinks, to hear him tell it." I left them with that.

I went back to the office, but there was nothing there. I went over to Mac's and had some meatballs with spaghetti. Mac watched me anxiously while I ate it.

"Something wrong?" I asked.

He watched me put the last mouthful away. "I guess not," he said, "by the way you ate it. I kinda thought that meat was spoiled."

Nice guy. "The Dodgers stink," I said, "and Mickey Walker couldn't punch his way out of a paper bag."

"Hah-hah," Mac said. "Your opinion, just your opinion."

"Besides which," I went on. "You run a crummy joint. The only reason I come here is because it's handy."

"The only reason you come here," he told me calmly, "is

because no other joint in town would let you in. A gumshoe, a shamus—they ain't so democratic, them other joints."

"Tonight," I told him, "I'm going to the Golden Pheasant. I'll bet they let me in. I'll bet I get a ringside table."

"That I want to see," Mac scoffed. "You should live so long."

"You should see me with my new suit on," I said. I paid him, and left.

The new suit was a dark blue cheviot, looking like more than it had cost—I like to think. With it, I wore one of my two remaining white shirts and a blue and silver striped tie. I hoped that this Pheasant wasn't one of those snobbish places where formal clothes only are admitted. Maybe the Dusy would impress them.

This Golden Pheasant was one of those snobbish places. The doorman looked down his nose at me, while he told me this. It was a long and thin and haughty nose. He didn't even glance toward the Dusy, parked just across the street.

"It's business," I assured him. "It's urgent business with Mr. Every and I'm sure he'll fire you if he hears you've kept me out."

"I'm sorry, sir," the doorman said. "I'm very sorry. Perhaps it would be better if you were to go some place and phone Mr. Every."

"O.K.," I said. "It's about Miss Harlin. You tell him that when you see him." I turned and started to walk away.

"Just a moment, sir." There was some urgency in his voice.
I waited.

"You didn't give me your name, sir. Mr. Every will want to get in touch with you, I am sure."

"I'm glad to hear it," I told him. "He seemed to be a hard man to approach. Tell him I might drop back. Or I might not."

He was worried, I could tell.

He said humbly: "Wouldn't you care to wait inside?"

"In *these* clothes?" I said wonderingly. "In these old rags? Jeeves, I'm disappointed in you. Just tell him I *might* drop back."

"You could wait in the bar, sir," he suggested. "I'm sure there'd be no complaint. I'll explain it to the bartender."

I appeared to consider this. I pursed my lips and wrinkled my brow. "They have whiskey in there?" I asked him finally.

"Of course, sir. Including some bonded whiskey."

"Well," I relented, "in that case, I might wait around for a while."

We went in together, and he went down to the end of the bar to explain it all to the bartender.

It was quite a place. There was silver in the decorating, and some pale blues. There was a misty, romantic quality in the atmosphere. All women would look glamorous in this light, all men interesting.

It was early, and there wasn't much of a crowd. Through the archway, I could see that most of the tables were empty. The bar was semi-circular, attended by five men in white. Only two of them were busy at the moment, the others stood around in a sort of parade rest position. They looked well-disciplined.

One of the men in white was standing before me now.

"Scotch," I said, "with seltzer." I examined my nails and pretended that I wasn't more at home in a spot like Mac's.

It tasted like all Scotch tastes—like liquid smoke, but I drank it manfully, while I surveyed the place.

Whoever said crime doesn't pay? He must have meant small crime doesn't pay much. Val Every had made the money for this joint in a variety of ways, all of them dishonest. He was probably making money here—just meeting the payroll would be big business. And Val wasn't the biggest operator in this town, not by a long, long way.

From the dining room, now, I could hear the sound of a violin—softly muted music, sad music.

It dug into me, inside, where I live.

3

No Logic in Love

THEN A FEMININE voice brought me back to here and now. "Were you waiting for Mr. Every?"

A blonde. She'd been some places and seen some things, I would guess. That was in the dark blue eyes. She wasn't hard. She was dressed daringly in a sheath of black satin, but she was dressed expensively. The humorous slant to her full mouth saved the face from being just another blonde's face. She had all she needed.

"I am," I said. "Has he come in yet?"

"Not yet." She climbed up onto a stool next to me, and gestured the bartender over. "Rye," she told him, "with a little water, Jim."

"Right, Miss Meredith—same as always."

She turned to me. "My first name is Judy, if you're interested. Did you bring some news about Flame?"

I shook my head. I told her my name. "I just wanted to talk to Every about it," I explained. "You work for him?"

She looked at me doubtfully. She smiled. "Work—why, yes, I guess it's work. You might say I watch out for his interests."

"Miss Harlin would be one of the interests?"

"Yes, damn it." Her drink came, and she studied it. "Yes, she would be the big interest. I was hoping she was dead."

I said: "The venom clamours of a jealous woman—poison more deadly than a mad dog's tooth."

"Was she poisoned?" Judy asked. "Tell me she was poisoned."

"No," I said. "At least, not to my knowledge. It's the music. I always quote the bard when I'm emotionally stirred."

She sipped her drink. "It shows, doesn't it—my jealousy? You noticed it."

"Nothing shows that shouldn't," I assured her. "But wishing her dead—that's a little rough, don't you think? Why don't you just wish she would fall in love with someone else?"

"Love?" she said, as though it were a foreign word. "Love? She's not in love with him. She's played him for a sucker ever since she started to work here."

"And him? He's in love with her, isn't he?"

"Hmmm. He could be. He wants her badly enough. I—it's hard to think of him in love with anything but money or power. If you know what I mean?"

"Just vaguely," I said. Her glass was now empty. "Could I buy you another drink?" I asked.

She shook her head. "It would bring me down a grade. My drinks are all free. If customers start buying them for me, well, you know—"

I ordered another Scotch, and she a rye. The violin had stopped and somebody was getting hot with a piano. Right out of the jungle, this piano, all left hand.

"What is she like?" I asked Judy.

"Flame? Like her name, sort of. I mean, there was fire there, there was a burning. Maybe it was just ambition, maybe it was just—greed."

"And maybe you're prejudiced."

"That could be." She looked at my glass. "You're a slow drinker."

I finished it in a swallow. "I think I'll have rye, too, this time."

The bartender filled mine up without comment. But he said to Judy: "Mr. Every isn't going to like this, Miss Meredith. You remember last time—"

"To hell with Mr. Every," Judy said. "If I can't get it here, I'll go somewhere else. Mr. Jones will take me, won't you, Mr. Jones?"

"Gladly," I said, and meant it. She was a comfortable girl to be with. Not quieting, but comfortable.

The bartender shrugged, and poured out the whiskey.

There was a silence, and then she looked over at me. "You know where she is, don't you? That's what you came to tell Val."

"I don't know where she is. I'm looking for her."

"You're working for Val, aren't you? He'd be afraid to have one of his own boys look for her." She stopped then, and I looked over to find the bartender glaring at her.

"I'm not working for Val," I said. "The guy who was is dead. He was killed in his office, this afternoon."

I scarcely heard the guarded intake of her breath. Her face was set rigidly, her eyes were blank, staring at the backbar but not seeing it. "Dead," she said in a whisper. "That fat man is dead?"

"That's right." I moved my glass around the circle of moisture on the bar. I kept my eyes from her stricken face.

Her voice was just above a whisper, now. "That's what will happen to Val. He's just like her—ambition is eating him up. He'll get in over his head on this."

"You love him, don't you?" I said, looking at her. She met my gaze blankly. "Is that bad, Mr. Jones?"

"Maybe, for you," I said. "I don't know him very well."

The bartender was back, the man called Jim. He said firmly: "You'll get one of your headaches if you have any more, Miss Meredith."

She smiled at him. "One more headache won't even be noticed, Jim. Another rye, please."

He looked doubtful.

"Or I'll take Mr. Jones away. And you know how Mr. Every will feel about that. You wouldn't want to be on the wrong side of Mr. Every, would you, Jim?"

His face colored. *No man,* I thought, *should ever need to be humiliated like that.*

I said quietly: "I'll be responsible, Jim. Don't worry about your job."

"O.K.," he said, and thanked me with his eyes.

It wasn't, I knew, his job he was worrying about. But I had let him think it was.

I said to Judy: "That rye's a man's drink. You should treat it with more respect"

I never heard her answer, if there was one. At that moment, a quiet voice at my side said: "You were looking for Mr. Every?"

THE MAN WHO spoke was short and round, dressed in beautifully-tailored dinner clothes. His face was round. It would have been a jovial face, excepting that his eyes were stone, just gray stone.

"I've been waiting for him," I admitted, "for some time. Though it has passed very pleasantly."

No expression in the gray eyes. "He's here, now. He'll see you. If you'll follow me?"

I followed him. Along the bar, and through a hall, past the

lounges. A door at the end of a short hall, here, and we went through it.

It was a big room. There was a mammoth desk in it, and one file cabinet, but it wasn't properly an office. There was a fireplace, with a long, low coffee table perpendicular to that, and davenports, a pair of them, flanking the coffee table. Heavy burgundy drapes and a wine-ish rug. Some leather overstuffed chairs.

This Val Every I had seen before. I tried to remember where. He was fairly tall, and immensely wide across the shoulders. He had a square, masculine face, which contrasted, with his black, curly hair and the soft brown eyes.

He was sitting behind his desk, and he didn't rise when I entered.

"I've seen you before," he said.

I remembered, then. A punk who'd held up a grocery store on the west side. I'd been on the force, then, in my first year. I'd nailed him at his rooming house.

"Sure," I said. "I'd forgotten your name. It was a long time ago."

"Where was it?" he asked me.

"In a rooming house, on Vine. It was about that business on 12th and Vine, that grocery."

"I'll be damned," he said. "You—" He used some naughty words. "How I used to hate your guts. And I'd forgotten...."

I said nothing. Stone-eyes said nothing. We both waited.

"That was the only time." His voice was reminiscent. "The only time I was ever nailed." He studied me like a specimen in biology class. "What do you know about Miss Harlin?"

"Nothing," I said. "That's why I'm here." There was some

sound from Stone-eyes, and Every's face seemed to freeze. He asked quietly: "Who you working for, chum? The city?" I shook my head. "I'm a private operative." His laugh was nasty. "That's a hell of a word for a shamus. Plumbers are sanitary engineers, and drummers are sales engineers. And you're a private operative. I asked who you were working for, laddy."

"My name is Jones," I said. "*You* can call me Mr. Jones. Who I'm working for would be my business. I'm looking for Miss Flame Harlin. I thought you might have something I could use." I turned to go.

"Just a minute, Mr. Jones." It was Stone-eyes' voice. It was gentle and quiet.

I turned to face him. He had a gun in his hand, a small gun. A Colt Bankers' Special, the kind that handles a .22 caliber long rifle cartridge.

It was a silly little gun, a toy, and I might have laughed. Only Moose Lundgren had been killed with a .22.

"Mr. Every wasn't finished talking to you, Mr. Jones."

Val Every nodded his head toward one of the overstuffed chairs. "Sit down—Jones."

I went over and sat down, trying to look more casual than I felt. I hadn't brought a gun in with me. My .38 was locked in the glove compartment of the Dusy. It had been parked there for some time, and I wondered if there was a parking limit. The damnedest things went through my mind.

Val Every rubbed his hands together and then studied the palms. He expelled his breath, and looked at me. "Miss Harlin worked for me. I took a personal interest in her career, you understand. Lot of people getting mixed up in this lately." He stopped and I waited. "Including the cops," he went on. "They were just up at my place. Two of them. One named Devine. I forget the big guy's name. I'll have to fumigate the place, now. I haven't had any trouble with the law for a long time. You tell them about me?"

"I told them what Lundgren had told me. I don't want any trouble with the law, either. I usually tell them all I can."

"Once a cop, always a cop," Every said. I made no comment.

"You're pretty solid with the boys downtown, aren't you, Jones?"

"We get along. I know most of them, the ones that matter, anyway."

"You and the Chief, huh?" I said nothing. "O.K.," he said. "I don't want any trouble with the law, not right now. And I don't want any trouble with you, not tonight. But stay out of my business, Jones. Keep your nose clean."

"I'll continue to look for Miss Harlin," I told him. "So long as my client wants me to. When she tells me to quit, I'll—"

"*She?*" Every said quickly. "You said 'she.' It's a woman?"

Quiet, again. Every looked over at Stone-eyes, and back at me. I cursed myself silently. I said: "No. I didn't say 'she'."

He was smiling. "Never mind. That's all for now, Jones." He turned to Stone-eyes. "When you go out, tell Judy I want to see her."

Stone-eyes walked with me to the door. I stopped, while he opened it. I said: "That Lundgren was killed with a twenty-two. You'd better have a good story, when the time comes."

"Wait," Every said.

I turned and waited. He had risen, and was walking towards me. Stone-eyes closed the door quietly. The gun was again in his hand.

Every came close enough to breathe in my face. "Lundgren was killed with a twenty-two? How'd you know?"

"I found him. I was with the cops all day."

Every looked at his boy. There was no expression in the gray eyes that looked back at him. "You know where I was, boss. You were with me, all the time."

"Not *all* the time."

"This guy's a cop, boss. This is what he wants. They'd rather lie than eat."

"If you guys can read," I said, "it'll be in tonight's late edition. Or whatever they call the sheet that's on the stands now. If you want me to hang around, I'd just as soon do it in the bar. That's good rye out there."

"A comedian," Stone-eyes said. "We'll tell you where to wait, gumshoe."

Every said: "Wait out in the bar."

I LEFT THEM and went out into the bar. There was a bulky, well-fed-looking man sitting on a bar stool, drinking a beer. I didn't need to see his face to tell it was Glen Harvey. His suits are even cheaper than mine, and fit worse.

He grinned when he saw me. "Have a drink on the taxpayers," he said. "This all goes on the swindle sheet."

Stone-eyes came out and walked down along the bar to where Judy Meredith was still sitting. She followed him back to the room.

"Whose idea was this?" I asked Glen. "You don't look any more like a cop than if you were wearing the blue. What do you hope to get out of this, except a hangover?"

"On beer?" Glen said. "I'm just sitting here. It's Devine's idea, and Devine's my boss, and you hadn't oughta run him down. If he wants me to sit here and drink beer, I will."

The bartender, not Jim, came over, and I ordered rye. "You should have a tuxedo," I said, to Glen.

"I'm no waiter," Glen said. "I'm a guest." He sipped his beer. "You know, that Moose Lundgren didn't have enough to get buried on. And not a relative. They're planting him in Potter's Field tomorrow, Jonesy."

The cold ground, I thought. *Deep and cold and all alone.*

The violin was back, crying in its throaty way, making the bartenders look unhappy again. "That fiddler gives me the willies," Glen said. Miss Judy Meredith, that lovely gal, would now be hearing the riot act. And from a joker like Every. There was no logic in love.

Judy came out after a few minutes looking no less happy than when she had gone in. She came directly over to where I was sitting, and climbed onto the adjacent stool.

Glen lifted his eyebrows, and coughed quietly, but I ignored him.

Judy said quietly: "Your friend's from headquarters, isn't he?"

"You'd have to ask him," I said.

"Val," she told me, "is burning out a bearing. He's not fit company for man or beast."

"Wait'll he sees the papers," I said. "You'd better find a place to hide, after that."

She ordered a rye and water. She said: "Mr. Every won't mind. He just said I could have one or two."

He went to get it, and she turned to me. "What's in the papers?"

"Lundgren was killed with a twenty-two," I said.

"So—"

"So that's what his boy carries, the little round man with the slate eyes."

"Don't others, too? Is that so unusual?"

"It's very unusual. At least, among torpedoes."

The man in white set her drink down in front of her. Glen coughed again, and I looked over at him, and then looked away.

"Do we have to stay here?" Judy asked. "We could get drunk anyplace, though it might cost you a little more."

"Every wants me to wait," I said.

"Oh. Then—you are working for him?"

"Let's go," I said. "Let's find some place where the lights are dim, and the music soft. Let's go some place and dance."

"I'll get my coat," she said. She left the bar. Glen said: "You're rude. You know that, I guess. You should be more familiar with Emily Post."

"She knows you're a cop," I told him. "I didn't want her to get the idea we were too thick."

He made no comment. He looked at me as though I had just crawled out from under a stone, and then looked away.

Judy came with her coat, and we left. The doorman looked surprised when he saw me leave with the boss's girl, but he made no comment.

We went to the Grotto, a fairly quiet spot on 41st, where the band is more concerned with danceable rhythms than trick arrangements, where there isn't any floor show.

We danced and talked and drank. We didn't get drunk. We didn't talk about Every, or Flame or Stone-eyes.

About eleven-thirty, we left, and drove out the drive, way out beyond Brown Deer, beyond the hills, to the bay. There, on a high point, overlooking the water, I parked.

I was aware of her, you can bet. I was ready to sign on the dotted at the moment. But I just lit us a pair of cigarettes, and turned on the radio, and we sat, looking out at the water.

There wasn't much conversation, and what there was I can't remember now. All I remember is the perfume she wore, and the way her voice seemed to match the quiet of the night.

Then she said: "You might as well kiss me. I've been kissed before I met Every, and I'll be kissed after he finds the grave he's headed for. There's no reason we should think of him."

I kissed her. And for the moment, I know she wasn't thinking of Every.

She sighed, as we drew apart again. She said: "You're all right, Mortimer Jones. You're the first man I've wanted to kiss in a long, long time. Maybe I ought to tell you about this."

"You don't need to," I said. "Every wanted you to go, didn't he? He sent you?"

"That's right. He wanted me to find out who you were working for."

"Do you want to know?"

"I don't give a damn, personally," she said. "And if Val wants to know, he can ask you himself."

I didn't kiss her again, though it was a struggle. We sat quietly listening to the radio and smoking, and about one o'clock we started back to town. We took our time, going back, and it was about two when I pulled the Dusy up in front of her apartment building.

It was a tall building, set back on a wide, deep lawn. Up around the seventh floor, there was a light burning in one of the apartments.

"That's mine," she said, "the one where the light is burning."

"You leave it on?" I asked.

"No," she said, "I didn't."

"Must be the maid," I said.

"No." She was getting out of the car, before I could get out to open the door. "No. It's not the maid. She comes in by the day."

"Look," I said. "You think—"

"There's nothing wrong, Mr. Jones," she said. "Nothing at all. Goodnight—and thanks. Thanks for the lovely evening." Then she was going up the walk, between the shrubs that bordered the lawn.

IT WAS BRIGHT the next morning. The sun, undimmed by clouds, ran the mercury up into the eighties. It felt like summer again.

Even Mac looked chipper this morning, when I ordered ham and eggs. "This is more like it," Mac said. "This is a day I might close up and take a drive out in the country."

I knew he wouldn't. He worked all the time, early and late. He would probably die with more hay in the bank than I'd ever seen. With no one to leave it to.

I finished my coffee, ground out my cigarette, and left. Sunshine flooded the street, and the kid was there, again, with the football. He still didn't have it.

I went out there. "Look," I said, "it's like this."

I took the ball from him, and took just one step, and put my foot into it. I could feel it was going to be all right, I could feel the solid impact of it. It went soaring, high into the cloudless sky, and dropped way down the block.

"See?" I said. "You've got to get behind the ball. You've got to get the feel of it."

"Thanks," he said. "Thanks a lot, Mr. Jones."

I felt pretty good. If the detective business fell off, maybe I could sign up with the Packers or the Bears. Or some college.

I walked back to the curb before I noticed the car that was parked directly in front of my office. It was a Mercury club convertible, a trim and sleek piece of fine merchandise.

There was a man behind the wheel. A neat little, round little man with stone-gray eyes. The window was down on his side, and he was looking at me.

I walked over there. "Quite a punt, wasn't it?" I asked him.

"You're cute," he said evenly. "You're quite a comedian."

"How's Every this morning?" I asked. "You two haven't been squabbling, have you?"

"Some day," he said, "I might put a hole in you. Just to see what comes out."

"You'd better get more gun, if you do," I said. "A guy with a twenty-two needs a lot of luck." I was feeling rough after that punt.

He was getting out of the car, now, on the curb side. We went up the steps together, Stone-eyes in front. I didn't want him behind me, even packing a .22.

Up there, he sat in the leatherette chair and I sat in my swivel chair. He looked at me gravely, rubbing his upper lip with the inner edges of his lower teeth, looking undecided. Then he said: "We got the papers last night, and we got them this morning. There was nothing in none of them about a twenty-two."

"What caliber did it mention?" I asked.

"It didn't mention any, none of the papers mentioned any."

"So?"

"The boss is unhappy. We're not as chummy as we were. I'd

hate to think you'd lied about that. We'll find out, understand. The boss has got contacts. He don't have to read the papers. But I keep remembering you said that at the wrong time."

"I was in a pretty hot spot," I said. "I wasn't worried about anybody but *me* at the time. I can't think of any reason I should worry about you."

His face hardened faintly. "When they figure out the *hour* it happened, the boss will be checking me against that, too. It might be rough, after that."

I wondered why he was telling me all this, so I asked him.

"Because I figured maybe you were a little smarter this morning. I figured if you'd tell me who you're working for, I could get things straightened out before the boss got any hotter. I could sort of wrap this up, and hand it to him."

I shook my head. "No soap. Judy tried to get that out of me, last night, and missed. You haven't got even half her charms."

"No," he said, "maybe not. But I've got a gun."

He wasn't lying about that. For it was in his hand, now. It was leveled toward a spot I estimated as right between my eyes. I didn't flinch, or move my head.

I said: "That would be dumb. The kid saw you come in with me. The cops have been watching this place since yesterday morning. All kinds of people may have seen you come up here."

He smiled a strange smile. "You wouldn't be afraid of a twenty-two, would you, Mr. Jones?"

I had no answer to that.

It was then the phone rang. I started to reach for it, but Stone-eyes shook his head. He kept the gun trained on me, as he went over and lifted the receiver.

"Hello," he said, "yes, this is Mr. Jones."

Then he smiled, a happy smile. "Of course, Miss Townsbury," he said. "I'll be out there right away."

He pronged the receiver. "Townsbury," he said. "That's the dame that runs the cure, isn't it? That's the old hag who cures the lushes."

"I don't know the name," I said. "It must be a wrong number."

"Sure," he said. "Of course. We'll probably meet again, shamus."

I nodded. "I hope so. I certainly hope so."

He stopped at the door. "You scare me," he said, smiling. "You scare the hell out of me." Then he was gone, and I heard his small feet, his light tread on the steps.

I phoned Miss Townsbury immediately, and told her what had happened. There was no answer from her for a few seconds. Then: "Perhaps you'd better run right out here. There are some things I had better explain to you."

I agreed that might be a good idea.

4

Knit One, Kill One

THERE WERE NO guests on the front lawn this morning, but I heard the sound of laughter from the rear of the house.

The Mercedes town car was near the entrance, and the tall dark chauffeur was dusting it leisurely. He nodded at me as I got out of the car.

"Miss Townsbury around?" I asked.

"In that same room. You can go right in."

The front door was open. I went through, and down the dim hall to the pastel green room.

Knitting, again. "Close the door, Mr. Jones," she said.

I closed the door and came over to sit in a frail-looking rocker.

"Who was that man who answered the phone in your office?"

"I don't know his name," I said. "He works for Val Every. He had a twenty-two on me, when the phone rang."

"A twenty-two on you?" She looked up from her knitting. "You'll have to be more explicit, Mr. Jones. What did you mean by that?"

"I mean this man had a gun pointed at me. The gun was a twenty-two caliber revolver. The same caliber that killed Lundgren."

The needles stopped. "Lundgren?"

"The detective Every hired. He was killed yesterday. Didn't you read about it in the papers?"

She shook her head. For the first time since I'd known her, her ice-blue eyes held apprehension. "Are we getting mixed up in this, in—murder?"

"I think we are. The police have been after me to reveal your identity. I'll hold out as long as I can."

She looked down at the floor, and up at me. "You're on good terms with them, aren't you? You can protect me in this?"

I had no answer for her, and said nothing. I had only questions.

Maybe she realized that, for she said: "You must be rather puzzled about this place. I feel that I should be frank with you."

"You can rely on my discretion," I said, in my smooth way.

"This place is used for curing alcoholism," she said, and the needles were back at work.

"Our patients are wealthy, all of them. We use a cure that might be frowned on in some medical circles. It's a—a *shock* cure. We have had exceptional success. But, of course, publicity would destroy any hopes we might have for continuing the work. You can understand that, Mr. Jones?"

I said I could. But I asked: "The fences, with the barbed wire? The heavy gate?"

The needles never stopped. "There is a period in the cure when they want to quit. Despite the solemn promises they made, before they were admitted, they try to run out during that period. They try to leave at night. We can't permit this. You may have wondered at Carl's vigilance. Carl is my watchdog."

I asked if Carl was the chauffeur, and learned that he was. I asked. "Is alcoholism the only thing you treat here, Miss Townsbury?"

"It is." She put the needles in her lap, and looked at me with eyes that were suddenly, surprisingly soft. "There's another story I've never told others, Mr. Jones. I'd like to tell you. I want you to understand that money doesn't motivate me in this work. I have all the money I'll ever need."

I waited, wondering at this new softness.

"There was a man," she said, "a young man, back when I, too, was young." She hesitated, smiling faintly, sadly. "He was gifted, Mr. Jones, a man of promise, of talent and breeding. He could have been one of our great composers. He was headed for the stars. Until that vile alcohol ruined him, dulled that brilliant mind, blunted his sensitivity." She paused. "It—killed him, finally."

There was some more conversation, after that. I promised her I would protect her as well as I was able, that I would contact the Missing Persons Bureau confidentially. I didn't tell her I already had.

I left her then, with her knitting and her memories.

Outside, the sun was hiding behind a cloud. I looked over at the stand of virgin timber, and over at Carl, still fiddling with the Mercedes. I heard the voices in the back, quieter, now.

Carl came over to stand next to the Dusy. "Everything's going to be all right, isn't it?" he asked me. "Miss Townsbury isn't going to get into any trouble?"

"Time will tell," I said. "Where's the redhead this morning?"

He smiled. "She's cured. She'll be all right, now."

"She was all right yesterday," I said. "She'll always be all right in my book."

His smile was still there. "Well, that's something else."

He went back to the Mercedes, and I started the motor. The Dusy went murmuring down the drive, talking to herself.

So the bootlegger and the lady in silk were at odds. One who had made his fortune selling it, and one who was using her fortune in curing it.

That's the way it looked, but there were so many angles, so damned many angles … And there was always Devine in the background, itching for my scalp.

Why couldn't I get Stone-eyes off somewhere, and work him over a little? He was the small type I could handle, if he didn't have the .22. But I was no longer with the department—I would need to use considerable finesse, instead of force.

And this Rodney Carlton, the poet with the nine iron? Who loved Miss Harlin desperately, but hadn't seen her for a month. He struck me as being a trifle on the phony side. But I could be wrong—I'd been wrong before, on lots of people.

I decided to go to Mac's first, to see if he had anything edible. There was a faint hollowness in my stomach. I upped the Dusy's pace a bit, and let my mind wander where it would while I kept my eyes on the road.

I can be wrong, all right. I'd been wrong about Mac. There was a crudely penciled sign in the glass of his locked front door. Gone for the day it read. Out where the grass was green, where the wind swept the hills, my Mac would be now. Sans apron, sans dialogue, sans frown, out where it might already be raining.

For there was thunder in the north.

There was dampness in the air, here on my poor street. There was that quiet that precedes a storm sometimes. And there was a Chrysler Highlander sedan parked at the curb in front of my office.

THE GIRL BEHIND the wheel got out when she saw me, and stood waiting. She was wearing something simple in a printed blue, some draped material that did her proud.

"Good morning, Hawkshaw," she said.

"Hello, Judy." I feasted my eyes a while. "Won't you step into my parlor?"

"Let's sit in the car and watch the storm come up," she suggested.

She climbed back in, and I followed her. "Every send you again?" I asked.

"Mmmmm. He didn't disapprove." She looked at me and smiled. "I think you did me some good last night."

The first drop of rain hit the windshield, and there were others, on the metal top. "The kiss?" I asked. "Or the dancing, or the brightness of my conversation? Or just my generally seedy appearance? That could be good for your ego, in a comparative way."

"Just you. Just Mortimer Jones, that easy, gallant, good guy."

"Enough," I said, looking into the dark blue, the knowing eyes. "I'm blushing. I'm no ladies' man."

"I wouldn't know about that," she said. "I'm no lady. But for a while, last night, I could have been. You treated me like a lady, Jonesy. It's kind of early to tell, but you might even have cured me. Wouldn't that be fine, wonderful?"

I said: "It could be temporary. Nobody's ever confused me with Tyrone Power."

Her laugh, a low musical chuckle from her lovely throat. "No, your charm isn't that tangible. Don't be frightened, Philo. It's not only you. There must be lots of other wonderful guys like you."

I said stiffly: "I don't remember coming off a production line."

"Jonesy!" Her hand found mine. "I didn't mean that. I meant, there must be other tolerant, gentle, decent men who'd find me attractive. I'm not hopeless, am I?"

"You could do all right," I assured her, "in any league. If you really think this stupid infatuation of yours with Every is finished, you could do all right."

"It could be," she whispered. "I'm hoping it is. Will you hold your thumbs for me, Jonesy?"

"I will," I promised. And then the thought hit me. "Do you know Miss Townsbury? The nice little old lady who runs that place for alcoholics?"

"Know her!" Her laugh was short and sharp. "I was up there for treatment. Why do you think—" And she stopped. She stared at me. "Never mind," she said. "I'm no stool pigeon, whatever else I've been."

I said: "How would you like to take a drive with me out to a poet's house?"

"Is he interesting?" she asked. "Is he handsome?"

"He's handsome," I said. "I think he might prove interesting."

We drove out in the Chrysler, slowly, over the wet streets, the wipers working diligently to sweep the torrents of water flooding the windshield.

There was a riot car parked in front of the cottage. There was the meat wagon, and a department coupé, and a cop standing up on the porch, out of the wet. The Chrysler braked to a halt, and I got out. I told Judy: "I'm going in there. If I'm not out in three minutes, you'd better take off. That'll mean I'm right in the middle of it."

She looked at me wonderingly.

"Something," I said, "must have happened to the poet."

I closed the car door, and ran.

The man in uniform, on the small porch stopped me. I told him who I was, and that I wanted to see the officer in charge.

I got in, finally. Harvey was there, but not Devine. Adams was there and an assistant M.E. Rodney Carlton was there.

There was a small but bloody hole in the side of his neck.

The assistant M.E. thought it had nicked the jugular, and he had died within a very few minutes.

Harvey nodded. "He was alive when I got here." Then he saw me. "Well," he said. "You're in this, too, aren't you?"

"I was going by," I lied. "I saw the wagon out front."

"You're a liar," he said. He was glaring at me. "This guy talked to me, before he died. Most of it I couldn't understand, but your name was clear enough."

"All right," I said, "I'm a liar. You want to run me in?"

Some of his quick anger was melting, and he looked uncomfortable. "Just hang around," he said. "I'll see you later."

I WALKED LEISURELY over to the window, and saw Devine step from a department car. I saw Judy ride off in the Chrysler. Devine looked wet and miserable as he came scurrying up the walk, his head down.

He didn't look any happier when he saw me. But he ignored me, at first, while he got the story from Glen. I listened.

Somewhere, Devine had got a lead on this Carlton, and he had sent Glen over. Glen had got here in time to hear a shot, a sharp little spat like a .22 makes. He had opened the door, when he heard that, and found Rodney Carlton on the floor, the hole in his neck.

Devine said: "Nobody in the house? Just him?"

"That's all."

"*Somebody* must have been here," Devine said. "Somebody shot him."

My eyes measured the distance from Carlton's body to the kitchen arch. I saw the line of blood-drops leading from there. At least, it looked like blood, though it wasn't very noticeable on that rug.

I went out into the kitchen. There was blood, a mess of it, on the floor near the door in here, I called them out.

"How's this?" I suggested. "Somebody rings the doorbell in the rear. He goes to the door, and—"

I looked from Devine to Harvey.

"Let's see what it looks like out there," Devine said.

There was a pair of trellises flanking the doorway, back here, effectively screening the view of the door from the neighbors. There was a small back yard, which was bordered by an open alley.

Devine looked at Glen Harvey. "Whoever it was," he said quietly, "he could be in Hoboken, by now. He could be in Paducah."

"Sure," Glen said. "I called the Doc, after I got the guy's story. He was still alive. I wasn't chasing out, while he was still alive."

"And what'd he tell you? Did he give you the murderer's phone number, too, so we won't have to go and get him, so we can just call him and have him drop down to the station? You're armed, aren't you? You got any reason for not going out that back door?"

Devine's face was red, and getting redder. He would probably work himself into a frenzy, the way he was going. I said mildly: "He did tell Glen something. He mentioned my name, for one thing."

Devine looked over at me, in his nasty way, and then looked at Glen. "That right? Jones in this one, too?"

Glen said evenly: "Carlton mentioned his name. He said something about putting *her* on a train. I don't know who he meant by her. He said I should tell Jones that. And tell him she never came back from *up there*. The way it sounded, he thought, at first, that Jones was working for Every. That's why Carlton told him he hadn't seen her for a month." Glen was looking at me, though he was talking to Devine.

"All right," I said, "here's something for you. This Carlton was engaged, at one time, to the girl Val Every's looking for. Every's number one torpedo carries a little Bankers' Special, a Colt twenty-two. That could be a twenty-two hole in his neck. And Lundgren was killed with a twenty-two. What more do you need?"

"Just your part in it," Devine said. "What about the train? And not coming back from *up there*. What's that mean?"

"Nothing to me," I lied. "The man was probably in a delirium."

"And you're not working for Every?" Devine said.

"That's right."

"Who are you working for, then? Now would be the time to open up, Jones. With two murders in two days, you could start playing it smart about now."

I looked at him, and away. I said: "Grab Every. Keep him on an open charge. I think I got something."

Devine said: "We'll take care of the law, in this town. If you've got something on this, I want it."

"What about Every?" I asked. "You've looked up all the files on him, haven't you? What's his big number, now?"

"Dope," Devine said.

That tied it up. It was beginning to make sense. I said: "Grab him. Somebody'll talk. Hold him. And I'll want four men, maybe more. More would be wise. Two of them can ride in the back of the Dusy, under cover. The rest, I'll place."

"You?" Devine asked. "You giving orders, Jones?"

"Not if you don't want me to," I said. "You can take it from here, if you want."

They were taking out the body of Rodney Carlton. Devine looked at Glen, started to say something, and then changed his mind. He looked at me quietly.

Finally, he said: "We'll talk this over down at the station."

I agreed to that, and I rode down there with him in the department car. We had no dialogue, on the way down.

While he went in to see the Chief, I phoned Judy Meredith. I hoped she had gone right home.

She had. I asked her: "Would you mind answering just one question, one very important question?"

"Try me," she said, "and see."

"Did you ever take dope?"

It was a hell of a question, and put very bluntly. But I think she understood there was no malice in my asking it. I heard no sound excepting the rumble of thunder, outside, and the clack of a typewriter from somewhere inside.

And then she said: "Not for long. I found out, in time."

Only that, and the click of the phone on her end as she hung up.

I phoned Miss Townsbury. "Something's come up," I told her. "I must see you, right away."

She would be at home all day, she informed me.

Devine was still in with the Chief. I told Harvey: "I'm going across the street and get a sandwich. I'll be back."

I was still there, in the counter lunchroom, when Devine came in. He said: "The Old Man said O.K. Who do you want?"

"You and Harvey in the tonneau," I said. "Melkins, Red Small, Jackson and Schulte. One of the M.E.'s, prepared to make an examination right on the spot. I think we can forget the warrants."

"What's it all about," Devine said, "or am I being personal?"

I told him what I thought, and why, and he looked skeptical. But he didn't discourage the trip. He would have liked to see me miss this one—the stage was properly set for me to look very silly if I missed.

WE RODE UP that way, three of us in the Dusy, the others following in a squad car. I moved along at a smart clip. Without conversation, it was a boring trip, and neither of my riders seemed to be very much interested in conversing.

I put Schulte at the gate. We rode around the entire estate, and I put the others where I thought they should be, though only the gate really needed watching. But I hadn't known this before coming up. Then Devine and Glen ducked down in back, while I drove up the gravel drive.

Carl wasn't in sight this afternoon. Miss Townsbury herself came to the door. She was wearing the steel-rimmed glasses again. We walked back together to the pastel green room. There was no knitting in sight.

I sat in the same rocker, and she in her knitting chair. I told her about the death of Rodney Carlton.

She showed no emotion at the news.

I said: "He didn't die right away. He talked, before he died."

There was emotion now—fear in the cold eyes, and a stiffening of the spine. "To—whom did he talk, Mr. Jones?"

"To me," I lied.

There was some relaxation in her posture, some relief.

"Miss Harlin is dead, isn't she?" I asked her suddenly.

Again, the stiffening. "Are you insane, Mr. Jones? If I knew she were dead, would I have engaged your services?"

"You might. You knew I was in with the department. You could do that to make the police think you were worried about her, as a sort of advance alibi. If you went directly to the police, they'd be coming up here. They'd be nosing into your business."

"That's ridiculous," she said, without expression. She was only mouthing words.

"Maybe. Or maybe you wanted Every to think you were worried about her. Is he getting out of hand, Miss Townsbury?"

"I don't know the man," she said.

"You knew he was a bootlegger, though he was never well known by anyone outside of the department. You knew him, all right. He worked for you. His little fat friend knew you, too, though he tried to pretend in my office that he'd only *heard* of you. And Miss Meredith knows you, too. The tie-up's there, all right. It's clear enough."

Light glinted off the lenses of her glasses. She was studying me, all pretense of indignation gone, sizing me up. She said: "You've managed to put quite a few unrelated facts together, haven't you, Mr. Jones?"

"A few," I admitted. "That redhead was the tip-off. I could see you had her well on the road. You bring the wealthy drunks up here, and cure them of their alcoholism. But you start them on something worse. Is it morphine? Opium?"

"And why would I do that?"

"So you can sell it to them. Or so Every can, through your cooperation. They aren't likely to talk, your customers, are they?"

"Talk to whom?"

"To the police."

"No," she admitted. "They aren't likely to go to the police. And neither are you, Mr. Jones. This place is well guarded."

There was somebody else in the room. The chauffeur, Carl. The gun he had in his hand was a Colt Camp Perry model, a single shot pistol with a long barrel, a hell of a long barrel. It was a .22.

"That's the gun that killed Lundgren and Carlton, isn't it? Is that the one that killed Miss Harlin, too?"

Carl said nothing, the long barreled gun held unwaveringly in his hand.

Miss Townsbury said: "All three of them made the mistake of trying to blackmail me. Is that the mistake you were trying to make, Mr. Jones?"

"No," I said.

"Both Lundgren and that poet," she went on, "knew that Flame came up here. That poet put her on the train that took her up here. Both of them know that was when she disappeared." She looked down at the floor. "That's why they died. They tried to blackmail me. That's why she died, too, that night—" Her voice trailed off.

"Carl took care of them?" I asked. "All of them?"

Carl said: "What difference does it make to you, shamus? What difference is anything going to make to you, where you're going?"

There was a sharp intake of breath from Miss Townsbury.

I said: "The man in the doorway will take care of me."

Carl's laugh was low. "That's a pretty dusty gag, Jones. That's a little old for me."

From the doorway, Devine said: "You'd better put that toy away, big boy. This thing in my hand is a *man's* gun."

Carl never even turned before he dropped the gun to the carpet. It would be a long time, I knew, before Devine would let me forget this.

THE DEPARTMENT BUILT up a case, all right. Some of Miss Townsbury's patients talked, and after that, some of her former patients. Some of the organization's small fry talked enough to sew all of them up—Every and Carl and the old girl and her staff. Judy wasn't in on any of it. Carl's gun had killed Lundgren and Carlton, but not Flame.

They found Flame the next day. In a shallow and poorly concealed grave in the woods. No coffin. In the cold, wet ground, with a knitting needle through her left eye, embedded in her brain....

A Murder for Mac

Some peeps start out to look for stolen cufflinks and come back with cufflinks. Not Mortimer— he always came back with a murder. He tried his best to keep his clients alive, but they always turned up dead in the morning. Someone was certainly playing hob with his clientele.

1

One On the House

IT WAS A fall day, fairly late in fall, but unseasonably warm. The kids were in school, most of them, and the street outside was quiet. I was drinking a beer, small, and gabbing with Mac.

Mac was polishing glasses. They didn't need it, but he thinks it puts him in a thoughtful mood if he polishes them when he's discoursing with me. When he says something he considers particularly profound, he'll take his eyes away from his work and look at me. An awful lot of ham in Mac.

I had ordered a second beer when he said, "It's going to wreck your racket, some day. People will be afraid to come to you. They want to find a missing collar button, or something, and they'll be afraid you'll ring a murder into it. What's going to happen to your racket, then?"

"Profession" I corrected him.

"Huh," he said. "A gum shoes, a shamus—profession, huh!"

"Booze-peddler, huh," I countered. "Seller of forgetfulness to derelicts, peddler of desire to minors and opiates to adults."

"I don't sell no minors," Mac said indignantly, looking up from the glass he was polishing. "And what's an opiate? That mean dope?"

"More or less," I admitted. "I just used it to get the proper flow in the sentence. No offense meant."

"Of course not," Mac said scornfully. "Just parading your high school education. What's a derelict?"

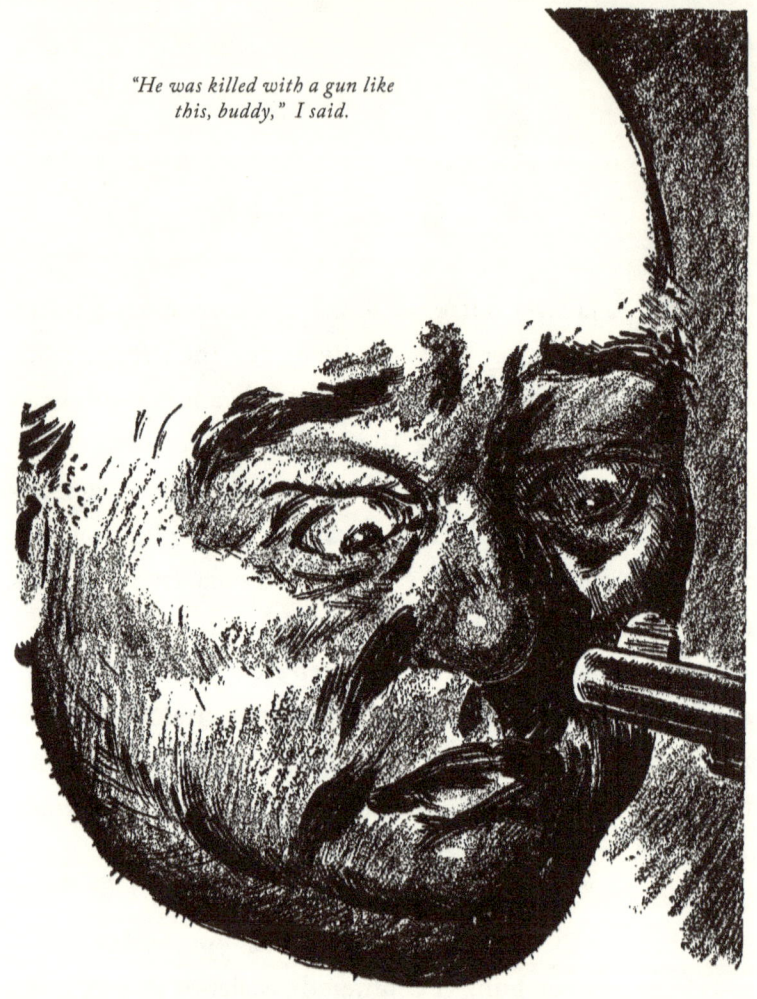

"He was killed with a gun like this, buddy," I said.

"Any of your customers," I said. "When am I going to get that beer I ordered?"

It was then that this girl walked in.

Dressed in some fuzzy wool dress of misty blue. Wearing a light coat of the same material, and a perky hat. Wearing gloves, like a lady. Looking like something better than a lady, one of those sleek blondes with slim legs and intriguing shoul-

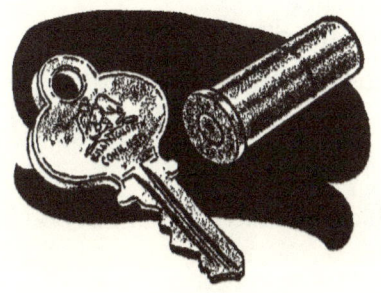

ders and like that. You know what I mean.

Mac was eating her up with his eyes. He said coyly: "At your service, Miss."

When she smiled I could tell she was enjoying the situation. She looked like a girl with the capacity for enjoyment. "Mrs.," she corrected him. "Though if I'd met you earlier—"

Mac colored and shuffled his feet and opened his mouth to say something, but nothing came out. He looked, at the moment, faintly like the village idiot.

The girl said: "I just dropped in to kill a little time. But I'll have a Manhattan while I'm waiting."

Mac still said nothing. Beer he had, whiskey, wine and a few mixes. But Manhattan, to him, was just a borough.

I said, to ease his discomfort: "It's warm enough for a Tom Collins. And he knows how to make *those*."

For the first time, she regarded me directly, taking it all in in her open, amiable way. The cheap suit and the inexpensive tie and the lean litheness of my graceful, fairly young figure. I didn't blush.

She smiled. "All right, a Tom Collins. And it better be good."

"It will," Mac said.

"Neither of you," she said, "I suppose, know when that detective up the block gets to his office. He's the man I came down here to see."

Mac had his poise back. "You came to the right place, Ma'am," he said grandly. "Shake hands with Mortimer Jones."

Her eyes were laughing now. "Why not?" she said, and extended her hand. I took it in mine.

It would be superfluous to say something electric passed through me at the contact. *Any* presentable female between sixteen and fifty can send variable degrees of voltage charging through my susceptible body with a handshake.

The voltage in this case was high. I aped Mac, in saying, "At your services, Mrs.—?"

"Douglas," she supplied. "Mrs. Malcolm Douglas." The sparkle was still in her dark blue eyes. "Though your friend can call me Sheila."

Mac dropped a glass.

"Would you like to go over to the office now," I asked, "or after you've had the drink?"

"The drink first," she said. "I really think I need it." She climbed up onto a bar stool. "It is warm, isn't it? Too warm for this three piece suit. But it's new, and I had to show it off. How do you boys like it?"

Mac said, "classy", to which I added, "It was designed for

somebody exactly like you." Mac sneered at me.

There wasn't much conversation after she got her drink. Mac went back to polishing his glasses, occasionally looking up, as though he were about to speak. But he never did.

I timed my beer to last as long as the Tom Collins. It wasn't hard. She was no dawdler.

And then the glasses were empty, and she said, "Shall we go?" and I nodded agreeably.

Mac said, "Thank you, and come in again," and she smiled and winked, and we went out into the sunshine together.

There was a big convertible parked in front of my office, a black job, light top, with whitewall tires. In fine taste, I thought, and said so.

"I like it," she said, "though it's no Duesenberg."

How had she known that? How did she know I drove a Dusy? I asked her.

"Don't be modest," she said. "You're known all right, Mortimer Jones. Do you think I'd come down to this shabby neighborhood for just *any* detective?" I tried to look smug.

TOGETHER WE WENT up the worn wooden steps to my office over the cigar store. I opened the window, while she seated herself in the leatherette chair on the retail side of my desk.

She was smoking a cigarette when I sat down. Her glance traveled from the end of her cigarette to my face, to the window behind me, and back to my face.

"Trouble?" I asked.

She smiled, and shook her head slightly. "Curiosity, perhaps." She paused. "I don't honestly know, to be frank."

"Your husband?" I suggested.

Her laugh was quiet. "That's it. Only don't think it's jealousy. Anything we may have had is dead. I couldn't be jealous of him."

"You want a divorce," I suggested. "I don't really relish that kind of business. I—"

"No," she said, "I don't want a divorce. I don't even want any evidence that would permit me to use divorce as a threat. I'm just—just curious." She gestured impatiently. "Aren't you ever curious? Doesn't it bother you when people act queerly?"

"Not too much," I answered. "Not enough to pay twenty dollars a day and expenses to some snoop."

Her eyebrows lifted. "Your rates?"

"My special fall rates."

"All right," she said. "Well, here's the way it is."

Her husband, who was head of the accounting department at the Nero Pressed Steel Company, had been going out a lot, nights. He was very frank about it—he was going out to play poker with some of the boys. He'd been winning, he told her, and he wanted to ride his luck. This had gone on for six months, and his luck hadn't failed yet, according to him.

"An honest man," I commented. "He could use the working overtime gag, you know."

"He should have," she said. "Because he wasn't playing poker. I found that out. Why, one of the men he claimed to be winning from consistently hasn't been in town for a year! If there were even the remotest possibility that a woman might be involved— But that's impossible." She shook her fair head. "Malcolm simply wouldn't look at another woman. I'm all the woman he wants—or can handle."

No lie, I was sure. "He loves you," I said. "He must."

"He does. Too much. I'm not worthy of a love that strong." She laughed again. "It's more than I deserve or want."

Poor Malcolm, I thought. I said: "I'm not sure I want your business, Mrs. Douglas." I stopped. I couldn't explain just why I didn't want it, excepting that it seemed sort of malicious.

"Ethics," she scoffed. "Mr. Jones, at your age—"

"You're not telling me the complete truth, are you?" I countered.

She shook her head. "I just want to know what he's doing. It's pure and simple curiosity."

Neither pure nor simple, I thought.

She was studying me. "I don't understand you, Mortimer Jones. You're not making sense." She crushed out her cigarette in the tray on my desk. "Have I asked you to do anything illegal? Is there any reason I shouldn't know what my husband does with his two evenings a week?"

"I suppose not," I said. "I suppose a married man really hasn't any freedom. The retainer will be fifty dollars."

She gave it to me in one piece, a fifty dollar bill. Her smile was mocking. "Men," she said, "how they stick together."

"In self-defense," I added. "You could drop in tomorrow, or I could come out there. Tonight is one of the nights, isn't it?"

She nodded. She said good-bye and headed for the door. She stopped there, with fine dramatic instinct. "Until tomorrow," she said, and left.

I heard her dainty feet click-clacking down the wooden steps. Poor Malcolm, I thought again.

I sat a while, smoking, after she had left. I turned on the radio for the news report, but my mind wasn't on it.

I went back to Mac's for lunch. Or rather, for the split pea soup and liverwurst sandwich I can get there and call lunch.

"What a broad, huh?" Mac said. "She sure sailed for me. What have I got, Jonesy? What is it I've got?"

"Just a tavern, so far as I can see," I told him. "What more do you want?"

"Huh," he said. "You saw the play she made for me. When's the murder?"

"Murder?" I said, and then remembered. "No murder," I told him. "A routine case. A missing collar button."

With great ceremony, Mac went to the register and withdrew a bill. He laid it on the bar. A ten dollar bill. "That sawbuck says there will be a murder," he said.

"Don't be foolish."

"Haven't you got ten bucks?"

"O.K." I took out a ten from my wallet, and placed it on top of his. "You hold the money. Now I'd like my soup."

"Yes, sir," he said. "Of course, sir."

Back at the office, I studied the penciled address of Mrs. Malcolm Douglas. I looked up the family in the city directory, but there was no information there I didn't already have.

I phoned Brenda Forbes. Brenda handles a social chit-chat column for a local paper and knows about everybody. I asked her if she knew the Douglas pair.

"Only faintly," she told me. "Nouveau riche, Jonesy. They haven't climbed up there, not yet. Not high enough for Brenda, though that blonde will make it, one day, I'll bet. When are we going out to get drunk, Jonesy?"

"As soon as you can afford it," I said. "I can't."

"Louse!" she said, and hung up.

Newly rich. The blonde hadn't looked like one of those. She'd looked like a girl with a background. You never can tell.

I went out, and walked up two blocks to where the Dusy was parked. The day's heat was lifting, there was a breeze from the east. Autumn was reverting to type.

The Dusy made no comment as I headed her home. In my small and undistinguished apartment, I pulled down the bed and took a well deserved nap. It had been a trying day.

2

Downpour of Death

FEW CARS WERE on the drive. The Dusy moved in and around and through it in her regal way, purring softly in smug self content. Up the drive to Barclay, and down the tree-lined wideness of Barclay to Westchester Boulevard. Near the corner of Westchester and Ogden, I parked.

There was a quarter moon overhead. There were the branches of a huge oak overhead. I wasn't much more conspicuous than a church spire.

I turned the radio on softly, and waited. A quarter of a block away, in full view, was the Douglas home, a large white house on a wide lawn, visible from here because of the bulge in the street directly in front.

The big convertible was parked in front, and a sedan was standing in the drive.

I listened to The Voice, wondering what kind of income tax he must pay, and if I'd mind paying that kind of tax with that kind of income. The air was cool and promised to get cooler.

The Voice was through. I turned the dial to The Killer's Circle and followed the trail of a midwestern homicidal maniac to his inevitable doom at the hands of the broad-shouldered, handsome, brilliant, semi-humorous detective Fred Fairplay. Never misses, that Fairplay. What a man!

The air got cooler. I waited. A leaf drifted down from the tree overhead and fell on the hood of the Dusy.

The door of the Douglas house opened, and a man came out. He didn't walk down to the sidewalk, but cut directly across the lawn from the porch.

I kicked the Dusy into life.

The glare from a pair of headlights cut at right angles across the street ahead, and then the sedan eased out onto the boulevard, heading east.

I waited until it was two blocks ahead before following. When he cut into the stream of traffic on the drive, I followed more closely, keeping two or three cars between us all the time.

He continued along the drive. Traffic grew thinner, and I was forced to drop further behind. My car is too conspicuous. I should buy a light, inexpensive sedan. But I won't.

Then the sedan made a sharp turn into the winding road that threaded up the bluff over the bay. I followed as discreetly as possible, hoping I wouldn't lose it in the apartment-studded streets on the bluff.

He was just turning down Iona Court as I achieved the final upward turn of the climb. I cut down to about ten miles an hour and followed.

I almost over-ran him. The sedan was parked near the entrance to the Court. I drove by, trying to appear uninterested.

Two blocks up, I turned. I went over one block, and came back and parked. I left the Dusy there, and walked over to Iona.

He was still sitting in the car. He was wedged in between another sedan and a coupé, near no apartment building, but with a view of all the apartments lining the street.

There was a small park across the street. I found a bench, and tried to appear casual. It was beginning to look as if Malcolm

Douglas was playing my game, though I doubted if he was getting paid for it.

He waited and I waited. A radio blared somewhere, and traffic moved by. The moon moved behind a cloud, and heat thunder rumbled from the west. It was cool, after the humid day. I was sorry I hadn't brought a topcoat.

The headlights of a car swung into Iona from the hill road. Across the street, Malcolm ducked for cover, as the car went by. It was a big convertible with whitewall tires.

That completes the cycle, I thought. She paid me to watch him watch her.

The convertible went down to the end of the block, and stopped. The figure getting out was indistinct from where I sat, but it was undoubtedly a woman. Malcolm was up and watching now. The figure disappeared into the lofty apartment building on the corner.

Malcolm waited for nearly thirty minutes. Then he left the car and walked down toward the apartment building. I remembered she had told me he loved her—too much. She was all the woman he wanted or could handle. I wondered how he was going to handle this.

Twenty more minutes, I waited. Then the tall, thin figure of the man I assumed was Malcolm Douglas appeared again from the doorway of the corner apartment. He walked steadily, almost mechanically, down to his sedan. I moved as unobtrusively as possible to the Dusy, hoping it would take him some time to maneuver out.

He was turning the corner at the other end as I drove into the entrance to Iona Court. Perhaps, I thought, my mission is complete. And perhaps this was a prearranged meeting. I followed.

Down again to the hillside road, down to the drive, through the evening pleasure-driving traffic to the lower east side. The sedan stopped there, directly in front of Teddy's Tap.

He's going to drown his sorrow, I thought. He has come face to face with *life*, and this is his answer.

I parked the Dusy, and followed.

A MAN WHO was probably Teddy was behind the bar. A fat, bald man, medium tall, wearing a white shirt, white apron and a red nose.

Three men were playing cards and drinking beer at a corner table. The tall thin man was in front of the bar, and I got my first close look at him.

A baby's complexion, a healthy baby. Blond hair, too fine and blond for a man, for my taste. Eyes a candid blue, now dark with anger. A man in his late thirties—physically.

Teddy said: "Well, Mr. Douglas, what'll it be?" I knew then I had the right man.

"Double Scotch," he said, with bitterness.

"Scotch-type, I got," Teddy answered. "No real Scotch."

"It's got alcohol in it, hasn't it?"

Teddy's bland face held surprise at the roughness in Malcolm's voice. He hesitated, a moment, then said: "Sure, sure, it's got alky in it." He set a bottle of Scotch-type whisky on the bar, and a small glass.

He came down to me. "Rye," I said, "with a little water."

"Yes, sir." He went to get it.

One of the men at the table called another man a lucky so-and-so, and there was laughter. The radio behind the bar was playing a love song, blue and lowdown, sung by some throaty contralto.

Douglas scowled at the radio, but said nothing. Teddy, noticing the scowl, looked at the radio doubtfully. But he didn't turn it off. He came up to stand near me.

"Quite a change in the weather, ain't it?" he commented. I admitted it was.

"Wouldn't be surprised if we got some rain," he went on.

I said he was probably right. "We could use it," I added.

"Sure could. Not so bad tonight, though. But if it stays damp, it'll be a heller tomorrow, I'll bet."

Down the bar, Malcolm Douglas deposited some change on the counter. He stared at it a while, and then his hand reached out and picked up a key from the pile on the bar. He held it up for a moment, staring at it.

His face was hard, the corners of his mouth tightly compressed. Suddenly he turned, and his right hand moved through a swift arc. The key went skidding along the floor, coming to rest in a corner of the room.

One of the men at the table looked up, in surprise. The others hadn't noticed. Teddy said: "Something wrong, Mr. Douglas? Something wrong with the Scotch?"

Douglas didn't look at him. "Nothing. I'll have some more." He was reaching for the bottle.

Teddy went down to pour it for him. He made no comment about the weather at that end of the bar. He picked the proper amount of change out of the pile, and rang it up on the register.

From the radio came *I Walk Alone*. Outside, there was a rising wind, and the door of the tavern swung in a few inches.

Teddy came back to me. "This wind'll bring the rain," he said. He was talking to me, but his eyes were on Douglas wonderingly. Then he looked over at the key in the corner of the room, squinting his eyes in the dim light. Douglas ordered more Scotch.

There was a pay phone on the wall. I walked over and called my office number.

After a proper interval, I said: "I'll be home a little late, honey. About a half an hour or so." I hung up.

Douglas still stood at the bar. Teddy was bringing a round of beer to the men at the table. Quickly, I stooped and picked up the key. When I came back to the bar, Teddy was back there, too. He stared at me for a few seconds. He started to say something, and stopped.

I took out my wallet, and extracted a bill. I let him see the buzzer, pinned inside, as I did this.

I said: "Another rye, please."

He didn't move. There was suspicion in his placid eyes—there was a new hardness to his wide, smooth face.

"It's all right," I said. "Haven't you got any more rye?"

"Sure," he said. "Sure, I got rye." He hesitated another moment before going to get the bottle.

Malcolm Douglas said: "Some more of the same."

The bartender was pouring my drink. "In a minute," he said. Outside, it was beginning to rain.

Teddy went down to pour some more Scotch. Malcolm Douglas said: "The dirty, rotten—"

Teddy looked up at him, the drink half poured. "What's that, Mr. Douglas?" he asked.

"Nothing, Teddy. I was talking to myself."

Teddy finished pouring the drink. The men at the table had forgotten their game for the moment, watching the incident at the bar.

Douglas finished his Scotch in a gulp, and headed for the washroom.

The bartender said to me: "You from Headquarters?" I lied, with a nod.

"Douglas in trouble? He's sure acting queer."

"It takes all kinds," I said.

Teddy was chewing his full lower lip. "Could I see that badge again?" he asked.

"You could phone Headquarters," I told him. "You could ask if Glen Harvey works there. Anybody could steal a badge."

Douglas came out of the washroom and headed directly for the front door. Teddy said, "Good-night, Mr. Douglas," but there was no answer.

I waited about ten seconds before following.

The sedan was in motion by the time I got to the Dusy. As I went by the door of Teddy's Tap, I saw the wide figure of the proprietor standing in the entrance, shielding himself as well as he could from the driving rain. He was still standing there, as I turned the corner, his apron and shirt a white contrast to the black night.

The Dusy shivered, as lightning flashed. I followed the sedan down to the drive, and down the drive to Westchester again. When it turned in at the white house on the wide lawn, I kept going. I went up to Ogden, turned, and parked.

For an hour, I waited, while the rain hit its peak, and tapered into drizzle, while lightning danced through the heavens, and thunder laid out its heaviest barrage.

Once, during a lull, I heard a report that could have been a backfire or could have been a gun. I waited, after that, for lights to go on in the white house, for some sign of activity, but there was none. I assumed it was a backfire. For surely a house of that size would contain servants. If it had been a gun, they'd have known it. After an hour of waiting, I went home, and to bed.

It wasn't until I was eating my morning egg at Mac's, and reading the morning paper that I realized it hadn't been a backfire.

Malcolm Douglas had been killed in the night—killed with a .38.

MAC WAS BRINGING my coffee as I finished the article. I showed him the pictures, the pale, blond Malcolm Douglas and his wife.

Mac almost spilled the coffee. "Hey," he said, "that's the babe. That's Sheila." I nodded.

Mac shook his head. "Jonesy—you think maybe she bumped him?"

"Your guess is as good as mine," I said. "I don't think she did."

Mac expelled his breath. "Neither do I. She's O.K., that dame. Nothing wrong with her. Though you can't never be sure with women. You through with that paper?"

I gave it to him. I said: "You can keep the ten dollars. You guessed right, for a change."

"I don't want no part of that ten," he said. "The bet's off." He was still shaking his head, as he walked back to the bar.

I drank my coffee slowly, smoking a cigarette and wondering if I was in the middle of this mess, if maybe I had been a professional stooge for Mrs. Douglas.

Outside, the sun was back. The stickiness was gone, though, and there was a faint breeze.

In my office, I pulled down the shades, and opened the windows a bit from the bottom.

It was quiet in here, now, and dim. I tried to think it all out, and the way it looked to me seemed logical, but there was no reason why. Nobody had entered the house in the hour after he had. Yet that had been a shot I'd heard in the storm's lull. The neighbors confirmed that.

There were only two servants, a housekeeper and a handyman. Both of them had been away last night. He had been alone, except for the murderer.

Mrs. Douglas had come home at three. Where she had been was not disclosed in the morning papers. But a neighbor had seen her convertible drive in at that time.

Somebody was coming up the stairs. It was not a woman's light tread, but the heavy tread of a big man. I lit a cigarette and leaned back in my chair, facing the door.

A fairly tall, enormous fat man bald as an egg, came in. He was dressed in a cheap serge suit and wore a cunning expression. Teddy, of Teddy's Tap. He hadn't wasted much time.

"Good morning," I said. "You're up early." I indicated the leatherette chair. He took it, and sat staring at me. I waited.

"Headquarters," he scoffed, finally. "I had you tagged for a private eye right off."

"You couldn't have gone to the auto license bureau this early," I said. "How'd you find me?"

"I saw that Detective Harvey," he said. "I figured, the way you were throwing his name around, he must be a friend. I asked him to recommend some private dick." He smiled a self-satisfied smile.

"So," I said. And waited, my eyes concentrated on his red nose.

He spread his hands in an expansive gesture, and tried a smile.

"Is it money, Teddy?" I asked quietly. A silly question. I'm sure he didn't want my honor.

He was at a crossroads—this was something outside of his previous experience. "Mr. Douglas was a customer of mine." He licked his thick lower lip. "I want to find out what happened to him."

"He was killed," I said. "He was killed with a .38." I reached into a top drawer of my desk, and pulled out a revolver. "A gun like this, Teddy."

The muzzle was pointing directly at the red nose.

Sweat beaded the bald dome of his head, and his small eyes were concentrated on the revolver. He didn't look at me, as he said: "I just wanted to find out about Mr. Douglas. You can't—"

I put the revolver away, and he seemed to come back to life.

"I can't what?" I asked him.

He was licking his lower lip again. "I don't know—nothin'—"

"Teddy," I said, "you should stick to running the tavern." I threw him the phone book. "Look up the police department number."

He hesitated, puzzled. "I don't want no trouble," he said.

"You're not getting any," I told him. "I'm trying to save myself some."

He gave it to me, and I phoned Headquarters. I asked for the Chief. Teddy didn't miss any of it. When the Chief's pleasant, after-dinner voice was on the wire, I said: "This is Mortimer Jones, Chief. I've got a client, and he wants a character witness."

He mumbled something about being a little out of line, but that was just for his conscience. "Put him on," he said eventually.

I handed the phone to Teddy. Teddy said "Hello," and listened.

When he pronged the receiver again, the look of cunning was gone from his eyes. He looked unhappy—he had come a long way on a warm day for nothing. He rose, and said: "Well, I just wanted to know. Mr. Douglas was a pretty good customer, and—I wanted to know."

"Sure," I said. "I know exactly what you mean." I opened another drawer. "You should have a drink before the trip back."

He sat down again. "Don't mind if I do." He blew out his breath plaintively. "This weather—"

My best rye, this was. I went to the sink in the corner, and got some water to go with it.

Over the rims of our glasses, our eyes met.

"To better understanding," I said.

"Yeah," he said, and drank. He relished it, I could tell.

"This Douglas," I said, "He was really in love with his wife, wasn't he?"

Teddy nodded, and his pale eyes took on a reminiscent glow. "He sure was. Every dime he ever made was for her."

"No outside stuff for him, huh?"

Teddy shook his head. "You know, he wasn't much of a drinker. Couple drinks, and he was talking to himself. That's all he ever talked about then." Again, he shook his head. "A funny guy. But not tight, no guy to nurse a nickel."

"He was always alone when he came to your place?"

He considered this. He looked up at the ceiling, and over at the bottle of rye.

I poured him another drink, and he studied it. "Couple times he came in with another guy. They didn't stand at the bar.

They always sat at a table. Guy named—let's see— Gosh, I've forgot." He downed the drink.

The smooth forehead wrinkled. "Yeah, yeah— Let's see— Mark, he called him. That's it—Mark."

I filed it in that active brain of mine. "And this Mark was the only one?"

"That's all?" He was still looking at the whiskey.

"All right," I said, "one more. But that's expensive whiskey, Teddy. That's no current stuff."

"I know," he said sadly, "I know."

He had his third drink. His nasal barometer was taking on a fine sheen. He rose, and took another look at the bottle, but I firmly pretended not to notice.

"Good-bye, Teddy," I said.

"Good-bye," he said, not looking back.

EVERY DIME HE ever made was for her...

There was no other girl in his life. All I had was a man named Mark, who would, undoubtedly, prove to be innocent and clear of it all.

I still had the key I had picked up last night. I had the routine hunch about that, of course, and it was true, I learned later. But now it was just a key, and that had been a big apartment building.

Again, there were feet on the stairs, two pairs, this time.

It was Devine, boss of Homicide. Devine, who hated my guts. Glen Harvey was with him; Glen's always with him— through no choice of his own. Devine's the boss. He lets you know about that.

Devine said: "We were trailing Scully. We know Douglas

spent a lot of time there, and when he came asking for a private dick, we figured he'd bear watching."

"Scully?" I said.

"Don't be any dumber than nature intended," Devine said. "He just left your office."

"Oh," I said. "You mean Teddy, of Teddy's Tap."

"That's right. What's his business with you?"

"Private," I said. I made quite a ceremony of putting the whiskey away. I made an insult of it. "Anything, else, before I go out to get a haircut?"

Glen Harvey coughed, and looked uncomfortable. Devine looked ugly. Devine said: "We could get it out of him. We were being nice. Because he's your client. Because you used to work in the department, and we wanted to give *your* client a break."

All he needed was a fiddler playing *Hearts and Flowers*. "Well," I said, "if you put it that way, all right. Somebody's tapping his till. He thinks it might be his wife. He wants me to hang around the joint and see."

Devine looked as skeptical as he had a right to look.

"But," I went on, "he couldn't stand the tariff. Nobody's going to pay twenty dollars a day to find out why he's losing an occasional ten."

Devine snorted. "O.K.," he said. "We'll work it out of him. I guess you know about obstructing justice."

Glen said: "Why don't you play it smart, just once, Jonesy?"

"That's a complicated question," I said. "It would require a long answer."

"We're in no hurry," Devine said.

"When people come to me," I explained, "they come because they've got trouble the law doesn't cover, or they want privacy.

That's all I've got to sell—help and privacy. If I turned all my cases over to the police, there'd be no need for me."

"Maybe," Devine suggested, "you could add that you haven't much regard for the Homicide section, too."

"Maybe," I admitted. "I haven't had much cooperation there. But it's been your baby when I was ready, hasn't it? You haven't seen *my* picture in the paper."

Devine colored, and Glen coughed again, a habit of his when he's embarrassed. "That bother you?" Devine asked.

I shook my head. "The less publicity the better, for me."

"O.K.," Devine said. "You've told us all you're going to, then?"

I nodded, keeping my eyes on his face. He had turned, and was heading for the door, when I said: "If I get any more, you'll get it, though."

"Keep it," he said from the doorway. And some more which couldn't bear repeating.

Glen was shaking his head sadly as he followed Devine out.

They'd be back, I knew. After they shook down Teddy, and he told them about the night before, they'd be back. With the cuffs ready, probably. But before I revealed anything I shouldn't, I wanted to talk again to Sheila Douglas.

I had a key on my key ring that had no purpose, so far as I knew. I took it off, and put the other key on, the one I'd picked up last night. When they came back, they'd be asking for a key.

I went out to get a haircut.

3

—

Cell Service

FROM THE BARBER shop, I drove to the Nero Pressed Steel Company. Not with anything in mind, particularly, but just following a faint and elusive hunch. It was a cluster of fairly new buildings on the edge of town—the modern type of plant, one floor and sky-lighted.

There were few trees, and the lawns around the offices looked newly seeded. I went into one of the offices, the one marked *Personnel.*

The stout blonde behind the reception desk in the outer office took one look at my buzzer—and turned white.

"No trouble, honey," I said easily. "It's about Mr. Douglas."

She breathed heavily. "What is it you want to know about Mr. Douglas?"

"I'd like to see his employment record."

She rose, and hesitated. "I suppose it'll be all right." She looked at me more closely. "Your name, please?"

"Glen Harvey," I said.

She turned, without further conversation, and walked toward a row of file cabinets on a far wall. She walked lightly for a heavy woman. When she returned, she had a large, rectangular card in her hand, which she handed me.

Nothing much here. Malcolm had been with the firm for seven years. He'd done all his climbing in the last four. He had been thirty-two years old when he died.

I said to blondie: "How old is this firm?"

"Seven years this summer," she said. "I've been with them all the time." She was grinning, now. "Used to work for Mr. Harvest, until he got upper class."

"Harvest?" I said.

"The president. The boss."

"Oh," I said, putting what inference I could into that exclamation. "He a young man, too?"

"Young enough," she said. "Young enough for me, anyway."

"Hmmm," I hummed, leering at her. "Who's this Mark that Mr. Douglas was so chummy with?"

She looked thoughtful. "I didn't know Mr. Douglas very well. He was very businesslike. Mark—let's see— Unless it could be Mark Callaway, from Quincey Steel—"

"Could be," I said.

She sighed. "Mr. Douglas was sort of clannish. I guess all the girls wished he'd been a little more friendly."

I gave her back the card, and thanked her, and went out again into the warmth of the day. Mark Callaway, from Quincey Steel....Mark was not a common name. Perhaps blondie had given me something. And, then again, perhaps it was all the way the papers stated. But it so rarely is.

Devine and Harvey would be interviewing my fat friend about now. Or maybe they were through, and waiting for me at the office. I decided to go back there, anyway; it was too early for lunch.

The kids were all in school, so I parked right in front of the office. Vacation time, that isn't a wise thing to do—it's too much car for them to ignore.

There was nobody at the office when I got there. Devine and

Harvey didn't arrive until about ten minutes later.

Even Harvey looked sour. Devine looked almost happy, in his grim way, as though I were finally where he always wanted me—right behind the eight ball.

He was chewing an unlighted cigar. He said, around it: "Let's go."

"Go?" I asked. "Where?"

"Down to the clink, down to the place you've been heading for a long time."

"And the charge?" I asked, as casually as I could.

"Intimidating a witness, obstructing justice, impersonating an officer of the law—don't worry, the D.A.'ll take care of that."

"I'm under arrest?" I asked.

He nodded. There was satisfaction in it. "You're under arrest."

Harvey started to say something, and stopped.

I reached for the phone. "I'm going to phone my lawyer first."

I heard some ejaculation from Harvey, and looked up—to see a gun in Devine's hand, a .38 Police Positive Special.

Devine's voice was almost gloating. "You wouldn't be resisting an officer, would you, Jones?"

Harvey said: "Easy, boss. Don't make any mistakes."

"No," I said quietly, "don't make any mistakes, Devine. Too many people are waiting for that." I took my hand away from the phone. "You haven't got enough friends."

His voice was hoarse. "You coming—*now?*"

"I'm coming now," I said. "I'm never going to forget this."

"You can bank on *that.*" He put the gun back in its holster. "Let's go."

We went. In the department car. Without dialogue, without looking at one another, with ill will and embarrassment all around. Neither Devine or I looked as uncomfortable, however, as Glen Harvey. Glen and I had always been friends. We'd often worked together, back when I was with the department.

Sergeant Deering was at the desk when we entered. He started to make some jocular remark, I'm sure. But he saw Devine's face. Devine said: "I want him booked for—"

"Just a minute," I said. "You'd better see the Chief first, Devine. Let's all run in and see the Chief."

He didn't even look at me. "For intimidating a witness, impersonating a police officer."

Deering's glance moved from Devine's face to Harvey's and then to mine. I said: "You got a clean cell, Art?"

He nodded, smiling faintly. He looked again at Devine. "Let's just hold him, without booking him, for a while, huh?" He looked at me. "That all right, Jones?"

"It's all right with me," I said. "I may be back here working soon, and I'd hate to get my name on the blotter."

Devine seemed to freeze. If I came back, it would be his job I'd have. He knew that—the whole department knew that. He said: "Just so he's here when I want him. Just so he's here when Whitney comes down." He turned away, and walked toward the Chief's sanctum.

Whitney was the D.A. Whitney was also Devine's cousin. A lot of his crummy relatives were working for the city.

Harvey was breathing heavily. "Jonesy, you damned fool," he said. "What ever got into your skull?"

"Let me in on it," Deering said.

Glen looked at me. "Go ahead, tell him," I said. "I'd like to hear it myself."

"This Scully guy, this bartender, claims you threatened him

with a revolver. He says you picked up a key in his place last night that belonged to Douglas. He says you claimed to be me."

"I picked up a key," I said. "The rest of it isn't true."

Glen shook his big head. "You'd better start planning your alibis." He went over to sit on a bench near the door.

Deering said doubtfully: "How about this cell business, Jonesy? You want me to lock you up?"

"You'd better," I said, "or Devine will be out for your scalp." He shrugged, and beckoned to the turnkey.

I was following him down the corridor when the flash bulbs went off. This kind of publicity I could use. I didn't like it, but I could use it. As somebody said, no publicity is bad publicity.

The door clanged. I said to the turnkey: "Tell Art that I want Harry Sylvester down here right away." He nodded and walked away, the keys jangling. I sat on the bunk and smoked and thought and quietly cursed Devine.

HARRY SYLVESTER, MY attorney, is a thin faced, small and grave young man, with big, dreamy brown eyes. Some quiet people just give the impression of being thoughtful. In Harry's case, it's different. I was ably represented.

I told him how it was. He sat on the stool in my cell, and I sat on the bunk, and explained it all to him.

When I'd finished, he said: "We'd better get the Chief on our side. I've talked to Whitney. Election year, you know—he's out to kick up some dust."

"What kind of a case have they got?" I asked.

"Not much of a case. Enough to be troublesome. Whitney's no fool, though." He looked at me gravely. "What say we all get together in the Chiefs office? I'll get Whitney and Devine, and maybe we can make some kind of a deal."

"We can try," I said.

He left, and I waited. I had expected, in the hour or so I'd been locked up, that the Chief would have called. But I remembered that I'd used him as a character witness this morning. He must have thought, now, that I'd been using him as a stooge.

Harry came back with the turnkey in about ten minutes. The door opened, and I went out. I winced only a little as it clanged behind me.

As we walked down the corridor, Harry said: "The Chief seems hot about something. You've been neglecting him lately?"

I told him what had happened.

"My cross," he said. "I don't suppose all my clients could be sane. If I'd known that—"

The Chief's office was large and quiet. Devine and Whitney sat in a pair of chairs near the windows. The Chief's eyes met mine, as we entered, and then moved away.

There were a couple of chairs on the far side of his desk. Harry and I appropriated these.

The Chief's big, white-thatched head turned our way. He didn't look at me, but at Harry. "I understand you have some kind of proposition to make, Mr. Sylvester?"

Harry said carefully: "Proposition isn't quite the word. I wondered just what the charges were against Mr. Jones."

Devine started to say something, but Whitney laid a restraining hand on his arm. Whitney said: "I think we talked that over, Mr. Sylvester."

Harry nodded. "We did. That was before I heard my client's story. I can't quite see a case here, after hearing that."

Whitney's handsome, excessively masculine face hardened.

"Do you deny you threatened Mr. Scully with a revolver?"

"Mr. Scully," I said, "asked me what happened to Mr. Douglas. I told him he'd been killed with a .38. I showed him one of my .38s. If he says I threatened him, he's lying. He came to blackmail me, and I had him call Chief Logan, here, to check on my character."

Whitney's smile held no humor. "Do you deny you claimed to be Detective Harvey?"

"I do. He thought I was some kind of a phony. I told him to phone headquarters and ask for Detective Harvey. This Teddy was always doubting me, it seems. I used what friends I *thought* I had."

"And the key?"

"Douglas threw a key away. I picked it up. Is that illegal?"

Devine cut into the conversation. "What about that fairy tale you told me in your office? About this Scully coming to you as a client, about his till being tapped?"

"A lie," I said. "But I figured this was probably his first attempt at blackmail." I emphasized that last word. "I hated to turn him in."

"Blackmail," Devine said scornfully. "Who you trying to kid, Jones?"

"He didn't go to you," I pointed out. "He knew Douglas had been killed, and he'd found out who I was. Why didn't he come to the police?"

Devine had no answer for that.

Whitney said: "It seems to be your word against his."

"That's right," I agreed. "That's your case."

Harry was smiling faintly now. He was the only person in the room who was. He knew Whitney was ambitious—he knew

Whitney didn't like doubtful cases.

Whitney looked at the Chief. So did Devine. All of us seemed to be waiting for him to say something. He didn't speak. He just looked out the window. I was his boy. I had been his boy. But no longer.

"Well—" Whitney said, and stopped.

Harry said easily: "If murder's been done, I'm sure my client is going to cooperate with the department. And I'm sure the department will welcome the cooperation. Wouldn't it be better if we just dropped this silly business?"

"*Cooperate,*" Devine said. "Not that damned—"

Something red burst inside my brain, and I was up and going for him.

WHEN I CAME back to sanity, Harry was holding one of my arms, and Whitney the other. The Chief was standing behind his desk, his eyes startled.

The Chief said: "Mort, for God's sake... What's—"

Devine still sat in his chair. He looked hard and nasty. He didn't look scared.

Whitney said: "Nothing is settled that way, Jones."

"Tell your cousin that," I advised him. "It's the only way *he* knows. I've cleaned up his last three cases for him. I've worked with and for the department ever since I set up my office. All I ever hear is cooperation, cooperation, cooperation— What the hell do they want me to do, sweep out the joint every night?"

The Chief was chewing his lip. He looked a bit worried. Harry was still smiling.

The Chief said: "Just what did you expect from us, Mort?"

"It's your word," I said. "I wouldn't think of using it."

Annoyance clouded his wide, intelligent face. "Don't be flippant," he said.

"O.K., I apologize for that. But *one* thing I want is a little respect around here, as a *citizen*. There are plenty of labor-spying divorce business private operatives around this town who get more respect than I do. They *never* work with the department. Nothing happens to them."

The Chief's face was friendlier now. He was almost smiling. "They don't seem to get mixed up with murder like you do."

"No," I said, "I seem to get the tough ones." I paused. "O.K., I'll stay out of this. I'll stay out of all of them. Homicide can work alone from here in—I won't get in the way."

The Chief frowned. Harry said: "Well, what's the verdict? We dropping the charges against my headstrong boy, here?"

Whitney looked at the Chief. They'd accept his judgment in this.

The Chief nodded. He said: "I'd like to talk to Mr. Jones alone, if you gentlemen don't mind."

They filed out. Harry and Whitney seemed satisfied, but Devine's thin, long face was heavy with discontent.

I sat down again, watching the Chief. He took his gaze away from the windows and let it rest on my face. "You're glib, aren't you?" he asked quietly.

He didn't expect an answer, and I didn't give him any.

"You're glib and flippant," he went on, "and not too concerned with normal dignity. You haven't enough respect for the ordinary processes of law. We're all human, Mort. We all make mistakes—but we're all doing the very best we can. That includes Devine."

I said nothing. He likes to talk. It's good talk, and sincere, and he's a good, sincere and capable man. "This word—this cooperation you say I use too much—"

"I didn't say that," I objected.

"You inferred it. Perhaps you're right. Perhaps it's a mania with me. But we need it, we all need it, most of our troubles arise out of a lack of it." Which was as true as any generality. I nodded.

He smiled. "You sort of used me for a stooge this morning over the phone, didn't you?"

I shrugged, and smiled. "Cooperation," I said.

He chuckled. "All right. Sure. You win." He paused. "You weren't serious about getting out of this case, were you?"

"I don't know," I said.

He shook his big head. "Don't. I like your touch. Stay with it, slugger." He rose. "And now, if you'll give me that key I'll have something to pacify Devine with."

I gave him the phony key, feeling no more like Judas than usual. I shook his hand, and accepted his blessings, and walked quietly out, a free man again.

4

Gumshoe for Sale

OUT IN THE sunlight, Glen Harvey was waiting. "I'll drive you back to your office," he said.

We were threading through the traffic on Fifth, when I said: "I used your name another place, Glen. Out at the Nero Pressed Steel Company."

"Oh," he said. "What's out there?" He was watching the traffic.

"A chubby blonde," I told him. "A blonde with lots of past and still some future. You should look her up."

"That's where Douglas worked, at Nero?"

"That's right."

"I'll look up that blonde." He was smiling.

"She's in personnel," I told him. "Drop me at Mac's, will you? I'm starving to death."

Mac had the early edition of the afternoon paper spread out on the bar in front of him. He looked surprised when I entered. "I thought they'd have you strapped in the chair by now," he said.

"If you've got a small steak," I said, "and you can serve it without dialogue, I'll take it."

"If I had a small steak," he answered, "I'd open a butcher shop." He held up the paper. "Read this while I fix you a hamburger."

I took it over to a table and read it. The picture of me wasn't so hot—it failed to show my proper profile. The story wasn't so hot, either.

INVESTIGATOR HELD IN DOUGLAS SLAYING, the headline read. The story didn't *say* that I was a double-dealing, criminal-fringe, self-seeking bloodsucker, but it left the reader with that impression, through some subtlety I couldn't diagnose. It didn't mention the work I'd done with and for the department. But it was a chain paper, trying to beat up circulation the only way it knew. The other papers would be kinder—I hoped.

I ate what Mac had termed a hamburger, and some French fries with it. I ate a quarter of lettuce, crisp and cold, with French dressing. I tried to ignore Mac's awkward attempts at humor, while I finished my coffee.

I took the paper with me when I went back to the office. My office door is rarely locked, and all kinds of people are apt to drop in—salesmen and con men and even collectors.

The man sitting in the leatherette chair was none of these, though he had a faint touch of the con man in him, I was sure. A tweedy gent, thin and tall, losing his hair, getting a wrinkle here and there. With the coldest, damnedest blue eyes I'd ever seen.

He looked at the paper under my arm, and then up at my face. "A poor likeness," he said easily. "It doesn't do you justice."

"Thank you," I said. "I felt the same way." He rose. "My name is Douglas, Nelson Douglas." He paused. "Malcolm's brother."

I said, "Oh," and some words of condolence I don't remember. If the tweeds were indicative, Nelson was doing all right—these were no domestic rags.

We both sat down again. There wasn't anything I could think of to say, so I waited for him.

He said: "Mrs. Douglas hired you to follow Malcolm, didn't she?"

I shook my head, saying nothing.

The cold smile again. "Oh, I know you're not at liberty to divulge that information to *everyone*. But Malcolm was my brother."

I still said nothing. There was something about the man that put me on my guard. Maybe it was the eyes.

He didn't seem ruffled by my stubbornness. The smile again. "You see, I know what was going on. I know what a cute deal they all had—Malcolm and Callaway and Harvest. It doesn't interest me. But one thing does." The eyes were alive now, cold but alive. "I want to know who murdered Malcolm."

"You came to me for that information?"

"That's right."

"I haven't got it. I don't know any more than the police do. Probably not as much."

"But you're going to find out?"

"I've no reason to."

He reached into an inner pocket and brought out a bill-fold. He extracted five bills from it and laid them on my desk. "You've a reason to, now."

The bills were hundreds.

I didn't pick them up right away, though it was a supreme effort of will. I said: "What did you mean by 'cute deal'?"

"I won't say. Not now. Maybe it has nothing to do with it. I've no desire to blacken my brother's name. But you check those two, Harvest and Callaway. You stick with them, and you'll probably get the picture." He rose.

I still didn't pick up the money. "The police," I told him, "are going to put some time on this case. You wouldn't have to pay them."

"I want *you* on it," he said. "I've no particular respect for that Homicide section."

I smiled, and said: "You haven't had any experience with them?"

"No," he said. "Excepting with that Devine who quizzed me this morning." He paused, studying me. "Though I have had some contact with the rest of the department." Another pause. "You see, Mr. Jones, I gamble for a living. That happens to be illegal, when done professionally."

I said "Oh," again, and rose, as he left.

In my snobbish way, I went to the window, to see what he was driving. But there was no car down there, none at all. I saw him leave the building and walk north. North was where the busline was.

He was a gambler, I thought, and he was playing a hunch. The five hundred was a gamble, not a payment. He didn't seem to be the kind of guy who'd pay out money without expecting a return. Though I could be wrong, and often am.

MY ANGLE OF the entire business so far was fairly firm in my mind, but it was just that, an angle. I had nothing to support it. I would have one hell of a time getting proof.

I looked up the Quincey Steel Company in the phone book, and asked for Mark Callaway. His voice, over the wire, seemed frightened. I identified myself, and asked if it would be possible to see him this afternoon.

"Why—yes," he said. "Would you—is there any reason—" A silence. Then: "Is it in connection with Douglas' death?"

"More or less," I answered. "My office, around five?"

"I'll be there," he promised. "Make it five-fifteen."

I made it five-fifteen.

The Dusy snickered a little as I started her. She thought I was stuck again. She was chuckling to herself all the way out to the Nero Pressed Steel Company.

I went in another door, this time, into the executive offices. There was a redhead behind a desk in here, a thin and hungry-looking girl with more freckles than are considered captivating. Whom did I wish to see, she wanted to know.

"Mr. Harvest," I said.

She looked doubtful, but asked me my name.

I told her my name and my occupation, and she disappeared through a door marked *A. J. Harvest, President.*

When she came out again, she told me that Mr. Harvest would see me, and indicated the door with a nod of her head.

This Harvest was a broad-shouldered man in early middle-age, with a fine conservative suit and a dull, conservative look. His hair was black as ebony, and well arranged. You could tell he took some time with it—the wave was designed to take about ten years off his apparent age. His face was broad and well cared-for. His handclasp was professionally firm and hearty.

Sheila, Sheila, I thought, *you can do better than this.* Even Mac would be better than this.

"And what can I do for you, Mr. Jones?" were his opening words.

"You could give me some information, if you will," I answered. "Particularly about Malcolm Douglas."

He shrugged. "What sort of information?"

"Whether he had any enemies, business enemies, whether his death would affect your business here, whether—" I hesitated. "Well, anything that might throw some light on what happened."

His smile was tolerant, patronizing. "Isn't all that something for the police, Mr. Jones? Aren't you overstepping your authority?" He looked at his nails. "Or is authority the proper word? You really haven't any authority, have you?"

"None," I admitted. "I've been putting a few facts together, here and there, and I thought you could add a few more. I don't work for the department, but I usually work with them. And I'm being paid for my time."

"Mmm-hmmm." He studied his nails again. "Well, nobody pays for mine, and I really haven't any information outside of the routine employment record." His voice was suddenly hard. "And you've already seen that, haven't you, Mr. Jones?"

I nodded, sizing him up, figuring him. He'd never overlook his gums, or vote a split ticket—but would he commit murder?

His voice continued on the new note. "You came snooping in here this morning, using another man's name. You're snooping again, now." He rose. "Just what did you have in mind, Mr. Jones? Just what few facts have you put together?"

"Relax," I said. "You're not in jail, yet."

"Jail?" he said. The well-groomed executive was no longer his front. He was reverting to form. "*You* talk about jail? Be very careful, Mr. Jones. I'm not without influence in this town. Don't make the mistake of threatening me."

"I'll bet you know the district attorney," I guessed.

He nodded. "It so happens I do. I'm sure he'll be interested in all this."

Two of a kind, he and Whitney. Same club, I'd bet. I said: "Neither you nor Whitney scare me, Mr. Harvest." I used the Chief's word then. "I came here expecting some cooperation." I rose. "I won't take any more of your time."

"Good." We were both standing now, and I saw he was a half head taller than I was. "Just stick with your dirty little business, Mr. Jones, and leave mine alone."

"I'll try," I promised him. "But it seems my client's business is mixed up with yours. If it's dirty, you've done your share in making it so." I paused, and gave him my hard glance 2-B. "And don't try to scare me—with your influence or your beef. You haven't nearly enough of either."

He was spluttering something when I left him. In the clinch, he was a splutterer.

It was now only four o'clock. I wouldn't be seeing the Callaway gent until five-fifteen. On an impulse, I phoned Sheila Douglas from the office.

She didn't sound like a recently bereaved widow. She sounded chipper. I told her that it was very important I see her this afternoon, and asked her if five-thirty would be all right.

"I don't see why not," she said. "Everything seems to be under control up here." A silence, then: "Does that include an invitation for dinner?"

I shivered a little. I hemmed, and hawed, and mentioned the neighbors, and her friends. How would it look?

"If *I* don't mind, I don't see why *you* should," she argued. "Leave the neighbors out of it."

"All right," I said. "Some little place. Some little *cheap* place." I heard her chuckle as I hung up.

Time to kill. With rye, with the radio, with cigarettes, and my own thoughts and conjectures, against the background of the muffled shouts from the street. The kids were playing ball.

A MINUTE OR two before 5:15, Mark Callaway put in an appearance. I'm a little hazy as to what I was expecting, but certainly not this. A man young in years, but certainly not in spirit, I thought. A thin and carefully dressed man with watery, small blue eyes and an apologetic air, now thoroughly frightened.

I sat him in the leatherette chair. I considered taking him in my lap, but discarded that. I gave him the full benefit of my piercing eyes. "We seem to be in trouble, Mr. Callaway," I opened.

He nodded, gulping. "I—guess so. I— You're not the police, are you, Mr. Jones?"

That was the second time this afternoon that question had come up. "No," I said, "I'm not the police. I'm a professional man, working for a client. But murder's been done, Mr. Callaway, and we can't very well keep the police out of that, can we?"

"I guess not." He licked his lips. "Is—your client Mrs. Douglas?"

I didn't answer. I studied him. I decided he wasn't bad looking, in his adolescent way. He had a certain charm. If he wasn't such a mouse… I said: "I'm not at liberty to divulge the name of my client, nor how much information I already have. I phoned you for an appointment because I wanted your story. If, in protecting my client, I also protect you, I'd expect additional remuneration." Lord, I was sounding stuffy.

He seemed to relax. "There isn't much I can tell you. Malcolm was a friend of mine. We—had some deals together—I guess you know about those. I was—terribly shocked to hear what had happened." He looked at me beseechingly. "Do you think *I* might be in danger?"

"It's very possible," I said smoothly. "That's why I want your *whole, true* story, Mr. Callaway."

He spread his hands helplessly. "What is there to tell? What can I tell you that you don't already know?"

"What kind of deal you had with Douglas, or rather, how you worked it."

He looked troubled. His gaze went to the floor, and then up to meet mine. He smiled, a child's smile, timid and asking for approbation. "You wouldn't understand, unless you were a bookkeeper. You're not, are you, Mr. Jones?"

I shook my head.

"Well, then, you wouldn't understand. We made some money—not nearly as much as you might think. But we made some—" He paused. "It was legal enough—I think." He paused, seeking words. "It's not something, maybe, that would benefit by too much publicity. If Malcolm's murder brings it all out into the open—" He shook his head.

I said nothing, waiting.

From the doorway, someone said: "How cozy!"

The blonde, Sheila Douglas. No three-piece suit this warm day, but something white and soft that set off her tan, and emphasized what wanted, but certainly didn't need, emphasizing. Her teeth gleamed whitely against the carmine lips—she was enjoying her entrance.

"Mrs. Douglas," Mark said, in a shocked voice. He had probably expected mourning, and she wasn't falling into the pattern.

"Mark, honey," she answered. "Has this cold man been

threatening you?"

He flushed. "He's trying to help me, Sheila. I'm sure he's trying to help me."

She chuckled. "For how much, Mark? Enough for a dinner?"

He looked confused and unhappy. "I—haven't offered him any—retainer, as yet."

"Offer him one," she said, "and watch what happens."

I rose, and got her a chair. I said stiffly: "You're joking, I hope, Mrs. Douglas. That isn't your impression of me."

"If you're human, that's my impression of you," she answered. "Or anyone else."

Mark cleared his throat. He said quietly: "As a matter of fact, I was considering employing you, Mr. Jones. On—" He looked at Sheila. "On—this thing that happened last night. If you can clear it up before the police delve too deeply into our affairs— Don't you see, it would—" He looked from Sheila to me and back.

Sheila was smiling. "Offer him a couple hundred as a retainer, Mark."

"Keep your damned money," I said roughly. "Nobody's buying me."

She was laughing now. "Not even renting you?"

If I weren't such a sucker for women, I'd have slapped her. If she didn't have that hair and figure, if I weren't such a gentleman… "Not even renting me," I said.

"Just for the evening? Just for dinner, and maybe a drink, and—"

Mark was blushing again. I was almost blushing, myself. "O.K.," I said. "I'm up against more than I can handle."

Mark rose, and said: "I'll see you again, Mr. Jones. I'll keep in touch with you." He almost tip-toed out.

There was a silence. Outside, some kid cursed fluently and lengthily. Otherwise, silence.

"Well," she said, "you were going to report. I see by the papers that you followed Malcolm last night."

I nodded. "I followed him. Over to an apartment house on Iona Court."

Silence, again. I had the swift, transient impression that for the moment she was frightened. But it was too fleeting to be sure of.

She nodded. "That key, the one the detective was questioning me about, do you think—"

I said: "Malcolm spent a lot of time setting the trap, didn't he? Six months, you said, he'd been going out nights."

"I've been careful," she said. "I don't know why, excepting that he was so—so unpredictable. A strange man—" She shook her head. "Where do you suppose he got the key?"

"He probably had a duplicate of yours made," I said bluntly. "It looked like a duplicate." I paused. "After he had that—"

She was staring into space. Her voice was no more than a whisper. "Spying on me—he was spying on me—"

"He loved you," I told her, "more than you're ever likely to be loved again."

She shook her head dazedly. "Let's get a drink. I need a drink."

WE HAD THE drink at Mac's. Mac's eyes almost popped out when we walked in. He had no words, for a change.

At a table in the corner, Sheila said: "The police have that key. Do you think they can trace it?"

"Maybe," I said. "If they get a lead, they can. Do you want to tell me the rest of it?"

Her eyes were almost green in the dim light. "No. Damn it, there's nothing to tell. Where's that drink?"

"Right here," Mac said, at my elbow. He set a pair of drinks on the table, rye and water, and walked away again.

Sheila's smile was tight. "Mac," she called, "we're still friends, aren't we?"

Mac had no answer, not for a widow so recently bereaved who was acting as she was. Mac had his standards.

The tight smile was still on her face. She was going to bluff this through. She held the drink high. "To love," she said, and gulped it down.

"I had quite a talk with Harvest this afternoon," I told her. "What an awful stuffed shirt he is."

She nodded. "My impression, exactly." No emotion on her face, nothing.

"He lives over on Iona Court, doesn't he?" I said.

Again, a shadow of something on her face, but was it fear? She said levelly: "I believe he does. Are you working for the police now, Mr. Jones?"

"I try not to work *against* them," I answered.

"Try not to work against me, too, will you? Or weren't you adequately paid?" She was reaching for her purse.

I shook my head. "I was paid. Your case is closed. You wanted to find out where Malcolm went, and now you know."

Her glass was empty. She said: "Well, then—is your interest personal? Does it matter to you what happened to Malcolm?"

"It matters to my client," I said, "to my new client."

She was immovable for a moment. Then her head turned

stiffly, and she called: "More rye, Mac."

When she turned again to me, her gaze met mine fully. "What did your new client pay you?"

"It doesn't matter," I said. "I've accepted his money. I can't be bought off, if that's what you had in mind."

"That's what I had in mind," she said. "I'm sure you wouldn't regret it, Mortimer Jones. I can almost guarantee that."

It's a good thing Mac wasn't hearing this. I felt uncomfortable—don't ask me why.

The implication of all she hadn't said was in the air around us like a perfume. But, no, not like a perfume, not that sweet.

She was smiling now. "Nelson, I suppose. Nelson Douglas—he always watched over Malcolm. Is it Nelson?"

I said nothing.

Mac brought the drink and left.

"He's a gambler," she said, "and Lord knows what else. You're not very particular about the source of your income, are you, Mortimer Jones? You'll be in trouble if you get mixed up with Nelson."

"I've been in trouble before," I said.

The smile again, the green eyes glowing. "Why? Do you like trouble? Relax—why don't you relax?"

"All right," I said. "Let's find a place to eat."

"I know just the place," she said. She finished her drink, and rose. "We'll take your car, shall we?"

Mac didn't even look at her as I paid him. He didn't say good-bye.

The Dusy purred in her self satisfied way. Sometimes, I don't think the Dusy is a lady. She (or he) is too susceptible to blondes.

The place she'd picked was a small place on Fortieth, a basement place with subdued lights, with dancing, with not much of a crowd. We ordered another drink and a pair of steaks. We danced, not talking. We ate and drank, not talking much. All the things we didn't say were there, waiting to be said. But she worked by indirection.

She left me for a while, to repair her makeup, and I sat alone at the table, wishing things were different. When she came back, she said: "I suppose I should be getting home. I suppose I should observe the conventions a little."

"All right," I said. "You've nothing to tell me, then?"

The smile. "Is there anything I have to tell *you?*"

The Dusy murmuring through the night, through the traffic. Sheila smoking quietly, and I fuming inwardly. Past the lighted front of Mac's, to the dark corner where the black convertible was parked.

She threw the cigarette out, and smiled up at me in the dimness. Then she reached up and took my head between her two hands. I felt the softness of her lips on mine, and smelled her perfume.

Then she was out of the car, and laughing softly. "Jonesy," she said, "quit fighting. Quit fighting yourself." And her heels were clicking across the road. I watched the convertible move down the street, thinking of nothing much, knowing little more than I had three hours before.

I went up to the office and used the City Directory. There it was—Harvest did live on Iona Court. I sat there a while, and then went over to Mac's.

He didn't have much to say, but it wasn't conversation I was after. It was rye. I had enough of it to get drunk, but didn't get drunk. I got irritable and quiet and ugly, but not drunk.

The Dusy was snickering at me on the ride home.

I slept without dreams, and woke to the glaring sun of another unseasonable day. The shades were up, the sun pouring through the open windows. I was wringing wet with perspiration.

I took a shower. I made the bed and shoved it back up into the wall. I dressed in the coolest suit I had and drove over to Mac's.

He was a little more amiable this morning.

I had some eggs—I forced myself to eat them. I had a roll and coffee.

Mac said: "You should have better manners, Jonesy. Squiring a widow around like that— And her wearing white."

"It takes all kinds," I said.

"I'm disappointed in her," he said. "I'm certainly disappointed in her." He shook his head grimly. "You think she done it?"

"Your guess is as good as mine," I said, and left him with that.

There was an old coupé parked in front of my office, holding a fat man. My guest of the morning before, Teddy of Teddy's Tap.

He stepped out onto the sidewalk as I came up. His eyes were faintly fearful. "Mr. Jones, I want to explain about yesterday. I didn't mean to—"

"Forget it," I said. "You've got to protect yourself."

"I know," he said, "I know. But that skinny faced guy, that Devine—he's trying to get me."

"Get you?" I asked. "For what?"

"For blackmail." He was licking his thick lower lip again. "Did you— I mean—"

"I told them you were trying to blackmail me, yes. I've got to protect myself, too, Teddy."

"Yeh, sure, I know—but—" He paused. "Could I hire you? Would you see that—"

I put a hand on his shoulder. "Go back and run your joint, Teddy. Forget about protection, or the police, or me. Just stick to the business you know. You'll be all right."

"O.K., O.K." He was reaching for a billfold.

"And keep your damned money," I said. "Put it in the bank."

I sat in my office a while, sulking in my childish way, feeling sorry for myself for no reason I can think of. I looked up Nelson Douglas' number in the phone book, and called him, but there was no answer.

I contemplated turning the whole thing over to the Chief. Let them work on it for a change, I thought. Let them put their agile minds to work. The taxpayers were paying them for that.

Outside, the kids were raising hell. It was Saturday—there was no school. I watched them for a while, wondering how many of them would get tangled with the police before they died. Some of them already had. I thought, *if we'd spend more for playgrounds, we'd spend less for crime prevention.* But that had been thought before, by better minds than mine.

I called Nelson Douglas again.

A man answered, a man who said he was Nelson Douglas. I was suspicious at the time, but not suspicious enough. "Could I see you this morning?" I asked, and told him who it was.

"Right," he said. "Get over here as fast as you can."

I got over as fast as I could. In the Dusy, that's fast. I was parked in front before I noticed the meat wagon across the street.

And Glen Harvey on the curb.

I looked at him, and knew. "Dead," I said. "Nelson Douglas is dead."

"Right," he said. "How do you want your sixty-four dollars?"

5

Make Mine Murder

GLEN LOOKED TIRED. His gaze didn't meet mine. "Devine's up in the apartment," he said dully. "He's waiting for you."

I walked up with Glen to the second floor. Doc Walters, the ancient and weary M.E., was still bending over Douglas' body, slouched in a chair. Even from the doorway, I could see the hole in Nelson's neck.

Devine was smiling—Heaven knows why. He looked at me and smiled, and over to the body, and the smile didn't leave.

"Did you want to talk to him?" Devine asked me.

I said nothing.

"You phoned him. What was your business with him, Jones?"

"He lost his cuff links," I said. "If you want to talk to me, let's go some place where we can be alone."

He colored, and the smile faded. "Stay polite. That's the way I want you. What was your business with him, Jones?"

"Murder," I said. "He hired me to find out who murdered his brother."

"That would be Homicide's business, wouldn't it?"

I nodded. "But he had no faith in Homicide. He said the section smelled. He said he'd had experience with the department and he didn't want them messing in anything as important as this."

Devine was white, and something incoherent came from his throat.

"I told you I'd rather talk to you alone," I reminded him. "Now you know why."

Glen Harvey coughed. Doc Walters didn't look so weary for the moment. I had the feeling he was enjoying Devine's discomfiture.

Devine said: "You were mixed up with both of the men who were killed. Any reason you shouldn't be the logical suspect?"

"Sure," I said. "I killed Nelson Douglas, and then phoned him. I wanted to find out how he was. I'm in this, the same way you are, as an investigator."

Glen Harvey said: "Chief, it isn't going to hurt, having Jonesy working along with us. We can—"

Devine looked at him scornfully. "Shut up."

Glen stiffened. He's a big man, and a hardworking man, and nobody to fool with. But he loves that city paycheck too well. He stood there, hate in his eyes. But he didn't move, or say another word.

Doc Walters said: "I'll bring the boys up. Take it easy, Devine."

Devine looked at him, and then back at me. To me, he said: "Beat it. I'll be seeing you later."

"The later the better," I told him, and beat it. The boys in white were coming up as I went down the stairs.

Still hot, outside. Like a July day, and this wasn't July. I felt faintly sick, remembering the blood on Nelson's neck, remembering the slack stupidity on his dead face. I took a deep breath of the sticky air and wished it would rain.

The whole picture was plain enough—the motive, the sequence. All but one thing—which one had done it? Who was the murderer?

I turned the Dusy toward the east side, toward Teddy's Tap.

There was nobody in the place but Teddy. He was standing behind the bar, staring into space, when I entered.

I asked him: "Did Malcolm Douglas ever bring his wife in here?"

He nodded. "Couple of times. The three of them would come in for some shrimp, once in a while. I got good shrimp."

"Three—?" I said.

He looked at me. "Sure. Him and his wife and his boss. What's his name again—?"

"Harvest," I supplied. "A.J. Harvest."

"Yeh. Big guy, handsome—"

I nodded. "Handsome enough. Got any drinkable rye?"

He reached down into a lower cabinet and brought out a bottle that was a duplicate of the one in my office. He opened it carefully, almost reverently. "On the house," he said, and poured a pair of drinks.

It was too hot for rye, if it's ever too hot for rye. But we drank.

Teddy said: "That Harvest, he tried to borrow money from me once. Mr. Douglas wanted to give me a note for it. That was a long time ago, the early part of the war."

"You didn't give it to him?"

Teddy shook his head. "I didn't have it, not before the war."

"Funny they should hit you for it."

He shrugged. "Guess he was desperate. Wanted to keep that business going. Guess he'd hit anybody that he figured might have it." He poured another pair of drinks. "On the house," he said again, and shook his big head. "I kind of liked that Mr. Douglas. There was something about him I kind of liked."

"How about his wife?"

"A bag," Teddy said. "The shape and the face, but just a bag."

"Everybody's girl," I guessed.

"Yeah." He nodded. "Yeah, I suppose… Everybody handsome enough, or rich enough."

I LEFT HIM and drove back to the office. I sat around there for a while, thinking about them all—Teddy and Callaway and Harvest and Sheila and Nelson and Malcolm. I started to think about Mac, and realized I was hungry.

Mac looked hot and tired. I asked him if he had any shrimp. He shook his head. "Got some good liver sausage."

"All right," I said. "On whole wheat bread. Why haven't you got some shrimp? The good taverns have shrimp."

"That's the place to go for it, then," he said. "You want some coffee, too?"

I told him I did. If it was fresh.

When he brought the sandwich, he said: "I never should have bet you. I should have shut my big mouth."

A kid came in, bringing the early edition of an afternoon paper. He laid it on the bar. There was a picture of Nelson Douglas on the first page. There was a picture of the apartment building in which he lived.

I showed the paper to Mac. "No," I said, "you never should have bet."

Mac looked sick. "Jonesy," he said, and stopped. He was staring at the paper. He swore. "Jonesy—what do you think—"

"I'm not thinking of anything right now," I said. "I've been thinking too much today."

When I was through, and was paying him, Mac said: "It wasn't *her*, was it, Jonesy? You know, don't you?"

"I don't know a damned thing," I said. "I'm even dumber than usual."

I drove out to the Quincey Steel plant, way out on the south side. It wasn't much of a place, a small foundry going to seed. I asked the girl at the door in there if Mark Callaway was around.

"He's about all that's left," she said. "But he isn't here this afternoon. He's at a funeral."

"How about the boss, then? He around?"

"You just asked about him," she said. "He's the *big* boss."

You never know. You can never tell, just by looking at them. I thanked her, in my gracious way, and left.

The Dusy was trying to tell me something on the way back to town, but I wasn't listening. I was thinking, revolving everything in my mental hopper, sifting and analyzing, getting nowhere except more confused.

At my office, I used the city directory again. And there it was. I phoned Glen Harvey at the station, and he was in.

"Going to be busy tonight?" I asked him.

"What's cooking?"

"I need your help. Not Devine's, but yours. Can you get away?"

A pause. Maybe he was wondering how *his* name would look in print, instead of Devine's, for a change. "I can get away," he said finally.

"What was Nelson Douglas killed with?" I asked him.

"A knife," he said. "We haven't got it yet. Why tonight, Jonesy? Why not this afternoon?"

"Because," I told him, in all seriousness, "the nights were made for love."

He sounded annoyed as I hung up.

An afternoon to kill. There were lots of football games on the radio, and I listened for a while. Then I went back to the apartment and took a shower and a nap. But the nap was too short. I re-read some Saroyan.

I didn't go to Mac's for supper. I scrambled a couple of eggs and made some toast and coffee, and waited for Glen to pick me up. He came around eight, full of questions.

I answered as many as I could on the drive over to Iona Court. I told him what I thought, and why, and what I wanted from him.

When I'd finished, he said: "Devine's going to be awful hot, if you're right. He's going to think I'm after his job."

"Well?" I said.

He didn't answer—he was smiling.

There was a black convertible parked near the entrance to the apartment building, a big job, with white-wall tires. We went into the lower lobby.

It was a self-service apartment, with rows of mailboxes in this part of the lobby. I studied them and found what I wanted. The key I had in my hand opened the lower door.

We went up in the self-service elevator, up to the fifth floor, to the apartment of A.J. Harvest.

There was no one in the hall up here, but I was nervous, just the same. I slipped the key into the lock of the apartment door.

It didn't turn.

I looked at Glen, and he shrugged. "I was hoping it would fit," I said.

Together, we walked down the hall, around the bend, to another apartment on the same floor. Here again, I tried the key. Softly, so as not to disturb the tenant.

This time it turned.

I took the key out again, and gave it to Glen. "Give me five minutes," I said. "Maybe a little more."

He nodded, and went back along the hall, out of sight around the bend.

I rang the bell.

IT WAS ONLY a matter of seconds before Mark Callaway opened the door. Attired in a dressing robe, wearing with it an uncertain look. The faint smell of perfume came with him, a perfume I had noticed before, in front of my office, that night.

"Well," he said.

I said: "Can I come in?"

"Of course, Mr. Jones." This last a little louder than necessary, loud enough to be heard in the apartment behind him.

I thought I heard some movement in there as I came in.

An ordinary apartment, in ordinary taste. Roomy and comfortable, but no movie set. I sat in an overstuffed chair in the living room, and he sat about five feet away, in another. He didn't ask me why I was here.

The perfume still lingered in the air. "I thought it was Harvest, all along," I told him. "You met him here, didn't you? It was just a geographical accident that you cooked up your little scheme."

He looked at the floor, and frowned. "What are you here for, Mr. Jones?"

"In behalf of my client, the late Nelson Douglas," I said, "whom you killed this morning."

He was white. I thought I heard a sound from the direction

of an archway that led off the living room. Callaway didn't move or say anything. He simply stared at me.

"Malcolm," I went on, "suspected his wife. I'm sure he didn't suspect you—at first. But after he'd had the duplicate key made from his wife's key to this place, after he'd used it, and had seen whatever it was he did see, it was too much. He committed suicide."

No words from him.

"He went home and killed himself. In the suicide note he probably left, he not only revealed what he knew about his wife's infidelity, he revealed the set-up you and Harvest had a few years back. That was during the war, wasn't it?"

Callaway gulped, and continued to stare at the floor.

"Sheila came home and found him. She got rid of the note and the gun. It looked like murder. You were all safe, then."

A voice from the archway, then. "None of this can be proven, Mr. Jones. None of this will do you any good."

Sheila Douglas. Wearing white again, a white terry cloth robe. Looking properly seductive, dominating the scene. She came over to take a cigarette from the box on the coffee table. She lighted it slowly, showing very little strain, and no emotion.

"There'll be accountants who can figure it out," I said. "There'll probably be a Congressional committee interested in this. Malcolm handled the books—that's why you had to cut him in, isn't it?"

He said nothing.

I nodded. "War contracts. Before the war, neither of you were doing so well. But why Nelson? Did he threaten you?"

Callaway's voice was hoarse. "He—threatened to expose us, Sheila and I— He—" He leaned forward, and put his head in his hands.

Sheila said: "Are *you* threatening us, Mr. Jones? What's your part in this?"

"I always work for my client," I said, "even if he's dead."

She smiled. "What's your price? Name it. Name it, and leave us alone. There's just enough truth in what you say to make it worth buying."

"I'm not for sale," I said. "Just my services, not me."

I wouldn't have believed the pocket of that terry cloth robe would hold a .38. I wouldn't believe it, until I saw it there in her hand.

The eyes plainly green now, the hand steady, the voice steady. "Tie him up, Mark. We can get out of this town. There are lots of towns. Tie him up."

From the doorway, Glen Harvey said: "Hold it. Don't anyone move."

The .38 was the same one. She hadn't got rid of it. It was a choice then of going to court for murder, or admitting the suicide. She admitted the suicide. Mark Callaway didn't have the stuff to take what they must have dished out to him down in Devine's special room. Glen looked pretty good, in the newspaper pictures—which Devine didn't share. Nor Mortimer Jones.

The books Malcolm kept for Harvest were a mess, and very transparent to the CPA's. There were padded expense accounts, non-existent steel bought and paid for with the taxpayers' money. They might have got away with it—only for Sheila and her roving affections. Or if Malcolm hadn't loved her so much—too much.

Mac mourned for a week. At his age....

The Constant Shadow

Death is a shadow, living with us, waiting to envelop us—a disembodied, intangible thing. But Death has his agents, professional and amateur. It was these Dr. Randolph feared—and why he hired Mortimer Jones. For murder loves company.

1

—

Death Is Waiting

THIS DR. CURTIS Randolph was a nervous man. He wasn't too tall, about my height, and he had a thin, unlined face with dark and probing blue eyes. He sat in my office, this hot summer afternoon, telling me his troubles, and chain-smoking cigarettes.

So far as I could tell, his troubles were mental, and I'm no psychiatrist.

He said: "You can understand, then, why I can't take all this to the police. I've nothing definite. It's as though a constant shadow travels with me, wherever I go." He tried a self-deprecating smile. "I—have always had a rather irrational fear of death. That, no doubt, is what motivated my going into medicine." He shook his head. "But the man with the scythe has never been such a constant companion as he has recently."

The man with the scythe was rather hackneyed. I liked "the constant shadow" better. Because death is that, a shadow, living with us, waiting to envelop us, waiting for us to step in front of a truck, or go out without our rubbers. I thought of Mr. Saroyan's tiger.

I said: "You've seen death enough, I guess, Doctor. You've no *reason* to think he's closer now than he's ever been?"

"Well—" Hesitation now in the smooth face, doubt, and the dark eyes covered my face thoughtfully. "Only this—this intuition." He took in a lungful of air through his mouth. "As a medical man, as a scientist, Mr. Jones, I hesitate to speak of intuition. But my medical training hasn't seemed to dull this sense I have, this superstition."

I asked bluntly; "There's nobody out to get you?"

Surprise in the smooth face now. Fear? I couldn't be sure.

"I don't quite—understand."

"This death," I said, "is an intangible thing. But he has agents, professional and amateur. Is there any *one* person you particularly fear, Doctor?"

He hesitated before he said no, and because he hesitated, I knew he was lying. He was a surgeon, one of the best in town and perhaps in the nation. He wouldn't come way down to my grubby office on the wrong side of the tracks just on a hunch. There was nothing I could do about shadows, and I explained that.

He nodded. "Of course, of course— But I said, Mr. Jones, that I felt the presence of death." He paused. "You spoke of agents, professional and amateur. I'm hiring you for that end, for the protection of your services from these, these—agents." That mechanical smile again. "The boss, himself, I believe I can fight. I've been fighting him a long time."

Outside, in the street, the kids were playing ball. Inside, in my office, it was quiet. I said: "What you really want, then, Doctor, is a bodyguard?"

He nodded. "Something like that." He frowned. "Or perhaps, Mr. Jones, I want the knowledge that somebody else is always near, somebody friendly."

"Twenty-five a day and expenses," I said. "Rather expensive friendship."

"Money doesn't matter," he said casually.

Dr. Randolph was slumped in the chair, his shirt soaked with blood.

He paused, then went on. "You were highly recommended, Mr. Jones. This is, you understand, a job that will require a man of exceptional ethical standards. I was assured by Mr. Ziegler that you met those qualifications adequately."

Ziegler was connected with a local insurance company for which I occasionally worked.

I didn't like it. I didn't like any part of it, but it was a job, a job for the trade I'd chosen, and there was no logical reason I could give for turning it down. I said: "When did you want me to start?"

"Tonight," he said. "About seven? I'll be out of town until then. Shall I expect you at my apartment, at seven?"

I said he could, and he rose, and I accompanied him to the

door. When he'd left, I went to the window; a compulsion neurosis of mine, this watching people leave the building.

His car, I saw, was a Cadillac coupé, a black, new one, and there was a kid sliding down the front right fender. That's why I park a couple blocks away, because of the kids. My Duesenberg has long, sweeping fenders, being old.

The kid climbed off the fender as the doctor stepped into the Caddy. I didn't see any shadow getting into the car with him, but in a car, the shadow's always there. With thirty to forty thousand killed by cars every year, any motorist can tell you he's not riding alone.

Well, he had this fear, this phobia, an exaggerated and irrational fear of death. There was a word for it, and I searched my mind. *Thanatophobia*—that was the word. All of us probably have it to some degree. But not like the doc, I hope.

I FELT HUNGRY, and it was nearly noon. I put what papers I had on my desk in my file and went out without locking the door. Down the steps, past the tobacco store, and I stood on the curb a moment, watching the kids. In this neighborhood, that was the only place they had to play.

After a while, I walked down the block to Mac's.

Mac was talking to a customer, a fattish gent in a loud suit and an expensive panama hat. Mac said: "Mortimer Jones, shake hands with Ed Byerly."

I shook hands with Ed Byerly, as directed. His hand was broad, but not soft.

"Used to know Ed," Mac explained, "in the old days." He winked. The *old days*, to Mac, meant Prohibition, when he'd really made money. To Ed, my boy said: "Mort, here, has an office over that cigar store."

Byerly nodded. "Oh—a shamus, huh?"

I nodded, and decided to ignore him. "One beer," I said to Mac, "and what have you got to eat?"

"Beans," Mac said. "Good beans, with pork. Made 'em myself."

"Some of those," I told him, "with rye bread, with *fresh* coffee." I took my glass of beer and went over to a corner.

I hoped, by this move, to discourage Ed Byerly. To no avail. He followed me right over, bringing his own beer along.

"Some life you must have," he said, taking the chair opposite mine. "I mean, with those divorce cases and all. I'll bet you've seen some sights, huh?" He smiled. "I mean—setting 'em up."

"That work's a little too raw for me," I said. "That end of divorce and labor trouble I steer clear of."

His broad face looked puzzled. "Yeah? What can a private eye do, besides that kind of work? I figured that's all you guys did."

"Not quite," I said. "It's all some of them do, I guess."

He sipped his beer, and shook his head. "Beats me. What kind of work do you handle, then?" He made a wet ring on the table with the bottom of his beer glass. "For instance, if it ain't too personal, what kind of work you on, right now?"

How subtle, I thought. *How deft.* I waited until his eyes came up to meet mine. Then I asked: "Who you working for, Ed? Yourself? Or for pay?"

He knew what I meant, though he pretended he didn't. "Why, I got a little racket of my own. I—"

I held up a hand. "Save it. You know what I'm talking about. Why're you nosing into *my* business?"

His brown eyes glazed over. "Didn't know I was."

Mac brought by beans and bread then. Mac pretended he hadn't heard the conversation. I said: "Nice friends you introduce me to. Got any more like him?"

Mac looked startled. Ed Byerly said: "Easy, gumshoe. If you're looking for trouble—"

"Shut up," I said. "Go some place else. If you've got some trouble, start unloading it. If you haven't, beat it."

There was one of those silences. Byerly was glaring at me, and Mac was making some inarticulate sound.

Byerly stood up, finally. He said: "You talk pretty rough for a little guy, Hawkshaw. I'll be seeing you again." He threw a half dollar on the table and stalked out.

I smiled at Mac. "I'm sorry I was rude to your friend. But it's a hot day, and he was so damned crude. Where'd you get friends like that, Mac?"

Mac shook his head. "Look, Jonesy, you hadn't oughta blow up the way you did. It ain't like you. Ed's a windbag and all that, but he's no punk. He ran with the roughest boys in town, back during Prohibition. You shouldn't take chances like that."

The constant shadow, I thought. "You're right," I said. "I don't usually let guys like him get me. But he was waiting here for me, wasn't he? He was asking questions about me before I came in."

Mac's mouth was open. "How'd you know that?"

"Because when you told him my name, when you told him I had an office over the cigar store, he knew I was a detective. I haven't much of a sign up there. You must have been talking about me."

Mac wiped off the table top with a rag. "O.K. So we were.

He didn't know you were a friend of mine. He and I did some business back in the old days, and he figured I'd be the guy to pump, I suppose."

"What'd he want to know?"

Mac straightened out a chair. "Oh, what it really amounted to, he wanted to know if you could be had. Bought, that is."

"I see," I said, though I didn't. "And you, no doubt, told him of my unimpeachable standards."

Mac went back to the bar. "Matter of fact," he said, "I told him just about anybody could be bought, that it was mainly a matter of the right price."

I stared at him, but he wasn't looking my way. I said: "I'll have my coffee, now."

"Coming right up," he answered.

Another customer came in after that, and Mac proceeded to get involved in a discussion of the merits of Bruce Woodcock and Billy Conn. I turned my thoughts to this morning's business.

This would be a twenty-four hour job, undoubtedly, and I'd need some help. I thought of Jack Carmichael. Jack had had a lot of bad luck, since he'd opened his agency. Some mess over a woman, a woman with connections. But Jack was a good operative. Besides which, he was into me for a couple hundred. I'd get some of that back. The doc was paying me five a day over my standard rate, and he probably hadn't meant a twenty-four hour day.

I decided to look up Jack. But first, I wanted to see Doc Enright. Doc was a friend of mine; he'd give me the low-down.

DOC'S OFFICE WAS over on Atwater near Vine. It was

a big office with a lot of windows, but Doc's name was on only *one* of them. That ethical he is.

He was busy, this warm day, but not too busy to see me. He's a short, fat gent with an angelic smile. He's a rough man in a poker game.

He said: "Some repugnant disease brings you here, no doubt. But you can rely on my discretion."

"Don't give me that quack-quack," I said. "I'm here for information."

"Free, no doubt"

"I've been hired," I went on, "by one of your colleagues. Relying on your self-asserted discretion, I will reveal his name. It's Dr. Curtis Randolph."

His face stiffened, and he studied me sharply. "Well?"

"Well, yourself. I wondered about him, that's all."

Doc studied his hands, rubbing them. Then he looked up again at me. "Maybe in the top five in America for surgery." He paused a moment, his eyes thoughtful. "You relied on my discretion. I'm relying on yours now. How long Dr. Randolph will keep his license is controversial. He's squashed two malpractice suits, but they were some time ago."

"What's his specialty?" I asked.

"It was plastic surgery, then. Some think it might still be his specialty, but not for the public, generally."

"Criminals?" I said.

Doc Enright smiled that angelic smile of his. "Jonesy, I've already told you more than any respectable doctor should. I've told you this because I know you and have a deep respect for your standards and your work. I will see you again, and next time don't bring any embarrassing questions with you."

I left him and went out to the Dusy. When I started her, she chuckled, in that nasty, mechanical way she has when I'm perturbed. I ignored her.

I drove over to Jack Carmichael's office, but nobody was there. There was a note on the door—*Out for Lunch*. I went down to the Dusy to wait.

Malpractice, Doc Enright had said. In plastic surgery, that could be horrible. That would be motive enough for murder. There was a chance the shadow had more than one agent gunning for Randolph.

There must have been a definite threat, to bring Dr. Randolph down to my office. If it was mental, if it was as nebulous as he would have me believe, he wouldn't be taking a trip, today, without some protection. It was some human he feared, and dealing with criminals, it could be any one of a number of potential killers.

I always get the easy ones, I reflected. *I always get the clean, simple cases.*

A Chev club convertible was stopping at the curb behind me now. In my rear view mirror, I saw Jack Carmichael lean over to kiss the blonde behind the wheel.

Then he stepped from the car.

He saw me and came over as the Chev gunned off. He was waving at the blonde.

I said: "You do all right, don't you?"

"This time, it's different," he told me. "With this one, it's wedding bells. If I can rustle up a few honest dollars." He was a tall, engaging sort of lad, dark and casual. He opened the door of the Dusy and slumped into the seat beside me. "You want something on account, no doubt, Jonesy."

"Not quite," I said. "I got a job that's a little too much for one man. I thought we could make some kind of deal."

"If it's honest," he said, "and doesn't involve physical labor, you came to the right guy." He shook his head. "This love is a wonderful thing, Jonesy, you know that? It's got to be honest."

"Would I be handling it if it weren't?" I asked.

He grinned. "Well, probably not. Let's have it."

I told him what it was, omitting any reference to the information Dr. Enright had given me. I told him what I thought would be a fair division of the spoils, including that portion of his pay I wanted on account.

He nodded when I was through. "Fair enough," he said. "And I'm not forgetting the two hundred, Jonesy. Or the good word you put in for me with the Chief when the boys down at headquarters were out for my scalp."

It was Devine who'd been out for his scalp. And any time I can buck Devine, I do. We have a reciprocal agreement; he hates my guts and I hate his.

I said: "O.K., I'll take the night shift, seven to seven. I can sleep days, even in this weather." I thought a moment and added: "I'll phone you after I see Dr. Randolph tonight. You'll be at home?"

He nodded. "I'll make it a point to be."

I left him, and went back to the office. There, for lack of anything better to do, I drank a bottle of beer, and sat near the window, watching the kids play ball.

A little later, I turned on the radio and listened to the Yanks. But St. Louis had too much for them that day and I turned it off.

About five, I went over to Mac's and had some beef stew.

Mac was still a little miffed about the way I'd talked to his friend, but he greeted me pleasantly.

It was cool in the tavern, and Mac was talkative once I got him started on Joe Louis. It was after six before I noticed the time.

I had to hustle, then. I went home for a quick shave and shower (one room and bath—but I call it home). I wore a neat and cheap blue suit and a neat and not cheap white shirt. I wore a bow tie and white shoes. I thought I looked pretty efficient when I rang the bell to Dr. Curtis Randolph's apartment that night.

2

Night Shift

IT WAS A top floor apartment in a fairly new and impressive building on the exclusive upper-east side. These were all studio apartments on the top floor and the cream of the lot.

A short and amiable Filipino in a white jacket opened the door. "Mr Jones?"

I admitted it, and he opened the door wider, saying: "Doctor busy now. Follow me, please."

We were in a hall and to our right was a mammoth living room, but he went the other way, toward a small office or den at the rear of the apartment. I could hear Dr. Randolph's voice, and the woman's, in the living room as we walked back.

I could still hear them when the Filipino had left me. But only the sound of the voices, not the words.

Then the voices grew louder, and I began to pick out a word or two. "Love" was one of them, and it was said scornfully, by the doctor. "Money" was another and it was said twice, neither time scornfully, by the woman. She had a pleasant, throaty voice, despite its angry pitch. Then I heard a door slam, a door I could not see from this angle, but it sounded like the front door to me.

The doctor was suddenly standing in the doorway to the den. He was smiling. "Mr. Jones. I'm sorry I kept you waiting. Some rather unpleasant business—" He shook his head. "My wife has decided to come back and live with me. Shall we go into the living room now?"

I followed him down the hall. The living room had full length windows, towering windows. It had a large, soft Royal Sarouk on the floor and two low, long davenports that seemed to wall off one corner of the room. There was a massive coffee table between them. We sat on one of the davenports.

I told him about my arrangement with Jack Carmichael.

He nodded absently. "Of course. I never stopped to realize it couldn't be handled adequately by one man." He was chewing his lower lip. "My wife will occupy the room down the hall. The door to *my* room is right there." He nodded toward a door about eight feet away from where he sat. "I'll be in there alone; you'll need to be within sight of it at all times."

I said: "I don't imagine you get up before seven? I can have Mr. Carmichael come here?"

He nodded. "I rarely get up before ten, as a matter of fact. I have some work out of town, some nights, and—" He frowned. "Well, I'll explain about that when the occasion arises. If you want, you can phone your assistant now."

Jack answered the phone almost immediately, and I told him how it was. He promised to be there on the dot.

When I came back into the living room, the doctor was smoking one of those monogrammed cigarettes. He said: "I suppose you slept this afternoon?"

I shook my head. "But I'll bet I will tomorrow. Don't worry about my falling asleep, though, Doctor. I've done this before."

He looked at me, and away. He put his cigarette out in a heavy, green glass ashtray and considered lighting another, looking at it for moments. Then he put it away and looked at me again. "You like Chopin?"

I didn't know whether I did or not, but I didn't lie. "I like any kind of music," I said.

He went over to a Capehart and put on some records.

I didn't know what to expect. What I got was a lot of brilliant piano. It was probably more artistic than Frankie Carle, but I can't say I preferred it. We sat there listening, not saying very much. After about ten minutes, he shut it off and came back to the davenport. He said: "You must think I'm crazy."

I shrugged. "You're playing a hunch. I play them myself."

He smiled a smile without meaning. "I've been thinking about what I told you this afternoon. I've been thinking about 'the constant shadow.' I've been thinking—a man's conscience could be called that. All of us have to live with that, don't we?"

"Most of us," I admitted. "Though there seem to be some who've done pretty well without it."

He nodded, only half hearing me, I thought. He was about to say something, when the Filipino returned.

No white jacket now, but a form fitting, sleek burgundy jacket, well-creased white flannels. The amiable grin was on his face. I thought, *he looks just like any other dance hall Romeo now.*

"O.K. I go now, Doctor? Big dance tonight. Contest."

"O.K., Juan," the doctor said. "Give 'em hell. I want to see you bring home another cup."

The Filipino nodded. "I bet I win. I got Rosa, tonight." He stopped at the archway. "Juan maybe late. Goodnight." He left.

Dr. Randolph shook his head. "How he stays as chubby as he does is a mystery to me. Working all day and dancing all night. The nights he's free, at any rate."

I said: "Which would indicate a clean conscience—or none."

He turned his gaze on me fully. "I suppose you've done some

investigating about me, this afternoon?"

"I check all my clients," I said.

"You heard that I was sued for malpractice—twice?"

I nodded.

His eyes closed, and he rubbed his forehead nervously with the heel of his hand. His voice was hoarse. "I—botched a couple of jobs. I was young and confident beyond my—my ability at the time. I—" His voice broke. "Oh, Lord. It was horrible, horrible—" His whole body seemed to shudder.

This was no act, I was sure.

He sat erectly now, and seemed to have control of himself. But his eyes were straight ahead into the gathering shadows at the far end of the room. "My moral code isn't at the church level, I'm afraid. But one thing I can't condone, in myself or others is a lack of surgical skill. Particularly in my—my previous specialty."

"You've given it up, now?" I asked.

"Not—completely."

"Well," I said, "I guess all of us have a skeleton or two in the closet. I've been told about your skill, Dr. Randolph. You've that to be proud of."

He nodded. "It's all I take *any* pride in." He seemed to shake himself of his memories. "You play gin rummy?"

WE PLAYED GIN rummy. It's a silly game, and an unpredictable one to my mind, but it does kill time. It killed three hours, at which time I was a little over nine dollars ahead. At our stakes, that was a lot. But the doctor's mind wasn't on the game. Your mind has to be a long, long way off to make any mistakes at gin rummy.

After that, the doctor went to bed.

I turned off all the lights but the large table lamp near one of the davenports. Then I went over to the window, the tallest, center window. Far below, I could see the traffic of the drive. To the west, north and south the lights of the city spread. I was in the shadows, here. At the other end of the room, the table lamp illumined the davenport and Dr. Randolph's bedroom door. It was a strange arrangement, I thought, a bedroom leading off the living room, with no hall. Or perhaps not *strange*, just *uncommon*.

The windows were open, but there was no sound from the traffic below, no city noises reaching this high. I went back to the davenport, and sat facing the door. I read what there was to read in the evening paper.

I was going through the want-ads (Miscellaneous for Sale), when I heard the key in the front door, the sound of the door opening, and a light, feminine tread along the carpeted hallway.

She stood in the archway a moment later. Blue-black hair and dark eyes, the hair up, the eyes gravely considering me. About twenty-five, I'd say, with a slim, arrogant figure, high breasted, fairly long legged. A fine morsel in the arch-way.

She smiled, a friendly smile. "You're the detective…?"

I rose. "That's right. And you're Mrs. Randolph?"

The smile again, and there was some bitterness in it now, I thought. "For the time being. It's nothing I'd care to make a career of. Aren't you drinking?"

I must have looked startled, for she chuckled. "I thought all private detectives drank," she said, "all the time. And talked out of the corners of their mouths. I thought they were all big hulks."

I'm not short, but then again I'm not tall. I'd like to be tall. I said: "I drink as often and as heavily as most, I guess. This didn't seem to be the proper time nor place."

"Nonsense," she said. "Sit right there. I'll get us something. Curtis doesn't use it. He should, poor dear, but his hands, you know, his marvelous, steady hands—" She went back into the hallway.

When she came back, she had discarded her wrap. The dress she wore was some pale shade of blue. A filmy material, and cut low, with a bare midriff. She was tanned in all the places I could see. She went over to a cabinet at the shadowed end of the room and brought back some bottles. One of them was a squat, pinched bottle of Scotch.

She held it high. "This all right?"

It tastes like liquid smoke to me, but I nodded agreeably.

"Ice," she said. "I'll need some ice. Is Juan back in the kitchen?"

I said he'd gone out—to dance.

"Well, would you run back, then? I can't seem to master those trays at all."

"After seven o'clock," I answered. "I can't move away from that door until then."

"Nonsense," she said. "I'll be right here." Her smooth forehead wrinkled. "Or am I under suspicion, too?" The chuckle again. "The sinister female, huh? Sending the poor gullible detective back to the kitchen while she slips into her husband's bedroom, gun clutched firmly in hand—"

I lighted a cigarette, and yawned, covering my mouth politely.

"All right," she said, "all *right*—" She went out, through the archway. She moved with just a suggestion of a swagger. It was entirely possible she'd had quite a few drinks already, tonight. Though the aroma from one is about the same as that from many. There was the sound of water running, and the clank of the closing refrigerator door.

Then she was back with a silver bowl of ice cubes.

"Will you mix them? You'll be sure, that way, that they're not drugged, and it's a man's job, anyway, you know."

I mixed them, Scotch and seltzer. She didn't use much seltzer, I was told. When she came to sit on the davenport, I caught another odor, her perfume. I stared at my drink. There is a lot of goat in me; there is also in me a decent regard for my trade. The two could come into conflict any moment now, I thought.

"Well," she said, "to success." She lifted her glass high.

We drank. I tried to think of something to say, but nothing came, nothing bright, at any rate.

"No bumps, no grinds," she said.

I stared at her doubtfully.

She laughed quietly. "I was thinking aloud. I was remembering a sign in the old Bijou. They were very strict at the old Bijou."

"That's a burlesque term, isn't it?" I asked.

She nodded. "And the Bijou was a burlesque house, one of the best. That's where Curtis first saw me. Three years ago."

She was getting into that alcoholic-confidential mood, I saw. She must have been three-quarters gone when she got home.

"And you gave up your career for marriage," I said.

She looked at me suspiciously. "I suppose you think that's cute. I suppose you don't know about all the entertainers who've come up from the burlesque stage."

"Gypsy Rose Lee, I've heard of," I admitted. "But you're

doing all right, now. You've come pretty far, from what I can see."

She said scornfully: "Married to *that?*" Her dark head inclined toward the bedroom door. "I like my men with a little life. If he wasn't rolling in the long green, I'd have left him. I'll leave him yet, when I get a better deal, when I get the kind of settlement I want." She considered me gravely. "Am I boring you?"

"You're embarrassing me," I answered. "And you'll be embarrassed, yourself, in the morning when you remember this conversation."

"You think I'm drunk?"

"A little."

Her full lower lip rubbed her upper lip now. "Maybe I am." She was staring into the darkness at the other end of the room. She rose, finally, and put her empty glass on the coffee table. "I like you, Philo," she said softly, "but I won't bother you, tonight." Her hand ruffled my hair.

Then she was gone, through the archway.

She bothered me all right, but only mentally the rest of the evening. I'd brought a pocket-sized edition of Saroyan along to kill time, but even he had nothing for me this night. I began to get sleepy around four, but I fought it off.

Jack Carmichael was on time, and I told him to phone me at home if anything happened I should know.

THAT WAS THE routine for a week, and nothing happened. On Tuesday night made some house calls with him, but I didn't go in. I stayed in the car.

Jack told me that most of his time was spent in the doctor's outer office with his receptionist. The receptionist admitted to the inner office only those patients she knew. Any doubtful arrivals were checked with the doctor before admittance to the inner office.

Twice, Jack had accompanied the doctor to some small, lodge-like building in the country. Where it was, however, Jack couldn't say. "I had to sit in that damned rear deck, with the lid down, both ways," he told me. "Something mighty fishy cooking up there, Jonesy."

I could guess what it was, but I didn't tell Jack that.

On Friday, Mac told me that Ed Byerly had been around again, and asking for me. Mac said: "I don't see much of you, Jonesy. You find a better spot?"

"That wouldn't be hard," I said, "but the truth is, I'm working all night and sleeping days."

"Huh," Mac said, "a night watchman. I figured you'd have to find honest work one of these days."

I didn't see Mrs. Randolph much that week. She came in late, usually, and she'd go right back to her bedroom, after a few words of greeting.

The doctor's brother, a short, squat man named Alex, I had the doubtful pleasure of meeting Saturday night. He was some sort of promoter, I learned. He and the doctor spent Saturday night over a chessboard. They were both very good. Their openings I could follow, and their end game. The moves in between were too subtle to follow at the time, though I could enjoy them, after I saw what they led to. Either one of them could have given me his queen and beaten me.

The doctor was the master, here.

Mrs. Randolph came in while they were playing. I mentally

compared her body to the doctor's brain, and thought, *it's the old, old story. Of Human Bondage*, I thought. But said nothing.

There was some three-sided dialogue, yours truly not participating, and then Mrs. Randolph retired, as the phrase goes.

Only she retired to the doctor's bedroom.

I glanced at him, and he must have been anticipating the glance. He made no gesture and said nothing—but I knew, when he looked at me, that it was all right.

Alex left, after a while, and Juan came in, wanting to know if there was anything the doctor wanted. He shook his head. "But you could mix a drink for Mr. Jones, here. Your preference, Mr. Jones?"

Rye, I told him, with seltzer.

Juan brought it, and the doctor told him he could go to bed now.

When we were alone, he sighed. He said: "That shadow's been a lot less constant these last few days. Nerves, I suppose, and I'm getting over it. I should have gone to a diagnostician in the first place, instead of a detective." Then he added; "Not that I haven't enjoyed your company, Mr. Jones."

He couldn't know at the time, of course, that he would be dead within thirty-six hours.

I said: "This sounds like a termination of contract talk."

He smiled. "Not at all. I'll want you for another week, at least. I feel better—but not that much better." He rose. "Good-night, Mr. Jones. If you'd care to play the phonograph, it won't bother us, if you keep it low."

I told him I'd brought something to read, and he left me. When his bedroom door closed, I walked over to the tall windows. The heat had persisted through the week, but it was fairly cool up here, with an almost constant breeze coming in.

I stood there a long time, trying to analyze the why and what of his words tonight. I arrived at no conclusion.

Sunday night was a dead night. Mrs. Randolph wasn't there. The doctor wanted to know if I played chess, and I told him I did. But it didn't take him many moves to discover how badly I played. We listened to some music, Goodman this time, and he turned in early.

Monday noon, I got the phone call from Jack. He was at the doctor's office, and would I get to hell over there right away?

The constant shadow, it seemed, had finally caught up with Dr. Curtis Randolph.

3

Caught by a Shadow

I GOT TO hell over there right away. I made the Dusy talk, on the way over, jumping two red lights and otherwise ignoring the law.

The office was lousy with officials. Glen Harvey was there, and the M.E., Doc Waters, and Glen's boss—the chief of Homicide, Devine.

Devine's thin, nasty face looked nastier than usual. He said: "I'll want you and Carmichael both down at Chief's office when we're through here."

"Check," I said.

Jack was pale and nervous, his face wet with perspiration. He said: "That guy's really been giving me a work-out."

"That's the only routine he knows," I said. I looked over to the chair in which Dr. Curtis Randolph was slumped. His eyes were open, his shirt soaked with blood. There was the handle of a knife protruding from his throat.

Devine was talking to Doc Waters. I motioned to Jack, and we went out into the hall. He told me how it was.

The receptionist had gone to lunch, but the doctor was still in his office. "This little fat guy came in," Jack said, "and wanted to see the doctor. Well, he was a friendly little gent, and I couldn't figure him for any harm, but I wasn't taking any chances. I asked him his name, and he said: Just tell the doctor his conscience is here. He'll understand. I went in and told the doctor that."

Glen Harvey was in the hallway now, and looking at us suspiciously, but Glen's all right. He went away.

Jack said: "The doctor sort of smiled, and said, 'Is he a little fat man?' and I said he was. The doctor said to send him in. I sent him in." Jack took a deep breath, and wiped his face with a damp handkerchief. "Well, the girl came back later, and was surprised to see me still there. She wanted to know if the doctor hadn't gone to lunch. I said he hadn't, that he'd had a visitor who'd left only a few minutes ago, and he was probably washing his hands. He did that a lot. The girl went in." Jack shook his head. "You could hear her scream all the way down to the city hall, I'll bet."

Jack's eyes were haunted. "I phoned the police, and then you. I'll bet the Chief will pick up my license, now."

"I'll do what I can," I promised him. "I'd have done the same thing in your position. You exercised all the caution that seemed reasonable."

Glen Harvey and Devine came out into the hallway. Glen said: "Shall I take the coach back?"

"You'll go with them," Devine said, "in Jones' car. I wouldn't ride with vermin like that."

Jack was white now. He took a step toward Devine, but I stepped in between them. I said: "Easy, Jack. We'll play this smart."

"That's right," Devine said, "like you guarded the doctor."

"You'll keep your license," I said to Jack, "and I'll probably wind up with Devine's job."

There was one hell of a silence. When I turned to face Devine, I almost winced. He looked ready for murder, right then. He knew, you see, that I wasn't talking complete nonsense. He knew the Chief wanted me for the job.

Harvey said: "Well, let's go." He looked uncomfortable.

Devine said: "Let's." And to me: "You're not much of a man, are you?"

"Only when I'm treated like one," I answered. "There's nobody else at the department who ever brings out the rat in me like you do."

He had no more to say, at least, nothing audible.

Jack and I and Glen Harvey went down the steps and out into the glare of the day. The Dusy's motor-murmur had a bit of a smirk in it, I thought.

Through the early afternoon traffic in silence, all the way down to the station. There, we went right in to the Chief's office.

The Chief's a big, fairly windy and competent man. He looked at us all sadly as we entered. "Mort," he said, and shook his head. When he turned to Jack, his eyes were hard. "Let's have it."

Jack told him just the way it was.

When he'd finished, the Chief said to Glen: "Take him to a steno and get it all down and signed. Mr. Jones will stay here with me."

IT WAS QUIET in the room after the others had left. The Chief, I noticed, was getting grayer every day. He was looking out the window, a habit of his. Then he swiveled around to face me.

"You could start at the beginning, Mort."

I gave it to him straight, right from the time Dr. Randolph had come to my office. I told him everything excepting what Doc Enright had told me.

The Chief's eyes were thoughtful. "It sounds kosher enough. Only hiring an incompetent like Jack Carmichael could almost be called criminal negligence."

"Jack's a good operative," I argued. "You know he is. It's just because he left the department they don't like him around here. I'm going to need him, if I work on this, Chief."

"Work on this? Why should you? Your client's dead. There's no money in it for you, now."

"Call it my professional pride," I said.

Devine stuck his head in the doorway, and the Chief beckoned him in. The Chief said: "Jones tells me he's going to help you with this, Devine."

Devine colored. "I can get along without that."

The Chief smiled. "I'm sure we can."

"O.K.," I said. "If that's an order."

Devine snorted. The Chief frowned, and said doubtfully: "It's no order. You can work on anything you want to that doesn't conflict with our department work." He paused. "I know you hate the word, and I guess I've used it enough with you, Mort, but *cooperation* is what we want and expect from—"

The voice went on, and on. I didn't show my boredom; I've a lot of respect for the Chief.

When he'd finished, I was looking properly humble.

Devine said: "We've got a lead on this, Chief. There's a guy been bothering the doc, and he's got a record as long as your arm."

"His physical description fit?" the Chief asked.

Devine nodded.

The Chief said: "All right, Jones. We'll leave things as they are for the time being. But keep in touch with us."

Which was my dismissal, and I took it. Devine didn't start talking again until I was out of the room and the door was closed. It's a heavy door; I could hear nothing.

I went down the hall to Devine's office, and Glen Harvey was there, as I'd hoped he'd be. He grinned at me. "Some day, that Devine is going to scalp you. Some day you're going to needle him once too often."

"He should keep out of my hair," I said. Then: "I hear you boys have a lead on this one already. Fast work."

"You hear the damnedest things," he said, and his eyes were blank.

"I'm going to work on this, Glen," I said. "I'm not going to get in anybody's way, but *I've got to know* about this one."

He shook his head. "I'm not saying a word. Excepting that I like to eat. I like to eat every day. Nothing personal, Jonesy."

"O.K.," I said, "nothing personal." It would be, I thought, in poor taste to tell him of the time I got *him* in the papers, picture and all. I did not want to be guilty of that.

I went out, and down to the Dusy. Jack Carmichael was sitting in the Dusy, smoking a cigarette and staring into space.

When he saw me, he said: "They showed me a million pictures in there, Jonesy, and some of them were pretty close. But I wasn't sure about any of them. I think, even in a picture, I'd be sure of that little, fat mug."

"I'm going to stay with this," I said, "at my own expense."

Jack said quietly: "The way I botched this, you probably won't want me around. But I've nothing else to do, Jonesy. I'd like to stay with it, too."

"I'd be grateful for the help," I told him. "I can't see a guy staying in town when he knows you got his picture in your brain. Unless he plans—" I paused. "You be careful, Jack. You keep your self armed."

"From here in," he promised, "all the time." Then: "And thanks."

I wasn't tired, now. I should have been, with only four hours' sleep, but I kept seeing that knife handle protruding from the doctor's throat. There's something about a knife...

The air was sultry and depressing, but it would be cool at Mac's, and so would the beer.

THERE WERE A couple of customers in the place, and one of them was the proprietor of the tobacco store under my office. He was reading Mac's paper, and so was Mac. It was a new edition.

They both looked up when we entered. Mac said: "Tough luck, Jonesy."

The murder was all over the front page.

"It happens to the best of us," I said. "Two beers."

Mac drew them, and brought them over. I asked: "Ed Byerly been in to ask about me lately?"

He shook his head. "You think maybe, Jonesy, he—"

"I don't know what to think," I said. "What have you got to eat?"

He had chili, and so did we. It was good chili; Mac would make somebody a good wife. We had rye rolls. Jack had another beer, and I had some coffee despite the heat.

When we were finished, I said: "I'm going up to see the widow. You find out what you can about this Byerly. Still got that jalopy of yours?"

He nodded, "Runs like a new car."

I gave him a twenty, and he left.

I went up to the office to check the mail. There wasn't much, mostly ads and a few bills. The phone rang, and it was Doc Enright. He said: "I've been reading the paper.

"Didn't know you could read," I said.

"They probably had you down at headquarters grilling you."

"I was down there."

"Jonesy—you didn't tell them anything I was foolish enough to tell you?"

"I didn't. You didn't tell me anything that Dr. Randolph didn't tell me himself, the first night I saw him. You can put your ethics right back in mothballs."

"All right, Sherlock. I suppose we'll get the whole juicy story tomorrow night?"

Tomorrow night was poker night. I said: "You'll get all the papers will tell you. I've got ethics, too."

"Huh," he said. "A man who'll check and raise. Ethics, huh." He hung up.

I decided not to call Mrs. Randolph first. There was a chance she wouldn't be home, but it wasn't much of a trip, anyway. The Dusy made it in eight minutes.

Juan opened the door. I said: "It's rather important, Juan, that I see Mrs. Randolph. Will you tell her that?"

He nodded and went toward the living room, leaving the door ajar. I heard the murmur of voices, and then he was back.

"Mrs. Randolph see you." He nodded toward the living room.

She was sitting on one of the big davenports, smoking. There was a half emptied glass of liquor in front of her, and the familiar shape of the Scotch bottle next to that. She was wearing a dressing gown. What was under it, I couldn't know. I would guess it was nothing.

"Philo," she said. "It's been a bad day, hasn't it? I suppose you're here for your check?" The dark eyes were mocking.

"I'm here," I said, "for what information I can get. This must have been a blow to you, Mrs. Randolph."

She stared at me levelly. "Nothing I can't bear up under. Don't let that little incident the other night give you any ideas, Philo. I *was* his wife, you know."

"I thought perhaps—" I said, and stopped.

She smiled and shook her head. "Drink?"

"If you've got some rye."

She inclined her head in the general direction of the cabinet at the far end of the room. "Would you mind getting it yourself?"

I went over and got a bottle of rye. I brought it back and mixed a drink. It was excellent rye.

She sipped her drink, and asked: "What kind of information were you looking for?"

"About his enemies, if any. About anyone who would have reason to be an enemy or who might benefit from his death."

"You could take the phone book," she said, "and pick every other name. He was a man with an unusually high quota of enemies. I guess I'd benefit the most from his death. Have you thought of that, Philo?"

"I've thought of it," I admitted. "And the name is Jones, Mortimer Jones. You wouldn't want me to call you Cleopatra, would you?"

That chuckle of hers and the dark eyes merry. "O.K., Mortimer." She considered me. She reached over to set her glass down, and I modestly averted my eyes. It took some will power. She said quietly: "How would you like a drive this afternoon?"

I knew what she meant. I said: "I'd like it."

She rose. "O.K. I'll be dressed in a jiffy. I've already had my shower." She walked over to the archway, and turned. "But I'll be damned if I'll wear black in this heat."

Even in burlesque, I reflected, they had to have their exit lines.

It was hot. *I* was hot, and I thought it must have been the chili and the coffee, for it was far cooler up here than it had been outside. I smoked a cigarette and finished my drink. I didn't mix another.

SHE DIDN'T WEAR black. She wore white, a revealing type of material. No stockings, white shoes, a white flower in her blue-black hair. She was something to see.

I said: "Won't you be needed this afternoon?"

"Alex is taking care of everything," she explained. "I don't know what I'd do without dear Alex."

Alex, I remembered, was the doctor's brother and chess opponent.

We went down in the elevator, and out into the humid day. I opened the door of the Dusy for her.

"Lordy, lordy," she said. "What in the world is this?"

"It's a Duesenberg," I said proudly. "It's an orphan, but still the finest car in the world."

"You must be doing all right," she said, and got in.

It was, I told her, my only extravagance.

"Besides women, of course. A car like this would be wasted, if you weren't on the prowl."

"A car like this," I told her, "makes women unnecessary."

She looked at me doubtfully, but said nothing.

It was a nice drive, up along the river to Brown Deer and out the Brown Deer road to a gravel road that led north. She directed me all the way. The gravel road was narrow and winding, flanked by some second growth stuff that wasn't used for farming nor grazing, so far as I could tell.

After about a mile of this, we came to another, even narrower road, and she indicated that I should take it. There was a gate here, and I got out and opened it.

I drove through, and stopped. But she said: "Never mind closing it. There's nobody here, and we'll be coming right back."

We came, finally, to a low, white building about the size of a five room cottage. But it was no dwelling, I felt sure. It looked too utilitarian. The windows were evenly spaced, the door was directly in the center of the end nearest us.

The door wasn't locked, and we went in.

Three small rooms, just cubicles, with a single bed in each, white, hospital beds. A small laboratory with a big sink, the walls lined with shelves, the shelves lined with bottles. A minute bathroom.

And the biggest room—the operating room.

We stood there, and my glance covered the operating table, the light above it, the white equipment.

"Here's where he made his money," she said. "He did some fine work, but he might have slipped from time to time. With these kind of people, it's best not to slip. Murder isn't always outside their line of work."

"He had an assistant here? He must have had at least one."

"If he did, I never met him—or her. If he did, he—or she—is probably in Paducah by now." She shook her head. "I've seen some of his better work. Your own brother wouldn't know you, when he got through." She shook her head again. "Let's get out of here."

We went out and got into the car. I asked: "You've told the police about this place?"

"Not yet. They didn't spend much time with me."

I set the speedometer on the Dusy. I wanted to give the Chief directions as accurate as possible.

We didn't talk much on the way back. When I stopped in front of the apartment, she said: "Come on up. I'll give you a check for what Curtis owed you. I don't want you to lose that."

I went up with her, and she wrote out the check.

She was standing close to me as she handed me the check, and she was smiling.

I was looking down into those blue eyes, and I must have swayed towards her. I'm only human.

"Why don't you kiss me?" she asked mockingly. "You want to."

I kissed her. The pressure of her firm, round body was constant and demanding. I hated my business, at the moment.

I pulled away finally. I said: "Won't expect a bonus for that." I took the check and got the hell out.

But I heard her say, before I closed the door: "Are you still satisfied with just the car?"

4

Murder Makes the News

THE DUSY MURMURED to me as I drove back to the office, but it wasn't anything I could understand.

From the office, I phoned the Chief and told him about the hidden hospital, giving him the mileage I'd copied off the Dusy's speedometer.

As I was hanging up, I heard the feet on the stairs. A few seconds later, Alex Randolph's squat figure was framed in my open doorway. I rose.

He looked sad, as he would. He also looked angry and determined. He said: "They've been giving me the run-around down at headquarters. They don't like me too much down there, I guess."

"Nothing personal, I hope," I said.

"Nothing but a couple of promotions of mine they couldn't solve. They hate you down there, when you're too smart for them."

I said nothing. I indicated the chair on the retail side of my desk.

He sat down, and said: "I want to hire you. I want you to find out who killed my brother."

"I'm working on it," I said.

"That's good. There's nothing they'll ever discover down there. They get anything tougher than a parking ticket, they start running around in circles."

Which wasn't true and I knew it. I said: "Did you know an Ed Byerly?"

He hesitated. "Sure. I mean, I know who he is and who his sister is. You think…?"

"Could be," I said. "Why did you mention his sister?"

"Because that's why Curt was paying Ed. This sister was a beauty, at one time, you understand? And she had this automobile accident. It left a scar or two on her cheek. They weren't too bad, but Curt talked her into an operation. He was younger, then." Alex Randolph shook his head. "God, what a mess he made of that."

"And that's why he was paying Ed Byerly?"

Alex frowned. "Not—quite. Ed got nosey. He found out some other things about Curt. He was trying to find out more, lately. I think that's why Curt hired you." He stared at me. "Say, that Byerly answers the description all right, doesn't he?"

So do you, I thought, but didn't say. I nodded.

"Stick with it," he said. He rose, and laid a couple of bills on the desk. They were hundred dollar bills. "If you need more, let me know."

I told him my rates.

"Never mind that. I got three more like that for you if you crack this." He expelled his breath. "Byerly, that son of a—"

"We're not sure it is Byerly," I warned him.

"Who else?" he asked. "Can't understand why I didn't figure him right away." He left.

Who else, I thought. Well, yes, who else…

I went over to Mac's. I left a note on my door for Jack, telling him I was there. I stood on the curb in the sun for a minute or two, watching the kids, and then walked down to Mac's.

It was cool in there, and the beer was exactly right. Mac was explaining to a customer about the artistry of Tommy Loughran. "You notice any marks on him?" Mac asked his listener.

The customer said, no, he never had.

"An artist, that's why," Mac said. "Like a shadow he was, in the ring, moving so easy and quiet and nice—"

Like a shadow, the constant shadow, I thought, and sipped my beer. A kid came in with some papers and put them on the bar. The door swung listlessly behind him.

There was a picture, I could see, on the front page of the paper. I moved closer. It was a picture of Ed Byerly. It was, the story with the picture stated, a man whom the police were looking for, right now. I remembered this morning, in the Chief's office, and the lead Devine had. This was the lead.

"Friend of yours in the news, Mac," I said.

He picked up the paper and read a moment. "Jonesy, my gosh, it's—"

"You and your friends," I said.

He was pale. "Jonesy, you gave 'em this. If Ed thinks I told you—"

"He'll come and get you with a knife," I finished for him. "No, I didn't give it to them, Mac. They've got their own sources of information."

Jack came in at that moment. I showed him the paper. He nodded. "I've already seen it." He looked sick. "And I saw his sister, this afternoon, Jonesy. I was over at her house. Lord—"

"I heard about her," I said. "What did you learn?"

"He hasn't been home since this morning. He told her, when he left, that he was taking a little trip in the country. If it's true,

Jonesy, he couldn't have—"

"If it's true," I said. "Did you see the picture?"

"Sure. I picked it out as one of the possibilities, down at the station this morning. But it's only a possibility. I'd be *sure,* I think, if I saw the picture of the real killer."

"As I remember Byerly," I said, "this isn't too good a likeness. It's probably an old picture."

Mac was listening in, and he nodded. "That's the way Ed used to look, though. He seemed to put on a lot of wrinkles, lately."

My lack of sleep was getting to me now. I said: "I think we'll give this business a rest tonight. I've had enough for one day."

Jack said: "If you won't want me, I think I'll give the blonde a ring. I'd like to look at something that'll take that picture of Mary Byerly out of my mind"

"I won't need you." I said. "I'll see you in the morning. And Jack, *remember to be careful.* You're the number one witness— don't forget that."

He promised he would, and left. I worried about him. I knew what an easy, fearless sort of gent he was, and how lightly he valued his life.

Mac said: "I wouldn't want to be him. That guy could very easy be victim number two, from witness number one."

"In our business, you never know," I said. And, because I was tired and not too sharp: "We live with the constant shadow."

Mac was staring at me when I walked out.

IN THE ROOM I call home, I pulled the bed out of the wall. I took a shower first and listened to the radio a while, but Morpheus kept calling. I hit the hay early.

In the only dream I remember, I was in a sort of circus procession made up of baby elephants with smiling faces. All of them cast big elephant shadows, and I couldn't figure out quite why.

The sun was high when I woke. It was still damp out, but the sun was there, working. I put some coffee on to boil before taking another shower.

Down at the office, I opened all the windows wide to get what breeze I could. When I turned, after opening the last one, I saw the girl standing in the doorway.

A tall, dark and serious girl, dressed plainly. A handsome girl, despite the plainness of her dress and hair-do. She said: "You're Mr. Jones?"

I nodded, and indicated the customer's chair.

She took it, and said: "My name is Ella Hamilton. I worked for Doctor Randolph." She paused. "I read about Mr. Byerly in the paper."

I said: "You're not Dr. Randolph's receptionist, are you?"

She shook her head. "I worked for him at that place up in the country. I was his nurse up there, and general assistant."

I could only stare at her. She hadn't looked, to me, like a girl who'd stray outside the law.

Some of my disbelief must have shown, for she said: "Would you come over here, please?"

It could have been a trap, but her hands were empty, her purse on my desk. I came over to stand close to her.

Her hands were above her head now, and then she pulled the hair above her ears high. "See," she said.

I could see the fine, hair-like scars there. "I see," I said.

Her smile was dim. "I owed Dr. Randolph a lot. I'm just trying to justify myself, I suppose, but before Dr. Randolph did that, I never appeared in public without a veil. Do you believe, now, that I worked for the doctor up there?"

"I believe you."

"Yesterday, around noon," she went on, "this Mr. Byerly drove into the yard up there. I didn't know what to do. I was frightened, but he seemed harmless enough. He told me he'd been looking for that place for a long time. He seemed to be—gloating. He looked everything over and asked if I was expecting the doctor."

"Around noon?" I interrupted.

"That's right. He didn't leave until one o'clock."

I said: "But then, he couldn't have—"

She nodded. "That's why I'm here. I couldn't go to the police. You can understand that?"

I admitted I could.

"But I saw his picture in the paper, and they seemed so sure he was the man. I couldn't just stand by, knowing what I did."

I asked: "Where were you yesterday afternoon, when I was up there?"

"As soon as Mr. Byerly left, I left. I wanted to warn the doctor. When I got to town, I learned what had happened. I couldn't go back to the hospital after that." Her voice shook. "It's not a nice thing to say, I know, but in a way, I'm glad he's dead. I'm free of that, now."

I said quietly: "A time will come, probably, when you'll have to tell all this to the police, when you'll have to sign a statement to all this."

She nodded. "I suppose so. But—" She shrugged.

I said: "I'll try to make a deal for you."

She reached for her purse, but I shook my head. "There'll be no charge for that. If I accepted money for that, *I'd* be making the deal, not you. Can you understand ethics as involved as that?"

The dim smile again. "I think I can. I've had some personal experience with involved, with *twisted* ethics. There was this gratitude, this loyalty, you see, on one side, and still—"

"I understand," I said. "It might take some talking to make the police understand, however. But I might manage it."

She gave me her address and telephone number.

Then I asked: "Dr. Randolph was a strange man, wasn't he? Had he ever displayed any thanatophobia before?"

She looked at me blankly.

"Irrational fear of death," I explained.

"Oh, yes. He was quite morbid about it. He hated death and feared it. He talked of it, often. You aren't the first detective he'd hired."

After she'd left, I contemplated calling headquarters. But I decided against it. If they found Byerly, he might have some good information. If they continued to look for Byerly, the real murderer would feel safe, and might—just might—make a mistake.

I phoned Jack Carmichael, and told him: "I want you to stick with Alex Randolph all day, Jack. At least, until midnight. I want to know every place he goes in that time. I'll get it from you tomorrow."

He said: "I can probably pick him up at the house, this time of the day."

"Right. If you need me, and I'm not at the office, leave the message with Mac. That blonde give you a rough time last night?"

"Ah, Chief," he said, "it's not *that* late. And she's a lady."

"O.K.," I said. "It's still early enough to get in a full day's work. And be very, very careful. You're a valuable man right now."

I HUNG UP, feeling like a tough employer. Well, Byerly had finally found what he wanted, what he'd probably been looking for for a long time. That's why he hung around the doctor, to get something with more financial potentialities than the doctor's conscience and a threatened malpractice suit. He'd found it—too late.

I thought of Ella Hamilton, and hoped I'd be able to do something for her. The longer I delayed telling the police what she'd told me, the less I could do for her. Withholding information from the law isn't the brightest thing in the world to do.

Doc Enright phoned and wanted to know, would I be at the game tonight? I said I thought I would. Unless something came up.

He asked: "What's new on the Dr. Randolph business, Jonesy?"

"Just some rumors," I kidded him. "I hear half the medicos in town are going to be mixed up in that mess, before it's finished."

There was a silence. Then: "You're kidding, Jonesy."

"No more than usual," I told him. "Bring a lot of money, tonight. I've revenge due me, and I mean to get it."

"Huh," he said, and hung up.

It was right after that the silly rhyme began running through my mind. Nothing that made sense, but it sounded like it was trying to. The pattern was forming.

I wondered about Byerly, where he was now. If he wasn't guilty of murder, he was guilty of blackmail, and the police would have the story on that by now. He had reason enough to hide.

But, still, he had Ella Hamilton as an alibi witness... Maybe, he'd get in touch with her. Damn it, I had no right to keep information like this from the police.

I fretted, and the rhyme ran through my mind, and the day grew warmer and more humid. This indecision is one hell of a state.

I decided, finally, to go out and park near the address Ella Hamilton had given me.

It was a lower-middle-class section of town, west of the river. I parked the Dusy about two blocks away, and walked over. I was in luck.

For, right opposite the rooming house in which she lived there was a small branch library. This library had a large, plate glass window on the street side, and I could see the reading tables behind it. I went in and read some Hemingway.

Of course, I wasn't reading it too closely. I was playing private detective and feeling exceptionally cunning. Any moment, Byerly should have come along and sneaked up those steps to the front door. Or Juan, or Alex Randolph, or any other little, fat man who might be involved in the death of Dr. Curtis Randolph.

Nobody like that came along. There was a laundryman who went up the steps and came down again, carrying a bundle of laundry. There was a fat woman who went up, carrying a bag of groceries. She didn't come down again, and I could deduce that she probably had enough groceries to last for some time.

I might not see her again for days. There was a thin, shabby gent with a briefcase who looked like a collector to me. I'm familiar with the breed.

But there was nobody who looked sinister or suspicious or even little and fat. I went up the steps, finally, myself.

Ella Hamilton's room was on the second floor, in front, and she was home. The room was shabby, but clean. Most all rooming house rooms are shabby, I think. But she kept this one scrupulously clean.

I tried a winning smile, and said: "I've been worried about you. I've been watching the front door."

"About me?" She looked puzzled. "Am I in danger?"

"If Byerly isn't the murderer," I explained, "and the real murderer knows you're Byerly's alibi, it would be to his interest to—visit you, wouldn't it?"

She looked frightened. "I never thought of that."

"Frankly," I went on, "I've been expecting Byerly. But he probably doesn't know where you live. I'd prefer it if *nobody* knew where you lived. You've a car?"

She nodded.

There was only one person I could think of who'd have room. Doc Enright lived with a maiden aunt in a mammoth house on this side of town. He'd have room, and the maiden aunt was the hospitable sort.

I phoned Doc from the pay phone in the hall downstairs and told him what I wanted.

It was all right with him. "Some babe of yours?" he asked.

I didn't answer that, but went up again and explained it all to Ella Hamilton. It didn't take her long to pack. I gave her the address and told her I'd meet her over there, in front of the house.

Nobody followed her, so far as I could tell. Nobody but me, that is.

Doc phoned his aunt by the time we got there, and she was a marvel. She even made me feel at home, and I wasn't staying. I said "so long" to Ella Hamilton and drove over to Mac's. All the way over that silly rhyme went running through my head.

Mac was mopping out the joint. He had his shirt off, but he was still wringing wet. "What a life," he said. "If you want beer, you'll have to draw one yourself."

I went behind the bar and drew a tall, cool glass of beer. There was a slip of paper on the bar with a phone number on it, and I picked it up, idly.

"Oh, that's right," Mac said. "Some babe in a Chev convertible left that number for Jack to call. 'If he isn't dead,' she said. Now, what could she have meant by that?"

5

A Very Nasty Racket

IF HE ISN'T dead... "I don't know what she could mean," I told Mac. "What'd she look like?"

"Like just another blonde to me," Mac said. "Not anything you'd ignore in a crowd, understand, or leave your wife for. Just a blonde, just another dame."

Mac's cynical.

"Jack can't be dead," I said. "He's being careful. He promised he'd be careful."

"Lots of formerly careful guys are dead," Mac said, and then he was staring at me. "Hey, Jonesy, you think—"

But I was already putting a nickel in Mac's phone.

A man answered, and I said: "I'm looking for a blonde with a Chev coupé."

"I'm looking for one with a Lincoln, myself," he answered. "You're easy to please."

"This is important," I told him. "I don't know her name, but she left this number to be called, and I have to get in touch with her. It's a matter of life and death, maybe."

He said: "Our hat check girl here's a blonde, and she's got a Chev convertible. She just started day before yesterday. That the one you mean?"

"Probably," I said. "Could I talk to her?"

"She doesn't come on until five."

"You got her home address?"

"Sure thing. But I don't know you, buddy. And I'm not handing out something like that over the phone."

"If you'll tell me the name of the place," I said, "I'll come down and prove to you that it's all right."

He told me the name of the place, and I went over. With some, the buzzer works, and with some it doesn't. I flashed it, just on the off chance, and it worked.

"Oh," he said, "a detective," and gave me the address.

It was a small, four apartment building on Ellsworth, near Hubbard. The blonde was home, and Mac was right. She was just another blonde. She told me what she meant by "if he isn't dead." That he would be within twelve hours, she had no way of knowing, then. And neither did I.

I spent the afternoon looking for Jack, and not finding him. I inquired at the residence of Alex Randolph and learned that the boss had gone out of town for the day, wasn't expected home until late tonight, and nobody at the house knew where he had gone. He was just "out of town."

Jack, I hoped, was out of town with him.

I went back to the office, but it was hot up there. I sat there for almost an hour, despite the heat, wondering if I'd get a phone call. I didn't, and the heat grew worse. From the north, I heard the rumble of thunder. We could use some rain.

I went to the window and saw the kids below. It didn't look much like rain, but you couldn't be sure. I hoped it would rain. I went over to Mac's.

I had a cheese sandwich and another beer and some words with Mac, but my heart wasn't in it. I was feeling sick. One thing I could do, I could work, but where would I start?

I went over to the tall apartment building, finally. There was a switchboard in the lobby. There was an operator here, who kept a record of all outgoing calls, because outgoing calls cost the tenants five cents a piece, and if the tenant complained, why, there was the number and here was the day you called it.

There was the number, on a couple of days.

They're so smooth, and then they overlook something as simple as this. They're so clever, and then they do the dumbest, damnedest things.

In a murder, it's best not to be smooth. In a murder, it's best to be as impromptu as you can. It's the careful planning that trips you up.

And all the time that silly rhyme was running through my head.

I went home and took a shower. I tried to take a nap, but that was impossible. If Alex Randolph wouldn't be home until late, there wasn't much I could do. At eight o'clock, I was on Doc Enright's front porch.

"Come in," he said. "Come in, as the spider said. I hope you brought some money or your checkbook."

"Both," I told him. "How's Ella?"

"Ella's fine. She and Aunt Aggie went to a movie. That was all right, wasn't it?"

I said it was all right, and we went down to the basement, to the rumpus room.

The boys were all there, all of them a lot wealthier than yours truly, but all of them played this quarter limit game as though it meant milk for their starving children.

I played it, that night, as though I didn't care if I won or lost. So naturally, I won. Doc was about the only guy who bucked me successfully that night, and on the really big pots I beat him out. I was nearly fifty bucks ahead when Aunt Aggie came down and told me I was wanted upstairs.

GLEN HARVEY WAS waiting for me up there. "We found Ed Byerly," he said. "We've been looking all over town for you and Jack. I had a hunch you might be here. I remembered your Tuesday nights."

"Where'd you find Byerly?" I asked.

"In a vacant lot. His face was bloody, as though he'd had a battle with someone, but we got him cleaned up now. He was strangled, Jonesy."

"He's—"

"Dead," Glen finished. "Jack here? We want him down at the morgue to identify Byerly as the killer, if he is."

From below, I heard the voices of the boys. "Byerly isn't the killer," I said. "I'll go with you now, and we'll wait for Jack. He should be back in town pretty soon."

"What the hell's he doing out of town?" Glen asked. "The Chief won't like that."

"He's chasing a wild goose," I said. "Let's go."

It's an ill wind, I thought. This is the first time in months I've been able to leave here, money ahead.

We took the department car. Glen said: "There's one bloody thumbprint on Byerly's collar, but it doesn't check with anything in the files."

I said nothing. The thunder was really rumbling now, in the north, and there was a damp breeze blowing in the sedan window. Clouds overhead blanketed the moon and stars completely. It was a depressing, miserable night, a night to match my mood.

Glen said: "Devine's got the screaming meemies. He thinks you guys are hiding out on purpose."

I told him what I thought of Devine. I said: "This is a nasty racket we're all in, Glen."

"It's a living," he said.

We didn't go over to Jack's rooming house to wait. We parked near Alex Randolph's big home, and turned off the lights.

Glen said: "I'm not the only one working overtime. The Chief's waiting down at headquarters, too, Jonesy."

"And Devine, no doubt?"

"And Devine." He peered through the gloom. "Is that a filling station open up there?"

"It looks like it," I said.

"I'd better run up and call in, tell them what we're doing. You wait here." He left the car.

I waited, while the thunder grew worse, while the wind rose. Then, as the first drops of rain spattered against the windshield, Glen was back. "They'll be waiting down there," he said.

We didn't wait long, though it seemed long. The rain was falling steadily when a huge sedan rolled up the street and turned in at the Randolph home.

About twenty seconds later, another pair of headlights came down the street. Glen looked at me for confirmation.

They were old, dim lights, and Jack's car was a jalopy. I took a chance. "That's Jack," I said.

Glen stepped out into the center of the road. I wasn't far behind him.

The jalopy ground to a halt, and Jack's head came out the side window. "What the hell's cooking?" he wanted to know.

"Murder," I said.

Glen was over at the car now. "Ed Byerly's been killed. They want you down to identify him."

"O.K.," Jack said, "let's go. But don't stand out there in the rain like that."

"You'd better come in the department car," Glen said. "This heap of yours doesn't look like it'd make it."

"Hmmm," Jack said. "That showcase of Randolph's couldn't lose me. And he was really logging."

On the way down, I asked Jack: "What'd you find out about Alex Randolph?"

"After thirteen hours of constant supervision by this trained and skilled operative," Jack said, "it was learned that Alex Randolph, brother of the deceased, owns a fox farm."

"And that's all?"

"That's all. Foxes, hundred of foxes, and I'll bet he'll take a beating, the way furs have been dropping, lately. But that's all I learned."

I said nothing more. I hadn't anything fitting to say.

Glen said: "You guys sure love to play cop, don't you? And without pay. It beats me."

"With pay," I said. *But without reward,* I thought. *Money isn't enough to pay me for this, tonight.*

Lightning split the sky, and the rain was really lashing the windows now.

Jack said: "I really should phone the blonde. She worries about me."

"Women," Glen said. "You can have 'em all."

"I'll take 'em," Jack said. "How about you, Jonesy?"

"Some of them are all right, I guess," I said.

We were in front of the station, now. The morgue was in the basement, the cool, dim morgue.

WE WENT IN, hurrying to get out of the rain, but I didn't want to hurry. We went down the worn, stone steps, and past Doc Waters, who was bending over one of the slabs. Doc Waters worked late, too, it seemed.

Then we came to a slab, and Glen pulled the sheet down, and Jack stared. We waited.

Finally, Jack said: "That's different than the picture all right. That's him, for sure."

He wasn't there again, today, I thought, *Oh gee, I wish he'd go away.* The silly, silly rhyme.

Glen said: "We'll go up to the Chief's office."

We went up slowly, thinking our separate and various thoughts. Mine weren't pleasant.

Devine was in the Chief's office, and so was the Chief. The Chief said: "Well…?"

"That's the man," Jack said.

Devine smirked, and the Chief nodded. "All right, we'll have a statement prepared in a moment. If you gentlemen will sit down?"

We sat down. I said: "Never mind the statement."

They were all staring at me. I thought of the rhyme. "He's the little man who wasn't there. I know that. Byerly was miles away from Dr. Randolph's office when the doctor was killed."

Devine snorted. The Chief said: "You sure of that, Mort?"

I could feel Jack's eyes on me. "I'm sure of it. There were lots of little, fat men involved in this case. None of them were there."

Jack said: "Are you crazy, Jonesy?"

"I went to see your girl today, Jack," I said. "She thought you might be dead. *She hasn't seen you for a week.*"

He started to say something, and stopped.

"Some girl must have been seeing you," I went on. "You couldn't go a week without some babe, could you."

He was looking at the floor.

"I checked Mrs. Randolph's outgoing calls," I said. "Quite a few of them were to you, Jack. That thumbprint on Byerly's collar is probably yours. Did he threaten you?"

He nodded, his eyes still directed toward the floor.

"What the hell—" Glen Harvey said.

"Dr. Randolph had these spells," I said. "There wasn't any danger to his life, really, but he thought there was. That was a nice set-up for a guy needing an angle. Lots of *previous* suspects. In the week we guarded the doctor, Jack met his wife. That would be a mutual attraction. Jack's got all he'll ever need, where women are concerned. And Mrs. Randolph will have all the money Jack will ever need, now the doctor is dead. Love at first sight, to use the polite phrasing. But Jack made a mistake."

I went on, hating myself. "Jack remembered a phrase Byerly had used, one time when he came to milk the doctor. That's the words he put in the non-existent fat man's mouth—'Just tell the doctor his conscience is here.' When Byerly saw that in the paper, he thought Jack was trying to frame him; he could guess that Jack was the killer, himself. Byerly had an alibi, but he couldn't find her. When did he come to see you, Jack?"

His voice was just a whisper. "Last night. He knew about Jean and me, too. He'd been watching the doctor pretty close, and he saw Jean and me, together."

Jean was Mrs. Randolph.

It got through to Devine, finally. "You mean, there never was a little fat man? Jack did the knife work, when the girl was out to lunch?"

"That's right. And later, Jack and Jean would probably get married. Is that the way it was, Jack?"

He nodded.

"You didn't want to identify Byerly as the killer," I said, "not until you knew he was dead. You couldn't afford to."

"Women," Jack said, and shook his head. "If I hadn't neglected the blonde." He made a gesture with his hand, and suddenly there was a gun in it, a .38.

I'd told him to arm himself, I remembered. I thought, *there are a lot of guns between here and the front door. He can't get through all of them.*

Then I knew he wasn't going to try.

For the barrel of his gun was moving toward his own mouth. Out of the corner of my eye, I saw Devine pull his own gun, and my hand smashed up, to knock off Devine's aim.

There was a hell of a racket, as both guns went off. Devine's tore plaster from the ceiling. Jack's blew out a good section of the top of his head.

"That was a hell of a thing to do," Devine told me.

"If he was going to die," I said, "I didn't want a guy like you killing him."

I hoped he'd make something of that, but he didn't. The thumbprint on Byerly's collar later proved to be that of an intern who had handled him.

The poker game was still going on when Glen drove me back to the Dusy. But I didn't want any more poker, not tonight. I drove right home. It had stopped raining.

The Case of the Sleeping Beauty

Mortimer Jones never expected his circulating-library knowledge of Freud would lead to murder. But amateur psychologists rush in where angels—or policemen—fear to tread.

HE WAS ABOUT fifty, I'd say. He wasn't the wealthiest man in town, perhaps, but he was close to it. His social position didn't match his wealth, the result of his recent marriage to a much younger woman of—well, call it doubtful background.

He said: "Sergeant Delaney recommended you, Mr. Jones. He spoke very highly of your ability." He paused. "And your—tact."

Pop Delaney handled the Missing Persons Bureau. I said nothing. I couldn't think of anything modest to say to that.

He looked thoughtful, before he began again. "This—business will require a great deal of—tact, I'm afraid, Mr. Jones."

"Privacy is what I sell, Mr. Greene," I told him.

He nodded, only half hearing. "Before my daughter—disappeared, you see, she went through a period of very—unusual behavior. Dr. Allencort diagnosed it as hysteria." Again, he paused. "There is no history of—insanity in either branch of her family, you understand."

I understood, of course. I said: "Do you know of any emotional disturbance that might have brought on this…"

He shook his head. "It began about three weeks before she disappeared." He looked down at the floor. "I haven't been, perhaps, the father I could have been. Patricia didn't always confide in me." He shrugged. "Since her mother died, Patricia has gone in for social work. I assumed she was perfectly adjusted to the change."

The "change" might mean the death of her mother, and it

might mean his marriage to a show girl. I didn't pursue that topic. I said: "I wonder if you'd give me a note to Dr. Allencort? Medical men are so bound up with their ethics, you know, and psychiatrists particularly. He may know something that would give me a clue."

"I'll phone him," he said. "Would that be all right?"

We entered the room as Red shot—he shot twice.

That would be all right, I assured him, and he phoned Dr. Allencort from my office. After that the rest of our business was tedious, having to do with a retainer and my rates, and other unimportant details. About as unimportant to me as my right arm.

He rose then, a thin and elegant gent in fine tweeds. I accompanied him to the door. There, he paused, and turned. He looked old, older even than he was, as he said: "I hope you'll have something to report and soon, Mr. Jones."

I told him it was a hope I shared, and he left.

I phoned Pop Delaney, and thanked him for the business. I asked: "What have you got on it so far, Pop?"

"Just a picture he left. Want it?"

"I've got one myself," I said. "That's all, huh, Pop?"

"That's all," he answered. "I smoke El Toros, Jonesy, but there's no hurry on that. Any time today is fine."

"Sure," I said. "Of course. You smoke too much for a man your age, Pop."

The picture Sturtevant Kenneth Greene had left was an expensive picture, done by the best portrait photographer in town. Even a kid with a Brownie couldn't have spoiled that face, though. Dark, with luminous eyes, a full mouth, suppressed fire seeming to shine from the paper which even this inanimate replica couldn't dim.

Suppressed fire, and I thought of the social work and sublimation, analyzing it all from the depths of my circulating library knowledge of psychology.

Maybe all social work isn't sublimation, I thought. Some perfectly adjusted people go in for it, Mortimer; don't be so damned cynical, so worldly, so suspicious of motives. But that's the way I am. That's what an exposure to Freud will do to a man of limited mental ability.

I told myself sternly to stick to the facts at hand which were few so far. Perhaps Dr. Allencort would have a few more.

At the cigar store below my office, I bought a box of El Toros. I sent them over by messenger to Pop Delaney. Then I went to Mac's for lunch.

It was a late spring, a practically early-summer day, and Mac was pensive as he polished glasses.

"Is it love, Mac?" I asked softly.

He looked startled, and then he shook his head. "Them Dodgers—how they could drop a easy one, like yesterday—"

It's guys like Mac who help to make me cynical. "Have you got anything light to eat?" I asked him. "Like a salad or some clear soup?"

"I got hamburger," he said. "I got chili. I got salami." He sniffed. "You could try the Waldorf if that's not good enough."

"It will do," I said. "A thin and well-browned hamburger on a delicately toasted bun, please."

He stared at me a moment and then went back to fry it.

With the hamburger, I had a glass of beer, and after the beer, some coffee. All the while, I was thinking about that picture, and about Sturtevant Kenneth Greene, and my mind kept getting ahead of the facts.

Another customer came in, and Mac got into a discussion with him regarding Brooklyn. I drank another beer slowly, and then walked up to where the Dusy was parked.

She sighed when I started her, as though in memory of her lost youth. She murmured deep in her steel throat, but it wasn't anything I could understand. I headed her east toward the Drive. It was a beautiful, beautiful day.

The office of Dr. Jerome Allencort was in a new and modern building on the Drive. It was a quiet, low-ceilinged place of subdued colors and modern furniture. Behind a bleached mahogany desk in the outer office sat an unbleached blonde.

Was it a professional call?

"No," I said, "it's private, however, and confidential. Would you tell the doctor Mortimer Jones is here?"

"Mortimer Jones?" she said doubtfully.

"Please," I said patiently. "I realize it isn't much of a name, but what can you do with 'Jones'?"

She took another look at my inexpensive and wrinkled gray

suit and then disappeared into the inner office. It was plain that I didn't measure up to their usual trade.

She came out again almost immediately and said the doctor would see me.

DR. JEROME ALLENCORT was a short, stout man with troubled brown eyes and a small mustache. He had a neat, mobile mouth and excellent taste in clothes.

He said: "Mr. Greene has phoned me about you, Mr. Jones. Just what sort of information were you seeking?"

"Whatever information you might think significant," I told him, and went on to explain about possible clues to her disappearance in her behavior.

He told me about the temporary paralysis she had imagined in the third finger of her left hand. About the shift in her sleep pattern; she slept days, but couldn't sleep nights. I asked him what significance he attached to the imaginary paralysis.

He hadn't definitely decided, he told me. He didn't look at me. He wouldn't want to say, definitely, because of the lack of sufficient time to study Miss Greene's case.

And the sleep?

He had some names for those I had to look up later. Hypersomnia was one of the words he used, and hyposomnia and insomnia. The last was the only one I knew; I learned later that the others meant an increase and a decrease, respectively, in the total hours of sleep. There was, he said, a possibility that Miss Greene hadn't been entirely truthful; there was a possibility she had slept both night and day (hypersomnia to you).

I didn't like Dr. Jerome Allencort. There wasn't any reason I should feel that way or suspect he was a phoney.

He smiled in his professionally patronizing way, and said: "I'm afraid I haven't been much help to you, Mr. Jones." His smile said that laymen weren't trained or equipped to follow the scientific mind in problems of this sort, and why didn't I run on about my business?

I said: "I run into disappointment quite often in my trade, Dr. Allencort." I picked up my hat, and rose. "You have a really impressive office here," I added.

"Thank you," he said, and looked at me sharply.

"Nice couch there," I continued.

His voice was cool. "It serves its purpose quite adequately." He rose. "Was there anything else, Mr. Jones? I've quite a full calendar for today."

"Nothing else," I said. "Thank you again, Doctor."

In the outer office, the blonde was examining her nails. Her eyes lifted as I came through the door, but then went back to her nails. She yawned.

"Beautiful day," I said.

She nodded and I thought she sighed. "It is," she admitted.

"A day to drive through the country," I went on. "To see the buds bud and the streams stream, to see nature…"

She made a face and shook her head.

"You could walk right out of here," I said, "and find a new job tomorrow."

"Didn't he tell you what you wanted to know, Mr. Jones?" she asked.

I shook my head. "And I thought I was being clever."

"Well," she said, "you weren't. And very few offices or professional men pay what Doctor Allencort pays, Mr. Jones. So take your Saxon coupé out in the country and see the buds for yourself."

"Don't judge me by my clothes," I said. "If you will step to the window, you'll see it's no Saxon I'm driving."

Again, she shook her head. But she was smiling. She went to the window, and I pointed out the Dusy to her.

"Why—it's a—a—" She tapped her forehead. "Don't tell me. I know what it is. It's a Duesenberg, isn't it?"

"Right," I said.

She turned to face me. "This is ridiculous, of course. But—do you dance?"

"With grace and deft ability," I replied.

"And do you know where the Colonial Haven is?"

I nodded. "A lovely spot, out where the buds are budding."

"There's a dance there, tonight," she said, "my brother's lodge is throwing. And the lucky boy I've asked had to go out of town, and if—"

"Where and when shall I pick you up?" I asked. "And is it formal?"

She told me where and when and that it wasn't formal. She smiled her nicest smile then, and said: "You're the first live wire who's walked in here since I started to work for the doctor. I hope you'll overlook my being so brazen."

"It's spring," I said.

She nodded. "I was beginning to forget that."

I went out into the spring to the Dusy. She sighed again as she started. I drove down to the station to see Pop Delaney, to see if there wasn't something he knew he hadn't wanted to tell me over the phone.

HE WAS IN his office burning one of the El Toros. They smell even worse than they look and they look like licorice sticks. He's a bulky man with a red face and hair gone white in the service of the city. He must be older than I hope to get.

"Jonesy," he said. "Got the cigars. Thanks. Anything on your mind?"

"I thought there might be something about this Greene girl you knew and wouldn't reveal over the phone."

He studied his cigar, and chewed his lower lip. "Well, there's nothing much more than a rumor, Jonesy. Schmidt picked it up from a pigeon. Claims this girl had been seen in a couple of spots with Red Bishop. Remember Red?"

"Gambler," I said. "Good-looking guy."

"Right. Rough, too, in his own way. Not in the Greene circle, I'd say."

"This Greene's got plenty, huh?"

"More social position than money," Pop said. "His wife had the money. I don't know if she left it to him or the daughter. But we're checking that now. Anyway, this Greene was right up there in the register until he married his current frau. His first wife was a Hokanson, and you know what they had."

I knew or could guess. About half the mint. "How did she die?" I asked.

"Heart. Always had a bad heart. Nothing up that alley, Jonesy. First thing we checked."

Maybe, I thought, that's where I got my skepticism, from the department. I'd worked with them for quite a while.

Pop said: "It's a queer mess, isn't it?"

I agreed it was. I asked: "What's in the files on Bishop?"

"Nothing. He's no bookie, you know. The big private games are his meat. He's never been on the blotter."

I thanked Pop and left him. I went out into the sunshine

again, wondering where I could find Red Bishop. I didn't have to wonder long.

He was sitting in the front of the Dusy. He looked like hell. He's a handsome gent, neatly and smoothly dressed. But his clothes looked like he'd slept in them and he had a full day's beard.

He wore no hat; his short, red hair was tousled. He said: "Going my way?"

We were acquaintances, but never more than that. "Glad to take you anywhere you're going," I said, and climbed in behind the wheel. "You look like you've had a rough night."

His laugh was short and bitter. "I did. In there." He jerked his head back toward the station. "They were grilling me most of the night."

Pop hadn't told me that. I wasn't with the department any more, I reminded myself, but I felt bad about Pop not telling me.

He said: "I recognized your car. I hope you don't mind about this."

I shook my head. I said: "Do you know where she is, Red?"

"I know about it," I said. "I'm looking for her. It's worth money, Red, to know where she is."

"Money——" he said. "It's worth my life to know where she is. I've been looking for her night and day since she left."

"Why?" I asked.

"Why?" he said, and again he stared at me. "Why would I be looking for her? Because I sail for her, because she's the one girl in the world I've met who isn't a twenty-two carat pain in the neck."

The Dusy started with a sad whimper, and I asked: "Where to, Red?"

"There's a sawbones over on the drive I'd like to talk to," he said, "if you've got the time, if you're not doing anything."

"I've got the time," I said, "but you'd be wasting yours. You mean Dr. Allencort, don't you?"

For the third time he stared at me. "What the hell are you, psychic?"

"I told him I was looking for her," I explained. "Give me what you've got, and I'll tell you my end of it."

He looked at me thoughtfully, and said: "I can't tell you all of my end of it. But not because I don't trust you, Mort." His voice was low. "I owe that much to her. But why was she going there, to that bughouse medic?"

Her hours of sleep were twisted, I told him. I put the Dusy into gear. "She had a paralysis of one finger," I went on, "and it was mental. I mean, there was no injury to the finger, it was a physiological reaction to an emotional tension."

"English, please," he said.

"Dr. Allencort's words," I said. "He meant the paralysis wasn't physical."

Red shook his head, then rubbed his face with both hands. I headed out into the traffic stream. He said: "Take me to the apartment, will you, Mort?"

The Dusy murmured to herself as we wove through traffic. There was no conversation from either of us. This Red, I could see, was a heart-sick boy. He wasn't simulating that.

When we stopped in front of the apartment, I said: "You'd do better to come clean with me. I'm not with the department any more, you know."

"I know," he said. He was getting out of the car. He turned, both hands on the door, and faced me. "Maybe, I will, Mort—

but later. I wish I knew she felt as I do. I wish I could be sure—"

He turned then, and walked wearily up and through the apartment door.

2

Motives and Means

I DROVE BACK to the office. The kids would be out of school now, so I parked a couple blocks away and walked the rest of the trip.

There was no mail at the office. I went over to Mac's. His mood had changed. The Dodgers had won that afternoon.

"Some clear soup?" he asked me. "Some humming-bird wings or unborn pheasant?"

"Some chili," I said, "if it's today's."

He must have noticed my downcast expression. "I didn't mean to be nasty before, Jonesy," he said. "I was in a bad mood at lunch-time."

"And I'm in a bad mood, now," I answered. "Why do I always get all the dirty linen? Why do I get the sad stuff?"

"Here?" he asked.

"No, not here. In my trade."

"Trouble's your trade," he told me. "If people didn't have trouble, you'd have to find another job."

He spoke the truth. It was a nasty trade, but I didn't want any other. After the chili and some rye rolls, I felt better. After some beer and thinking about my approaching engagement with the blonde, and after a shower in my little apartment, I felt almost human.

Norah, standing in the front doorway of her south side duplex a half hour later, her blonde hair artfully and beguilingly piled high, looked fine.

"Good evening," she said. "You look different, you look good."

"You look the same, but better," I answered. "I'm a lucky man."

It was a lovely night and a fine dance. The floor was dim enough to be romantic and underpopulated enough to make dancing a pleasure. The bar was uncrowded, the table service excellent.

I should have been joyous, but I wasn't. I kept thinking of the sleeping beauty.

I asked Norah about her, while we were alone at the table.

"A good kid," Norah said, and studied her drink. "A beautiful girl." She looked at me. "But definitely punchy."

"So I've heard," I said. "I wonder why."

"A good kid," Norah repeated.

"Frustration?" I said.

"I'm no doctor," she said. "Speaking for myself, I'd say a gal has to raise a little mild hell once in a while. This Patricia Greene might have worked her energy off at the mission and those places, but she looked like a lady who could conceivably devote her waking hours to love."

"No boy friends?" I asked.

She looked at me quietly a moment. "You're a detective, so I suppose it isn't quite as unethical to reveal a patient's case history. But what the doctor had on paper, what I saw of it, no boy friends, not one."

"Who told you I was a detective?"

"Dr. Allencort."

"He's quite a boy, isn't he?" I said.

She smiled mechanically. "Let's have another drink."

I was quiet on the ride home.

Norah said: "It can't be that bad. Whatever it is, it can't be that bad."

"I'm not very good company," I admitted. "Not tonight. I've been thinking about Patricia Greene." I shook my head. "I can't seem to get a lead."

When I took her to her door, she said: "It's been a wonderful evening. You can't be boring, even when you try." She was smiling and looking up at me.

I kissed her and forgot the sleeping beauty for that moment. I said: "I'll be seeing you again, you can bet. I'll be better company, next time."

"You were all right tonight," she told me, and closed the door.

Going down the steps, I was thinking of Norah. But in my little rat's nest, I looked at the picture of Patricia Greene again before pulling down the bed.

Bad night, tossing night, half asleep, half awake, half crazy, like a man in love. But I couldn't be in love with a picture. I considered the possibility of seeing Dr. Allencort again, but as a patient.

I made some coffee. The kitchenette was cold; the wind had shifted to the north-east. My white shirts were all dirty. I was out of sugar; I drank the coffee without. A bad start to another bad day.

THE PHONE WAS ringing when I got to the office. It was Sturtevant Greene, and would I get out there right away?

Greene came to the door himself. "If you'll come into the study?" he said. "I don't want the servants to hear."

We went into the study. There was a woman standing next to

the fireplace in there, a woman about thirty, slim, with beautiful blueblack hair and brilliant black eyes. Mrs. Sturtevant Greene. She was pale, too, as pale as her husband.

His hand trembled as he gave me the note. "It came in the mail this morning," he said simply.

It was a request for ransom. The letters, it appeared, had been printed with a child's printing set, huge letters, all caps. It read:

DON'T CALL THE COPS OR THE GIRL DIES. FIFTY THOUSAND. NOTHING BIGGER THAN A TWENTY. AT YOUR HOUSE, 8 O'CLOCK FRIDAY NIGHT. SOMEONE WILL CALL FOR IT. REMEMBER—NO COPS!

"It could be a fraud," I said. "Some angle shooter who knows your daughter is missing could be working a racket."

"This came with it," he said.

It was a piece of yellow silk.

"It was cut out of the dress she was wearing when she—" His voice broke.

His face was gray as ashes, his voice a whisper. "My wife will verify—"

I caught him as he started to fall. I helped him over to a huge chair, and told Mrs. Greene: "You'd better phone a doctor right away."

He was gasping for breath now, and his eyes were closed. Then his hands gripped the leather arms of the chair he was slumped in, and his eyes opened. He said, "Never mind the doctor. I've had these attacks before." He took a deep breath. "My heart—"

"The doctor can't hurt you," I answered, "and he'll probably help you. This is quite a blow, Mr. Greene."

His eyes closed again. "At least I know, now. At least I know she's alive."

I didn't think it the time to point out that he couldn't be sure of that. With kidnapers, you can't be sure of anything. Except that hanging's too good for them.

The doctor came and ordered him to bed.

I waited in the study until Mrs. Greene came back. She was still pale, but under admirable control. She asked: "What would you recommend, Mr. Jones?"

"Call the police in secretly," I said. "Kidnapers aren't people, Mrs. Greene. They're not human. Every snatch they work successfully encourages that many more to try it."

She shook her head, and went to sit in the overstuffed chair. "I don't know what to do. I wouldn't want to do anything that might jeopardize—" She put a hand to her forehead and stared at the rug on the floor.

"Get the money," I said, "today if possible. Has he that much available?"

She looked up at me and nodded. "I'm sure he has. You— plan to pay it then?"

"That's right. And nail them after they drive away."

"*They*—you think there's more than one?"

"Probably. It's risky coming here. Someone would need to be waiting in the car; as a look-out, to keep the motor running, to help fight their way out in case we do call the police."

She lit a cigarette and inhaled deeply. She said: "I can't, I just can't decide what's best—"

"The decision would be yours," I pointed out. "I can only advise, and it wouldn't be the proper time to disturb Mr.

Greene with the decision. I'm afraid you'll have to decide, Mrs. Greene."

She bit her lower lip. Then she looked at me. "I'll do what you think best."

"I don't want it to be *my* decision," I told her. "I've advised you, but I want a direct order from you before I go ahead."

"Call in the police," she said, finally. "I—think it's best." Her face was set and strained; she was breathing deeply.

I nodded in agreement. I said: "There are some things about her disappearance I still haven't got straight, Mrs. Greene. Would it be too much for you if I talked about it, now?"

She shook her head. "I want to do anything I can to help."

My questions had to do with exactly when and under what circumstances Patricia had left the house, when it was first suspected she wasn't coming home.

It wasn't much clearer to Mrs. Greene than it was to me. No one in the house had known where Patricia was going that day. Her hours depended on the work she was doing currently; there was no definite schedule to her activities. She'd been last seen on the morning of her disappearance by Mrs. Greene at the breakfast table. The cook had seen her leave the house later.

"She didn't mention any place she was going that day?"

"Just what I told the police—she mentioned some family named Scarlatti, but I've no idea who they are."

Another little thing Pop hadn't told me. I thought of how the Chief was always talking cooperation. I wondered if he thought it wasn't reciprocal, this cooperation.

I thanked Mrs. Greene and told her I'd get in touch with her later. She said she'd go to the bank to get the money. I drove directly down to the station.

I wanted to see the Chief, but I dropped in on Pop first. I said: "One box of cigars wasn't enough, huh?"

"I don't know what you mean," he said, and there was honest curiosity on his broad, red face.

I told him what I meant. About Bishop being grilled at the station while I was there, about the Scarlattis.

He said: "I didn't know it, either, and that's the gospel, Jonesy. But I'll damned well find out why I didn't know it. Let's go in and see the Chief."

WE WENT IN and saw the Chief. "Mortimer, boy," he said, "it's almost a pleasure seeing you again." Then he saw the wrath in Pop's face. "Something wrong?" he asked quietly.

Between us, we told him what was wrong. I managed to work the word cooperation into it. It's his favorite word, and I thought he winced when I used it.

Pop finished with: "Maybe, sir, you think I'm too old for this job. Perhaps that's why—" Pop was just *one* year older than the Chief, and he knew it.

The Chief looked uncomfortable. "I'll get to the bottom of it right now." He pressed a button. He didn't look at either of us, as he said: "I gave this one to Devine, since he asked for it, because he wasn't busy at the time and your section was, Sergeant."

"Devine—?" I said, and it was all clear. Devine was chief of Homicide, a triple-plated jerk who hated my insides. Devine *would* want this one; there were wealthy people involved.

Devine didn't come in answer to the summons. His number one man and the brunt of his foul disposition came instead— Glen Harvey.

"Perhaps," the Chief said, "you can explain why Sergeant Delaney wasn't kept informed about the developments in that case. I think the entire department is aware of my views regarding cooperation." He didn't look at me. "We can hardly expect cooperation from outside of the department if we don't practice it within the department itself."

Glen looked properly humble. This much I'll say for him; he hated Devine as much as the rest of us, but he tried to cover for him then. He explained how busy they'd been, how rapidly new angles had popped up in the case, how much time Devine had had to spend out on the street. I'd always admired Glen's loyalty, but not the object of it.

When he was finished, I told the Chief about my part in the case, and laid the ransom note on his desk. He read it.

When he'd finished, there was silence. Glen coughed. The Chief said: "Tomorrow's Friday." He picked a cigar out of the humidor and looked at it without lighting it. He looked at me. "They want us there tomorrow night?"

"I convinced Mrs. Greene that would be best," I said. "She's getting the money today."

There was some more talk after that. We laid out the plan for tomorrow night, the men we'd need, and the arms. The Chief gave me a little talk, using the word 'cooperation' only once, and I left them.

Glen Harvey came out while I was getting into the Dusy. He said: "Devine will be after your scalp now. The Chief'll dress him down."

"Devine's been after my scalp a long time," I answered. Then I asked: "What did you learn at the Scarlatti place?"

Glen shook his head. "Not much. She was there, all right, but that's all we learned. They thought a lot of her, all but the old man, that is. The old man's a lush; this Greene girl was trying to work on that too, I guess."

"Devine go with you, down there?"

He looked puzzled. "Sure. Why—?"

"Nothing," I said. "I just wondered."

"What difference does it make now?" Glen asked. "I guess I understand you, all right. Devine isn't one to get the best out of witnesses. But if the girl's been snatched, if they're going to pay, what—"

"Nothing," I said again. "No difference. It's a hell of a day, and I guess I'm moody."

"It is a hell of a day," he agreed.

I went over to Mac's for lunch. I was in there, drinking some fresh and flavorful coffee with sugar, when it started to rain.

It wasn't much of a rain—just enough to be annoying, a gusty, chill drizzle. I went from Mac's to the office.

I was sitting there, relishing a fair hooker of rye, when the phone rang. It was the Chief. He said: "You can forget our plans for tomorrow night, Mort. The Greene girl was found in the woods near Mauston."

"Alive—?" I asked.

"No. She'd been stabbed in the throat with something sharp and thin, something like an ice-pick."

"The papers got it? If they haven't, we could still work that—"

"The papers have it," he interrupted. "Some farmer up there found her, and the local paper got it the same time the police did."

"O.K. Chief," I said. "Thanks."

He didn't hang up. A pause, then: "I suppose that washes you up on the case, Mort?"

"I suppose it does," I admitted. "It would be Devine's baby, or would it? That's outside of our jurisdiction, isn't it?"

"We don't know where she was killed," the Chief said. "She was *found* up there. She's been dead some time."

"Some time" meant they didn't know how long, not yet. I said: "It doesn't sound like a snatch to me. But it could be, especially since they took some trouble to hide the body."

3

No Silver Lining

AFTER HE'D HUNG up, I had another hooker of rye. I tried to forget the picture I had in my mind of the sleeping beauty now sleeping the dreamless, final sleep. Now on a slab at the morgue.

I wondered how they'd keep it from her father. This would be a bad time to tell him with his heart as critical as it was.

The rain had stopped, but not the gusts. Nobody was paying me any more; it wasn't any of my business, but I decided to go over and have a chat with the Scarlatti family. I phoned the station and got the address.

It was on the south side down near the freight yards, a section of squalid, soot-covered frame hovels. The Scarlatti house was a two story affair, leaning precariously to the south, with broken windows and a sagging porch.

There were two girls, both under seven, playing in the high weeds of the front yard. Mrs. Scarlatti opened the door to my knock. She looked at the girls in the weeds, and at me.

I told her my business, I told her a lie with it. I told her I was a friend of Patricia Greene's.

She was a tall, thin woman with weary eyes. "Come in," she said.

I came into a dim parlor, furnished with a faded, frayed sofa and some kitchen chairs. I sat on one of the chairs. From the rear of the house, I could hear a baby squalling. From the next room, I could hear snoring.

Yes, Miss Greene had been there Tuesday. It was the first time in a couple weeks. She'd heard Miss Greene had been sick for those weeks.

I nodded. "She worked pretty hard. Did she come by street car?"

Mrs. Scarlatti frowned. "I—suppose so. She usually did. Is there—the police were here yesterday. Is there something—? Is Miss Greene missing?"

"Miss Greene is dead," I said.

Mrs. Scarlatti's thin face was tight in shock and grief. Her pale lips moved. She's been hit hard and often, I thought. She must have known all the hardship there is to know, all the grief. But she can feel like that about Miss Patricia Greene.

"She—was an angel, that's what she was. Who—could— what happened?"

"She was murdered," I said. "I want all the help you can give me, Mrs. Scarlatti. There may be something, some detail you don't think important which could be a real lead."

She told me about Miss Greene, all she knew about her in great detail, and all she thought about her. There wasn't anything, in any of it, that would help.

I thanked her, when she'd finished, and told her she'd been a help. I took my last twenty from my wallet and handed it to her. "It'll go on the expense account," I said. "I'm permitted an allowance for testimony like you've given me."

She said: "I don't—"

"Please take it," I said. "It isn't the first I've handed out. You've been more help than any of them."

She took it and thanked me. As we walked to the door, the baby was still in fine voice, but the snoring had stopped.

A man stood in the open bedroom door, a bleary-eyed, thin, nasty-looking gent about a half head taller than myself. He was wearing a pair of greasy trousers, and that was all, so far as I could see.

"What the hell's goin' on here?" he asked.

"A motorcycle race," I said. "You missed it. It was a piperoo."

He took a step forward, one fist clenched. "Wise guy, huh?"

Mrs. Scarlatti said, "Sam, don't—"

I put a hand up near my shoulder, movie fashion. I said in my coldest, bleakest voice: "Don't worry, Mrs. Scarlatti. Sam isn't going to do anything. Anything but shut his mouth. Are you, Sam?"

His face sagged, and his blood-shot eyes filled with apprehension. His clenched fist unclenched. In those few seconds, all his belligerence was gone. He turned and went to the bedroom.

There was surprise on Mrs. Scarlatti's face. Maybe she'd never seen him talked back to before. After the surprise, I thought she showed relief. She said: "I'd like to do—flowers—or something to—" She held out the twenty.

"There'll be a lot of flowers," I said. "Too many flowers. But you could pray. I'm sure that's what she'd want."

"I'll pray," she promised.

Next to the Dusy stood a boy above twelve. He said: "What kind of car is that?"

"A Duesenberg," I told him.

He shook his head. "Some jalopy."

"Are you a Scarlatti, too?" I asked him.

He nodded. "Sam, Jr." He climbed up on the running board to stare at the instrument panel. "Boy," he said.

"Do you remember Miss Greene?" His face tightened, and he

didn't look at me. I put a hand on his shoulder. He shook it off. There was something here; I knew there was something here.

"Sammy," I said, "what's the matter? Didn't you like her?"

HE STILL WOULDN'T look at me. "Sure, I liked her. Everybody liked Miss Greene. But, Pop—I don't know anything." He finally looked up at me. "You a cop?"

I shook my head. "I'm a friend of Miss Greene's. I thought you were, too."

He looked back at the house, indecision plain on his young face.

I said: "Let's go down and get a banana split. I'm hungry, aren't you?"

His eyes lighted up. "In—this? In the car?"

I nodded. "Slide in."

He opened the door and slid in. He said nothing as I started the motor. We moved down the street. Two blocks down, he said: "There's a drugstore, up this street." He nodded toward the right.

Sammy ordered the Special DeLuxe Banana Split Royale at my urging.

When it arrived, he looked at it. He didn't make a move for his spoon. He said: "You're not a cop?"

"No, Sammy. On my honor, I don't work for the police department. But I'm an investigator."

"That's all right," he said. "Pop said I shouldn't tell the cops a damned thing. That's all he said, just the cops." His eyes didn't leave the Special DeLuxe Banana Split Royale.

His voice was low. "That day the cops were asking about. Tuesday, it was—I saw Miss Greene. I saw her leave the house and walk up toward the car line. I saw this car stop, this Olds coupé, and I saw Miss Greene get into it."

"A new Olds?" I asked.

He shook his head. "A '41 or '42. You know, from before the war."

"You didn't see who was driving?"

Again he shook his head. "I just saw the back of it. It was about a half block away. I was watching Miss Greene. That's why I knew it was her."

"Why aren't you in school, Sammy?"

He stopped eating and looked up at me suspiciously. "I thought you weren't a cop. I'm *through* school. I graduated in winter."

"How old are you?"

"Twelve."

"Aren't you going to high school?"

"Pop won't let me. Pop says it's a waste of time."

He'd graduated from eighth grade when he was twelve, maybe before he was twelve, but high school was a waste of time... Well, I wasn't a social worker. I said: "Anything more you can tell me about that, Sammy? Think hard, now."

"Nothing," he said.

"Don't you think it's strange your pop didn't want you to tell the cops?"

He shook his head. "Pop don't like cops. Nobody likes cops, do they?"

"Some cops are all right," I said, "lots of them. But you should go to school, Sammy. You'll have to go nights, anyway. You'll never get a Duesenberg if you don't go to school."

"Joe Fazio's got a Caddy," Sammy answered. "And Joe never went past sixth grade. He told me so, himself."

Joe Fazio was a welter, a rugged, brawling mixer.

"Joe won't have the Caddy after he meets Danny Burke," I said. "Joe won't have his marbles, either. Danny's a *college* man."

Sammy looked up at me scornfully. "Joe'll murder him. Danny Burke's a bum. Joe told me so."

"You want to bet?"

He shook his head. "I'm broke."

"A bet like this," I said. "If Joe wins, I'll buy you a banana split every day for the next year. If Danny wins, you go to school. Any kind of school, night school or high school."

He grinned up at me. "O.K.," he said.

"I'm serious," I said. "I mean you'll go to school and *study*. You'll work at it. A guy who backs out on a bet is a welsher, Sammy."

"I know," he said, "and I'm serious, too."

We'd finished and I drove him home.

When he got out, he said: "So long. And thanks a lot. I'm— glad I told you about Miss Greene."

"So am I," I said. "Miss Greene is dead, Sammy. She was murdered."

I left him there, standing on the curb, watching me drive off. His eyes were wide. I adjusted my wings and my halo and turned north on Water Street.

I drove directly down to the station. There, I headed directly for the Chief's office. He was in, but he wasn't alone. Devine was with him. *Nobody likes cops*, I thought, *and here's the reason.*

THE CHIEF GREETED me amiably enough, but Devine said nary a word. I explained about the Olds to the Chief while Devine listened in.

When I'd finished, the Chief asked: "Who told you this?"

"A reliable witness," I answered. "I can't tell you any more than that."

Devine snorted.

I ignored him. "I'll probably drop this deal now," I told the Chief. "But I thought the Olds might be a lead for you. I thought you might have *somebody* in the department who could use it. This witness doesn't like cops. He thinks cops are unqualified scoundrels. He's probably wrong about that, but it wouldn't do any good to let the *usual* kind of cop see him."

The Chief looked at me, at Devine, and out his wide window. He looked back at me. "All right, Mort. Thanks for the information." He smiled, and shook his head. "I hope somebody pays you to continue. Or I hope you get some heart, so you'll work on it without pay. But thanks for what you've given us."

Outside, the wind had stopped, which changed it from a windy, unpleasant day to a quiet, unpleasant day. I drove back to the office, talking to myself, for some reason.

The office was unlocked; I'd left it that way. The office was occupied; I hadn't left it that way. Red Bishop sat in the leatherette chair.

He'd looked like hell last time I saw him, but he looked worse now. He was shaved, and the expensive suit he wore was impeccable. But his eyes were just blank spots in his face, and his face itself was a frozen grimace of grief and shock.

"Who did it, Jones?" he asked hoarsely. "What do they know down there at the station?"

"They don't know a damned thing," I said, "and neither do I. It could have been somebody in an Olds coupé." I told him about that.

He looks like a man who's lost everything, I thought. *He looks like a man who's seen the end of the world.* I don't know why, but I thought of that finger paralysis at that moment. And I had one of those hunches.

"You were married to her," I said, "weren't you?"

His head tilted to one side. He looked like a wax dummy, staring at me. "Where'd you find that out? Do *they* know, down at—"

"Nobody knows," I said. "I just guessed it."

That's where she'd wear the wedding ring, on the third finger of her left hand. That would symbolize, for her, the shameful thing she'd done. But...

"Was she sorry after she'd done it?" I asked. "Was she ashamed of being married to you?"

He didn't say anything for seconds. I began to get the jitters. He didn't have the reputation of a violent man, but you can never tell.

Then, suddenly, he put his head down between his hands. His body shook. He could bet ten grand on the turn of a card without batting an eye. But this was too much for him. He loved her, all right. No doubt about that.

His voice sounded like it was coming through a tunnel. "We were married across the line, at Helenville. One of those marrying parsons. Coming back, we stopped at the Grotto. You know, that spot on the edge of town. I got drunk. I had to drink that night. I got stinking. The next thing I knew, I was sitting out in the parking lot in the car with, well—a bag I used to kick around with." He raised his head and looked at me. "Pat was standing next to the car. She'd come out to look for me—and found *us*. I swear I don't know what I'd been doing."

He shook his head and gulped a mouthful of air. "Maybe we'd been... oh, lord, I don't know, Jones—"

Night, I thought. It had happened at night. That's why she couldn't sleep. Night was part of the humiliation she suffered, and the ring a symbol of her error. After all the frustration of the years of waiting for marriage with the right man, he wasn't—or so she thought.

He straightened in his chair now. He was fighting for control. He asked, in a dead voice: "Do you think she might have committed suicide?"

"No," I said. "What happened after that, Red?"

"There was a cab there. She took it home, I guess. After I came back to normal, I tried to get in touch with her. I phoned her, but she'd hang up on me. My letters came back, unopened."

"Who knows you were married?"

"Nobody. Anyway, I didn't tell a soul. It was up to her, Jones. I wanted a chance to prove to her that I was all right. But I wanted it to be her decision. I—wanted it to be right."

He said: "Do you think that bug doctor? I mean, who else? Who'd want to—what reason—"

"One of your old girl friends?" I suggested. "The one in the car?"

"No. Hell, no—" His voice trailed off.

"Somebody who hates you?" I went on. "Somebody who took this way to—"

"Nobody hates me that much," he said. "And nobody knew about it."

"You going to work on this?"

I shrugged. "I don't know. It's not really my business. I've no reason to want to work with Devine."

"Here's a reason," he said.

I turned. He had his wallet out, and he pulled some bills from it. Five bills, five one hundred dollar bills. He laid them on the desk. "Stay with it, Jones."

I told him what my rates were.

"Never mind," he said. "That's yours. Just stay with it. And could you let me know if you find out anything? Could you let me know before the cops?"

"I'm afraid I couldn't," I said. "The reason I get the cooperation I do from the department, the reason they leave me alone, is that I always work with them, never against them."

"O.K.," he said. "I'll be doing some checking myself. I'll keep in touch."

He went out, and I heard his feet going down the hall and down the stairs. I stayed at the window and watched him leave the building. I watched him walk up a few hundred feet and climb into the car that was parked at the curb—the Olds coupé.

4

One Motive More

I STILL COULDN'T shake the mood I was in, the lousy, cynical mood. I phoned Dr. Allencort's office and Norah answered. I asked: "Could you think of something bright and cheerful to do tonight? Something that would lift a man out of the dumps?"

"I could," she answered. "But we could go to a show, too. That would be a more acceptable and respectable way of spending the evening. Speaking from my vast medical background, that is.

"How's the boss?" I asked. Still busy?"

"Busy enough. I could get some tickets for *The Gay Forties*. I know a guy. Would that fill the bill?

"That would be fine," I said. "I could almost fall for you, you know it? You're so beautiful—and normal."

"You're not so beautiful," she answered, "but you're normal enough. About seven-forty-five?"

"Fine," I said. "We won't dress, huh?"

"Not formally," she said.

I was smiling as I pronged the receiver. Tomorrow, I'd go to work in earnest. Tonight, I wanted to forget the whole rotten mess.

I almost did. *The Gay Forties* was a good revue; good music, good gags, good legs all the way down the line. Norah looked out of this world, in black again with gold accessories, with her hair a new way, but still up. After the show we danced and drank.

But she'd read the afternoon papers after I'd called, and she knew the story too, now. We both tried, but we couldn't get the proper, festive spirit.

When I took her home, she said: "This was my fault, this time. Maybe we'd both better consult the doctor."

"Next time will be different," I promised, "and it wasn't your fault."

In the morning, I called Glen Harvey and asked him what they'd dug up on the printing set that must have been used for the ransom note. They'd dug up nothing, so far. And what did they have on Sam Scarlatti, Sr.?

They had an old desertion rap against him and a string of drunk and disorderlies. They had an open mind which could go either way on Sam Scarlatti, Sr.

How about the Olds coupé?

Nothing, yet. They were working on it, of course, but nothing, yet.

I didn't say anything about Red Bishop, because Red was my client now. But I thought it damned funny Glen didn't say something about Red Bishop and his Olds coupé.

"That's all you've got, Glen?"

"That's all. You still on this, Jonesy?"

"I'm still on it. Give my regards to Devine." I hung up.

Motive, means and opportunity, I thought. There's got to be a motive in this, somewhere. Means and opportunity can be proven, later, but a murder without motive… There's got to be something, somewhere.

Kidnapping was a motive. Fifty thousand dollars was a

motive, all right. If a man's poor enough, degenerate enough, he'd do about anything for that kind of hay. Only Sam Scarlatti didn't have an Olds coupé.

I wondered how much Red Bishop knew about the Greene fortune. Red seemed to be in the upper brackets, himself, but with gamblers it's hard to tell. And gamblers love cinch bets. Marrying a couple of million, marrying a beautiful girl with a couple of million would appeal even to me, a man of high ethical standards.

I phoned the Greene home.

I identified myself to the maid who answered the phone, and asked if it had been possible to keep the papers from Mr. Greene.

It hadn't. Mr. Greene was suffering a relapse of his attack of the day before. The doctor was there now. Did I want to talk to the doctor?

I said I would talk to Mrs. Greene.

Mrs. Greene's voice on the phone was controlled, but her tension was evident. She told me: "My husband's condition is extremely critical, Mr. Jones. He seems to have developed an obsession about this Bishop person. The police rather think he's involved, don't they?"

"It's hard to tell what the police think," I said, "and especially from a reporter's account of what the police think. But Bishop isn't one to be overlooked. That's why I phoned. I wonder if you would phone your husband's attorney for me and explain my position. There's some information in his files I need."

She said she'd do that. She also said, "My husband wants you to stay with this affair, Mr. Jones."

I told her I intended to. I said it was too bad about the papers.

Then I asked: "You don't know of any—acquaintance of Miss Greene's who drove an Olds coupé, do you?"

A pause. "No—although, of course, I don't know much about cars. Does that mean... Is that kind of car involved—" Her voice faltered. "There was nothing about it in the papers."

"There won't be," I said, "unless there's a leak. A car of that kind is involved."

She said: "I could try to find out, if it would help—"

"Try to find out, if you will. But don't use the name, 'Oldsmobile'. That would be a tip-off. Just find out *what* kind of cars her friends and acquaintances drive."

It would have to be a friend or acquaintance, I thought as I hung up. It would almost have to be for her to get into the car without protest. She was no pick-up, from what I knew.

I WENT OUT and down to Mac's. It was an in-between day, not gloomy, not sunny, neither warm nor cold, a run-of-the-mill day.

At Mac's I had some coffee. Then I drove over to the auto tag bureau. I've a friend there, a cooperative, obliging friend, and he knew my business was semi-official.

I checked the cars of everybody I knew who could have the faintest connection with the case. I got two Buicks and a Chrysler, a Lincoln Continental, one Olds and a Pontiac. The Olds belonged to Norah's brother, and his connection with the case was so negligible that I didn't bother to look him up.

The Pontiac I ran across was a coupé, listed as Red Bishop's. Sam Scarlatti had no car at all as I suspected.

I thanked my obliging friend and left. I drove over to the offices of Dykstra, Keeling and Grant, on Lincoln Avenue.

Mr. Dykstra was what I like to think of when I think of lawyers. He was tall and spare and his blue eyes were keen, though friendly. He had dignity without pomposity and poise without arrogance. He told me all I wanted to know, simply, without reverting to legal terms.

The will of Emily Greene, who had been a Hokanson, left most of the Hokanson money to Patricia Greene, when and if she should come of age. Until that time, it was in the hands of Sturtevant Kenneth Greene; he and his daughter were the only heirs.

Unless Patricia should marry, in which case her heirs and assigns (as they say) would gain priority. In the event Patricia didn't marry, thus having no heirs or assigns, so to speak, Kenneth Sturtevant Greene would get his adequate (by my standards) share, Patricia the bulk. The death of either would make the other complete beneficiary.

Patricia had been twenty-two at her death. She had been of age.

I said: "If she should have a husband, he'd be in line now for all of this money, wouldn't he?"

He looked at me sharply. "Yes. But, of course, she hadn't a husband. Unless—" There was a question in the word.

I shrugged. "I just wondered. I don't want to overlook anything."

I thanked him and left. I wondered if it was my business to tell Red Bishop he was a millionaire. I wondered if perhaps, he didn't know it. And I wondered if it hadn't been my duty to tell Mr. Dykstra that Patricia had a husband.

I ran them all over in my mind, fitting what I had to each one. But those were only the ones I knew of, people who had a connection in some way with Miss Greene. It could have been kidnappers, any of a host of unknown criminals, people I hadn't met and wouldn't meet.

I'd mistaken a Pontiac for an Olds. I was reasonably sure of that. I'd seen Red's car from the back and mistaken it for an Olds. Perhaps Sam Scarlatti, Jr., had, too. It explained why Glen Harvey hadn't said anything this morning about Red Bishop. So far as the police knew, Red's car was a Pontiac.

On an off chance, I drove past Red's apartment. I was lucky; the car was there, the same one he'd been driving yesterday. It was a Pontiac all right. I'd been wrong.

Fisher Bodies, I thought. General Motors cars; they almost overlap in their price fields. At a casual glance, they look alike. Not the Chev and the Caddy, of course, but going up through the list, one resembles the other, more or less. Sure, sure...

Chevrolet, Pontiac, Oldsmobile, Buick, Cadillac, I thought. *Buick,* I thought. If I could mistake the big Pontiac for the small Olds, couldn't Sammy mistake the small Buick for the big Olds? From the back and half a block away?

Motive, means and opportunity... Oh, Lordy, yes... It hit me like a club, the realization that all of them fit, all of them were tailored, almost.

I swung the Dusy around and headed for the station. Glen Harvey wasn't there, but all the testimony of the persons inter-viewed in the case so far was there and available. The Chief had it in his office.

"I'm still with it," I said. "Somebody's paying me."

He held up a sheaf of papers. "Want to look at this?"

"That's what I'm here for," I told him.

I looked it all over, and the gap was there, all right. The police are just as suspicious as I am, I realized. That's where I'd learned it.

"You're hot," the Chief said, "and I can tell it. You've got a lead."

He cleared his throat.

Here it comes, I thought. *Here's where he uses the word again. Here's where I hear about cooperation. And if I'm right, Devine will get his picture in the papers, again.*

I said quickly: "I want to handle it alone, Chief. With your cooperation for part of it, but the rest of it alone. It will take a trick, and the department can't stoop to trickery."

He looked displeased.

I said quickly: "I don't want the pinch or the credit. Harvey can have that. And I want you to let me know the moment a complaint comes in, the moment you hear about a threat. That way, I'll know."

He looked puzzled. He said: "This is damned irregular as usual, Mort. Why in hell can't you do *something* the routine way?"

"Because it wouldn't work. Because the law is too complex and juries too susceptible to a smart attorney. Don't you trust me? Don't you think I'm capable of handling it?"

His smile was less paternal than annoyed, though there was some paternalism in it. "O.K., Mort," he said.

I went back to the office and phoned Red Bishop. I told him what I wanted from him. I told him he'd have to play it smart; he'd have to hide what he felt, because I wasn't sure and he could gum the whole thing up if he should lose his temper. I told him I would write the letter.

He said: "If you think you've got something, Jones, I'll play along. I'll be all right if it leads to what we're looking for."

After that, I wrote the letter. I worded it very carefully. Then I phoned for a messenger. When he arrived, I told him that I wanted it delivered without his divulging the sender's identity. I wanted it delivered to one person, only.

WHEN HE LEFT, I went over everything in my mind, planning it all, looking for the weaknesses, trying to decide on the best way to lay the trap, the surest way.

I poured a drink, a small one, mostly water. I turned on the radio and waited.

Red was the first to call. He'd had action from his end, he said. "It doesn't add up, though, Jones," he protested. "Not to me, it doesn't."

"It will," I said. "I'm almost sure it will."

The Chief didn't call. I sat through two soap operas and a jive program, and still the Chief hadn't called. So I phoned him.

"Nothing stirring," he told me. "I hope you know what you're doing."

I said: "Send Glen Harvey over to my apartment, will you? I'm going home now."

He promised he would. And that he'd phone me there if he got a call.

I was frying some eggs when Glen arrived. I fried a couple more for him. "Devine's not going to like this," he told me. "He might make things rough for me."

"You're a big boy, Glen," I told him. "I don't want Devine to like this. But if you'd rather I got somebody else—?"

"I'll do it," he said. "I'll be the martyr."

"The big, bold hero, you mean," I said. "With your name spelled out in all the papers, and the pictures, and everything."

"More salt, please," Glen said.

We went over to Bishop's apartment.

We talked the whole thing over. I said: "The kidnapping was just a gag. If that farmer hadn't found the body, if we'd waited with the money, no one would have shown up for it, anyway. If they found the body after that, it would look like the kidnappers had learned the police were waiting. I'd bet there's another note, somewhere, that would have been delivered saying just that."

"A theory, only, Jonesy," Glen said.

"A theory only," I admitted. "But so was my guess at the murderer. And you didn't get a call at the station, did you?"

"Not yet."

"You won't. And maybe we won't get a confession tonight. That's what I can't figure out, how to sew it up."

Glen said: "Maybe we'll have to sew Red up, after it's over. Have you thought of that? The first murder is the toughest one; it comes easier, after that."

"I'll take that chance," Red said. "I've got a .45, right in that desk over there."

"Too big for your pocket," I told him. "I brought you a little one." I handed him one of mine I'd brought for the purpose, a .32 automatic.

I said: "You'll have to change your story, Red. In the letter to which I signed your name, I said you wanted no part of the estate. Now, you can say you just wanted to be sure of the murderer, and you intended to claim the entire portion belonging to your wife. If anything will get action, that should."

I could see the trembling start in him again. I said: "Don't go off half-cocked, boy. We're not sure, you know."

It was at that moment his bell rang.

Glen and I went back to the dark kitchenette to stand behind the open door in there, as Red went to press the buzzer.

A little later we heard Red say "Good evening," and we heard the murderer's answering greeting. We heard the door close.

There was some dialogue we couldn't get, and then Red said clearly: "I wanted to see if you'd go to the police with my letter. My mind's clear enough on you, now. I intend to claim the entire estate due my wife. I—don't think you'll have any kick about that, will you, Mrs. Greene? You might have too much explaining to do."

"I don't understand," she said.

"I saw you pick up Pat," Red lied.

That was his own idea, that was one of those simple but effective ideas that come on the spur of the moment.

"You're lying," she said.

His voice went on evenly. "The police think it was an Olds, but it was your Buick, wasn't it? You knew she was going to the Scarlattis. You'd benefit plenty from her death. Only an amateur like you would use an ice pick."

Her voice was low now, dangerous. "You've told this—this ridiculous story to the police?"

"No. I'm not interested in vengeance, Mrs. Greene. I'm interested in the estate. I suppose we're two of a kind, in that, but I'm the one who wins in the end. Because you'll never fight me, will you? Not when I know what I do."

It was costing him plenty to say these things, I realized. I could see that he was a poker player, all right.

He was still talking. "Don't think you're safe. One word from me and those police experts will take that Buick apart, they'll put every stitch of clothes you own under the microscope. They'll find blood, somewhere, there. They can check the dirt on your tires, and they might even find the ice pick and the printing set. Once you're named, you're nailed, Mrs. Greene."

Her voice was still low. She said: "I'm an amateur, all right, Mr. Bishop. But I didn't come unprepared."

I nudged Glen. "Here's where the Marines arrive," I whispered.

We stepped out into the hall in time to hear the first shot. We entered the room as Red shot. He shot twice.

He turned to us as she crumpled. He said: "I was hoping she'd do that. I was hoping she'd give me an excuse." Then he crumpled, himself.

Red pulled through, after some high-class abdominal surgery by high-priced docs. Mrs. Sturtevant Kenneth Greene, who had married what she thought was millions, lost out here as she had before. She lived for a while, but it was a losing fight all the way. She talked before she died. She blamed her husband for all of it. If he had had the money he apparently had, she reasoned, none of it would have been necessary. Glen Harvey got his picture in the papers.

Red didn't personally use a dime of the Greene millions. He established a social center with it, a big modern place, and named it the Patricia Bishop Memorial Foundation.

Sturtevant Greene died of heart disease two months later.

Oh, yes—and Danny Burke, who'd gone to Centerville Teachers' College for two months, decisively whipped Joe Fazio, who'd gone to P.S. 38 for six years. Which goes to show what an education will do.

The third time I took Norah out, things *were* different.

Red Runaround

The Dusy-driving dick is up to his hub-caps
trying to crack a thrill-girl kill and save
his client from the hot seat—but it looks
as if his only chance is to hire a sitter!

ODDLY ENOUGH, I saw him fight Jackie Benson. That was the last fight he had, before the police picked him up, before the D.A. went into action and nailed him clean and tight.

He looked good against Benson. Benson was a buller and a hitter, a flatfooted wader, and that's the kind of man Tod relished. Tod hit him almost at will, counter-punched him silly, marked him up. He didn't put Benson down; nobody had ever put Benson down. But he won twelve rounds of the fifteen. He won a chance at the title. Four days later, they picked him up for the murder of Lila Abbott.

A wealthy family, the Abbotts. Prestige and power. Lila—the tabloids called her the "Thrill Girl"—had been something of a blot on the family shield, married twice, once to a wrestler and once to a count. Neither marriage had lasted longer than a year. She was spending her time with Tod Nelson just before she was killed. It was rumored they were engaged.

She was a thin and hungry-looking blonde and not to my taste, but I could guess at the appeal she may have had for some men. Her thinness was a patrician thinness and her hunger was not for food, I would guess. She was way out of Tod Nelson's social sphere and that would be a lure too, you understand. Perhaps he'd forgotten she'd been married to a wrestler.

Well, they made a case. I didn't get too much of it from the papers; I was busy at the time with a hotel skipper. But I saw Devine's picture in the paper the day they picked Tod up, and

I could guess that if the evidence wasn't strong enough, Devine might manufacture some. There are lots of homicides in this town, and very few of them are my business. They're Devine's business. He can have them.

The countess was holding a gun very steadily in her hand now. It was pointed at the count.

ON AN EARLY fall afternoon it became my business. The girl in my office was fairly short and finely built, with red hair and deep blue eyes. Clothed in green, she looked haunted and unhappy.

She said her name was Joan Nelson, Tod's sister. She said I'd been recommended to her by a Nels Keeling who was her brother's attorney. She wanted me to find the murderer of Lila Abbott.

I said: "Your brother's already been convicted of that, Miss Nelson. There isn't much time—"

Her face maintained its composure but I could tell it was an effort of will. "No, there isn't. I—had assumed they wouldn't

convict an innocent man. I didn't realize until yesterday how wrong I'd been." Her voice was higher now and her face showed her grief.

I hesitated a few moments before saying more. Not because I needed the pause, but she did. She was tense, fidgety.

I said: "I may uncover nothing. Private investigators cost money, Miss Nelson, and they aren't nearly as infallible as some people believe. I wouldn't want to hold out any false hope in anything as important to you as this."

Her mouth was trembling.

"Do you need all those words to say *no?*"

I looked down at my desk top.

She rose. "I understood you were in good standing at Headquarters, Mr. Jones. I didn't realize it was *that* good."

"Please sit down," I said. "Please—" I said. "I'm sorry, Miss Nelson. I'd like to hear your side of the story."

She sat down and told me her side in a dry, flat voice. A few times she had to stop for control, but her voice didn't waver very often. Tod had been in love with the Abbott girl, all right. He'd told his sister that.

"I tried to talk him out of it. I tried to show him what she—was. That count—and then that wrestler—Tod's a good boy, you understand, Mr. Jones. He hasn't had experience with girls—with women like that, and she was clever. Oh, Lord, she was clever enough." The blue eyes were almost black now. "I'm glad she's dead."

I said: "Do you know where Tod was on the night the Abbott girl died? Two witnesses have claimed they were together, and that they were quarreling."

"They weren't together when she was killed," she said. "Tod wouldn't lie to *me*, not about something like that."

"You think the witnesses were lying?"

"One of them was—that man who claimed he saw Tod leave the building at three o'clock, that Al Coleman, the cab driver. He said he knew Tod, you'll remember, and he couldn't be mistaken."

"And where was Tod at three o'clock?"

"Walking the streets. He'd had a fight with Lila—he was restless and unhappy—"

They're always walking the streets. They're never in a crowd of friends or a public, inhabited place or at home with the family. They're always walking the streets. Well, maybe if they weren't there'd be fewer convictions.

I said: "We've only his word on that."

"That's right," she said, and the words were a challenge. Her eyes searched my face. "Don't you believe it?"

"I'll have to believe it if I'm to go ahead," I said. I didn't say that I believed nothing that I heard and only half of what I saw. But that would have been the truth.

She told me more. I put it all down—names and addresses. The count and the wrestler and the cab driver and the waiter who'd heard them quarrel and even the address of the Abbott home and Tod's manager. She had it all in a book.

I said: "You came prepared."

"I've questioned them all myself," she said. "I didn't get anywhere."

No, and I probably wouldn't either. Because I wouldn't have only the facts to search for, I'd have Devine to buck—and Devine's cousin Whitney, who was the D.A. They'd look bad if this case exploded. The papers would give them hell. It was a typical Devine-Whitney job, full of holes they'd probably plugged with intimidation.

I didn't want it. But I couldn't tell that to the girl with the trusting blue eyes and the flame-colored hair. I couldn't take off my armor and throw away my sword in front of her. I couldn't even get down off my white charger.

I said: "I'll do all I can. I'll keep you informed, Miss Nelson. I want to see Tod first."

"I don't think you can," she said quickly. "They won't let you."

"I'm going to try." She rose and I accompanied her to the

door. There, she started to say something but stopped. She said "Good-bye," and then I was listening to her heels going down the hall.

I WENT BACK to the phone and called the chief. "I want to see Tod Nelson this afternoon," I told him.

"He's not here, Mort." A pause. "Or did you know that?"

"I knew it. I want a letter from you to the warden up there. I want it to appear as though I'm on a semi-official mission, if you're agreeable to that."

Another pause, a longer one. Then: "Why, Mort?"

"For a client," I said simply.

"His sister?"

"For a client," I repeated.

"The case is finished. He dies in six days. You don't want to stir up anything there. Mort. He's been convicted."

"All right," I said. "I just thought, considering how I'd always worked with the department, considering that I used to work for the department and knowing your views on coopera-tion, you'd be willing... Oh, well, you're not interested in that. Thanks for listening anyway."

"Where's the fiddle?" he asked me.

"I don't understand."

"The fiddle music that goes with that heart-rending ballad," he explained.

I laughed politely. "O.K., I'm sorry. I guess it wouldn't be good politics for an outsider to mess into that case. I can see your point."

His voice was quiet now and there was no humor in it. "You're not by any chance inferring that I'd obstruct justice, are you, Mort?"

"No," I answered. "But it was Devine's baby, wasn't it? And it would be a poor chief who wouldn't back his own man."

No answer.

"So long," I said.

"Get over here," he said. "I'll have the letter ready. You skate on very thin ice at times, young man."

"Let's forget the whole thing," I said. "I'm not going to buck the department. I never have and I won't now."

"The letter will be waiting for you in my office," he said, and hung up.

There'd be a little speech waiting for me, too. About the dignity of my profession, about cooperation and respect for others and whatever else might come to his careful, tradition-bound mind. But he was a good man and I liked him.

I'd already had an early lunch, so I drove right over. He was in his office dictating the letter when I got there. He didn't smile at me. I sat down. He gave me a short lecture on respect and tact, and then asked: "Why are you digging into this, Mort? Do you really feel that Tod Nelson's innocent?"

I considered that question before answering. Then I said: "I've really no opinion on it at all. But my client thinks he's innocent, and my client's willing to pay me to work on it."

He put his finger-tips together and studied them.

"I'll be tactful," I promised, "And if anything new should develop in the investigation, anything important, I'll see that the proper authorities—"

He interrupted me with a wave of the hand. "I know all that. I'm thinking of Whitney in this, not Devine."

Whitney was Devine's cousin, but he was also an important

man and very sharp politically. He was as shrewd as Devine was stupid. It didn't look good for the chief to be on the other side of the fence from the D.A.

"Whitney might not ever know," I said. "You don't want any doubt in *your* mind about Tod's guilt, do you?"

"No," he said heavily, "I don't. I'd give up this job tomorrow to prevent an innocent man from being punished."

He would, too. I know him well and respected him always. If Devine hadn't been in the department, I'd almost have been satisfied to work here for the chief. But even if I took Devine's job, he'd still be around. My stomach wasn't strong enough for that.

"All right," he said. "Well—luck, Mort." And now he smiled though there wasn't much happiness in it.

Outside at the curb, Glen Harvey was just climbing from a department car. "Greetings," he said. "Down on business?"

Glen's a good boy, even if he is Devine's right hand. I said I'd just dropped in to get something from the chief.

He stretched and glanced over at my car. "Still got the Duesenberg, I see," he said companionably. "It would be a nice car to take fishing. My vacation starts next week. How about you, Jonesy?"

"I'm on a case," I said. "I can't loaf on the taxpayers' time like you boys."

"Sure," he said, "sure. Your racket I should have."

"Yeah," I said. "Well, give my love to Devine."

He made a face and then shook his head. He looked weary as he walked up the steps to the big door. He looked like he needed a vacation.

The Dusy was murmuring to herself as we moved through

traffic, through the afternoon sunlight down Eighth. It was a fine afternoon, sunny but not hot, an afternoon for golf. It was no afternoon for a mission like mine.

He'd been sentenced in July. He now had six days before the man pulled the switch. I was starting on a cold trail, and I'd get very little help from the department on this one. The fact that I was being paid for my time, win, lose or draw, didn't compensate me enough to let me forget how hopeless it was.

I prodded the Dusy gently and she surged. Up the Boulevard to the Drive now. I kicked her and she soared, singing to herself. More than ten years old, my baby, and there still isn't anything on the road that can even give me a fair race.

I made it in excellent time. It was a clear road. The Dusy seemed to sigh, when I cut the ignition, as though she was just beginning to enjoy life.

I WENT THROUGH a long, long corridor and up some concrete steps and down another corridor to the warden's office. I gave him the letter from the chief and waited.

He was frowning as he read the letter, and he was still frowning as he looked up at me. "This is a little unusual, you understand, Mr. Jones."

I agreed to that.

He sighed. "But—of course—" He tapped the letter, and the frown changed into a near-smile. "For *him*, of course, I'd go a long way."

I said I would, too.

He looked at me. "Didn't you used to work there in Homicide?"

I nodded.

"I know you, now. Mortimer Jones, of course." He pressed a button. "There's—ah—something new on Nelson's case?"

I couldn't tell him I was just working for pay—for Joan Nelson. He wouldn't want a private eye nosing into this. I said: "We're not completely satisfied, for some reason."

He nodded. "Yes. I can see that perhaps—" He shrugged. "Oh, it's probably personal. Maybe, it's just because I used to watch his fights."

"He's a fine boy," I said. "I can't see murder and particularly a woman." I realized, as I said it, that I must have felt that way all along without being aware of it.

Then I was walking along another corridor smelling of disinfectant and food.

Past a guard, past a priest to the cell of Tod Nelson, welterweight challenger. He was sitting on the bed, his head in his hands, when the turnkey let me in.

He looked up slowly, and stared at me. Finally he said: "I've seen you around, but I don't place you."

"Mortimer Jones," I volunteered. "I'm a private detective. Your sister has hired me, Tod."

He looked away, down at the floor. "It's pretty late for that, isn't it?"

"Maybe. I didn't encourage her. I mean to do all I can and I need your help."

He looked up. "I can't tell you anything I didn't tell the jury time after time. You must know all I've got to tell."

"I can get it. But there might be something else. I thought you might have some ideas on it." I paused. "I thought maybe you could give me a lead to the real murderer."

He stared at me. "If I knew that, don't you think I—"

"Maybe you don't know it," I said. "But if Miss Abbott had had any enemies, she might have mentioned it to you. There may be lots of things you know about her that the police don't." I stopped, trying to read his reaction to all this. He didn't look like a murderer, not to me, but a lot of them don't. Most of them don't. He didn't look like a man who was going to be very cooperative, either.

After a moment, he said: "There isn't anything, anything at all. I think that ex-husband of hers, that Count Terrati still saw her. That's what we were quarreling about. But he's clean; he was out of town that night."

"That didn't come up at the trial, did it?"

"Terrati? No, but they had him locked up with me back in town for a while. They had that Greek there, too, that grunt-and-groan artist. I don't know what his alibi was."

The Greek was Nick Theosophulus, the wrestler, a man of supposedly violent temper. But that may have been only a publicity gag. I studied the slim, quiet lad sitting on the cot, wondering what I should say next.

He got up and went over to look out through the front of the cell. With his back to me, he said: "How's my sister taking it?"

"*She's* fighting," I said.

He turned to face me. "You mean I'm not?"

I nodded.

"In June they picked me up," he said. "In July they railroaded me up here. Now—with five days to go, you come up here asking questions. You think my lawyer didn't put me wise about Devine and Whitney? You think I don't know when I'm up against a fix? Why should Sis pay out what dough she's got left to you?"

"She thinks I can do something," I said.

He shook his head and turned his back on me again.

"A lot of fights have been won in the last five rounds," I said.

"Not fixed fights."

For the second time he turned to face me. His voice was quiet but tense. "Look, it's taken me a long time to reach this state of mind. I'm almost ready, now, for what's going to happen. Don't get me worked up or think something that isn't true." He came over to stand close to me. "And don't get Sis all stirred up about any chances. I know you private eyes. I know how you make your living."

There was no anger in the eyes staring into mine. They were the dead eyes of a resigned man.

"I thought I knew fighters, too," I said.

"Beat it," he said.

I left him. I walked along the concrete corridors, the quiet, grim corridors, and up the clean concrete steps that led to the warden's office.

He said: "Well, Mr. Jones—?"

"Nothing much," I said. "He's not part of this world any more. He's quit."

The warden nodded. "He's been reading the Bible a lot. He's convinced, I think, that he was the victim of a police conspiracy."

Conspiracy was a strong word to use. But he may have been the victim of police stupidity, I thought. Not police stupidity, but Devine stupidity. Maybe the chief thought so, too. And the warden. These were all my unspoken thoughts and undoubtedly were his.

I thanked him and left. I drove down the wide drive to the

gate and out through the massive, guarded gate to the highway. It was late afternoon—a pleasant time of day. But my mind was back in that pile of stone, that gaunt, gray mausoleum of men's hopes.

2

Big Chair Cool-off

I DECIDED IT wouldn't be the count I saw first or the Greek. It would be that taxi driver, the cabbie who'd recognized Tod leaving the apartment building at three o'clock. That was the time he was supposed to be walking the streets. Al Coleman was his name and the prosecution had built a large part of their case on his testimony.

The Dusy began to whine as I prodded her with my right foot.

This Al Coleman lived in a sad-looking duplex near the end of Vine Street. It was a high, narrow place, a converted single-family dwelling. Al lived on the second floor.

The door lock buzzed in answer to my ring and I went in and up a flight of narrow, rubber-carpeted steps to the landing above where a woman waited.

She was a thin and vacantly pretty woman in a colorful house dress. A peroxide blonde, I would guess. She waited quietly and disinterestedly while I told her my name and explained my business.

"Al won't talk to you," she said. "Al's done all the talking he's going to."

Through the open door, I could see a child playing in a pen in the middle of the living room floor. I could see cigarette smoke and hear a radio playing.

"There's a boy who's going to die in five days," I said. "Surely, if your husband can help to prevent that—"

"Al's not interested," she interrupted. She started to close the door.

"I *am*," I said quickly, and flashed my buzzer.

"Save it," she said. Her laugh was short, and scornful. "A private dick, geez." The door closed.

I went down the steps again and out to the Dusy. There was a new car here I'd noticed before, a '47 model in a popular make—clean and shiny. I wondered if it was Al's. I wrote the license number down in the book with the addresses.

Maybe Al was fed up with questions. And maybe Al was afraid of questions. I'd seen him again.

The license bureau would be closed now. I could maybe get it through the chief but I didn't want to bother him any more than necessary. This guy I knew in the license bureau would give it to me tomorrow.

I was hungry, but I drove down to the big garage at 4th and Edison first.

It took some finagling. It took some double talk to convince the boss down there that I was on semi-official business. But I finally got the route sheet I wanted.

Al had had a fare at two o'clock from the Harmony Hut to an address out on 53rd. He'd had another at two-thirty from the stand on 12th to a suburban address. At three-twelve, he'd been back at the stand, because he'd picked up another call from there.

Nothing else between two-thirty and three-twelve. Maybe he was cruising. But if he wasn't, he'd taken a strange route from the suburban address back to the stand. Cabbies don't take the long way around, not on their own time.

I phoned Nels Keeling, Tod's attorney, from a drug store but his office didn't answer. I phoned him at home and his wife said he was out of town. I left my office number with her for Nels to call later.

I wondered if Keeling had investigated the strange route of Al Coleman. I didn't think so. He didn't have my suspicious nature. He was a good lawyer, but a bad one for a murder case.

A lot of my work would have to wait until tomorrow. I wanted the testimony in court and Doc Waters' verdict as to the death and I wanted to talk to the technical men personally.

I went over to Mac's for supper. Mac was talking to a customer about Tunney. "A credit to the profession, that's what he was," Mac was saying. "A gentleman, that's what. He marked Dempsey up plenty, both fights. Don't get the idea he was a powder-puff."

"This place open for business," I asked, "or is it your discussion hour?"

"Ha-ha," Mac said hollowly. "You're so funny, Jonesy. Did you want to buy something?"

"Something to eat." I admitted, "and something to drink—if it's not too much trouble."

"I got hamburger," he said. "A hamburger sandwich?"

"With onions. And a glass of beer while I'm waiting."

He drew the beer and set it on the bar in front of me.

"I was just up to see Tod Nelson, Mac," I said.

He was all interest. "You working on that. Jonesy? When'd you start working on that?"

"Today. What do you think of Tod, Mac?"

"A good boy." He nodded emphatically. "He got robbed, Jonesy. Tod's a clean kid. Best damned welterweight in the world, too." He paused. "How's he taking it?"

"He isn't," I said. "He quit."

Mac's eyes were round. "You don't mean—not suicide—?"

I shook my head. "Just mentally. He thinks it's foolish for me to work on it, it's hopeless."

"He don't know you, Jonesy," Mac said, and went down to fry the hamburger.

My boy, my Mac… After the humiliation of this day, I had to come here to feed my stomach and my ego.

I had another beer with the hamburger and some coffee after that. Then I went back to my little apartment to shower and shave and put on another suit. I decided I might try to see the count this evening.

THE COUNT HAD married again, but not for money this time. He'd married a woman from his own background, the world of impoverished royalty. She was a duchess who'd foresaken her use of the title, a slim, dark woman with enormous brown eyes. It was she who opened the door of their apartment to my ring.

"Countess Terrati?" I asked.

She nodded.

I told her who and what I was and that I'd like to talk to the Count.

She sighed. "About that frightful business, Mr. Jones?"

I nodded.

She hesitated. "I can't see, Mr. Jones, what's to be gained by this—"

"Perhaps a man's life," I said.

She sighed again. "Well, all right. But hurry, won't you? We're due at the theatre in half an hour." She led the way to the living room, a vast studio living room furnished in bleached woods and soft colors.

The count sat in an overstuffed chair, reading. He looked up, then rose as I entered.

He was extremely tall, aristocratically thin, with a high, narrow but somehow handsome face. The countess introduced us and explained my business.

He said: "I'd be glad to help in any way I can," and indicated a chair for me.

I sat down and he sat down. The countess went over to stand near his chair. She lit a cigarette but all her attention, I could sense, was on me.

I said: "It isn't my purpose to embarrass you, but you were married to the Abbott girl, count. You were her first husband. If there's anything in her background that might prove helpful in this business, I'd appreciate it."

He was frowning. "I don't—quite understand."

"If I'm to assume Tod Nelson didn't kill her," I went on, "it's reasonable to assume she had some other enemy. It may have been an enemy of long standing or it may have been a prowler. If it is some enemy out of her past, you might know of it."

I was talking to him, but watching her. She was perfectly poised and apparently indifferent, but I could feel her tenseness just the same.

The count was still frowning. "She had all the petty, malicious enemies a woman in her station is heir to, Mr. Jones. I can't believe they were guilty of any crime more vicious than gossip. I certainly don't intend to name any of them."

The countess expelled a cloud of faintly perfumed smoke.

I said: "I wouldn't expect you to, count. It's not a gossiper I'm looking for. It's a murderer."

I thought he flinched.

The countess said quietly: "That was tactless, Mr. Jones. You've forgotten the count was married to Mrs. Theosophulus."

She accented the wrestler's name. She made a savage bit of irony out of that. Again I thought the count winced.

"I'm sorry," I said.

The count didn't seem to be hearing us. He was thoughtful. He looked sad. He said softly: "If she had to die, it's too bad she didn't die before she met that—that animal."

"The wrestler, darling?" the countess asked.

He looked at her and away. He looked at me and said: "I'm sorry Mr. Jones. But there's really nothing I can tell you. I've told police all I knew, which was little. I'd prefer not to talk about it at all."

"I see," I said. "I don't suppose you saw very much of her after the divorce." I rose.

They seemed to be turned to stone. Both of them staring at me.

The count's voice was hoarse. "What did you mean by that, Mr. Jones?"

The countess said evenly: "I'm sure it was another of his tactless remarks." She turned to him. "We'll be late for the theatre, dear."

He seemed to shake himself. "Yes—of course—"

Nobody walked with me to the door. I said good-bye, but the countess only nodded. The count seemed to be still in his daze.

I left them and went down to the car. It was still early and Nick Theosophulus didn't live too far from here. I had never seen a Greek wrestler up close. It should make an interesting study.

The Dusy went purring up Prospect to Kane, down Kane to Newhall and out to a section of small homes and flats. There was a light on at 4534 Newhall. It was a small, frame cottage.

I don't know what I was expecting, but certainly not this. Perhaps I'd been unconsciously expecting a fat and sweaty man in a pair of faded trunks, a bald man with a bullet head. But not this—this Adonis, this Apollo… This tall, broad and handsome young man in the sport coat standing there in the open doorway grinning at me.

He was blond and tanned and amiable, right out of *MGM*. He said: "Well, you must have something to say. Say it."

"I'm looking for Nick Theosophulus," I said.

"You're looking *at* him," he answered. "You're a collector, no doubt."

"No," I said. "No, I'm a private investigator, Mr. Theosophulus, and I'd like a little of your time."

"I've enough of that," he said. "Come in."

I went in to a small living room furnished for comfort. I took a chair and he sat on the davenport.

I TOLD HIM I'd just been to see the Terratis.

"That louse," he said, and his good nature was gone for the moment. He looked at me sharply. "What'd he have to say?"

"Not much. He seemed rather preoccupied."

"Sure, sure. But don't think his mind isn't going a mile a minute. He's fooled a lot of people, that fascist devil."

"Fascist?" I said. "I didn't know that."

"Not many did. But when the Moose was just learning to

speak from a balcony, Terrati was very, very close to him. Since Lantern-Jaw took the count, Terrati's changed parties, I hear. He's a red-hot Commie, now."

"Quite a jump," I said.

"Don't even think it," he answered. "It's just a change of name."

"Maybe," I said. "But I don't think my business has international complications. It's about your former wife, Nick."

"I guessed that," he said. "You working for Tod?"

"For his sister."

"Oh," he said, "Joan." His voice was gentle. He expelled his breath slowly and stared past me. "Tod got a rough deal."

"You know him."

"Sure. I've seen him fight. You don't think he'd use a club if he wanted to kill somebody, do you? You don't think he'd batter a woman to death with a steel bar or whatever the hell was used?"

"It doesn't seem likely," I admitted. "But who else?"

"Count Terrati would be my choice. I wouldn't know why and I know he's got a sound alibi for that night, but it would be his kind of work."

I smiled and said: "Maybe you're prejudiced."

"Maybe. Just don't underrate that yegg, is all. He's smooth, with his fine clothes and scholarly, gentlemanly manners. He's trained to be smooth. Just don't put murder past him."

I said: "You don't think this might have been a—political murder, do you?"

Nick shrugged. "Probably not. But: if she threatened to expose him—" He shook his head. "No. Lila wasn't a political type. She probably never knew what was going on."

There wouldn't be, I felt sure, much information from Nick

Theosophulus unless it was information about the count. I asked a few more questions and drew blanks.

I thanked him and prepared to leave.

At the door he said: "You need any help on this? I mean free help? Any errands to run or stuff like that?"

"I guess not," I said, "but thanks. For Tod, huh?"

"Partly. But for Lila, too. We didn't hit it off and she divorced me. But it was fun while it lasted. It isn't anything I'll ever forget."

I said there wasn't anything I could think of, but if I needed him, I'd let him know. I said, Good night and walked down to the Dusy.

They both remembered Lila, I reflected; both Nick and the count. She must have been some girl at that. And they hated each other. Because of Lila? Or because of politics? Because of Lila, I would guess.

There was a car parked up the block, one I hadn't noticed when I drove up. Nothing unusual about that excepting it was the same kind of car that had been parked in front of the cabbie's house this afternoon.

I couldn't read the license number from here. I climbed into the Dusy and the car up the block pulled away. Its lights flashed on as it swung around the corner and disappeared.

I went home to bed.

It was cooler next morning as the wind was from the north. I went over to Mac's for breakfast. I read the paper there and dawdled before walking the half block to my office.

Joan Nelson was waiting in front of my office in a Chev club coupé. She got out as I approached.

Her eyes searched my face. I said; "I've nothing much to report. Come on up to the office."

Up there, I told her what I'd done the day before. I said: "Do you think Tod learned something about the count from Lila? Did he ever mention anything like that to you?"

She shook her head.

I said: "How did Tod meet Lila?"

"Through Mike Bradford. It was at a party."

Mike Bradford was Tod's manager.

"That was after she'd divorced Theosophulus?"

The girl nodded. "It was only about ten months ago." Her hands were in her lap, one firmly locked in the other. Her face was pale, but the deep blue eyes were determined. "How about that Coleman, that cab driver?"

"He won't talk to me. I'm going to do some checking on him today."

"He talked to me," she said. "But I'm sure he was lying. He's the key to the whole thing. I think somebody's bought him."

"Maybe," I said, "but it wouldn't be anybody I'd seen so far. Al wouldn't travel in those circles. Remember this—from the police viewpoint, he's the perfect, uninterested witness. A cruising cabbie who just happened to recognize Tod leaving the apartment. There's no tie-up, there's no reason for him to lie."

"But he lied—"

"Or made a mistake."

"Mistake," she said in a low scornful voice. "Would he identify someone in a case as important as this if he wasn't sure? If he wasn't sure—or lying?"

"Probably not. Though I've had some strange experiences with witnesses."

Her head was bent now, and she was close to tears. "It's all so confused," she said, "so hopeless." Then she was crying quietly.

3

Red Tentacles

THE SUN GLINTED off her red-gold hair, glistened in the tears moving slowly down the pale, faintly freckled cheeks. I wanted to go over and take her in my arms, but I didn't. I sat there and said nothing.

After a few moments, she fumbled in her purse for a handkerchief. "I'm sorry," she said. "I don't often break down like that. But it's been such a rotten, *machine-like* business from the beginning. It's as though we're up against something too complicated and too well organized to fight."

"They all look tough until they're cracked," I said. "And the easiest ones to crack are the well organized ones. There's a pattern to those. We've just got to find out who wove the pattern."

She tried a smile, but it was weak. "I don't want you to think I haven't confidence in you, Mr. Jones. Mr. Keeling assured me you were the best detective in town."

I made some remark and told her I would do everything I could. I didn't tell her it might not be enough, and I didn't tell her not to worry, because there wasn't anything for her to do but worry after the deal Tod had received. I told her I would keep in touch with her right along and she left.

Then I sat there for minutes feeling like a knight without a horse. On an impulse I phoned Jack Elder.

Jack was an operative for a nationwide agency and I knew

he'd done some work on the Commies. I asked him about the count.

He didn't answer right away.

"All right," I said. "So it's agency business and Federal business and I'm just a jerk shamus trying to make an honest dollar. It wouldn't matter to you if Tod Nelson went to the chair. You'd get your salary just the same, and your expenses—"

"Stop talking so I can think," he interrupted me. "I'm trying to remember. That was some time ago I worked on that, Mort." Another pause. "If I remember right, the count was anti-Commie. It seems to me he was one of their favorite targets, the dissolute nobleman marrying a product of America's greed."

"That was before Mussolini began to wane?"

"Oh, sure, sure. That was a hell of a while ago. Look Mort, I can get you more on this, current stuff. One of our operatives worked on it recently."

"I'd appreciate it," I said and he told me he'd call me back as soon as he got it.

Then I went over to the courthouse.

The testimony in the Nelson case read like a play, or rather, like the rough first draft of a corny play by a college sophomore. Devine was there as the hero or sub-hero, perhaps, because District Attorney Whitney, one of Devine's crummy cousins, had all the long and hammy speeches. He's a pompous, fairly articulate man who knows more than his speeches indicate. His corn is a calculated corn, devised to swing a jury, and he had swung this one.

Because there'd been no confession, because Tod Nelson had a good name in the male public's mind, his vilifying of Tod had been by inference only. His relating of the evidence garnered by the able Devine and the (vast) resources of the specialists who'd helped Devine, was detailed, seemingly infallible. His summing up was a mixture of science, logic, corn and venom. It was, as I'd suspected, a Whitney wind-up to a Devine job. And with all the honest, capable, hardworking men in the department, it was a complete mystery to me how Devine hung onto his job—even considering the relatives. Of course, he'd been there a long, long time....

I got another idea and phoned a photographer I knew who worked for the local *Courier-Tribune*. I told him what I wanted.

"Not from the paper, Jonesy," he answered. "They wouldn't let 'em out like that. But I got some of my own."

Could I get three of them?

"Sure. Not this morning—I'm just going out. But I could meet you at noon."

I arranged to meet him at noon and went over to the license bureau. There I learned that the new car I'd seen in front of Al's house was his. The license had been granted only a month ago. I didn't know what a cabbie earned, but considering what a person has to pay for a new car these days, considering that he had a wife and child, it wasn't too unreasonable to assume Al might have had a recent windfall. Of course it maybe have been an uncle who died, or something like that. But I'm suspicious, by nature.

I made some other calls: on Tod's manager, Mike Bradford; on the restaurant where the waiter had overheard Tod arguing with Lila. The waiter wasn't there. He was home, sleeping. Mike Bradford was a short man with no hair and a scowl.

"We got a bum decision," he said. "But what can you do? The kid was railroaded by Whitney, and Whitney's sure as hell going to look bad if the case breaks open again. Homicide ain't going to give you any help. You can bank on that."

"They never have," I said, "outside of Glen Harvey. I thought you might know something about Tod and Lila that would give me a lead."

He shook his head. "Tod didn't talk about it. I think he wasn't too proud about getting mixed up with a dame like that. But she sure had the hooks in him."

Not only in him but in Nick and the count, too. And perhaps some others… Perhaps the killer, some gent out of her busy past I hadn't met and wouldn't meet. That's the angle you're always dealing with in murder. Some mental defective on the prowl, some minor character nursing an unvoiced grievance, some sudden burst of fury between normally friendly and reasonable people. That's what makes unsolved murders: not the cute and tricky contrivances of the premeditated jobs, but the senseless, illogical incidents of chance.

Only this one looked contrived; that was my only hope—that it was planned and had a pattern.

I went over to meet the photographer for lunch. He had the pictures I wanted, good shots, and from the neck up as I wanted them.

Then I went back to Vine Street, nearly to the end, to the duplex abode of Al Coleman, cabbie and key witness.

THE SAME BLONDE waited at the top of the landing and she didn't look happy to see me. "My husband's asleep," she said, "and he don't want to be disturbed."

"I won't disturb him any more than I need to," I told her, "but it's very important I see him."

"Important to who?"

"To him. And to the police."

That look of scorn came again to her blank face.

"You could call the police department and ask for the chief," I said. "You could ask him about me."

She looked doubtful now, a little frightened.

"Or I can go and get a couple of cops and come back?" I said.

She was frightened. She said: "What's Al done—? Is it about his being a—witness?"

"I don't know he's done anything he shouldn't," I said. "But it's about his being a witness, all right."

She stared at me and then toward the open door. "Come in," she said. "I'll wake him up."

I went into the living room, a room of mohair and cheap wall paper, a clean, dead room. The play pen wasn't in sight, nor the baby. I took a seat on the davenport while she went through an archway into the house beyond.

I heard a murmur of voices—a grumbling masculine voice, hers getting shrill. I heard some bad words. Then Al said: "Aw right, aw right, lemme get dressed."

She came back into the living room looking pale. "He'll be here right away." She sat on the davenport's matching chair and stared at the rug nervously.

We waited in silence.

Then there were steps coming through the dining room and Al Coleman stood framed in the archway. He was a fairly broad, medium tall man with dark, thick eyebrows and dark, unruly hair. He was wearing dark trousers, a blue cotton shirt and a scowl.

"O.K. peeper, what's the beef?" he said.

"Just some questions," I said, "about the Nelson case."

He was lighting a cigarette. He didn't sit down, but stayed in the archway. "So, go ahead."

"I wondered if you were sure it *was* Tod you saw. I thought you might be wrong about that. Did you know him pretty well?"

"I don't know him at all. I seen him fight lots of times and I know what he looks like. It was him, all right."

"Fights cost a lot of money," I said. "You see many of them?"

He looked at me suspiciously. "I see all the big ones. Maybe I make a lot of money, peeper."

"I see," I said. "We've got some other suspects in this case, too. Maybe it was one of them you saw." I took out the pictures and held them out to him.

He hesitated and then he came over to take them from me. He looked them over carefully, suspiciously.

"Could it have been one of those?"

"No," he said.

"You've seen those men before, though, haven't you?"

He shook his head. "Never." He seemed relieved.

"That's very strange," I said.

The blonde was staring at me. Al was staring at me. I said: "One of them is the lightweight champ, one the welter champ, the other the middle champ. They've all fought here, often. You see *all* the big fights, Al?"

"They're bad pictures," he said. He was breathing hard.

"They're good pictures," I answered. "You could recognize a welterweight contender on a dim street at three in the morning, but you don't know the titleholders."

"What you getting at?" he asked. His eyes were shining, hard.

"And you took a very strange route back from the Heights to the cab stand if you went past that apartment, Al." I paused. "I don't think you were ever there. I don't think you saw Tod that night or even anybody who looked like him."

The blonde said something inarticulate. Al said: "You calling me a liar, peeper?"

"Not yet," I said. "And don't get any ideas. I'm armed."

"Get out," he said. "If you come again, bring a warrant. But get out of here—*now*."

"Al—" the blonde said.

He didn't even look at her. "Shut up!" He was still glaring at me. "Get moving."

I rose. "Sure," I said. "Play it dumb, Al. Cover up for the killer. Let Tod go to the chair. They'll really nail you if that happens, Al. The D.A. will make it a point to see you get the book," I walked to the door.

He didn't say another word. He stood there glaring at me. The blonde had risen and her glance traveled between us, back and forth, back and forth.

I went out and closed the door quietly behind me.

When I was halfway down the stairs I heard his voice, loud and angry. He called her a name. The baby began to squall.

I went out, started the Dusy and drove down to the corner. There was an angle street here and I turned to park on that. From this position I could watch the new car in front of the Coleman house.

I waited an hour and nothing happened. I waited another half hour and decided nothing was going to happen. I'd banked on his wife not knowing. If she didn't, I figured Al would go to see the person he was covering for. If his wife knew though, he could use the phone.

Well, maybe he figured there was no hurry. Maybe he had only himself to cover, but I couldn't believe that. It didn't add up right.

I drove back to the office. There was some mail up there waiting for me, but nothing important. I was sorting through this as the phone rang.

It was Glen Harvey. He said: "Devine's heard about what you're doing, Jonesy. He wants you to wait at your office for him."

"O.K.," I said. "Thanks for calling, Glen."

I DIDN'T HAVE long to wait before I heard Devine's heavy tread on the stairs. Then he was in the doorway, his thin face sour but showing no anger so far.

As a matter of fact, I thought he looked more uncertain than angry which I didn't understand right away.

He took my customer's chair and said: "I've just had a call from Al Coleman."

I said nothing.

He rubbed the palms of his hands together, and studied them. He looked up. "I know Al. I've known him a long time."

So. No wonder he didn't look angry. I still said nothing.

"I might—" He shook his head. "Maybe I didn't go into his story as well as I should have."

"What did he say to you when he called?" I asked.

"He was complaining about you bothering him. He said you'd been checking his route that night, and you pulled some kind of trick with pictures on him. He said he's clean and he doesn't want any private eyes bothering him."

"And you come here to tell me to lay off?"

Devine shook his head. "I came here to see if I missed the boat."

I could only stare at him. This wasn't the Devine I knew, this reasonable, mistake-admitting searcher for a truth. This was a new characterization and I was wary.

He went through the palm-rubbing routine again. "Haven't you got anything to say?"

"Not much. You surprised me. I wasn't expecting this."

Some of the old hardness was in his voice now. "Just what were you expecting?"

"A dressing down. A few nasty words telling me to lay off or you'd have my scalp."

He looked at me fully. "You think I'd let a man go to the chair if there was a reasonable doubt in my mind about his guilt? You think I'd do that?"

"No," I admitted. "No, you wouldn't. I just can't get the quiet approach."

He ignored that last. He said: "What have you uncovered on Al?"

"Nothing you could jail him on." I went on to tell him about the car and the pictures and the strange route.

He took it all in, frowning; When I'd finished, he nodded. "I've been hearing some things about Al, lately. It's too bad I hadn't heard 'em before the trial. I bowl with him, you see, and I thought I knew him pretty well."

I was beginning to understand his attitude. He hated my guts but if I could help him, if I could help to get him out of a very bad hole... I said: "He should be watched."

He nodded. "I've got Glen Harvey on him right now." He

was still frowning. "But where does Al fit in? He hasn't any connections, so far as I know, with anybody who knew the Abbott girl. He looked like a Grade-A witness to me."

"He looked that way to the jury, too," I said. "That's probably what decided them."

Devine looked at the floor, his face rigid. "O.K., O.K.—what makes you think Nelson isn't guilty?"

"Just my belief in him. What makes *you* think so?"

He flinched. "I'm not saying he isn't. I'm saying I might have missed on Al. That doesn't open the case again not all the way."

Not all the way, I thought. *Just enough to worry him. Just enough to make him treat me like a friend.*

"That count," he continued, "was my first choice. That Greek my second. The count's covered all the way and the Greek is clean enough so a jury wouldn't convict him. That leaves Nelson."

"If it's that simple, it leaves Nelson," I said. "There's a hundred and thirty-odd million other people in the country. It could be almost anybody else."

"They were quarreling," Devine said. "The waiter testified to that and Nelson admitted it." He looked at me challengingly. "You got a better suspect?"

I had to admit I didn't have—not right now anyway.

"If you get one," he said, "you'd be in a good position, wouldn't you?"

I knew what he meant. He meant in a good position to embarrass himself and the D.A. He knew that what recent pinches I'd had had gone to Glen Harvey. He knew he hadn't many friends outside of his relatives. He knew the chief wasn't one of his friends.

I said: "I don't quite get you."

"You get me all right," he said.

I shrugged. "You're a part of the department, Devine. You know I never work against the department."

"I'm talking about *me* not the department," he said.

"The only times I've bucked you," I explained, "have been in defense."

"I'm not bucking you this time. Don't get the wrong idea. I'm not afraid of my job or you or the papers. You can believe that or not. I don't give a damn. But I'm admitting I may have missed on that Nelson-Abbott deal. I don't want to see an innocent man burn any more than you do. And if you've got something, I'll work along with you."

I almost admired him. For the first time since I'd known him, he was talking like a man, not an animated boil or an apple-polishing politician. If I hadn't seen him in so many other characterizations, this one would have won me all the way. But I'd known him so long....

"O.K.," I said, "I'll be honest with you. I haven't anything but a lot of angles, so far. When and if I fit them together into something that might help, it'll be Homicide's body and *your* baby."

He rose then and held out his hand. "I'll keep in touch with you. And you with me?"

I shook his hand. "I'll let you know anything I find."

4

—

No Pattern Yet

IT MUST HAVE made a hell of a tableau, me and Devine shaking hands and looking at each other like a brother act. I was glad nobody was watching.

Then I was listening to his heavy feet going down the stairs again. I shook my head for some reason. Maybe I'd surprised myself. But he had come to me openly and honestly.

The phone rang and it was the chief. "Devine there?" he asked.

"He just left," I said.

A pause and a cough. "You—ah—got together, all right?"

I closed my eyes. "What do you mean, chief?"

"I sent him over," the voice went on, "to tell you that Homicide is working right with you on this Nelson business. Didn't he tell you that?"

"Why—yes he did," I answered. "I probably wasn't listening as closely as I should, but he told me that all right."

"Weren't listening—?" His voice was gruff. "What does that mean? What are you talking about? Isn't this case important enough to merit your attention, Mr. Jones?"

That *Mr. Jones* is for when he's annoyed. "It's important," I said, "and I'm working like a dog on it, chief. And I'm working with Devine." I paused. "He and I understand each other, now."

"All right," he said. "You're making some sense." He went on with a few words about cooperation and vigilance and some other virtues he admires.

After he'd finished and hung up, I went over to open the window. The office, I thought, needed an airing.

Then I sat in my chair and thought of nothing. They all went around and around in my head, making no pattern—Tod and his sister, the count and his wife, the Coleman pair, the Greek and Mike Bradford and Devine and the waiter and even Nels Keeling, the lawyer, who hadn't phoned as yet.

So I phoned him at his office. He was there.

"I was just going to call you," he said. "What's the trouble?"

That's automatic with a lawyer, to think of trouble. I said: "You do any checking on the state's witnesses in that Nelson case?"

"Mmmm—no. They seemed disinterested enough to me. Something come up?"

I told him about Al Coleman. I asked: "Think you could get a stay of execution on that kind of information? I hate to be fighting time in this business."

He didn't think he could unless I got something a little more substantial to offer. The governor would want a recommendation from the D.A. "And Whitney and I aren't exactly lodge brothers," he finished.

I said I'd try to get something more substantial. I told him about Devine and his heart-breaking confession of possible incompetence. "The police will be working along with us now," I said, "and so will Whitney probably."

He said he was glad to hear that, but he didn't sound like he believed it. He repeated that he'd need more than I had so far before he'd start any action for a stay.

A careful, conservative lawyer, Nels Keeling. Probably a very good man for probate work.

It was nearly five o'clock and all I'd had for the day's labor was some suspicion regarding the honesty of Al Coleman.

I went out to eat, but not at Mac's. I wanted to see that waiter anyway, and I could eat at the restaurant. It was less than a block away from the apartment where the Abbott-Terrati-Theosophulus girl had lived. She hadn't gone back to her family after her last divorce; she'd lived alone.

The waiter was there and willing to talk. He was more than willing—he was eager. He'd never been this important before and the chances were he'd never be this important again. He told me all he'd heard in great detail. He told me all he'd thought with the same attention to detail. Then he took my order.

He told me the same thing Tod had told me. They'd quarreled about the count. Tod had accused her of infidelity.

I was just beginning to attack my shrimp cocktail when Nick Theosophulus walked in. He seemed startled when he saw me but headed right for my table.

"I didn't know you ate here," he said by way of greeting.

"First time," I said. "You eat here often, Nick?"

He pulled out the chair across from mine, and sat down. "Often enough. Lila and I used to come here all the time. Just—habit I guess." He picked up my menu. "You getting anywhere on that business?"

"Not very far."

He shook his head. "You haven't got much time."

I had four days, after tonight. And there was nowhere I could think of to go tonight. I'd checked everything there was to check and had seen everyone there was to see.

Before turning in I went down to headquarters. And learned that Glen Harvey wasn't tailing Al Coleman. He'd never found him; Al was missing.

That was Thursday night.

They didn't find him Friday though they were combing the town. They had his wife down at headquarters and I was there when they grilled her. She knew nothing about where he had gone. She said she was worried about him. But she didn't look worried to me.

Friday afternoon I talked to Joan again. She was a little more weary, but no less determined. The very fact that Al was missing seemed a good omen to her. Nels Keeling thought he had enough for a stay of execution now. But the governor didn't agree.

Friday night I went out to talk to Mrs. Coleman. Perhaps she'd tell me something she'd be afraid to tell the police. She wouldn't talk to me at all.

Friday night I didn't sleep so well.

Saturday, Jack Elder called and he had the story about the count's conversion. The count followed the party line like a true comrade. He told me how it came about that the count had been shown the light. He said he'd bill me for the research.

I WENT OVER to see the count. He didn't seem surprised to see me. He was home alone and he ushered me in like an old friend. He was smooth, all right.

When we were seated in the studio living room, I fired the opening gun. I said: "I've been wondering, Count Terrati, if this could have been a—a *political* murder."

He considered that, chewing his lower lip reflectively. Then he said: "I don't follow you, Mr. Jones."

"As a threat," I went on, "to you. As a warning that your recent conversion to a—a liberal viewpoint wasn't acceptable to your former friends."

He was watching me now. He wasn't taking his eyes off of me for a second. "Are you saying that Lila may have died as a result of some beliefs I hold? Aren't you being ridiculous?"

"I'm trying not to be. But I'm overlooking nothing. A blow at her would be a blow at you, wouldn't it? She still meant a lot to you."

"We were friends if that's what you mean. We were civilized people, Mr. Jones, and the separation was mutually agreeable. But there wasn't any of the—affection you infer."

"The night Lila died," I said, "she and Tod were quarreling about *you.*"

He smiled. "Am I to be responsible for a jealous man's hallucinations?"

"He must have had some reason to be jealous."

Again he smiled. "It has been my experience that reason or knowledge aren't necessary for jealousy. It's a sickness, Mr. Jones. It's unreasonable and misleading. You aren't trying to involve me in this mess because of a jealous man's accusations, are you?"

"I'm not trying to do anything but find a murderer," I said. "I thought you'd be willing to help me, in that."

He shrugged. "If I could have helped I would have before the trial." He paused. "You seem to have investigated my background rather thoroughly, Mr. Jones."

"That's right. But don't mistake my motives. I'm not on

a witch hunt. Your beliefs are your business. My job isn't concerned with that unless it helps to solve a murder. I'm a private investigator, not a Congressional committee."

"I see. And where did you get all this misinformation?"

I heard a door open, and close. I heard footsteps. I said: "It took some digging. It isn't too generally known. I wouldn't worry about it."

The countess was in the room looking composed and lovely. Looking a bit annoyed when she saw me.

Count Terrati said: "Mr. Jones has been accusing me of infidelity, darling."

She smiled at me, a smile as phoney as a lead dollar. "You meant mental infidelity, no doubt? I keep a very close watch on my attractive husband, Mr. Jones. But I can't stop his dreaming."

I said: "The count has misquoted me. A lot of other people have accused him of infidelity. I merely repeated what I'd heard."

Neither of them seemed as poised as they'd been a moment before. The count regained his first. He said quietly: "Mr. Jones has also been investigating my—political leanings. I'm not sure he approves."

"I didn't say that," I objected. "I'm a liberal, myself."

They both smiled then and looked at each other. I felt like a canary between two cats.

The count said: "Very commendable, Mr. Jones. We'll have to get together on that. But some other time, I'm afraid. We're leaving in a few minutes to spend a week-end in the country."

There wasn't anything I could do about that, except to say good-bye. I had no authority, no evidence. I had nothing but the mentally bruised feeling of having achieved nothing. I left them.

The Dusy growled as I started her and coughed as I eased out from the curb. She seemed unhappy.

I went down to Headquarters. On the way I drove past the Sports Bowl. There on a wall was a poster of Nick Theosophulus in all his half-naked glory. *"The Greek God,"* the poster read, *"versus Moose Mulligan. Two out of three falls."*

Devine and Harvey were coming down the concrete steps as I pulled up in front of Headquarters. They saw me and came directly over. Devine said: "We've just got a call. You can come along if you want."

I got out as Glen Harvey added: "A couple of kids found Coleman—out on Atkinson and Hubbard." We were walking toward the department car. "An empty lot. Knife in his throat. He's been dead for some time, I guess."

Glen drove. There was no dialogue on the way. Devine looked worried, but he had a right to look worried. The Nelson case was blowing up in his face.

It was a corner lot, high with weeds, littered with junk. It was in a more or less deserted section of town, comprising a few run-down dwellings and a deserted warehouse. This lot had formerly been used for parking the way it looked, for there was a break in the curb and a gravel driveway now thickly spotted with weeds.

AL COLEMAN LAY near the end of the gravel, his eyes open, his face slack. The eyes seemed to be surprised. There was a darkness staining his shirt, a darkness that had once been the color of blood. Doc Waters was bending over the body when we got there.

Out on the sidewalk two uniformed policemen were keeping a gang of boys and a few adults off the lot.

Devine said: "How long, doc?"

"Can't tell right away. More than a day."

The internes were coming with the stretcher. Devine looked at me and away. Glen said: "It looks as though you were right about Coleman, Jonesy."

There was no satisfaction in that, for what Al knew had died with him. We had no lead at all now. I walked back along the gravel, looking for a spot of mud, anything that would show tire tracks. There was nothing.

Devine walked along with me. He said: "Now that he's dead, maybe that wife of his will chirp. She's got nothing to hide now. Let's go over there."

The three of us drove over to Vine, to the duplex of the Widow Coleman. She was out in the front when we got there, sunning the baby in his buggy and sitting on the porch reading a magazine.

Devine said: "Let me do the talking."

The three of us went up onto the porch, Glen and I well in the rear. But not far enough back so we couldn't hear Devine say: "We've found your husband, Mrs. Coleman."

She must have guessed immediately. For her face drained of its color; the magazine dropped to the floor. She took a deep breath and tried to say something. She put a hand on the porch railing.

"He was stabbed to death," Devine said.

She started to sway on her chair and Glen moved past me. He caught her as she toppled.

Tactful, thoughtful Devine… and he'd known her husband.

I went through the open doorway and up into the kitchen. I was ready with a glass of water when she opened her eyes again.

She talked after a while. She'd been expecting something bad to happen. Al had been acting so strangely the past year, staying away from home on his nights off, talking so queerly.

She was near hysterics, talking, talking, talking—and saying nothing. She told about the money he'd said he'd won in a poker game, the money he'd used for the car. That was right before the trial and she knew he'd been lying about the poker game.

After a while, Glen and I went down to the car.

Something was digging at my mind, screaming to be recognized, but it wouldn't break through to the surface. In her words there'd been a tie-up, but I didn't see it, not then.

Devine came down to the car after a few minutes, and we started back to the station. Devine stared out the window saying nothing.

Then, just before we stopped in front of headquarters, he said: "What have we got that we didn't have before? What have we got but another murder?"

"And I was going on vacation next week," Harvey said. "I suppose this'll crack it wide open again."

"You mean the Nelson case?" Devine said.

Glen was pulling up to the curb. "That's right."

"I don't see it," Devine said. "We'd need more than this to take to the governor."

I didn't say anything. Under the new love-Devine policy, I was avoiding arguments. We went in and down the hall to Devine's office. The personal effects of the late Al Coleman were on his desk in there in a big envelope.

Devine went through them methodically, one by one. A ring of keys, some change, a ring, a cheap cigarette lighter, a wallet. He went through the wallet.

He smiled when he came across the card. He said: "No wonder Al's changed. No wonder he was away from home on his nights off." He tossed it over to me, and I read it.

It was a membership card in the Communist party.

That's what had been buzzing around my brain. That's the tie-up I'd been looking for right along.

I said: "Maybe this case is wide-open again."

"How do you figure that?" Devine asked.

I told him about the count.

"Let's get him," he said. "Let's bring him down and work him over. I never did like that jerk; he was too smooth."

"He's out of town," I said, "for the weekend."

"How long's that?" Glen asked. "How long's a weekend?"

"Some of them end on Sunday night," I said, "and some on Monday."

"We'll put a man on his apartment," Devine said. "We'll get him the second he comes home."

"Tod goes to the chair on Monday," I said, "unless Whitney asks for a stay on this information."

"I'll see," Devine said. "I'll talk to him. Glen, send Schultz over to that apartment right away. Maybe they haven't left. If they have, tell him to wait there until he's relieved."

After checking with the technical men with Doc and with the Chief, I went back to the office and phoned Joan Nelson. I told her what had happened.

"But," I finished, "nothing's settled, yet. We haven't got a shred of evidence besides the tie-up. No prints on the knife, no witnesses that saw anything strange, not a damned thing. And don't tell this to anybody. We're keeping it from the papers, too, for the time being."

"Everything's going to be all right," she said. "I know it, I know it—"

I was almost sorry I'd told her. For everything wasn't all right, not by a long, long way. Going up against the count was a man's work, getting anything out of him he didn't want to reveal was something for Superman.

I HAD MY thoughts on the matter, my own private unshared thoughts. Properly worded, properly presented, maybe it would work. Maybe and maybe not. I feared Devine's heavy hand though, and it was Devine's case. If he would listen to reason....

It didn't sound like reason to him when I phoned him. It sounded like I was trying to take the play away from him. "We'll talk about it, tomorrow," he said. "I've had a bellyfull today."

I went home and tried to sleep. It was tough work. After a pint of rye, I managed it. But even then there were dreams.

Sunday morning was a bad morning, windy, wet and dark. I fried an egg and made some coffee. I took a shower.

It was while I was taking the shower I began to wonder if it was just a weekend the count was on. Maybe he'd left town for good. Maybe things were getting too hot. I had to depend on his ego, on his belief that nothing could come up he couldn't handle.

I went down to the station and Devine was there. He said: "We'll take the evening shift over there. I'm waiting here for the call until then."

He puts in enough time, I'll say that for him. He isn't afraid of work. He's too fast and too careless and too apt to jump at an innocent conclusion, but he surely puts in the hours.

I said: "How about Whitney? Did you talk to him?"

Devine looked at the floor. "He—doesn't think we've got anything."

"How about the chief? He's got some weight?"

"He doesn't want to buck Whitney."

I didn't say any more about that. I went down to the press room. There was a game going and I got into it. I couldn't make a dime. My luck was sour. I hoped it wasn't symbolic. Luck was what I was going to need.

We ate some sandwiches right there for lunch and had some coffee. My luck never changed.

Around supper time Devine came in. He said: "We may as well wait out there as here. I'm getting fed up with this place."

We went out and the rain had stopped. But it was still damp and dark and windy. Devine drove, making time. He was nervous and jumpy.

I said: "Have you thought over what I asked you last night?"

"Yup. We'll play it that way until I think you're on the wrong track. Then we'll play it my way."

I said: "If you crack this, they'll forget about the other."

He didn't answer. He didn't even act like he'd heard me, but I knew he had.

We waited about a half block back from the entrance after sending Glen Harvey home.

It wasn't very entertaining sitting in the car with a man I'd never liked and who'd never liked me. There wasn't much we had to talk about, but it still wasn't boring.

Time passed slowly. Once we had a false alarm—a couple that looked like them, and that gave us some excitement for the moment. But they were a pair of innocents.

We'd been waiting three hours by my watch and three weeks by my imagination when they came walking up the sidewalk toward the apartment entrance. The countess was clinging to his arm and they were laughing about something. They looked like a pair of distinguished and carefree sweethearts.

We gave them ten minutes and then went in and up.

It was the count who opened the door. He saw me and smiled. He saw Devine and frowned. He said: "What is it this time?"

"A murder," I said. "A different kind of murder. A knife, this time."

Nothing on his face, nothing. "Well—? Does it concern me?"

"He was carrying the card," I said. "I thought you might know him. Man named Coleman, Al Coleman. He was the principal witness in the Nelson case."

Something in his eyes, now. Puzzlement? Wonder? "Come in," he said.

We went in to the vast modern living room again. The countess was in there smoking a cigarette standing near one of the high windows. The count said to her: "Al Coleman's been murdered, dear."

She turned to face us. Nothing in her face either. "That's too bad. Was it because of—of that business, you think?"

"We think it was."

There was something on the count's face, something hard to define. It looked like he was groping for something, trying not to believe where his mind was leading him. Then I thought I saw shock there. He said: "Sit down, gentlemen."

We sat down and I said: "We figure that Al was bribed to tell what he did about Tod Nelson. We couldn't figure who did the bribing. Anyway, the person who did began to fear that Al might crack. If Al cracked, the case against Tod cracked. Maybe Al was doing a little blackmailing, too. For one of those two reasons or both, he died."

THE COUNT'S FACE was stone-cold now, and stone-hard. He'd seen the picture. He'd loved her—they'd all loved her. She must have been some girl.

He put his face in his hands, and then took his hands away. He said: "You think it might be a 'political killin',' as you call it. Is that the reason you're here?"

"It's no political killing," I said. "You know that. Politics is the tie-up, but it's no political killing. But unless we get the murderer, it'll be a political mess. That would bring the F.B.I. in. That would be very, very bad for you—and for the party."

The countess said evenly: "I can't follow this. Are you trying to implicate my husband in this latest killing, too, Mr. Jones?"

"Not unless he wants it that way," I said.

She was looking at the count now and he at her. She must have read what was in his eyes for her poise was cracking. She said: "They're trying to trick you, Anthony. They're trying their best to turn you—"

Devine hadn't said a word, but he wasn't missing a word either.

I said: "You gave me quite a lecture on jealousy the last time I was here. You know about that, don't you, at first hand? You live with it."

The countess' voice was higher now. "It's persecution, Anthony. It's capitalistic trickery—"

I said: "Your wife converted you to the cause, didn't she, count? Surely she wouldn't want the party involved in her own jealous crime. She wouldn't want the party to suffer because *she'd* killed your former wife and then used Al Coleman to frame Tod Nelson. She hasn't got any protection coming after killing a loyal worker like Al."

There was the damndest smile on his face now, an unholy smile. He said: "You can believe, gentleman, that this comes as a complete surprise to me. But you've done a clever job, Mr. Jones, and I see the picture now." He turned to his wife. "Wouldn't it be better to confess, dear, and save the party embarrassment? They'll uncover it all. It's merely a matter of time."

The shock was on her face. She was standing near a long library table and she put a hand on that to support herself. "Anthony—" she said, and closed her eyes.

There was some viciousness in his smile. Maybe he was remembering Lila Abbott and what she'd always been to him.

His voice was dead as he threw the countess to the wolves. "It would be better for you to confess, dear. It would save me the unpleasantness of showing them that glove you neglected to destroy, that glove with the blood on it. It's Al's blood, isn't it, dear?"

She tried to say something now and then her hand was fumbling in the drawer of the table in front of her.

I started to rise and so did Devine, for she was holding a gun very steadily in her right hand now. It was pointed at the count.

She put three fast shots into him before Devine could come

up on her from the side. She toppled before Devine got to her.

The count died with that same damned smile on his face.

The glove and a little work-out in Devine's room were enough to break her down. She was going to be nailed for killing the count, anyway; the others probably wouldn't hurt her very much more.

Devine got to Whitney and Whitney got to the governor. Mortimer Jones got a nice check and a kiss from Joan Nelson. The kiss was almost as nice as the check.

Tod never fought again. His fight was gone, buried with Lila Abbott.

A Bier for Baby

She was a lot of corpse, I was a lot of cop.
We had our memories—and one other
thing in common—too much killer!

1

—

Death at Robber's Roost

I'D BEEN THERE two days. I'd seen the "Miracle Mile" on Wilshire and the U.C.L.A. campus. At the Brentwood Country Club, I had shot a respectable (for me) ninety-two. I had seen one movie star, whose name I couldn't recall. But I hadn't seen anyone I knew. I'd driven out alone in the Dusy, because I thought I needed the sun. What I needed most of all was company, being by nature a gregarious animal.

It was in this pensive mood, on Thursday morning, that I sat in a spot called Ben's Badger Bar, talking to Ben, who owned the joint. Ben's from some small town in Wisconsin, and he likes to dwell on the glories of that great state. But he stays in Santa Monica, just the same. Can't leave the business, he explains. California seems to have a certain resemblance to the army, that is, everyone complains when they're in it, but cherish it in their memories.

"I miss the snow," Ben was telling me this morning. "I miss the old pepper a guy gets when that mercury drops. Used to be quite a skater, back home."

I said they were skating, right now, not seventy-five miles from here, but Ben shook his head. "It's not the same," he said.

I never did find out why it wasn't the same. For, at that moment, a feminine voice behind me said, "Mortimer Jones, as I live and breathe."

I turned in happy expectation, to see who this was, living and breathing behind me. It was Myrtle Jessup.

Back in my town, Myrtle had helped me from time to time, for pay. Myrtle sold information. In the trade, she's known as

a stool pigeon, and held in contempt by many. But I liked her.

She hadn't seemed to age any, either above or below the neck. She was wearing a suit of some delicate green. She had on, in

On the tile floor lay Myrtle's body. Her sweater was red with blood....

lieu of a blouse, a turtleneck sweater of fine cashmere. Myrtle does all right by a sweater.

"It's been a long time, Myrt," I said, "but time has been kind to you."

"And you, Jonesy." She shook her head. "How's the big town?"

"Full of snow when I left," I told her. I was studying her all the while, the tight blonde curls, the warm brown eyes, the full mouth, now smiling.

"Do you still drive that Duesenberg?"

I nodded, and asked, "How's Sam?"

She looked at me queerly for a moment. "Sam—you mean Sam Whitnall?" And then, without waiting for a reply: "We're divorced, Jonesy. Over a year ago."

"I didn't know that," I said. "I'm sorry, Myrt. I thought Sam was strictly for you."

"So did I," she said. "When are you going to offer me a drink?"

She's a woman of rare discrimination; she drank rye, just like yours truly. She'd finished the first, and was studying the second, when she said, "Still in business, same business?"

"That's right. Though not out here. This is a vacation, the first in three years."

"You mean, if I put you in the way of a job, an easy, well-paying job that wouldn't take more than an hour, you'd refuse it?"

"I might," I said. "It would depend upon the pay, of course."

"You haven't changed," she said. "Well, we won't talk about it now. There is a chance that I won't need you."

So we talked of other things, and Ben joined in, after a while. It was surprising how the time slid by. I had more rye than I can comfortably handle; that I know. But how it happened that Myrtle and I wound up at that party, I will never know.

I don't even remember the trip over, though we must have gone in the Dusy. I do remember the redhead, though. She was the first thing I noticed.

There were six men there, and four women. Outside of the redhead, I didn't pay much attention to the women. And when I saw who the host was, I thought maybe Myrtle had exceeded the bounds of good taste. The host was Sam Whitnall.

He seemed surprised to see us, but not in any way annoyed. "I didn't know you were in town, Mort," he said. "Settling out here?"

"Just a trip," I told him. The last time I'd seen Sam, we'd been on opposite sides of the fence, but his face showed no animosity now.

"Welcome to Robber's Roost," he said. Then, as Myrtle passed into the living room, leaving us at the door: "Myrt isn't planning any trouble, is she? This is the first I've seen her, since the divorce."

"I couldn't guarantee anything, Sam," I said. "I met her in a bar. And now I'm here, and don't remember getting here. If you think she's got any ideas, that way, we could buzz right along."

"Hell, no," he said. "I should be able to handle anything she can start."

It was a remark I was to remember later.

We went into a living room longer than it was wide and it was wider than any I'd seen before. The ten people already there seemed lost in it.

But it couldn't hide the redhead.

She was standing near the piano, watching the gent who was hammering out some boogie. She had a drink in one hand

and a cigarette in the other, like one of those old John Held, Jr. cartoons. She had more curves than you're likely to get in a cartoon, though.

"Some girl, huh?" Sam said.

"Some girl," I agreed.

"Mine," Sam said, "all mine."

I had another of those alcoholic lapses, after that; the next thing I remember was sitting on a davenport with the redhead. Myrt was dancing with some gent even shorter than she was, and she's fairly short.

The redhead's name, I'd learned, was Rita, Rita Regan, and she'd come to this town to get into pictures. "But you know how those things are," she said.

I didn't, but I nodded sagely, being in a sagely nodding mood.

"And then I met Sam," she went on, "and I've been on the merry-go-round ever since." Some bitterness in the voice, now? "Sam acts as though he owns me. There are times—" She shook her head.

"Sam seems to be doing all right," I said.

"Past tense, you mean," she said. "He did all right. He's in a position now where he doesn't have to do anything. Though I suppose doing nothing would be called doing all right? Do you think so?"

"It's too involved for my present state of mind," I answered. "Couldn't we talk about something less complicated?"

"Well," she said, "what?"

"Well—you."

"There isn't much. I'm from Grand Forks. Do you know where Grand Forks is?"

"One of the Dakotas."

She nodded. "North Dakota. About twenty-thousand hard-working citizens, really a nice town. I was an innocent girl, of course, but possessed of certain charms, and the town seemed a little small to me. So I saved my money, and went to Chicago."

The story went on from there, through hat check girl, modeling, chorus, right up to Hollywood—and Sam. Sam she'd met at the home of one of the town's small producers. Sam hadn't given her a moment's rest since.

"I can't say that I blame him for that," I told her. "If I'd met you first, you'd be getting even less rest."

"I'm blushing. And now, how about you, Mr. Jones? You're a detective, aren't you?"

"More or less."

"You don't look like a detective," she said.

"How do detectives look?"

"Oh, fat and dumb, or tall and broad-shouldered with wise cracks. Or slim and debonair, and sort of brilliant."

"Type casting," I said. "I am a private investigator, and the less I look like those types, the more private I'll be, and the more privacy, the more business."

"And the more business, the oftener you can come out here for vacations?"

"Well, roughly, yes.

"But you probably haven't as much money as Sam, have you?"

"Very probably not. Why?"

"I was thinking you'd be more fun. Sam is awfully boring, at times, and—"

But Sam was coming across the room toward us, now, and any further complaints she may have had were stilled. Sam had a pair of drinks in his hand, and he handed one to each of us.

He had a smile on his face, but it was purely facial. "Making time with my girl, eh, Mort? Isn't she a beauty?"

I agreed to that.

"Beauty like that would be wasted in pictures, wouldn't it, Mort?"

Marriage versus a career, I thought. *This is getting like a soap opera.* "I'm sure no type of picture, moving or still, could possibly do her justice," I said tactfully.

Sam sat down on the davenport—between us. "See, baby," he said. "Why don't you give up this pipe dream, like a sensible girl, and—"

HE NEVER FINISHED the sentence. From behind us, at that second, came the muffled blast of what was certainly a gun.

Rita flinched. "Backfire?" she asked.

"That was no backfire," I said and looked at Sam.

"No," he said. "I'd bet on that. It came from the other room, or the hall, didn't it?"

"It sounded like a closed room to me," I said and stood up, as Sam got to his feet.

He nodded to me. "C'mon along."

The lad at the piano continued to play. Two couples who were dancing continued to dance. Rita stayed where she was, as Sam and I went to the front hall.

There was a dining room to the right here, and there was the door to the lavatory, right near the rear door. There was an acrid smell, and it seemed to come from the rear of this hall.

We went back toward the kitchen, but opposite the lavatory door, we both paused. The acrid odor was exceptionally strong, here.

The little gent who'd been dancing with Myrtle came out through the kitchen doorway. "What the hell was that racket?" he asked us.

It seemed like a delayed reaction to me. A girl came out through the same doorway and I saw the lipstick, now, on Shorty's collar.

For some reason all four of us were silent a moment, all four of us were looking with varying unease at the closed lavatory door.

It was Sam who tried the knob. The door swung open.

On the tile floor of this fair-sized room lay the body of Myrtle Jessup Whitnall. She was spread-eagled on that hard floor, and the entire upper half of her cashmere sweater was red with blood.

Sam said nothing, just stared. Shorty said, "Suicide. Why'n hell would she want to do a thing like that?"

There was no weapon in sight. There was a shoulder-high, casement window in the room, and the window was open.

"What makes you think it's suicide?" I asked Shorty.

His girl friend was already halfway to the floor when I turned to ask him that. She landed with a thud, before he even noticed her.

Lieutenant Duncan, out of homicide, was a big gent with a square face and soft, inquiring eyes. His voice was low and easy, but the brown eyes overlooked nothing. He'd talked to Sam and Rita, one at a time, in the kitchen. I was alone in there with him now.

"Private investigator, Mr. Jones?"

"That's right, Lieutenant."

"This the kind of company you keep in your home town, too?"

"Not often," I answered. "I knew this Mrs. Whitnall when she was Myrtle Jessup. I'd bought some information from her, a couple of times."

"A pigeon?"

"That's right."

"She hire you to come up here with her?"

"No, she didn't. I came here as a guest."

"Uh-huh. The department know you, personally, back East?"

"The Chief does. You could wire him. I worked out of homicide there for six years."

"Oh. You quit?"

"I quit. It was my own idea. I could go back to the department, any time."

Duncan's smile was wry. "Sure, only then you wouldn't be able to afford California vacations. Where were you, when you heard the shot, Jones?"

"On a davenport, in the living room, talking to Whitnall and Miss Regan."

"Who else was in the room, then?"

"Waterford was playing the piano, and two couples were dancing. I'm not sure of their names."

"Mmmm-hmmm. And this Ed Burrows?"

"He was in the kitchen, I think. Anyway he came out of there as Whitnall and I came out into the hall. That girl who fainted was in the kitchen with him. I'd say, offhand, they were otherwise occupied."

The brown eyes were mildly skeptical. "What gives you that idea?"

"Lipstick on his collar." I paused. "And that look people have."

Duncan said nothing for seconds, looking gravely thoughtful. Then he said, "Okay, Jones. Send in that Burrows. And hang around."

I went out and told Ed Burrows the lieutenant would see him next. Then I went over to sit next to Sam and Rita on the davenport.

Rita was pale, but under control. "Right back where we started from," she said. "Well, what did he have to say, Mr. Jones?"

"Just checking my background," I answered. "He seemed to think I was in bad company."

Sam was scowling, and my words didn't lighten the scowl any. Rita chuckled, and Sam said, "Cops. I don't like any cop, but I like a smart one least of all."

"He's smart enough," I said. "Who were the two gents who left, Sam?"

He looked at me suspiciously. "Why?"

"I'd say the rest of us are in the clear," I explained. "But Duncan's going to check those two very carefully."

Sam was looking at me steadily. "We'll let Duncan check 'em, if that's all right with you. You're not getting any ideas about playing cop, Jones?"

"I brought her here," I said. "I feel responsible, Sam."

I could almost feel him tense. Rita was smiling, and that probably angered him even more.

He said, "I'm in the clear on this. But my background isn't so right I'd want it dug into. I'm warning you, Jones, keep your nose clean."

"You know me better than that," I said. "You know me well enough to know I don't scare. And I'm not interested in your background. I'm only interested in what happened here, today."

Sam didn't say any more. But I didn't need a crystal ball to guess he and I weren't going to get along after this. He went over to talk to Waterford.

Rita was still smiling. "You like to play with fire, don't you, Mr. Jones?"

"It's a part of my trade," I told her.

She sighed. "It was refreshing, hearing someone talk back to Sam for a change. I'm getting awfully weary of that man." She stamped out her cigarette in an ashtray. "But he lives so well, so very, very well."

The short man, Ed Burrows, was coming out from the kitchen, now. He gestured to Waterford, then came over to where we sat.

He had a puzzled look on his face. "I think that cop's got me picked for the number one boy, you know that?"

"Imagine that," Rita said. "And why should he think that, Ed?"

"Because I was in the kitchen. And the kitchen opens up onto the back porch, and so does that bathroom where she was shot. But Babe was with me all the time, in the kitchen. He can't do nothing to me, can he, if Babe sticks with me?"

"I don't know," Rita said.

"I'm asking you, peeper," Burrows said.

He was sounding very tough for a man his size. I looked at him coolly. "No," I said, "there's nothing he can do, nothing but pinch you. The jury would do the rest."

Burrows' voice was rough. "Listen, Hawkshaw—"

It was Sam Whitnall who interrupted him. Sam, who had come up behind him, said, "Take it easy, Ed. This is no time for rough stuff." He paused, looking at me. "There'll be plenty of time for that, later."

Ed went over to talk to Babe, while Sam sat on the davenport again. He was smoking a cigar. He was staring out across the room, and saying nothing. Things were a little strained, to say the least.

Rita, for the first time, looked uncomfortable. I could imagine she'd have reason to fear Sam's wrath. I'd have reason, too. But in my trade it's best not to show any more fear than is absolutely necessary.

Back East, Sam had a reputation as a man to get along with. The one time I had gone up against him, it had been because of one of his lesser hoodlums, and he hadn't had enough at stake to make an issue of it. But we weren't friends, by any means.

The uniformed man at the door was talking to a newcomer, now, and it was clear the new man was another detective. He walked right through the room, and out into the kitchen.

Sam watched him idly, and then his gaze swung around to me. "Did Myrtle tell you just why she wanted to come up here?"

"Not that I remember. I don't even remember driving up here."

Sam looked more thoughtful than angry now. "You know, there isn't a soul here who'd have any motive for killing her. Not a soul but me." He shook his head.

"How about those two who left?"

"They don't even know her."

We didn't have any further dialogue after that. In a little while, Duncan came to tell me I was free to leave the place.

"But stay in town," he added.

He was, for the moment, interested only in Sam, Ed Burrows and the girl called Babe. The rest of us were free to leave.

2

Two Lippy Punks

IT WAS JUST chance that Rita and I went out together. On the front porch she said, "You wouldn't be going my way, I suppose?"

"I'd be glad to take you anywhere," I said.

"It's not too far—Santa Monica."

"That's my neck of the woods," I told her.

"The Miramar," she said.

Which wasn't my neck of the woods by about ten dollars a day. The Dusy started with an appreciative murmur, and Rita said, "Even out here, you don't see many of these. What is it?"

"A Duesenberg. America's finest car. The world's finest, if you'll pardon a little boasting. It's an orphan, now."

"Nice," she said, and no more.

I cut down Hilgard to Lindbrook, took Lindbrook to Westwood Boulevard, and Westwood to Wilshire. Still, no words.

Out Wilshire, toward the sea. At Sepulveda a hot rod pulled up alongside, while we waited for the light. Couple of young fellows in it, and the lad next to the driver looked over to grin at me.

"I'll bet that was some stuff in 'thirty-two," he said.

I could feel the Dusy shiver. Sensitive, she is, and proud.

"It's some stuff now," I answered. "Where do you put the hay in that heap?"

"Huh," he said, and no more.

We watched the light. At the amber on the cross street, the hot rod edged forward a bit, but I think that's cheating. I was waiting for the green.

When it came, I went into low, and so did the hot rod. Tires squealed, and we hit the far side of Sepulveda hub and hub. He was right there, losing nothing, gaining nothing, as I went into second.

I hadn't gone a hundred feet in second before I knew I had him. I had thirty feet on him before I went into third.

I slowed then, and he pulled up alongside. They were both still grinning. The lad on my side said, "Okay, we live and learn. You wouldn't want to sell it, maybe? I know a guy would buy it, rich guy—"

"My right arm I'll sell, first," I told him. "Nice job you boys built there."

"It's no Dusy," he said, "but for eight hundred smacks—"

They waved, and passed on.

Still no words from Rita.

"It's a nice day," I said. "Things are going to be all right. The way Myrtle operated, she was bound to get it, eventually. I liked her, and I feel sorry for what happened. But in her business there was always that possibility."

"I'm thinking about Sam," she said. "I'm thinking it wouldn't be very smart to be on the wrong side of Sam."

"I suppose not."

"Mort, he wants to marry me. I think I'm afraid to turn him down, now."

"And afraid to marry him, too?"

"Myrtle was married to him," she said.

"Myrtle was also a girl who'd risk plenty to make some

money. She wasn't a girl to overlook an angle, and one of the angles finally caught up with her."

She shook her head impatiently. She was staring straight ahead. "All right. Let's just say I don't want to marry him. Let's just say I don't want anything to do with him, from now on."

"You didn't act like this back at the house," I pointed out.

"I was on guard, then. I realize, now, I've always been on my guard around Sam."

We were on Ocean Avenue, then, and I stopped in front of the Miramar. "I'll see you again, I hope," I said.

She smiled at me. "I'd like that. You're not afraid of Sam?"

"It's a considered risk." I smiled. "But it'll be worth it. I'll call you."

She stood on the curb a moment, looking at me, one hand on the door. Finally she said, "Not that it matters, but I pay my own rent here."

She turned and walked off.

I drove back to Ben's Badger Bar. I was no longer drunk; the haze had left with the finding of Myrtle's body. But I was hungry and Ben advertised the best hamburger in town for only a quarter.

I had one of those, with some coffee. As I was finishing, Ben asked, "How was the party?"

"Not so good," I said. "How did you know I went to a party?"

"That dame called up, right from the phone on the wall, there. I couldn't miss her conversation, even if I tried."

"Who'd she talk to? Did you get the name?"

"Some guy named Ed. She asked for Sam, but this Ed must have told her Sam wouldn't talk. Weren't you listening?"

"I must have been drunker than I thought," I told him. "I

didn't even see her leave the bar. Ben, do you think you could remember everything she said?"

He looked thoughtful. "Let's see. She called and asked for Sam. Then it seemed like this guy who answered the phone, this Ed, must have told her Sam wouldn't talk to her. Because she said, 'He'll talk to me, if I come out there. And I'm coming out there right now, Ed.' Then she slammed the receiver on the hook and came back to the bar."

"And what did she say to me?"

Ben's eyebrows went up. "She asked you how you'd like to go to a party, and you seemed to think that would be just dandy." Ben was frowning, now. "Something wrong, Mr. Jones?"

"The girl's dead now, Ben. She was killed at the party."

He was staring blankly. "Accident?"

"No. She was murdered."

"Holy smokes! That must have been some party!"

"It was. And I've got a hunch it's not over." I paid him and went out to the Dusy. I drove slowly back to Wilshire, to the auto court room-and-bath I was currently calling home.

It was a pleasant place, all things considered. I tried to read some magazines I'd bought. I turned on my portable radio, and poured myself a small snifter of rye.

I couldn't relax. I kept seeing Myrtle on that tile floor, the blood soaking her sweater. I kept seeing little Ed Burrows coming out of the kitchen, and that empty-faced blonde he'd been mugging.

The back porch would have been a logical place for the killer to stand. The kitchen door led out to the porch.

I wondered if Duncan had found the weapon. He looked like the kind of gent who'd take the house apart in the search for it. If those two who left had nothing to do with the murder, the weapon would have to be somewhere in that house or on the grounds.

My thoughts went to Myrtle, the dead pigeon, and I realized she'd probably never have gone up to that robbers' roost if I hadn't been along. Myrtle, for some reason, had always considered me a kind of modern Galahad.

If she'd gone up there for purposes of blackmail, it was possible Sam wasn't the intended victim. Sam's friends would be equally vulnerable, unless he'd changed social levels along with his address. Taking Ed Burrows as a sample, this seemed unlikely.

That included six men and four women, outside of Sam. I know the piano player by name only. I knew Ed Burrows and the first name of his girl friend, if Babe can be called a name. Which left four men and two women about whom I knew nothing, not even their names.

But Duncan had them all catalogued by now, and this was really Duncan's baby, and no particular concern of mine.

I had almost put it from my mind, when the proprietor of my modest home came to tell me I was wanted on the phone in the office.

It was Lieutenant Duncan. "I'm still over at the Whitnall place," he said. "I'd like to have you drop over."

It didn't sound like an order. There was, as a matter of fact, a certain deference in his voice. It is something no private operative expects from a police officer, and I wondered what had prompted it.

I was there in ten minutes. He was waiting on the porch with the other detective. The uniformed man was gone.

"We got a report in answer to our wire, Jones," he said. "You seem to be well thought of, back there."

I couldn't think of anything to say to that.

"This is Sergeant Chopko," Duncan said. "He'll be on this case. With about ninety murders a year in this town, I don't know how much time he can give it. But I'd appreciate your cooperation."

I shook the hand Chopko extended. It was a big hand, and he was a big man, a man of about fifty with an unlined face and pale blue eyes.

For some reason, I didn't think we were going to get along.

Duncan said to him, "I'll be at headquarters. Check those two who left the shindig early. I'll hold Whitnall and Burrows and that girl as long as I can down there." He turned to me. "Like to ride along with Chopko? Maybe seeing those two guys will help to jog your memory."

His face was deadpan, and I couldn't tell whether the remark about my memory was malicious or not.

"I'd like to," I answered.

We went in a department car; I left the Dusy there.

"WE'LL GO OVER to Venice, first, I guess," Chopko said. "That's where this Joe Gillespie lives." He didn't look at me as he said this. He looked like a kid who'd been chastised by teacher.

We'd driven all the way to Centinela, and he'd turned south on that before any more words came from him.

Then he said, "Twenty-eight years on the force." He shook his head. He didn't look at me.

"So—" I said.

"Twenty-eight years on the force," he repeated, "and I got to take a private eye along when I go to look up a couple punks."

"It wasn't my idea," I said. "All I wanted out here was the sun."

He didn't say any more. At Venice Boulevard he turned west, toward the ocean. There were a couple more turns after that, but no dialogue.

The alley we were on now was supposed to be a street, but bore no resemblance to one, though it was called Speedway. It should have been valuable property, because of its proximity to the water, but it looked like little more than a varied collection of shacks, crowded and decrepit.

Finally, he pulled into a small yard behind an ancient and paintless row of units that must have been small apartments. He climbed out, said, "Come along, if you want," and headed for the rear door of one of the units.

I came along. He had already pressed the bell button when I stepped up on the building-long porch. He'd had no response.

He stepped over to a window near the door and peered in. "Radio going in there," he said.

He came back, and this time he knocked on the door.

From inside, someone said, "Okay, okay, keep your shirt on."

Chopko's face stiffened, and he muttered something.

The door opened, and we were facing a man who looked no more than twenty-two years of age, a thin-lipped, brown-eyed young man of medium height and more than medium good looks. He was thin, but looked wiry. I'd seen him at the party, I remembered.

"The law," he called back over his shoulder, and then his gaze met Chopko's evenly. "Something on your mind, Sergeant?"

"Don't be smart, punk," Chopko said. "Your buddy here, too?"

"My buddy? Who do you mean?"

"Dartanian."

The youth nodded. "He the one you want to see?"

"I want to see you both, Gillespie. I'll do the talking. You can confine your end of the dialogue to answering my questions."

Joe Gillespie's smile was scornful. "Sure, Sergeant. Come in and relax."

We went into the main room of the unit, a living room that was obviously furnished by the management; the kind of furniture only a rooming house or apartment proprietor would pick. There was a small kitchenette visible from this room. There was an alcove off it that held a double bed and a narrow dresser.

In a grease-stained, worn-upholstered chair sat another young man I'd seen at the party, a stocky, swarthy youth in slacks and a bright yellow sport shirt.

He surveyed us gravely without getting up from his chair, without showing an emotion on his broad, placid face.

"How's the rug business, Dartanian?" Chopko asked.

The dark youth yawned. "Holding up, thanks, Sergeant. How are things with you?"

"I make a living. And not selling phoney oriental rugs, either."

No emotion on the Armenian's face. "You know anything about oriental rugs, Sergeant?"

"I'm not here for that," Chopko said. "I'm here to check on a party you boys were at this afternoon."

Joe Gillespie had taken a seat on the room's wicker davenport, and he entered the conversation, now. "That party at Sam Whitnall's, Sergeant?"

"That's the one. Which one of you boys left first?"

"We left together," Gillespie said.

"At what time?"

Gillespie shrugged. "Three, three-fifteen. I couldn't tell you much closer than that."

"You couldn't make it about three-thirty?"

Gillespie shook his head. "Like to oblige, Sergeant, but it wasn't that late. What's the trouble?"

Chopko ignored the question, "What makes you so sure about the time, Joe?"

Dartanian answered for him. "Because I had a customer I had to see at that time, Sergeant, over in Beverly Hills, and Joe went with me. She even remarked about how prompt we were."

Chopko smiled bleakly. "A customer, or a friend?"

"A customer," Dartanian answered evenly. "She bought a Royal Sarouk, Sergeant. You know what a Royal Sarouk is?"

"I'm not interested," Chopko said. "What's this customer's name?"

Dartanian made a ritual of taking a check from his pocket and scrutinizing it. Then he rose and brought it over to Chopko.

It was a check for fifteen hundred dollars, signed by a Cornelia Schultz. "A widow," Dartanian explained, and gave the sergeant her address.

Chopko's face was flushed, and his voice just a growl. "I hope, for your sake, this rug's as represented, Dartanian."

"I wish it wasn't," Dartanian said. "I lost some money on the deal, Sergeant."

Gillespie said, "It wasn't the rug you came to see us about, was it?"

"No," Chopko said. "It was about a murder."

"Murder?" Gillespie asked.

Dartanian took his seat again in the worn chair. He said nothing, watching us both.

"Murder," Chopko repeated. "For a couple of punks, that's quite a step."

"It was just a party," Gillespie said. His voice seemed higher. "He's no particular friend of ours Sergeant. This Babe Norton's the one who told us about it. You know, Ed Burrows' girl."

Chopko transferred his attention to the stocky youth. "How long did it take you to peddle that rug?"

Dartanian shrugged. "I lose track of time on a deal. Hour, maybe."

"Maybe longer, too, huh?"

"Maybe. Why?"

"There's been a man waiting here for you to come home, right up to a half hour ago. Where'd you go after you sold the rug?"

"No place. Stopped at a drive-in, for a sandwich. That's all."

THERE WEREN'T MANY questions after that. Chopko told them to go down to the station to make their statements, and we left.

Outside, he said, "Punks, smart, lippy punks. I'd like to work 'em both over, personally."

It was getting dark, and he turned the lights of the car on as we backed out of the yard.

"We get a worse record every year out here, and it's not because of the natives, either. It's these mugs from the East. We ought to have a quota."

I suppose he was talking to me, but he wasn't looking at me, so I couldn't be sure. "I'll be going home soon, Sergeant," I said.

"I wasn't talking about you," he said. "I'm talking about guys like Whitnall and Burrows and those two hoodlums."

We drove back to Westwood without any further conversation. When I got out of the car, I said, "Lieutenant Duncan's got my address. But I suppose he'll want me downtown to sign a statement?"

"That's right. Tomorrow morning. About eight."

Driving through the shopping district of the village, I saw this sign, charcoal broiled steaks, and it reminded me I hadn't eaten for nearly three hours.

While I was waiting for the steak to broil, I phoned Rita.

She sounded glad to hear my voice. "I was afraid it was Sam," she said.

"He hasn't phoned you?"

"Haven't heard a word."

"In that case," I suggested, "you should be free tonight."

"Available," she said, "but hardly free, Jonesy. This is an expensive town."

"So I've heard," I said. "Any special place in mind you'd like to go?"

A pause. "I have. I've a place I'd like you to see. Though you might be disappointed."

"Not if you're with me," I promised. "About eight-thirty all right?"

3

A Classy Clip-Joint

RITA WAS READY at eight-thirty. I wasn't ready for that much beauty, and I had to stare for a few moments before I found my voice. "You're wasting your time with Sam Whitnall," I told her finally. "You should be signed up just to stand around and be admired."

"You've been drinking," she said. "And I'm not wasting my time with Sam Whitnall any more, I hope."

We cut down to the beach road and headed up toward Malibu, at her directions. It was a bright night, and the ocean was living up to its name, serving as a scarcely moving mirror for the moon.

I could smell her perfume, mixed with the sea air.

"Anything new on the murder?" she asked.

"Nothing startling. I went over with the detective to see those two young angle-shooters. But their alibi is cast iron."

"I've been wondering about Ed Burrows," Rita said quietly. "I've been thinking he's about the only possible choice, isn't he?"

"Or Babe."

"Not that simpering—"

"With murder," I interrupted her, "you can never tell. Some of the meekest mice turn out to be the fiercest lions."

"Slow," she said. "It's only a few hundred feet now. Here it is."

It was a wide driveway leading to a beach home set about a hundred yards back from the road. The place was brilliantly lighted, and obviously no longer used as a private residence. About fifty yards up the drive there was a chain stretched between two concrete pillars, acting as a gate.

A man in a trim, grey uniform came over to my side of the car. "Membership card, sir?"

"It's all right, Len," Rita said to him. "He's a friend of mine."

The man touched his cap. "Sorry, Miss Regan. Didn't see you." He went to pull back the chain.

The drive went around to the back of the building, where the parking lot was filled with cars. Expensive cars, all of them, convertibles predominating.

A youth in a uniform matching that of the man at the gate took the car over here, and we went up onto the porch that spanned three sides of the building.

From here I could hear the music of a piano. The pianist was playing a piece I'd heard this afternoon at Sam's.

Another man met us as we went into the lobby of the place, a man without a uniform, this time, wearing a dinner jacket.

"Miss Regan." He smiled at both of us. "You've come for dinner?"

She nodded and he led the way into a low-ceilinged, dimly lighted dining room, decorated in grey and green. On a stand in the center of this spacious room, Waterford was seated at the keyboard of a white-enameled concert grand piano.

It was a quiet place, well staffed and with the air of intelligent management. Soothing music from the piano, excellent service from the waiters, and good food.

"Very nice," I told Rita. "I can't see why you might think I'd be disappointed. Even on top of my recent steak, that lobster tasted good."

She smiled. "I thought it might be too quiet for you."

"That's the way I like it."

"I like it, too," she said. "And that's what I can't understand about it. It doesn't match Sam at all."

"Sam?" I said. "What's he got to do with it?"

"He owns the place. He runs it. With a manager's help, of course, but it was his idea."

I couldn't see it. Not for Sam Whitnall, who'd been in every racket that paid off, ever since I'd known him. I asked, "Is it really a private club, or is that gent at the gate just for show?"

"It's private. It's so private, members can't even bring guests. Some very big names in this town have been refused admission. And others, not so big, Sam has gone after. You figure it out. I've been trying to."

"I can't," I said. "But if he wants to go legitimate, we really shouldn't question him."

"Legitimate? I can't see him going legitimate, if it costs him money. If he figures his time worth anything at all, this place is a white elephant. And he's been running it for two years."

"It doesn't look like he's losing money tonight," I said.

"He doesn't usually have a crowd this large. Some nights, he may have only six or seven."

I looked around the room, and noticed one peculiar fact. There were no couples, here. There were no parties. Everybody was eating alone. If it was a social club, they weren't being social.

"You say this crowd is unusually large?"

"That's right. I think I know why, too. It's why I wanted to come out here, tonight. Usually, they come and go, you see. But tonight they're waiting for Sam."

A glimmer of something flickered in my brain. "They usually see him before they leave?"

"That's right. And tonight he isn't here." Rita was facing the entrance as she said this, and she added, "He wasn't here, I should say."

I TURNED TO see Sam, Burrows and Babe standing in the wide entrance to the dining room. They were all looking our way. Then Sam went back into the lobby with Babe, and Ed Burrows was walking towards us.

One thing I'd noticed, all the occupants of the room seemed relieved to see Sam.

I didn't notice any more than that; Ed Burrows was blocking my vision now.

It was Rita he addressed, though. "Sam's awful mad, Red. You know we don't allow guests out here."

"I'm a guest myself," Rita said. "I'm no member, Ed."

"You're the only guest that's ever been in here, up to now," Ed said. "It's been all employees or members, up to now. And if you were going to bring a guest, you could've been a little more choosy."

"You're too small to talk like that, Ed," I said.

"Shut up," he said, without looking at me. And to Rita: "Sam wants to see you in his office."

She looked at me.

"Don't go if you don't want to," I told her.

Her smile was forced. "Don't worry. I can handle Sam."

She rose, and walked through the quiet room to the entrance. I was still standing when she disappeared. *The land of make-believe, I thought, the land of the false front, of the mirage, the land where money doesn't talk, it shouts.*

"Nice place you've got here," I said to Burrows.

He nodded. "Sam's awful proud of it. Let's go, Jones."

"The bounce?" I asked. "You're going to throw me out of this elegant and refined place, Ed?"

He shook his head. "I want to talk to you. Sam's got a proposition he wants me to give you."

"So long as it's legal," I told him, "I'm always open to a proposition."

I followed him through the dining room, and into the lobby. I was uneasy; I wasn't armed and didn't think it would do any good if I was. We went back along the lobby to a closed door, and Ed opened it.

Ed went through first and turned on the light. It was a small room, with a desk and file cabinet, with a door in the opposite wall that must have led out onto the porch.

"Now's all right," Ed said. He was facing me, but he was looking past me. I turned to see if there was anyone else in the room.

I got about halfway around when the roof caved in. I could feel myself going, and I fought it. Another part of the roof landed then. I don't even remember hitting the floor....

About all I remember regarding that interlude was the flame and the sparks, and this damned drumming in my ears. The sparks went away after a while, but the drumming continued.

I woke to the sound of it; it was rain on the canvas top of the Dusy. A solid, steady rain without wind, a soaking rain.

I was sitting in the front seat; there was a man sitting next to me, behind the wheel. I was back at the auto court, parked in front of my unit. I could see, by the light of the court, that it was Joe Gillespie who'd driven me home.

From the back seat, a voice said, "He coming to, Joe?" It was Dartanian's voice.

"Mmmm-hmmm." Gillespie smiled at me in the dimness. "No hard feelings? Ed asked us to take you home. You must have had one too many, huh?"

"This is no time for bad humor," I said, and rubbed the back of my neck. "What time is it?"

"Eleven o'clock. You've been out for almost an hour." A pause. "You're alive, though. That's something."

"Don't scare me, boys. I've been in this business a long time, too long for that kind of talk to work. When you see Sam, tell him he made a mistake. Tell him he played it like an amateur."

"Sure," Dartanian answered. "Sam had a little message for you, too. He said he's got a nice clean business, and he doesn't want any trouble with you. Next time, Sam said, you won't be so lucky."

They were both climbing from the car now. Then they were running through the rain toward another car, whose headlights had just gone on.

I wondered who was waiting for them, there. It was an Olds sedan, and it pulled away, down the drive to the street, the moment they'd slammed the doors behind them.

My head was throbbing in rhythm to the beat of the rain. The Dusy was murmuring to herself, as her motor cooled. A light went on in a bathroom two units down, and a car went by on Wilshire, making time, its tires humming on the wet pavement.

I was more angry than scared, but I was scared some, too. Not only for myself, but for Rita, who was probably still out there. Then I remembered her smile when she'd said, "I can handle Sam," and I knew she could. She was no crossroads cutie; she'd been places and seen people, all kinds of places and all kinds of people.

I wouldn't have to worry too much about Rita. I could start worrying about myself. I wasn't getting paid to dig into the affairs of Sam Whitnall. Duncan didn't need me, and Chopko didn't want me. I was no amateur. I was a professional, and a professional who works without pay is of unsound mind.

I kept seeing Myrtle's blood-soaked sweater, though. I kept building up a peeve against Ed Burrows, and those two punks who'd just put on the B-picture act.

I took the keys out of the ignition, and found my door key. Then I opened the car door quickly, and bolted for the protection of the porch.

The fast movement was rough on my head, and I moved more slowly after I was out of the rain. I'd been slugged before, but for more reason, and never while I was on vacation.

Inside, I took a hot shower, and got right to bed. There were a lot of questions in my mind, but I didn't want to seek any answers tonight. I was asleep almost immediately.

It was still raining in the morning. Not as heavily, but just as steadily. It was a gloomy, chill day. There was a radio blaring in the next unit. There was an Olds sedan coming into the courtyard.

It pulled up in front of the office, and I got my .38 out of one of my grips. I'd been bounced around too much in the past twenty-four hours to want any more.

I returned to the window in time to see who was getting out of the car. I put the gun back in my grip. It was a girl going into the manager's office, a girl in a green knit suit and white shoes, without stockings. It was Rita.

She left the office in a minute, and came walking up the porch toward my door. I had it open when she got there.

I was wearing a robe and pajamas and slippers. I needed a shave. But she smiled at me as though I were human.

"Bad night, Jonesy?"

"Bad enough. Come in."

She came in and sat in the room's only comfortable chair. I sat on the bed. She pulled a cigarette out, lighted it. She seemed to be stalling, framing some words in her mind.

Finally: "I'm sorry about last night, Jonesy."

"Not as sorry as I am. That your car out there?"

She shook her head slowly. "It's one of Sam's. Why?"

"Did you drive it last night?"

Again she shook her head. "Why all the questions, Jonesy?"

"Don't you think I have some answers coming?"

She shrugged. "I suppose. No profit in it for you, though, is there? That's what you work on, isn't it, profit? Revenge may be sweet, but it's not very profitable, is it?"

"That's three times you mentioned profit," I told her. "Don't tell me what's coming next."

The smile again. "I suppose this situation is nothing new to you."

"You suppose right. How much is Sam offering?"

"Not Sam. Me."

"You?" I took a breath. "I never would have thought it, Red."

"Sam offered me my big chance last night, Jonesy."

I laughed. "He's a producer now, huh?"

"There's a director who comes out there," she went on. "A brilliant man. A little erratic, but brilliant and well thought of at Mammoth. He can make me, Jonesy."

"Sam talked to him?"

"So did I." She was watching me intently. "It's a long way from Grand Forks. It's been a long, rough trip, with some detours. I'd hate to think it was in vain."

"Where do I enter this tableau?"

She paused, studying me. "You just forget where you were last night, and what happened. Forget about all of yesterday. Just go on and enjoy your vacation."

"I'd like to, Red," I said. "This director who's brilliant and erratic and well thought of at Mammoth. Is it opium he uses, or cocaine?"

She was rigid in her chair. Her voice was very low. "You think that's what it's all about, out there? You think—"

"WHAT ELSE? THAT'S why Sam was so exclusive. Money wasn't enough. They had to be rich, and addicts, too. Beautiful front he's got there, and food good enough to make the place seem just what it was supposed to seem, a fine restaurant. Sam sold them the dope right from his office, and just the two of them knew of the transaction. I wouldn't be surprised if each member thought he was the only addict. He didn't want any of the riff-raff trade, just the ones who could control themselves. That's why he was so choosy."

"You're guessing at all this, Mort."

"Sure, sure. Maybe it's the lobster they come for. Maybe it's the piano playing. The law will find out, quick enough."

She didn't say anything for seconds. She was staring at the floor. Then she looked up to meet my gaze. "It's still not your business, is it?"

"No. It's something for the police."

"And you're going to them with this?"

"I haven't decided. You don't think I should?"

A pause. "No. Nothing's to be gained."

"And maybe a career would be lost?"

No answer from her.

"I should have known," I said. "I probably did know, but wouldn't let myself admit it. You're no child. You knew Sam Whitnall wasn't on the up and up. The first corruption is the hardest, Red. After that you can take it in increasing doses—until you'll accept murder."

Her voice was tight. "Mort! You don't have to say things like that. I had nothing to do with that murder."

"Maybe not. But you'll accept help from the man who did. This ambition can lead anywhere. Your ambition was your first corruption. I don't know how far beyond murder it can take you, if there is anything beyond murder. But there won't be any step you can't take if you take this one."

She was smiling now, a mocking smile, "If you will all open your hymn books to page twenty-three, we will sing—"

I got off the bed. My hands were shaking. I said, "Red, maybe you'd better leave. I just got up, and I've got a bad taste in my mouth. I don't want to feel any worse than I do. Go on back to your hoodlum friends, Red."

She stood up. "Don't make any decision in that frame of mind, Jonesy. Don't let your conscience lead you into something your pocketbook will regret, later."

I didn't look at her. "So long, Red."

"I'll be seeing you." The door closed.

It was still raining steadily. I watched her walk along the protected runway to her car. I watched her swing the Olds in a U-turn, the twin wipers working.

The land of make-believe, I thought. *The mirage, with sound effects. With sound effects— Of course, of course, that was it!*

I shaved, showered, and made some coffee on the gas plate. All the while I was doing this, I was thinking and realizing how stupid I'd been. Motive, means and opportunity. Something big enough for murder. Somebody capable of murder.

I drove down, after my coffee, to see Duncan.

Chopko was with him, in Duncan's office, and I gave a clerk my statement in there, and signed it. Then I said to Duncan, "I'd like to go out to that Whitnall house, again. There's something I overlooked."

Duncan looked at Chopko, and back at me. Chopko said, "This guy taking over the department's work? We all going to get laid off?"

Duncan kept his eyes on me. "You got an idea?"

"That's right."

He looked doubtful. But he was also looking thoughtful. "Is your car here?"

I nodded.

"Okay. You get out there with him, Mike, in his car. I'll be out, later, if the chief comes in in time."

Chopko nodded without saying anything, and we went out to my Dusy.

Chopko looked at it with some suspicion, but made no comment as he climbed in.

I moved out in low, goosing her, and he mumbled something.

I said, "No weapon, yet, huh?"

"No. She was shot with a thirty-two, but there wasn't even a thirty-two any place in the house. How we going to get in, out there?"

"Nobody home?"

"Wasn't, the last I heard. Had a man out there since seven-thirty."

"There'll probably be a window open, or something."

He just grunted in answer to that one. By the tone of his grunt, I guessed he didn't like the idea.

4

Five Grand Final

ONCE I GOT on Wilshire, I made time. There was nobody in sight when I parked in front of the Whitnall home, and no cars in the drive. We went up and rang the front door bell.

There was no response. I said, "Let's go around in back."

We went around in back. Not a window was open, or unlocked. The back door, like most of those older houses, though, had the kind of lock practically any simple key can open.

Only I didn't have any simple key on my key ring.

Chopko watched me fumble around with my key ring for a while, and then shook his head. From his pocket, he took one of those dime store skeleton keys and slipped it into the keyhole.

It worked like a charm.

We went into the kitchen. I said, "I'd always taken it for granted that these California houses didn't have basements. This one has."

"So?" he said.

"I just wonder if there's a laundry chute in that lavatory, leading into the basement."

"There is."

"Let's take a look at it."

He followed me into the lavatory. The door to the laundry chute was open, and I looked into it. It didn't end flush with the top of the door; there were a couple more inches of chute above that, and a plywood roof to it.

There was a hole in the plywood, and it looked like a bullet hole to me. I showed it to Chopko.

"I'll be damned," he said. He looked at me curiously.

"Let's go down in the basement."

The steps to the basement led from the kitchen, which also supported my theory. We went down, and over to the laundry chute near the gas furnace.

It was a straight chute, directly below the lavatory. I said, "Ed Burrows stood here, and fired directly up the chute, into that plywood top."

"And then ate the gun?"

My eyes were on the concrete floor, on the perforated grill to the drain there. Ed would pass right over it, on his way up the stairs.

Chopko saw the direction of my gaze. "Those things are cemented in, aren't they?"

"Not usually." I bent, got one finger nail under the edge of the light stamping that served as a grill, and flipped it clear of the opening.

It wasn't much of a drop to the bottom, but it was too dark to make out clearly whether or not there was anything there. I flicked my lighter.

By its flickering light I was sure I could see something solid protruding from the surface of the water in there. It looked like the barrel of a revolver to me.

I stifled my imagination, and put my hand down into the opening as far as it would go. I just made it with my finger tips. I pulled it out, and showed it to Chopko.

It was a revolver, all right.

Chopko looked at it for some seconds, before saying, "Only thing wrong with that, it's a .38. And she was killed with a .32."

"This wasn't the murder gun," I said. "This was the sound effects." I laid it carefully on the floor. I'd touched nothing but the barrel, so far, and didn't want any possibility of prints eliminated. "Whitnall killed his ex-wife with a silenced gun. He gave that to Dartanian or Gillespie when they left. They got rid of it, one way or another. Burrows goes down into the basement, here, after Whitnall is planted right in front of me, the perfect disinterested witness. Burrows shoots off this .38, making one hell of a racket, ditches it, and runs up to the kitchen in time to come rushing out of there with Babe and lipstick all over his collar. They're all covered, and the gun is gone, and what kind of a case can the D.A. make out of that?"

"None," Chopko said. "Not even now, he can't make a case out of it." He looked at me with something like good humor on his broad face. "You're all right, Jones. You'll forget an old man's peeve?"

I grinned at him. "I was a cop once myself. You said you'd like to work those two young punks over, Sergeant. Maybe that would be the weakest link, huh?"

He smiled. "Maybe. The smoke, here, would drift up through that chute into the bathroom, wouldn't it?"

"Right. There was already some smoke in there, from Sam's gun, so—"

I never finished the sentence. There was the sound of a door being opened, upstairs. It sounded like the front door to me.

I looked at Chopko. He shrugged.

"You hide," I said. "There, in the fruit cellar. They might

think I'm here alone."

Chopko went into the boarded fruit cellar, as I went back to the foot of the basement steps.

I heard the steps going through the tiled hall, now, and then into the kitchen. I heard Ed Burrows' voice. "Hey, Sam, this back door's open."

A silence that seemed to stretch into minutes.

I made a lot of intentional noise walking over to the laundry chute again.

From the top of the steps, Sam called, "That you down there, Jones?"

"Right," I said. "I just wanted to check this laundry chute. I found the gun."

Another silence, and then two pairs of feet were coming down the steps. Sam was first, Burrows right behind him.

"Who the hell do you think you are?" Sam asked. "You got too much guts for one man, Jones."

"That's what I've been told," I agreed. "Stay out at the opium den last night, Sam?" I had my head in the laundry chute, and I was looking up the passage as I said this.

No answer from them. I pulled my head out and turned to face them. "That must be some business you've got out there. Good enough to protect with Myrtle's death. Did she want in, Sam, or did she just want a lump sum?"

Sam was staring at me. Ed said, "Why don't we work him over right? What are we waiting for?"

"Sam hasn't got his gun," I said, "nor you yours, Ed. But I have mine."

They stood there at the bottom of the steps, neither one moving. Sam said, "I told you he was a bright boy. You've figured it all out, haven't you, Jonesy? What do you think it will get you?"

"About five grand," I said. "And that's cheap." I nodded toward the gun on the floor. "Ed's probably, and it wasn't the kill gun. But if I should take my theory to the law, they'd work the rest of it out of Gillespie, all right. That Dartanian might not crack, but you picked a lemon in Gillespie, Sam."

Ed said, "We going to listen to this yakety-yak all day, Sam? We going to fool with a punk like him?"

Sam smiled. "Punk? Not Jones, Ed. He's been around a long time, Ed." And to me. "Five grand, Jonesy, and that's the end of it?"

"Five grand is plenty for vacation pay," I said. "I—"

There was a gun in Sam's hand.

His voice was low and easy. "Five grand is cheap, Jones. But I couldn't trust you. I couldn't trust any private gumshoe. And I owe you something from before, you'll maybe remember. Not much, because the guy wasn't much. But he was one of mine, and you sent him up." He nodded to Ed. "Check to see if he was lying about the gun."

Ed came over to run his hands over me. "He sure was, boss. This jerk sure loves to play with fire, doesn't he?"

Sam came over to stand next to me, now. "He does," he said, and slapped me with his left hand. Then he stepped back. "All right, Ed, smack him."

Ed drew his right hand way, way back and from the fruit cellar Chopko said, "That'll be all, boys. Put that gun down, Whitnall."

I was right about Gillespie talking, after he'd had a few rounds with Chopko. And it was the way I'd figured it. Rita

Regan got her chance, just the same, and I understand she's quite a hit. I've never seen any of her pictures, so I can't tell you how she is, there. But she makes an awful lot of money, I understand.

www.ingramcontent.com/pod-product-compliance
Lightning Source LLC
Chambersburg PA
CBHW030932020726
47498CB00001B/212